PRAISE FOR

"Lee's flavourful and original settings range from competing starfaring empires in the far future to re-imagined histories."

—Aliette de Bodard, Introduction

"Yoon Ha Lee is an exciting new author who is one of those helping to move science fiction into the twenty-first century."

—Gardner Dozois, Hugo- and
Nebula-Award winning editor and author

"Like the sinuous road between the twinborn dragons, Yoon Ha Lee's fiction walks a delicate balance between opposing forces: the precision of math and the resonance of myth, the fiery glow of war and the cool reminiscence of history, the pacing and sweep of a space epic and the beauty and refinement of a lyric poem. Rich, evocative, and always undergirded by impeccable narrative logic, Lee's stories transport us to unimagined vistas that feel at once ancient and new."

—Ken Liu, Nebula-, Hugo-,
and World Fantasy Award-winning author of "The Paper Menagerie"

"Yoon Ha Lee writes with the heart of a mathematician and the precision of a poet."

—Lavie Tidhar, World Fantasy Award-winning author of *Osama*

conservation
of shadows

CONSERVATION OF SHADOWS

Prime Books

www.prime-books.com

For more information, contact Prime Books:
prime@prime-books.com

ISBN: 978-1-60701-387-7

conservation of shadows

YOON HA LEE

PRIME BOOKS

CONTENTS

INTRODUCTION...9

GHOSTWEIGHT 11

THE SHADOW POSTULATES 37

THE BONES OF GIANTS... 52

BETWEEN TWO DRAGONS... 80

SWANWATCH 93

EFFIGY NIGHTS 104

FLOWER, MERCY, NEEDLE, CHAIN.. 120

ISEUL'S LEXICON 129

COUNTING THE SHAPES 187

BLUE INK... 211

THE BATTLE OF CANDLE ARC...220

A VECTOR ALPHABET OF INTERSTELLAR TRAVEL.......................245

THE UNSTRUNG ZITHER..252

THE BLACK ABACUS..278

THE BOOK OF LOCKED DOORS 289

CONSERVATION OF SHADOWS 306

introduction

In my other life, I am a computer engineer; and I do a lot of mathematics. Mathematics, like most sciences, presents laws and models that are meant to hold true in reality—but, like most sciences, maths is constantly evolving and adapting itself to new observations that do not fit its models.

One thing I find amazing about Yoon Ha Lee's fiction is to see it so steeped in that same logic, and to find across her stories the same fascination about models. Models can dictate the behaviour of the universe, and yet at the same time fail to describe its complexity. Lee's stories present, over and over, this fundamental tension between image and truth; between myth and reality; between actual behaviour and model. This is nowhere more evident than in "The Book of Locked Doors," where the eponymous book draws magic from memories of dead people, forever frozen in misleading, one-purpose images: the dead are recorded only through their ability to practise magic, and this magic is the only thing that the book provides to its users.

Yoon Ha Lee has been one of those fairly discreet authors: her first story was published in 1999, long before I entered the science fiction and fantasy writing scene. She has since then been reprinted in various "year's best" anthologies, but to the best of my knowledge, seldom shortlisted for major awards, and Lee herself has remained relatively discreet. To my mind, this is a shame, as her talent for intricate world-building as well as writing multi-layered, subtle fiction has mostly gone unrecognised. Stories like "Ghostweight" or "Flower, Mercy, Needle, Chain," with their Asian-inspired Galactic empires, their original take on branching multiple universes, their idiosyncratic approach to ancestor worship and the preservation of the dead, are among the best and most memorable short fiction I have read.

Lee's flavourful and original settings range from competing starfaring empires in the far future to re-imagined histories, whether medieval or otherwise. Her characters are researchers and magicians, often forced into figuring out the rules of the world; but also generals and war-heroes, soldiers who do not necessarily have a taste for battle but do what they do for love of their people—and do it terribly well, with devastating consequences.

One thing Lee does not shy from is portraying the harrowing cost of war, genocide, and occupation, whether it is for the occupying forces or for those fighting for peace or independence. It is something I particularly appreciate in her fiction: far from glorifying war, Lee provides a thoughtful, nuanced examination of the cost of violence; of how war can be dehumanising but at the same time utterly necessary; of how a national identity builds and maintains itself in times of strife. That Lee is Korean-American, from a country that was devastated and separated several times by war, certainly informs and nourishes those narrations. As a Franco-Vietnamese, with roots in another country that has had its share of divisive and painful conflicts, I find this counterpoint to other more jingoistic narrations (sadly all too present in genre) both appreciable and much-needed. Stories like "Between Two Dragons" or "Blue Ink" are all the more striking because of this thematic undercurrent.

There are sixteen stories in this collection. In them you will find a war-kite pilot carrying the ghost of a compatriot in her head, a civilisation which kills others by taking and twisting their language, ships of soldiers passing through a black hole to reach a battle at the end of time, a dozen dizzying ways to travel through space, and many more such wonders, which I hope you find as breathtaking and as haunting as I did.

—**Aliette de Bodard**

ghostweight

It is not true that the dead cannot be folded. Square becomes kite becomes swan; history becomes rumor becomes song. Even the act of remembrance creases the truth.

What the paper-folding diagrams fail to mention is that each fold enacts itself upon the secret marrow of your ethics, the axioms of your thoughts.

Whether this is the most important thing the diagrams fail to mention is a matter of opinion.

"There's time for one more hand," Lisse's ghost said. It was composed of cinders of color, a cipher of blurred features, and it had a voice like entropy and smoke and sudden death. Quite possibly it was the last ghost on all of ruined Rhaion, conquered Rhaion, Rhaion with its devastated, shadowless cities and dead moons and dimming sun. Sometimes Lisse wondered if the ghost had a scar to match her own, a long, livid line down her arm. But she felt it was impolite to ask.

Around them, in a command spindle sized for fifty, the walls of the war-kite were hung with tatters of black and faded green, even now in the process of reknitting themselves into tapestry displays. Tangled reeds changed into ravens. One perched on a lightning-cloven tree. Another, taking shape amid twisted threads, peered out from a skull's eye socket.

Lisse didn't need any deep familiarity with mercenary symbology to understand the warning. Lisse's people had adopted a saying from the Imperium's mercenaries: *In raven arithmetic, no death is enough.*

Lisse had expected pursuit. She had deserted from Base 87 soon after hearing that scouts had found a mercenary war-kite in the ruins of a sacred maze, six years after all the mercenaries vanished: suspicious timing on her part, but she would have no better opportunity for revenge. The ghost had not tried too hard to dissuade her. It had always understood her ambitions.

For a hundred years, despite being frequently outnumbered, the mercenaries in their starfaring kites had cindered cities, destroyed flights of rebel starflyers, shattered stations in the void's hungry depths. What better weapon than one of their own kites?

What troubled her was how lightly the war-kite had been defended. It had made a strange, thorny silhouette against the lavender sky even from a long way off, like briars gone wild, and with the ghost as scout she had slipped past the few mechanized sentries. The kite's shadow had been human. She was not sure what to make of that.

The kite had opened to her like a flower. The card game had been the ghost's idea, a way to reassure the kite that she was its ally: Scorch had been invented by the mercenaries.

Lisse leaned forward and started to scoop the nearest column, the Candle Column, from the black-and-green gameplay rug. The ghost forestalled her with a hand that felt like the dregs of autumn, decay from the inside out. In spite of herself, she flinched from the ghostweight, which had troubled her all her life. Her hand jerked sideways; her fingers spasmed.

"Look," the ghost said.

Few cadets had played Scorch with Lisse even in the barracks. The ghost left its combinatorial fingerprints in the cards. People drew the unlucky Fallen General's Hand over and over again, or doubled on nothing but negative values, or inverted the Crown Flower at odds of thousands to one. So Lisse had learned to play the solitaire variant, with jerengjen as counters. *You must learn your enemy's weapons,* the ghost had told her, and so, even as a child in the reeducation facility, she had saved her chits for paper to practice folding into cranes, lilies, leaf-shaped boats.

Next to the Candle Column she had folded stormbird, greatfrog, lantern, drake. Where the ghost had interrupted her attempt to clear the pieces, they had landed amid the Sojourner and Mirror Columns, forming a skewed late-game configuration: a minor variant of the Needle Stratagem, missing only its pivot.

"Consider it an omen," the ghost said. "Even the smallest sliver can kill, as they say."

There were six ravens on the tapestries now. The latest one had outspread wings, as though it planned to blot out the shrouded sun. She wondered what it said about the mercenaries, that they couched their warnings in pictures rather than drums or gongs.

Lisse rose from her couch. "So they're coming for us. Where are they?"

She had spoken in the Imperium's administrative tongue, not one of the mercenaries' own languages. Nevertheless, a raven flew from one tapestry to join its fellows in the next. The vacant tapestry grayed, then displayed a new scene: a squad of six tanks caparisoned in Imperial blue and bronze, paced by two personnel carriers sheathed in metal mined from withered stars. They advanced upslope, pebbles skittering in their wake.

In the old days, the ghost had told her, no one would have advanced through a sacred maze by straight lines. But the ancient walls, curved and interlocking, were gone now. The ghost had drawn the old designs on her palm with its insubstantial fingers, and she had learned not to shudder at the untouch, had learned to thread the maze in her mind's eye: one more map to the things she must not forget.

"I'd rather avoid fighting them," Lisse said. She was looking at the command spindle's controls. Standard Imperial layout, all of them—it did not occur to her to wonder why the kite had configured itself thus—but she found nothing for the weapons.

"People don't bring tanks when they want to negotiate," the ghost said dryly. "And they'll have alerted their flyers for intercept. You have something they want badly."

"Then why didn't they guard it better?" she demanded.

Despite the tanks' approach, the ghost fell silent. After a while, it said, "Perhaps they didn't think anyone but a mercenary could fly a kite."

"They might be right," Lisse said darkly. She strapped herself into the commander's seat, then pressed three fingers against the controls and traced the commands she had been taught as a cadet. The kite shuddered, as though caught in a hell-wind from the sky's fissures. But it did not unfurl itself to fly.

She tried the command gestures again, forcing herself to slow down. A cold keening vibrated through the walls. The kite remained stubbornly landfast.

The squad rounded the bend in the road. All the ravens had gathered in a single tapestry, decorating a half-leafed tree like dire jewels. The rest of the tapestries displayed the squad from different angles: two aerial views and four from the ground.

Lisse studied one of the aerial views and caught sight of two scuttling figures, lean angles and glittering eyes and a balancing tail in black metal. She stiffened. They had the shadows of hounds, all graceful hunting curves. Two jerengjen, true ones, unlike the lifeless shapes that she folded out of paper. The kite must have deployed them when it sensed the tanks' approach.

Sweating now, despite the autumn temperature inside, she methodically tried every command she had ever learned. The kite remained obdurate. The tapestries' green threads faded until the ravens and their tree were bleak black splashes against a background of wintry gray.

It was a message. Perhaps a demand. But she did not understand.

The first two tanks slowed into view. Roses, blue with bronze hearts, were engraved to either side of the main guns. The lead tank's roses flared briefly.

The kite whispered to itself in a language that Lisse did not recognize. Then the largest tapestry cleared of trees and swirling leaves and rubble, and presented her with a commander's emblem, a pale blue rose pierced by three claws. A man's voice issued from the tapestry: "Cadet Fai Guen." This was her registry name. They had not reckoned that she would keep her true name alive in her heart like an ember. "You are in violation of Imperial interdict. Surrender the kite at once."

He did not offer mercy. The Imperium never did.

Lisse resisted the urge to pound her fists against the interface. She had not survived this long by being impatient. "That's it, then," she said to the ghost in defeat.

"Cadet Fai Guen," the voice said again, after another burst of light, "you have one minute to surrender the kite before we open fire."

"Lisse," the ghost said, "the kite's awake."

She bit back a retort and looked down. Where the control panel had once been featureless gray, it was now crisp white interrupted by five glyphs, perfectly spaced for her outspread fingers. She resisted the urge to snatch her hand away. "Very well," she said. "If we can't fly, at least we can fight."

She didn't know the kite's specific control codes. Triggering the wrong sequence might activate the kite's internal defenses. But taking tank fire at point-blank range would get her killed, too. She couldn't imagine that the kite's armor had improved in the years of its neglect.

On the other hand, it had jerengjen scouts, and the jerengjen looked perfectly functional.

She pressed her thumb to the first glyph. A shadow unfurled briefly but was gone before she could identify it. The second attempt revealed a two-headed dragon's twisting coils. Long-range missiles, then: thunder in the sky. Working quickly, she ran through the options. It would be ironic if she got the weapons systems to work only to incinerate herself.

"You have ten seconds, Cadet Fai Guen," said the voice with no particular emotion.

"Lisse," the ghost said, betraying impatience.

One of the glyphs had shown a wolf running. She remembered that at one point the wolf had been the mercenaries' emblem. Nevertheless, she felt a dangerous affinity to it. As she hesitated over it, the kite said, in a parched voice, "Soul strike."

She tapped the glyph, then pressed her palm flat to activate the weapon. The panel felt briefly hot, then cold.

For a second she thought that nothing had happened, that the kite had malfunctioned. The kite was eerily still.

The tanks and personnel carriers were still visible as gray outlines against darker gray, as were the nearby trees and their stifled fruits. She wasn't sure whether that was an effect of the unnamed weapons or a problem with the tapestries. Had ten seconds passed yet? She couldn't tell, and the clock of her pulse was unreliable.

Desperate to escape before the tanks spat forth the killing rounds, Lisse raked her hand sideways to dismiss the glyphs. They dispersed in unsettling fragmented shapes resembling half-chewed leaves and corroded handprints. She repeated the gesture for *fly*.

Lisse choked back a cry as the kite lofted. The tapestry views changed to sky on all sides except the ravens on their tree—birds no longer, but skeletons, price paid in coin of bone.

Only once they had gained some altitude did she instruct the kite to show her what had befallen her hunters. It responded by continuing to accelerate.

The problem was not the tapestries. Rather, the kite's wolf-strike had ripped all the shadows free of their owners, killing them. Below, across a great swathe of the continent once called Ishuel's Bridge, was a devastation of light, a hard, glittering splash against the surrounding snow-capped mountains and forests and winding rivers.

Lisse had been an excellent student, not out of academic conscientiousness but because it gave her an opportunity to study her enemy. One of her best subjects had been geography. She and the ghost had spent hours drawing maps in the air or shaping topographies in her blankets; paper would betray them, it had said. As she memorized the streets of the City of Fountains, it had sung her the ballads of its founding. It had told her about the feuding poets and philosophers that the thoroughfares of the City of Prisms had been named after. She knew which mines supplied which bases and how the roads spidered across Ishuel's Bridge. While the population figures of the bases and settlement camps weren't exactly announced to cadets, especially those recruited from the reeducation facilities, it didn't take much to make an educated guess.

The Imperium had built 114 bases on Ishuel's Bridge. Base complements averaged twenty thousand people. Even allowing for the imprecision of her eye, the wolf-strike had taken out—

She shivered as she listed the affected bases, approximately sixty of them.

The settlement camps' populations were more difficult. The Imperium did not like to release those figures. Imperfectly, she based her estimate on the zone around Base 87, remembering the rows of identical shelters. The only reason they did not outnumber the bases' personnel was that the mercenaries had been coldly efficient on Jerengjen Day.

Needle Stratagem, Lisse thought blankly. The smallest sliver. She hadn't expected its manifestation to be quite so literal.

The ghost was looking at her, its dark eyes unusually distinct. "There's nothing to be done for it now," it said at last. "Tell the kite where to go before it decides for itself."

"Ashway 514," Lisse said, as they had decided before she fled base: scenario after scenario whispered to each other like bedtime stories. She was shaking. The straps did nothing to steady her.

She had one last glimpse of the dead region before they curved into the void: her handprint upon her own birthworld. She had only meant to destroy her hunters.

In her dreams, later, the blast pattern took on the outline of a running wolf.

In the mercenaries' dominant language, jerengjen originally referred to the art of folding paper. For her part, when Lisse first saw it, she thought of it as snow. She was four years old. It was a fair spring afternoon in the City of Tapestries, slightly humid. She was watching a bird try to catch a bright butterfly when improbable paper shapes began drifting from the sky, foxes and snakes and stormbirds.

Lisse called to her parents, laughing. Her parents knew better. Over her shrieks, they dragged her into the basement and switched off the lights. She tried to bite one of her fathers when he clamped his hand over her mouth. Jerengjen tracked primarily by shadows, not by sound, but you couldn't be too careful where the mercenaries' weapons were concerned.

In the streets, jerengjen unfolded prettily, expanding into artillery with dragon-shaped shadows and sleek four-legged assault robots with wolf-shaped shadows. In the skies, jerengjen unfolded into bombers with kestrel-shaped shadows.

This was not the only Rhaioni city where this happened. People crumpled like paper cutouts once their shadows were cut away by the onslaught. Approximately one-third of the world's population perished in the weeks that followed.

Of the casualty figures, the Imperium said, *It is regrettable.* And later, *The stalled negotiations made the consolidation necessary.*

Lisse carried a map of the voidways with her at all times, half in her head and half in the Scorch deck. The ghost had once been a traveler. It had shown her mnemonics for the dark passages and the deep perils that lay between stars. Growing up, she had laid out endless tableaux between her lessons, memorizing travel times and vortices and twists.

Ashway 514 lay in the interstices between two unstable stars and their cacophonous necklace of planets, comets, and asteroids. Lisse felt the kite tilting this way and that as it balanced itself against the stormy voidcurrent. The tapestries shone from one side with ruddy light from the nearer star, 514 Tsi. On the other side, a pale violet-blue planet with a serenade of rings occluded the view.

514 was a useful hiding place. It was off the major tradeways, and since the Battle of Fallen Sun—named after the rebel general's emblem, a white sun outlined in red, rather than the nearby stars—it had been designated an ashway, where permanent habitation was forbidden.

More important to Lisse, however, was the fact that 514 was the ashway nearest the last mercenary sighting, some five years ago. As a student, she had learned the names and silhouettes of the most prominent war-kites, and set verses of praise in their honor to Imperial anthems. She had written essays on their tactics and memorized the names of their most famous commanders, although there were no statues or portraits, only the occasional unsmiling photograph. The Imperium was fond of statues and portraits.

For a hundred years (administrative calendar), the mercenaries had served their masters unflinchingly and unfailingly. Lisse had assumed that she would have as much time as she needed to plot against them. Instead, they had broken their service, for reasons the Imperium had never released—perhaps they didn't know, either—and none had been seen since.

"I'm not sure there's anything to find here," Lisse said. Surely the Imperium would have scoured the region for clues. The tapestries were empty of ravens. Instead, they diagrammed shifting voidcurrent flows. The approach of enemy starflyers would perturb the current and allow Lisse and the ghost to estimate their intent. Not trusting the kite's systems—although there was only so far that she could take her distrust, given the circumstances—she had been watching the tapestries for the past several hours. She had, after a brief argument with the ghost, switched on haptics so that the air currents would, however imperfectly, reflect the status of the void around them. Sometimes it was easier to feel a problem through your skin.

"There's no indication of derelict kites here," she added. "Or even kites in use, other than this one."

"It's a starting place, that's all," the ghost said.

"We're going to have to risk a station eventually. You might not need to eat, but I do." She had only been able to sneak a few rations out of base. It was tempting to nibble at one now.

"Perhaps there are stores on the kite."

"I can't help but think this place is a trap."

"You have to eat sooner or later," the ghost said reasonably. "It's worth a look, and I don't want to see you go hungry." At her hesitation, it added, "I'll stand watch here. I'm only a breath away."

This didn't reassure her as much as it should have, but she was no longer a child in a bunk precisely aligned with the walls, clutching the covers while the ghost told her her people's stories. She reminded herself of her favorite story, in which a single sentinel kept away the world's last morning by burning out her eyes, and set out.

Lisse felt the ghostweight's pull the farther away she walked, but that was old pain, and easily endured. Lights flicked on to accompany her, diffuse despite her unnaturally sharp shadow, then started illuminating passages ahead of her, guiding her footsteps. She wondered what the kite didn't want her to see.

Rations were in an unmarked storage room. She wouldn't have been certain about the rations, except that they were, if the packaging was to be believed, field category 72: better than what she had eaten on training exercises, but not by much. No surprise, now that she thought about it: from all accounts, the mercenaries had relied on their masters' production capacity.

Feeling ridiculous, she grabbed two rations and retraced her steps. The fact that the kite lit her exact path only made her more nervous.

"Anything new?" she asked the ghost. She tapped the ration. "It's a pity that you can't taste poison."

The ghost laughed dryly. "If the kite were going to kill you, it wouldn't be that subtle. Food is food, Lisse."

The food was as exactingly mediocre as she had come to expect from military food. At least it was not any worse. She found a receptacle for disposal afterward, then laid out a Scorch tableau, Candle column to Bone, right to left. Cards rather than jerengjen, because she remembered the scuttling hound-jerengjen with creeping distaste.

From the moment she left Base 87, one timer had started running down. The devastation of Ishuel's Bridge had begun another, the important one. She wasn't gambling her survival; she had already sold it. The question was, how many Imperial bases could she extinguish on her way out? And could she hunt down any of the mercenaries that had been the Imperium's killing sword?

Lisse sorted rapidly through possible targets. For instance, Base 226 Mheng, the Petaled Fortress. She would certainly perish in the attempt, but the only way she could better that accomplishment would be to raze the Imperial firstworld, and she wasn't that ambitious. There was Bridgepoint 663 Tsi-Kes, with its celebrated Pallid Sentinels, or Aerie 8 Yeneq, which built the Imperium's greatest flyers, or—

She set the cards down, closed her eyes, pressed her palms against her face. She was no tactician supreme. Would it make much difference if she picked a card at random?

But of course nothing was truly random in the ghost's presence.

She laid out the Candle Column again. "Not 8 Yeneq," she said. "Let's start with a softer target. Aerie 586 Chiu."

Lisse looked at the ghost: the habit of seeking its approval had not left her. It nodded. "The safest approach is via the Capillary Ashways. It will test your piloting skills."

Privately, Lisse thought that the kite would be happy to guide itself. They didn't dare allow it to, however.

The Capillaries were among the worst of the ashways. Even starlight moved in unnerving ways when faced with ancient networks of void-current gates, unmaintained for generations, or vortices whose behavior changed day by day.

They were fortunate with the first several capillaries. Under other circumstances, Lisse would have gawked at the splendor of lensed galaxies and the jewel-fire of distant clusters. She was starting to manipulate the control interface without hesitating, or flinching as though a wolf's shadow might cross hers.

At the ninth—

"Patrol," the ghost said, leaning close.

She nodded jerkily, trying not to show that its proximity pained her. Its mouth crimped in apology.

"It would have been worse if we'd made it all the way to 586 Chiu without a run-in," Lisse said. That kind of luck always had a price. If she was unready, best to find out now, while there was a chance of fleeing to prepare for a later strike.

The patrol consisted of sixteen flyers: eight Lance 82s and eight Scout 73s. She had flown similar Scouts in simulation.

The flyers did not hesitate. A spread of missiles streaked toward her. Lisse launched antimissile fire.

It was impossible to tell whether they had gone on the attack because the Imperium and the mercenaries had parted on bad terms, or because the authorities had already learned of what had befallen Rhaion. She was certain couriers had gone out within moments of the devastation of Ishuel's Bridge.

As the missiles exploded, Lisse wrenched the kite toward the nearest vortex. The kite was a larger and sturdier craft. It would be better able to survive the voidcurrent stresses. The tapestries dimmed as they approached. She shut off haptics as wind eddied and swirled in the command spindle. It would only get worse.

One missile barely missed her. She would have to do better. And the vortex was a temporary terrain advantage; she could not lurk there forever.

The second barrage came. Lisse veered deeper into the current. The stars took on peculiar roseate shapes.

"They know the kite's capabilities," the ghost reminded her. "Use them. If they're smart, they'll already have sent a courier burst to local command."

The kite suggested jerengjen flyers, harrier class. Lisse conceded its expertise.

The harriers unfolded as they launched, sleek and savage. They maneuvered remarkably well in the turbulence. But there were only ten of them.

"If I fire into that, I'll hit them," Lisse said. Her reflexes were good, but not that good, and the harriers apparently liked to soar near their targets.

"You won't need to fire," the ghost said.

She glanced at him, disbelieving. Her hand hovered over the controls, playing through possibilities and finding them wanting. For instance, she wasn't certain that the firebird (explosives) didn't entail self-immolation, and she was baffled by the stag.

The patrol's pilots were not incapable. They scorched three of the harriers. They probably realized at the same time that Lisse did that the three had been sacrifices. The other seven flensed them silent.

Lisse edged the kite out of the vortex. She felt an uncomfortable sense of duty to the surviving harriers, but she knew they were one-use, crumpled paper, like all jerengjen. Indeed, they folded themselves flat as she passed them, reducing themselves to battledrift.

"I can't see how this is an efficient use of resources," Lisse told the ghost.

"It's an artifact of the mercenaries' methods," it said. "It works. Perhaps that's all that matters."

Lisse wanted to ask for details, but her attention was diverted by a crescendo of turbulence. By the time they reached gentler currents, she was too tired to bring it up.

They altered their approach to 586 Chiu twice, favoring stealth over confrontation. If she wanted to char every patrol in the Imperium by herself, she could live a thousand sleepless years and never be done.

For six days they lurked near 586 Chiu, developing a sense for local traffic and likely defenses. Terrain would not be much difficulty. Aeries were built near calm, steady currents.

"It would be easiest if you were willing to take out the associated city," the ghost said in a neutral voice. They had been discussing whether making a bombing pass on the aerie posed too much of a risk. Lisse had balked at the fact that 586 Chiu Second City was well within blast radius. The people who had furnished the kite's armaments seemed to have believed in surfeit. "They'd only have a moment to know what was happening."

"No."

"Lisse—"

She looked at it mutely, obdurate, although she hated to disappoint it. It hesitated, but did not press its case further.

"This, then," it said in defeat. "Next best odds: aim the voidcurrent disrupter at the manufactory's core while jerengjen occupy the defenses." Aeries held the surrounding current constant to facilitate the calibration of newly built flyers. Under ordinary circumstances, the counterbalancing vortex was leashed at the core. If they could disrupt the core, the vortex would tear at its surroundings.

"That's what we'll do, then," Lisse said. The disrupter had a short range. She did not like the idea of flying in close. But she had objected to the safer alternative.

Aerie 586 Chiu reminded Lisse not of a nest but of a pyre. Flyers and transports were always coming and going, like sparks. The kite swooped in sharp and fast. Falcon-jerengjen raced ahead of them, holding lattice formation for two seconds before scattering toward their chosen marks.

The aerie's commanders responded commendably. They knew the kite was by far the greater threat. But Lisse met the first flight they threw at her with missiles keen and terrible. The void lit up in a clamor of brilliant colors.

The kite screamed when a flyer salvo hit one of its secondary wings. It bucked briefly while the other wings changed their geometry to compensate. Lisse could not help but think that the scream had not sounded like pain. It had sounded like exultation.

The real test was the gauntlet of Banner 142 artillery emplacements. They were silver-bright and terrible. It seemed wrong that they did not roar like tigers. Lisse bit the inside of her mouth and concentrated on narrowing the parameters for the voidcurrent disrupter. Her hand was a fist on the control panel.

One tapestry depicted the currents: striations within striations of pale blue against black. Despite its shielding, the core was visible as a knot tangled out of all proportion to its size.

"Now," the ghost said, with inhuman timing.

She didn't wait to be told twice. She unfisted her hand.

Unlike the wolf-strike, the disrupter made the kite scream again. It lurched and twisted. Lisse wanted to clap her hands over her ears, but there was more incoming fire, and she was occupied with evasive maneuvers. The kite folded in on itself, minimizing its profile. It dizzied her to view it on the secondary tapestry. For a panicked moment, she thought the kite would close itself around her, press her like petals in a book. Then she remembered to breathe.

The disrupter was not visible to human sight, but the kite could read its effect on the current. Like lightning, the disrupter's blast forked and forked again, zigzagging inexorably toward the minute variations in flux that would lead it toward the core.

She was too busy whipping the kite around to an escape vector to see the moment of convergence between disrupter and core. But she felt the first lashing surge as the vortex spun free of its shielding, expanding into available space. Then she was too busy steadying the kite through the triggered subvortices to pay attention to anything but keeping them alive.

Only later did she remember how much debris there had been, flung in newly unpredictable ways: wings torn from flyers, struts, bulkheads, even an improbable crate with small reddish fruit tumbling from the hole in its side.

Later, too, it would trouble her that she had not been able to keep count of the people in the tumult. Most were dead already: sliced slantwise, bone and viscera exposed, trailing banners of blood; others twisted and torn, faces ripped off and cast aside like unwanted masks, fingers uselessly clutching the wrack of chairs, tables, door frames. A fracture in one wall revealed three people in dark green jackets. They turned their faces toward the widening crack, then clasped hands before a subvortex hurled them apart. The last Lisse saw of them was two hands, still clasped together and severed at the wrist.

Lisse found an escape. Took it.

She didn't know until later that she had destroyed 40% of the aerie's structure. Some people survived. They knew how to rebuild.

What she never found out was that the disrupter's effect was sufficiently long-lasting that some of the survivors died of thirst before supplies could safely be brought in.

In the old days, Lisse's people took on the ghostweight to comfort the dead and be comforted in return. After a year and a day, the dead unstitched themselves and accepted their rest.

After Jerengjen Day, Lisse's people struggled to share the sudden increase in ghostweight, to alleviate the flickering terror of the massacred.

Lisse's parents, unlike the others, stitched a ghost onto a child.

"They saw no choice," the ghost told her again and again. "You mustn't blame them."

The ghost had listened uncomplainingly to her troubles and taught her how to cry quietly so the teachers wouldn't hear her. It had soothed her to sleep with her people's legends and histories, described the gardens and promenades so vividly she imagined she could remember them herself. Some nights were more difficult than others, trying to sleep with that strange, stabbing, heartpulse ache. But blame was not what she felt, not usually.

The second target was Base 454 Qo, whose elite flyers were painted with elaborate knotwork, green with bronze-tipped thorns. For reasons that Lisse did not try to understand, the jerengjen disremembered the defensive flight but left the painted panels completely intact.

The third, the fourth, the fifth—she started using Scorch card values to tabulate the reported deaths, however unreliable the figures were in any unencrypted sources. For all its talents, the kite could not pierce military-grade encryption. She spent two days fidgeting over this inconvenience so she wouldn't have to think about the numbers.

When she did think about the numbers, she refused to round up. She refused to round down.

The nightmares started after the sixth, Bridgepoint 977 Ja-Esh. The station commander had kept silence, as she had come to expect. However, a merchant coalition had broken the interdict to plead for mercy in fourteen languages. She hadn't destroyed the coalition's outpost. The station had, in reprimand.

She reminded herself that the merchant would have perished anyway. She had learned to use the firebird to scathing effect. And she was under no illusions that she was only destroying Imperial soldiers and bureaucrats.

In her dreams she heard their pleas in her birth tongue, which the ghost had taught her. The ghost, for its part, started singing her to sleep, as it had when she was little.

The numbers marched higher. When they broke ten million, she plunged out of the command spindle and into the room she had claimed for her own. She pounded the wall until her fists bled. Triumph tasted like salt and venom. It wasn't supposed to be so *easy*. In the worst dreams, a wolf roved the tapestries, eating shadows—eating souls. And the void with its tinsel of worlds was nothing but one vast shadow.

Stores began running low after the seventeenth. Lisse and the ghost argued over whether it was worth attempting to resupply through black market traders. Lisse said they didn't have time to spare, and won. Besides, she had little appetite.

Intercepted communications suggested that someone was hunting them. Rumors and whispers. They kept Lisse awake when she was so tired she wanted to slam the world shut and hide. The Imperium certainly planned reprisal. Maybe others did, too.

If anyone else took advantage of the disruption to move against the Imperium for their own reasons, she didn't hear about it.

The names of the war-kites, recorded in the Imperium's administrative language, are varied: *Fire Burns the Spider Black. The Siege of the City with Seventeen Faces. Sovereign Geometry. The Glove with Three Fingers.*

The names are not, strictly speaking, Imperial. Rather, they are plundered from the greatest accomplishments of the cultures that the mercenaries have defeated on the Imperium's behalf. *Fire Burns the Spider Black* was a silk tapestry housed in the dark hall of Meu Danh, ancient of years. *The Siege of the City with Seventeen Faces* was a saga chanted by the historians of Kwaire. *Sovereign Geometry* discussed the varying nature of parallel lines. And more: plays, statues, games.

The Imperium's scholars and artists take great pleasure in

reinterpreting these works. Such achievements are meant to be disseminated, they say.

They were three days' flight from the next target, Base 894 Sao, when the shadow winged across all the tapestries. The void was dark, pricked by starfire and the occasional searing burst of particles. The shadow singed everything darker as it soared to intercept them, as single-minded in its purpose as a bullet. For a second she almost thought it was a collage of wrecked flyers and rusty shrapnel.

The ghost cursed. Lisse startled, but when she looked at it, its face was composed again.

As Lisse pulled back the displays' focus to get a better sense of the scale, she thought of snowbirds and stormbirds, winter winds and cutting beaks. "I don't know what that is," she said, "but it can't be natural." None of the Imperial defenses had manifested in such a fashion.

"It's not," the ghost said. "That's another war-kite."

Lisse cleared the control panel. She veered them into a chancy voidcurrent eddy.

The ghost said, "Wait. You won't outrun it. As we see its shadow, it sees ours."

"How does a kite have a shadow in the void in the first place?" she asked. "And why haven't we ever seen our own shadow?"

"Who can see their own soul?" the ghost said. But it would not meet her eyes.

Lisse would have pressed for more, but the shadow overtook them. It folded itself back like a plumage of knives. She brought the kite about. The control panel suggested possibilities: a two-headed dragon, a falcon, a coiled snake. Next a wolf reared up, but she quickly pulled her hand back.

"Visual contact," the kite said crisply.

The stranger-kite was the color of a tarnished star. It had tucked all its projections away to present a minimal surface for targeting, but Lisse had no doubt that it could unfold itself faster than she could draw breath. The kite flew a widening helix, beautifully precise.

"A mercenary salute, equal to equal," the ghost said.

"Are we expected to return it?"

"Are you a mercenary?" the ghost countered.

"Communications incoming," the kite said before Lisse could make a retort.

"I'll hear it," Lisse said over the ghost's objection. It was the least courtesy she could offer, even to a mercenary.

To Lisse's surprise, the tapestry's raven vanished to reveal a woman's visage, not an emblem. The woman had brown skin, a scar trailing from one temple down to her cheekbone, and dark hair cropped short. She wore gray on gray, in no uniform that Lisse recognized, sharply tailored. Lisse had expected a killer's eyes, a hunter's eyes. Instead, the woman merely looked tired.

"Commander Kiriet Dzan of—" She had been speaking in administrative, but the last word was unfamiliar. "You would say *Candle*."

"Lisse of Rhaion," she said. There was no sense in hiding her name.

But the woman wasn't looking at her. She was looking at the ghost. She said something sharply in that unfamiliar language.

The ghost pressed its hand against Lisse's. She shuddered, not understanding. "Be strong," it murmured.

"I see," Kiriet said, once more speaking in administrative. Her mouth was unsmiling. "Lisse, do you know who you're traveling with?"

"I don't believe we're acquainted," the ghost said, coldly formal.

"Of course not," Kiriet said. "But I was the logistical coordinator for the scouring of Rhaion." She did not say *consolidation*. "I knew why we were there. Lisse, your ghost's name is Vron Arien."

Lisse said, after several seconds, "That's a mercenary name."

The ghost said, "So it is. Lisse—" Its hand fell away.

"Tell me what's going on."

Its mouth was taut. Then: "Lisse, I—"

"*Tell me.*"

"He was a deserter, Lisse," the woman said, carefully, as if she thought the information might fracture her. "For years he eluded Wolf Command. Then we discovered he had gone to ground on Rhaion. Wolf Command determined that, for sheltering him, Rhaion must be brought to heel. The Imperium assented."

Throughout this Lisse looked at the ghost, silently begging it to deny any of it, all of it. But the ghost said nothing.

Lisse thought of long nights with the ghost leaning by her bedside, reminding her of the dancers, the tame birds, the tangle of frostfruit trees in the city square; things she did not remember herself because she had been too young when the jerengjen came. Even her parents only came to her in snatches: curling up in a mother's lap, helping a father peel plantains. Had any of the ghost's stories been real?

She thought, too, of the way the ghost had helped her plan her escape from Base 87, how it had led her cunningly through the maze and to the kite. At the time, it had not occurred to her to wonder at its confidence.

Lisse said, "Then the kite is yours."

"After a fashion, yes." The ghost's eyes were precisely the color of ash after the last ember's death.

"But my parents—"

Enunciating the words as if they cut it, the ghost said, "We made a bargain, your parents and I."

She could not help it; she made a stricken sound.

"I offered you my protection," the ghost said. "After years serving the Imperium, I knew its workings. And I offered your parents vengeance. Don't think that Rhaion wasn't my home, too."

Lisse was wrackingly aware of Kiriet's regard. "Did my parents truly die in the consolidation?" The euphemism was easier to use.

She could have asked whether Lisse was her real name. She had to assume that it wasn't.

"I don't know," it said. "After you were separated from them, I had no way of finding out. Lisse, I think you had better find out what Kiriet wants. She is not your friend."

I was the logistical coordinator, Kiriet had said. And her surprise at seeing the ghost—*It has a name,* Lisse reminded herself—struck Lisse as genuine. Which meant Kiriet had not come here in pursuit of Vron Arien. "Why are you here?" Lisse asked.

"You're not going to like it. I'm here to destroy your kite, whatever you've named it."

"It doesn't have a name." She had been unable to face the act of naming, of claiming ownership.

Kiriet looked at her sideways. "I see."

"Surely you could have accomplished your goal," Lisse said, "without talking to me first. I am inexperienced in the ways of kites. You are not." In truth, she should already have been running. But Kiriet's revelation meant that Lisse's purpose, once so clear, was no longer to be relied upon.

"I may not be your friend, but I am not your enemy, either," Kiriet said. "I have no common purpose with the Imperium, not anymore. But you cannot continue to use the kite."

Lisse's eyes narrowed. "It is the weapon I have," she said. "I would be a fool to relinquish it."

"I don't deny its efficacy," Kiriet said, "but you are Rhaioni. Doesn't the cost trouble you?"

Cost?

Kiriet said, "So no one told you." Her anger focused on the ghost.

"A weapon is a weapon," the ghost said. At Lisse's indrawn breath, it said, "The kites take their sustenance from the deaths they deal. It was necessary to strengthen ours by letting it feast on smaller targets first. This is the particular craft of my people, as ghostweight was the craft of yours, Lisse."

Sustenance. "So this is why you want to destroy the kite," Lisse said to Kiriet.

"Yes." The other woman's smile was bitter. "As you might imagine, the Imperium did not approve. It wanted to negotiate another hundred-year contract. I dissented."

"Were you in a position to dissent?" the ghost asked, in a way that made Lisse think that it was translating some idiom from its native language.

"I challenged my way up the chain of command and unseated the head of Wolf Command," Kiriet said. "It was not a popular move. I have been destroying kites ever since. If the Imperium is so keen on further conquest, let it dirty its own hands."

"Yet you wield a kite yourself," Lisse said.

"*Candle* is my home. But on the day that every kite is accounted for in words of ash and cinders, I will turn my own hand against it."

It appealed to Lisse's sense of irony. All the same, she did not trust Kiriet.

She heard a new voice. Kiriet's head turned. "Someone's followed you." She said a curt phrase in her own language, then: "You'll want my assistance—"

Lisse shook her head.

"It's a small flight, as these things go, but it represents a threat to you. Let me—"

"No," Lisse said, more abruptly than she had meant to. "I'll handle it myself."

"If you insist," Kiriet said, looking even more tired. "Don't say I didn't warn you." Then her face was replaced, for a flicker, with her emblem: a black candle crossed slantwise by an empty sheath.

"The *Candle* is headed for a vortex, probably for cover," the ghost said, very softly. "But it can return at any moment."

Lisse thought that she was all right, and then the reaction set in.

She spent several irrecoverable breaths shaking, arms wrapped around herself, before she was able to concentrate on the tapestry data.

At one time, every war-kite displayed a calligraphy scroll in its command spindle. The words are, approximately:

I have only
one candle

Even by the mercenaries' standards, it is not much of a poem. But the woman who wrote it was a soldier, not a poet.

The mercenaries no longer have a homeland. Even so, they keep certain traditions, and one of them is the Night of Vigils. Each mercenary honors the year's dead by lighting a candle. They used to do this on the winter solstice of an ancient calendar. Now the Night of Vigils is on the anniversary of the day the first war-kites were launched; the day the mercenaries slaughtered their own people to feed the kites.

The kites fly, the mercenaries' commandant said. *But they do not know how to hunt.*

When he was done, they knew how to hunt. Few of the mercenaries forgave him, but it was too late by then.

The poem says: So many people have died, yet I have only one candle for them all.

It is worth noting that "have" is expressed by a particular construction for alienable possession: not only is the having subject to change, it is additionally under threat of being taken away.

Kiriet's warning had been correct. An Imperial flight in perfect formation had advanced toward them, inhibiting their avenues of escape. They outnumbered her forty-eight to one. The numbers did not concern her, but the Imperium's resources meant that if she dealt with this flight, there would be twenty more waiting for her, and the numbers would only grow worse. That they had not opened fire already meant they had some trickery in mind.

One of the flyers peeled away, describing an elegant curve and exposing its most vulnerable surface, painted with a rose.

"That one's not armed," Lisse said, puzzled.

The ghost's expression was unreadable. "How very wise of them," it said.

The forward tapestry flickered. "Accept the communication," Lisse said.

The emblem that appeared was a trefoil flanked by two roses, one stem-up, one stem-down. Not for the first time, Lisse wondered why people from a culture that lavished attention on miniatures and sculptures were so intent on masking themselves in emblems.

"Commander Fai Guen, this is Envoy Nhai Bara." A woman's voice, deep and resonant, with an accent Lisse didn't recognize.

So I've been promoted? Lisse thought sardonically, feeling herself tense up. The Imperium never gave you anything, even a meaningless rank, without expecting something in return.

Softly, she said to the ghost, "They were bound to catch up to us sooner or later." Then, to the kite: "Communications to Envoy Nhai: I am Lisse of Rhaion. What words between us could possibly be worth exchanging? Your people are not known for mercy."

"If you will not listen to me," Nhai said, "perhaps you will listen to the envoy after me, or the one after that. We are patient and we are many. But I am not interested in discussing mercy: that's something we have in common."

"I'm listening," Lisse said, despite the ghost's chilly stiffness. All her life she had honed herself against the Imperium. It was unbearable to consider that she might have been mistaken. But she had to know what Nhai's purpose was.

"Commander Lisse," the envoy said, and it hurt like a stab to hear her name spoken by a voice other than the ghost's, a voice that was not Rhaioni. Even if she knew, now, that the ghost was not Rhaioni, either. "I have a proposal for you. You have proven your military effectiveness—"

Military effectiveness. She had tallied all the deaths, she had marked each massacre on the walls of her heart, and this faceless envoy collapsed them into two words empty of number.

"—quite thoroughly. We are in need of a strong sword. What is your price for hire, Commander Lisse?"

"What is my—" She stared at the trefoil emblem, and then her face went ashen.

It is not true that the dead cannot be folded. Square becomes kite becomes swan; history becomes rumor becomes song. Even the act of remembrance creases the truth.

But the same can be said of the living.

the shadow postulates

Kaela Navus was reading a beginners' sword-dancing manual when a hand descended upon her own, blotting out the diagram. She looked up, mouth opening in protest, only to have the scroll plucked from her grip and rolled shut. The black lines faded into ricepaper-white. "Teris!" Kaela said.

Her roomsister, Teris Tascha, set the scroll down on the escritoire out of Kaela's reach. "You won't learn the pattern for the Swallow Flies Home from a diagram," she said. "It has to live in your muscles."

Kaela felt the heat in her face and averted her gaze, but did not argue the point. Of this year's magistrate-aspirants at the Black College, she was the least comfortable with the required physical disciplines. She would rather have been working on her thesis if it hadn't been for the difficulty her research topic was giving her. The college did not specifically ask magistrate-aspirants to learn sword-dancing, but since Teris had agreed to teach her, she had chosen it instead of any number of more staid alternatives, like archery or dance.

"Come on," said Teris. She nudged Kaela into standing up. Teris was the taller of the two, with great dark eyes and bright hair that she kept pinned up so it wouldn't get in her way. She was Kaela's only roomsister, although the Black College preferred to group its magistrate-aspirants in threes. One had dropped out during the first term. Teris compensated for the absence by venturing into the city most evenings, while Kaela was relieved, and spent her free hours in the garden or library.

Teris said, "Let's go through the Swallow Flies Home—only this time I'll mime, and you'll use my blades." She unsheathed one of the two blades at her hip and held it out. "The balance will be close to your practice-sticks, Kaela. Go ahead."

Although Teris was right, Kaela flinched from the weight of steel, the shining edge separated from her grip only by the slender, flower-embossed circle of metal. She accepted the second blade with better grace, wondering how she could apologize for her awkwardness.

"Just hold them for a few minutes until you get used to them," Teris said. And, after the tension in Kaela's arms and shoulders began to ease, "Ready?"

Kaela felt far from ready. She had put off purchasing her own brace of blades, despite having saved enough to do so, for this very reason. Nevertheless, she could not bring herself to turn away from her roomsister's encouraging smile. "Ready."

The first time through, sweating and trembling, she halted in the middle of the gliding steps through which she and her partner would exchange positions. Only the nakedness of her embarrassment kept her from blurting out, "I'm sorry," or "I can't," or some excuse. She had danced this pattern before, not clumsily, but not expertly either. She had done this before. Just not with blades.

Kaela started over, and her roomsister moved in perfect accompaniment. At the point where she had stopped earlier, exhilaration overtook her. The blades were in her hands, and Teris did not even have practice sticks. She did not have to worry about miscalculating and getting cut by a lunge, although Teris's reflexes were good enough to prevent such an occurrence. Through the weight of metal, the momentum of their turns as their shadows performed a projection of their dance across the floor and upon the wall, Kaela imagined that she tasted migration toward a season of beauty and poise.

The pattern ended. Kaela returned to the room, to the blades, to Teris's delighted smile.

"That was splendid," said Teris. "I don't know why I didn't think of it earlier."

"Think of what?"

Teris gestured toward the blades, although she seemed in no hurry to retrieve them. "Letting you wield them for the sword-dance. It's different, you see, even if you use the heavy wooden knife-sticks. You know what I mean, now."

Despite an unexpected reluctance to surrender the blades, Kaela did just that. She did not trust herself with them at the moment; she did not trust her voice or even her hands. She hoped that her eyes conveyed gratitude rather than giddy madness. And her hands no longer trembled. They must have stopped during the pattern, without her awareness.

Unfazed by Kaela's momentary muteness, Teris resheathed the blades with an admirable nonchalance, and smiled again. Neither of them glanced toward the scroll with its absent manual.

After that, Kaela returned to studying for the week's exam in judicial theory. She had neglected to do so earlier because she was puzzling over the problem of the shadow postulates, which she had brashly submitted as her research topic, and later because she had decided that, after months of dead-end possibilities, she would rather learn sword-dancing. She was paying for it now.

Tonight, she would rather have hidden in her room and studied. The Black College was hosting a trio of visiting scholars, however, and since the dinner talk was on mathematics, her specialty, she could not absent herself. Teris had disappeared after their practice session, heading for a festhall sword-dance with her lover, a college technician who shared her enthusiasm for the physical disciplines. Kaela envied them their revelry, even though she shied away from that bright, barbaric atmosphere.

Trapped at dinner, Kaela toyed with her chopsticks and reviewed canonical decisions while a senior magistrate introduced the scholars. When her seatmates started giving her irritated looks, she switched to teasing apart a tassel on her floor-cushion to keep herself awake.

Three scholars, the ever-present convention of rhetorical balance, in contrast to the undiluted pairing of the sword-dance, relic of earlier, more warlike traditions. The second scholar, at least, had an animated face and voice in contrast to the pedantry of the first. Even so, she felt her attention drifting. Maybe she should buy a new floor-cushion for her room, one with many silk tassels for the unraveling. On second thought, maybe not. Teris was sensitive to small nervous motions, but was too polite to protest. Kaela tried to return the courtesy by stilling herself. The sword-dancing did help reduce her jitteriness.

When the scholar went into a digression on mirror dynamics, Kaela sat straighter, the tassel forgotten. This intersected her research topic, after all.

"—what the mirror-war revealed," said the scholar by way of conclusion, "is that the relationship between source and image is mediated by these dynamics. An invisible third presence, if you like, satisfying the rule of three for Vorief's framework."

Kaela shivered at the name. Anje Vorief's studies in entelechy had resulted in near-instant communications and the ready production of silhouettes, which displaced scribes and the necessity of large-scale printing. They had also led to the continent's only mirror-war, which started with the assassination of several public figures by paring away their reflections hour by hour until they wandered lost in iterations of shattered identity and died.

Nevertheless, now that safeguards existed against those abuses, Vorief's treatise, *When Shadows Walk into the World*, was required reading at the Black College. Magistrates had a long history of primitive applications of entelechy theory, as the college's procession of shades showed. All magistrate-aspirants were warned that the shades, which belonged to past magistrates, paid them especial scrutiny. The shades' demands for inhuman honesty had driven careless aspirants into safer academic pursuits.

The third scholar had finished speaking. Kaela's body begged for sleep.

She stayed just long enough to show courtesy to the visitors before fleeing to her empty room. Tassels and their shadows, forming unbreakable knots on the walls, twined in her dreams.

"I'm hungry," Kaela said after her roomsister prodded her awake.

Teris gave her an exasperated look. "I bet you didn't remember to eat anything at dinner. I saved you a pastry from breakfast, but your tea's no longer hot."

"You're too splendid for words, Teris." Kaela didn't mind lukewarm tea.

Teris sniffed, but the crook of her mouth suggested she was not unflattered. "How was the talk?"

"The parts of it I was awake for? There were some interesting things about how mathematical applications affect the propagation of legal norms, models for ethical calculus, that sort of thing."

Teris had started stretching, palms to feet, and she straightened herself before saying, "Nothing controversial, then. I wish they would inflict these itinerant scholars on us less often. Let them ponder philosophy and leave applications to us."

"I'm sure they think their work is important. At least we're exposed to judicial research from all over the continent. Unless you think we should be sheltered from different paradigms until we have more experience?"

"See what happens when I give you a pastry? It's restday and here you are starting a policy discussion without a third participant."

Kaela changed the subject, despite her roomsister's teasing tone. "How was the festhall?"

"Ever so refreshing after poring over documents." She resumed her stretches, recounting the pleasure of her lover's surety of form, the consuming dream of motion they shared.

Soon sorry she had asked, Kaela made noncommittal noises in response. She thought Teris spent too much time trying to impress the technician. Still, she enjoyed watching her roomsister's lithe motions, although the topic of conversation had stifled her desire to join in the stretches.

Reluctantly, Kaela looked away and reviewed the last two days of notes, even if it was restday. She lost herself in her research problem. The shadow postulates, although they dated from an earlier era, extended the Vorief framework. Like those before her, Kaela suspected that the third of the three postulates, which dealt with incorporeal consequences, could be derived from the rest of the extended framework.

As a magistrate-aspirant, Kaela could have submitted a less abstruse, more *practical* research topic. The point was to prove herself capable of basic research methods, no more. Many scholars had lost years in the postulates' intricacies only to peel away into related studies. Kaela was too stubborn to admit that this might happen to her.

Last week, her sponsor, the senior scholar Roz Roven, had reminded her that she needed to submit a draft of her thesis by the end of this term. "I know you've sworn yourself to this," he said, "but you're running short of time. You may have to settle for a less ambitious problem. You won't be the first." The words belied the regret in his gaze, that the student he had taken in on account of her early promise should fall short, as he had decades ago.

Kaela found the prospect of his disappointment unbearable, even if the third shadow postulate was one of the outstanding problems in entelechy theory. Stymied, she wondered what had prompted the magistrate Brien, several hundred years dead, to append the postulates to a mundane schedule roster. Records from that time, according to Teris, spoke of war between nations now united. Of Brien, they said little concerning mathematics. In his time, he had befriended a traitor and the traitor's innocent lover, herself a magistrate. Beyond that, Kaela had never been able to follow the intricacies of intrigue.

If more of Brien's writings had survived, the shadow postulates might not have become such an enduring puzzle. Kaela shook her head. Too bad the magistrates' shades communicated through cryptic gestures and never in words, or she—and generations of mathematicians before her—would have asked Brien's faceless shade the everlasting *why?*

Although Teris invited her to a festhall dance after dinner, Kaela refused. "I might head out before dinner and eat there," Teris said, disappointed but forgiving, as always. "Don't worry about me, sister-mine."

Kaela could no more stop worrying about her roomsister than she could stop fidgeting. Since she delighted in symmetry, she saved tea and riceballs from dinner just in case. They grew cold as she hunched over her notes.

When the equations started to blur, she conceded that this was doing her no good. In a fit of recklessness, she shrugged on a shabby wool coat, located her boots, and ventured out of the room. Shadows clung to her footsteps. She shivered.

Fear of shadows was a common student phobia. During curfew hour, wherever light lived, shades paced along the college's walls and through its gardens. They were instantiations of past magistrates, a phenomenon from the Black College's earliest days. New students received the curfew-bell schedule upon arrival so they knew when to be wary. Rumors abounded of students losing parts of their reflections, or speaking in voices of dust and smoke, or getting lost on paths they had walked a hundred times, ending up on rooftops or behind doors that, once exited, were never to be seen again. According to the college, the curfew hours were the outgrowth of a religious practice to honor the shades. Teris had opined, when they first met, that it was really to keep revelers from irritating the shades into starting a second mirror-war.

Kaela, startled out of being intimidated by her new roomsister's confident bearing, asked, "Wouldn't it make more sense to have an all-night curfew, then? And aren't the shades only abroad during those particular hours?"

"Nothing ruins a judgment like the facts," said Teris, and they both laughed. That was when Kaela decided she might be able to share a room with Teris without stammering every time Teris glanced her way.

In any case, none of the shades troubled Kaela as she threaded her way from campus to city. The quarter that surrounded the Black College had its share of street lights, hazing the stars' distant shine. Kaela coughed behind her sleeve at the mingling of smoke, perfume, and cheap vintages with bouquets obscured beyond recognition. She skirted puddles and shied from laughing men and women who swept by her with disdainful looks at her clothing. *Student,* their glances judged her, *and poor at that.* Both were true enough, and she was not Teris to challenge them in her turn.

As Kaela was about to pass the first festhall, she realized she had forgotten which one Teris had said she would be at, or whether, indeed, she might not drift among several in the course of the night. This only firmed her determination. Kaela sought her roomsister at the more reputable festhalls that mushroomed around the college. Even then, the noise from the doorways appalled her.

She found no sign of Teris's bright hair amid the crowds. Men propositioned Kaela, or offered dances or drinks, but she refused them with polite phrases, unmoved by smiles or inviting eyes. Her training in sword-dancing helped her elude those who became more insistent before they could grab her arm or swing her close.

After a while, Kaela gave up and retraced her route, unwilling to check rowdier possibilities. She credited Teris with better taste. Obsessive about detail, she checked the festhalls in reverse order as she went. In the Spinning Rose, she found Teris Tascha at last.

The beat of hand-drums warned her of the sword-dance within, and her hands clenched in the folds of her coat. The rhythms, whose syncopation she analyzed instinctively, drew her toward the open entrance, the hushed voices, the lanterns blossoming in bold colors. She did not belong here, despite the invitation, but Teris—Teris was another matter.

Kaela edged into the Spinning Rose, and saw Teris with that bright-spun hair caught up in combs and beaded ribbons, blades gleaming in her hands. Across from Teris was the technician, likewise lithe, his motions timed to hers. Kaela was unable to remember his name, but here names didn't matter. Teris and her lover did not see the watcher by the doorway, shaking and flushed wordless. Their gazes were locked upon each other, but what they saw, Kaela realized, was not each other, only the dance's precise symmetries, the parabolic flight of flung blades, the coordination of movement with the drums' insistent voices.

Enraptured by Teris's laughing eyes and quickened breath, those choreographed geometries, Kaela almost stepped farther into the festhall, ready to meet the eyes of an unpartnered dancer and offer herself to the dance. The spinning blades, which would once have tightened her throat with dread, now reflected light into patterns that tugged at her hands, her feet, the pulse in her veins.

Then Kaela remembered that she had no blades of her own, because purchasing a brace would have meant committing herself to this bright, barbarous dance. If she walked a little closer and caught Teris's attention with the plea in her eyes, Teris would smile at the technician and draw away from him to loan Kaela her blades for a dance or two with the unthinking generosity she had always shown. Teris wouldn't mind; would, in fact, be delighted to see her roomsister join the dance at last. Kaela could not, however, bring herself to interrupt the pair, so splendidly matched, for her own brash pleasure. She left the festhall, and no one marked her departure.

Shaken, Kaela did not think to check the hour before she ventured back on campus. The street lights stretched shadows into spindly mockeries. Although no one shared the path with her, other shadows moved purposefully, undistorted by exigencies of distance and angle. Since she was halfway to her dormitory, she hastened rather than turning back.

Between one step and the next, a magistrate's shade brushed her shadow. For a terrible, unblinking moment, she understood the principle by which Vorief's framework could be used to kill from a distance, understood it in a visceral manner that her first-term reading of the treatise had failed to convey. What was a shadow, after all, but a shape in the moving world reduced to a projection of possibilities?

The dead magistrate had made his choices, Kaela was given to understand, and those choices collapsed into the single sharp fact of his death, the face of unflinching truth. What would her shade reveal after her heartbeat stilled?

She saw her life flattened to an ink-blot, her own shadow beginning to peel into shapes she did not want to confront, and fled the rest of the way to her room. Her hands shook as she spread her sleeping mat, and in the darkness, she laced her fingers together to still them. Only shadows, she told herself over and over as she sought sleep. Only shadows.

Kaela did not mention the Spinning Rose to her roomsister that day or the next or the next after that, even during sword-dancing practice. She reread *When Shadows Walk into the World*. She performed flawlessly on her next exam, which concerned the comparative history of execution and exile, although after she handed it in, she could not recall any of the questions, much less her responses. And, Teris told her one morning, she began talking in her sleep.

"What have I been saying?" Kaela demanded.

"Mathematical things," Teris said, and recited some of them back to her.

She relaxed, then wondered why she had been tense. "Oh, that. I've been trying to reformulate Brien's notation. I swear there's something going on with those definitions, if I could just see what he was doing. The entelechy framework didn't exist while he lived, so that third postulate must have seemed necessary to him. Why is it so hard to figure out how to derive it?" She swallowed. "I haven't been keeping you up, have I?" Kaela slept deeply, so Teris's comings and goings rarely woke her, but the reverse was not true.

Teris, in the process of unpinning her hair to brush it out before breakfast, paused and shook her head. The tangles were almost copper in the lamplight. "No. I'm just worried about you. I can't say I understand your research, but you've got to ease up on yourself."

Kaela averted her gaze from her roomsister's earnest eyes. "I'm nearing the deadline for that rough draft, and my notes, the structures I see, they don't quite come together. As if there's a gap, and I should know the shape of the bridge."

"Even so." Teris passed the brush from hand to hand with unthinking precision. "Tomorrow, instead of your paper, promise me you'll do something that hasn't the slightest relationship to research. Sit in the library and read torrid love poetry if that's what it takes. It'll help. You'll see."

"I want to buy my own blades," Kaela blurted out.

Forever after, Kaela would remember that her roomsister's expression, rather than being surprised or amused or smug, became thoughtful and not a little pleased. "Tomorrow, hells. We can go shopping after breakfast, if you like. Neither of us has class today until the afternoon, is that right?"

"Yes," said Kaela, thinking that, with blades of her own, she need no longer fear shadows.

That evening, and the evenings afterward, Kaela and Teris, both wielding steel, practiced true sword-dances. Teris showed her new exercises to ease her out of her self-consciousness. It helped for a while. She would never equal her roomsister's shining poise, but she approached it in her own slow way. Sometimes, laying alone in the darkness with the blades beneath her pillow, she even forgot her encounter with the magistrate's shade.

Scant weeks remained before her draft was due. Kaela resumed murmuring in her sleep. Teris continued to invite her to festhall sword-dances, but Kaela's fear of shadows held her fast. Finally, she retreated to the Black College's library after dinner to avoid the invitation, telling herself she needed to concentrate. As she slipped between the shelves, she avoided looking at the shreds of her shadow along the interstices of wall and floor. Teris, she was sure, had never struggled with phobia in her life.

She stopped by the shelves that housed the Black College's history and counted backwards by decades until she found the era during which magistrate Brien had held office. So few volumes to encompass the long dance of lives, all reprinted via silhouette. Originals that old were stored elsewhere, and here the usual must of aging paper was replaced by a cleaner smell.

Kaela knew that she would find little on Brien here; she had already looked. Her roomsister, better trained in historical methodology, would have told her if anything useful appeared elsewhere. Who had Brien's friend the traitor been, and what had he betrayed? She should have paid more attention, even if it seemed like gossip too ancient to have any relevance, especially to mathematics.

"Brien," she said into the rows of listening books, tasting the name. The ancient gossip had once been anything but ancient or irrelevant; had captured three people, at least, in its knots. She did not know what they had looked like or what their voices sounded like. She did not know the touches they exchanged or failed to exchange.

The archivist on duty, bemused by Kaela's interest, found no contemporary portraits of the three, but located a later woodprint of the execution, called *Between Shadows*. The first thing Kaela noticed was the utter absence of blades in the picture, although even today, full magistrates carried a ritual sword of office. "Who is who?" Kaela asked, captivated by the stark stiff lines and shadows, the contrasting fluidity of the falling leaves that framed the scene.

"Rahen the Traitor," said the archivist, pointing to the man who stared defiantly from the center of the picture, hands bound behind him. "Magistrate Kischa." A woman with a river-fall of dark hair around her averted face, to Rahen's left. "Magistrate Brien." A thin man with no expression except in his hands, with his fingers laced together. In those tense hands, Kaela, who had learned to read stances as a sword-dancer, saw a cry too broken for other expression.

And all around them, the falling leaves, each three-lobed. No, shreds of leaves. Even Kaela understood that symbolism, the implication of death and divided lives. She thanked the unknown artist for being straightforward.

The archivist said, "Shall I make you a silhouette of this?"

"Yes," Kaela said. "Oh, yes." Brien had a face now. She would settle for that.

She made it back to her room with a half hour to spare before curfew, clutching the woodcut-silhouette all the way. She laid it atop her escritoire and studied it more closely. For all she knew, the artist had invented the faces. But those tense, anguished hands had a truth in them beyond fact or fancy.

Next to the picture, she laid her silhouette of the shadow postulates in their earliest known formulation, although the archaic notation gave her headaches. Three postulates, braided around each other and into the entelechy framework. Three-lobed leaves. Three people, two lovers, one death.

The bell tolled curfew. Kaela was nowhere near ready to sleep. She stretched, then segued into the Wolf Approaches, miming the blade. Her shadow partnered her, a solitary shape against the wall. She stopped. No. Without Teris, it wasn't the same.

"I am not afraid," Kaela said to her shadow.

Kaela repeated the stretches to keep her muscles from knotting up. Idly, letting her mind drift free of her body, she negated the third shadow postulate, then followed the strands of logic in search of the inevitable contradiction. She knew the extended framework as intimately as her hands knew the unruly cascades of her hair. With practiced discipline, she began working through the consequences of a system identical save for that one negated postulate.

There was no contradiction.

Kaela sat before the escritoire. She laid her hands on her notes, intending to make sure she was remembering the postulates correctly, then snatched them back before they clenched and crumpled the sum of her work. Her gaze fell again on the woodcut-silhouette with its border of falling leaves.

No. She had not misremembered.

It was as though, having lived all her life in the belief that roomsisters or roombrothers must come in threes, she discovered they could live in pairs, as with herself and Teris, or quartets. The Black College organized itself around a rule of three, but why not a rule of two, or four?

A person cast one and only one shadow under most circumstances, but in the darkness, no shadows lived; in the light of several lanterns, shadows proliferated. Each scenario, for a given set of light sources, was equally valid. And so it was with the third shadow postulate.

Two shadows crossing and uncrossing while she watched, breathless, from the doorway of the Spinning Rose.

"Teris," Kaela breathed, eyes widening. She was in love with Teris Tascha, despite the sister-taboo.

Falling leaves, three-lobed leaves. Brien must have loved his friend's lover, the woman with the long, dark hair, although it had gone unwritten and Kaela, in the absence of textual evidence, would never be able to prove it.

Kaela began writing, scarcely conscious of her pen's outpouring. She knew the shape of the entelechy framework and the alternate structures that would result from the variations on that third, mutable postulate, from its possible negations. She knew, too, that she could not articulate the key insight, the silent cry that Brien had left within the single language abstract enough to trust with his anguish at standing outside his friends' romance.

Perhaps Brien had executed the traitor, friend and rival both, with a traitorously glad heart himself. Perhaps he had wished to discard himself in the traitor's place, after seeing what the execution did to that dark-haired woman. The artist, in drawing Brien's fingers as a cage of tension, convinced Kaela that the latter was closer to the truth.

Kaela remembered the name of Teris's lover, but it didn't matter. She put down her pen. Now that she understood what she had overlooked, she had time to formulate a coherent thesis. Roz Roven, her sponsor, would be pleased.

She also understood that she could never mention her insight to Teris in a language that the other woman could fathom. Kaela had no desire to break the paired beauty of hand meeting hand, blade meeting blade, to step between two sword-dancers' shadows intersecting beneath the eyes of light. But she could find her own dance.

I have loved you in your own language, Kaela thought as she picked up her blades, *so softly that we never knew it. Let your language be mine; let me cast my own shadows.*

No shadows interrupted her all the way through curfew hour that night as she walked to the Spinning Rose, or any night thereafter.

the bones of giants

Whatever else might be said of the sorcerer who ruled the rim of the Pit, he had never been able to raise the bones of giants. The bones lay scattered in the rimlands, green-grey with moss and crusted with crystals, whorled with the fingerprints of desperate travelers. The bones did not easily surrender fingerprints. The locals considered it bad luck to leave their marks on the giants' bones.

Tamim was sitting in the lee of a rock and had raised his gun to his head when the giants' bones embedded in the hill shook themselves free of earth. He knew that the gun wasn't going to be of any use against the bones. He knew of only two ways to destroy ghouls: lure them past the rimlands' borders so they would crumble into dust, or pierce them through the heart with jade.

The border was days away. Tamim had used the last of his jade bullets escaping a vulture patrol.

His finger hesitated on the trigger.

"You shouldn't do that," a girl's voice, or a young woman's, called from the other side of the rock.

He shouldn't have let his guard down, even for a suicide attempt. Maybe especially for a suicide attempt. The sorcerer's Vulture Corps was always happy to collect corpses.

Tamim edged around the rock. He didn't like leaving bones at his back, but they were taking their time assembling themselves, as though unseen ligaments were growing at each joint. Their clattering made him jumpy. *Assess the threat,* he reminded himself, *then decide.*

The girl was in plain sight. She had brown skin like Tamim's own and long black hair in tangles down to her waist, too long to be practical, the kind an aristocrat might have. No aristocrat, however, would have been caught in that high-collared black coat.

Tamim knew the rimlands' sumptuary laws, knew what the black coat meant: vulture, and necromancer besides. He aimed and fired.

He must have made some noise to alert her. She ran toward him, ducking at the right moment. The bullet missed her by inches; a lock of hair drifted free. "I'm not what you think, boy," she said breathlessly. She barely came up to his shoulder. Her hand, surprisingly strong, caught his and twisted the gun to point at the ground between them.

Five bullets left, but he wanted to save one for himself. Admittedly, at this range he was more likely to shoot himself if he tried again. That wasn't even taking into account the girl's reflexes. "What are you, then?"

"I'm no vulture," she said. "I'm alone out here. I need help, and I'll take what I can find, whether it comes in the shape of a giant or a boy who looks half-ghoul himself." She stared directly into his eyes as she released her grip on the gun.

Tamim made a frustrated noise and holstered the gun. A soldier wasn't supposed to feel curiosity, but today he had forfeited any claim to being a soldier. "You're the one raising the bones," he pointed out.

He had been wrong about the skeleton. There were two of them, not one, entangled oddly from aeons in the earth's embrace.

The girl took her attention off Tamim for a moment. She laced her fingers together, then pulled them apart. In a rush, the bones separated into two skeletons. Loam, uprooted grass, and glittering gravel showered both Tamim and the girl. Dust swirled in the shape of grinning skulls, then settled. The girl paid it no heed. Apparently she was as accustomed to the rimlands' behavior as he was.

"There," she said with evident satisfaction. "What do you think? One's yours, of course."

He stared at her stonily.

"It's not like I can ride two of them at once," she said, as if she made perfect sense and he was the slow one. "You haven't run screaming yet. That's always useful."

Clearly the world had plans for him other than suicide today. "I was reared by the undead," Tamim said. His mother, a woman with a brilliant smile and an aristocrat's long, slender hands, had given him into the care of a company of ghouls, reasoning that it would prepare him to survive in the rimlands and eventually take up her cause. But one by one his caretakers had fallen apart, rotting teeth and decaying eyes, a toe here and a loop of shriveled intestine there.

His mother had died attempting to assassinate the sorcerer when Tamim was a child. The undead did not fall apart immediately upon their creator's death, but lingered for a span of years proportionate to the creator's skill. Tamim's mother, for all her ambitions, had not been a particularly skilled necromancer. He had a dim memory of crying when the last of his caretakers ceased to move, even the mindless, instinctive creeping of a rotted finger toward the hand. It had been the last time he cried.

The girl nodded as though his childhood was unremarkable. Perhaps it was, from a necromancer's point of view. "Right or left?" she said.

Involuntarily, Tamim looked up at the giants. The one on the left had a long, narrow skull and cracked teeth. Curiously, spurs extended from the back, as though wings had been broken off. The one on the right had a broader visage and no spurs, and its left arm was longer than the right.

"I don't know your name," Tamim said. "Why should I take up with a necromancer?" He hadn't known that any necromancers remained in the rimlands who did not serve the sorcerer. The Pit was death, and the sorcerer controlled the Pit: ergo necromancers served he who ruled death. The rest had fled to the lands beyond the Pit, or died in a hundred small rebellions. The sorcerer was not notable for his sense of mercy.

"I'm Sakera," she said. "Pleased to meet you, I'm sure. I'll make you a bargain, O soldier"—her eyes alighted briefly on the gun—"who wishes to die. Help me bring down the sorcerer, and at the journey's end I will give you the death you desire."

The gun was an unbalancing weight at his hip. He had lived with such things all his life. "How long a journey?" Then, realizing that he was actually considering it, he added, "I don't need your help to kill myself."

"Months," Sakera said. "But I've seen what happens when you miss with a gun. You might live out the rest of your days as a mangled thing with less mind than a ghoul. With a necromancer, death can be certain. It can even be swift."

"I'm not that incompetent." He had long years of practice killing.

"No, I imagine not." Her voice was brisk. "Let's put it another way, then. There can't be many necromancers left in the rimlands. If you're no vulture-friend, I may be your best chance of getting rid of the sorcerer."

"I don't trust you," Tamim said. Tact had never been one of his strengths. Among other things, it was wasted on ghouls.

"You don't need to trust me," Sakera said. "You just need to believe me."

It disappointed him that she wanted to kill the sorcerer. Tamim had no fondness for the man's reign, but he suspected that Sakera meant to replace the sorcerer. Some traitorously sentimental part of Tamim had expected better from this girl, for all that he had met her only minutes ago.

Sakera made a fist, rotated it, then opened her fingers. The lopsided skeleton knelt before her. She clambered up the bones and sat on one of the kneecaps, legs dangling. "Or I could leave you to die in the giants' shadow, before I take this one away," she said. "Your choice. But I hope you come with me. It will be a lonely journey to the sorcerer's palace otherwise."

"What is your grievance with him?" Tamim said, on the grounds that he might as well be certain.

"He raised my family as ghouls," she said. "They're still not at rest."

It sounded plausible. Maybe she was a good liar. "You came here for the giants' skeletons."

"Yes."

"How did you know I'd be here?"

"I may not be a vulture," Sakera said, "but I can smell death on the wind."

"I could have used your help when I was fighting the vultures," he said. The company of ghouls had taught him how to fight—his mother, a pragmatist in her way, had sought out the corpses of veteran soldiers—but it had still been one against several.

Sakera grimaced. "If only. A necromancer is only as useful as the bones she can call to her service. I promised myself I would only touch giants, who are long gone from the world, and whose families will not miss them."

"That's an inconvenient promise," Tamim said, without approbation.

"I came here for the bones. I'm glad you came, too. Most people are afraid." She waved down at him. "Over here."

Tamim craned his head and regarded her skeptically.

"Oh, that's right." She made another gesture. The giant began lowering her to the ground, but her hand spasmed. The giant lurched. She somersaulted clear and rolled to safety, swearing in a language he didn't recognize.

Tamim helped her get up, more out of curiosity than politeness. Both her hands were shaking. "How long has that been going on?" he asked.

"Long enough," she said, embarrassed. "That's the other reason I need an ally. I can't draw the patterns by myself anymore."

Patterns? "You'd better show me how to work the—" What should he call it? "—the giant." As though it were a set of tools. "Why do you need patterns?" He didn't recall that his mother had ever drawn anything.

"Do you know how the sorcerer came to power?" Sakera asked.

Tamim shook his head. His mother had told him gilded tales of the sorcerer's court as though it had always existed, a place where enemies' skulls were made into banquet cups and musicians played upon lyres of bone or tortoiseshell.

"In the old queen's court, he was her most trusted general and a master calligrapher. First he conquered the Pit, which is death. Perhaps he made some terrible bargain there. Then, in the palace archives, he discovered some scrolls on ancient fighting forms, and applied those to the corpses he raised. Thus even ghouls who were once farmers and potters and prostitutes can fight, because they are aligned with the necromancer's patterns.

"As for the sorcerer, he had become smitten with his queen. When she refused to marry him—well. You can guess the end of that story."

Tamim was thinking of the patterns. "This implies that if you draw other fighting forms, you could apply those to the ghouls as well. Am I correct?"

Sakera nodded. "But you have to have an accurate hand and a knowledge of inner anatomies. Writing is troublesome for me, and drawing is impossible."

It didn't surprise him that a necromancer would be literate. Tamim had learned the alphabet from his mother, and could read and write, if shakily. He hadn't had much opportunity to practice. "Teach me," he said.

Her face lit. He had never seen anything like it, on the dead or the living. Carefully, she repeated the motion that had caused the giant to kneel. Although her hands shook a little, Tamim could tell what the gesture was supposed to look like. He did it several times until Sakera nodded her satisfaction.

"How do I get the giant to respond to me?" Tamim said. "Surely it doesn't move every time you twitch your hands. The ghouls I knew just followed orders. They didn't require constant guidance."

"Give the giant a name," Sakera said, "and use the name to address it in your mind. As for guidance, it's a thing of memory. The recent dead remember who they were, after a fashion. They remember how to do the things they did in life, for a time. Or they're instructed by patterns. The giants have been dead so long that they do require constant guidance."

When he died, would she raise his bones and—

"No," Sakera said. "I wouldn't do that. I am a necromancer, yes, but I made a promise. I told you, the death you desire." Her tone was almost cheerful. "Come on, give it a try."

Tamim looked at the giant with spurs. *Ifayad,* he thought, which meant *bird of prey.* He could see the letters in his head: *iro-fel-alim-yod-alim-dirat.* Then he made the gesture Sakera had shown him.

The giant knelt. He climbed up and up, into the skull, along the ridge of an abraded tooth in the open mouth. He wondered what it smelled like: earth, probably, and crushed flowers, and the tang of minerals newly exposed to air. His sense of smell was deadened from so many years among ghouls, and his adolescent years among the few remaining resistance fighters had not restored it.

If something went wrong and the great jaws closed, he would be crushed. It comforted him. "Now what?" His voice echoed oddly in the space of the skull.

"How are you supposed to see anything from in there?" Sakera said. He couldn't tell whether she was laughing or exasperated. "Come down again and we'll learn to ride the giants properly. Then, when we have paper, I can show you how to scribe your own patterns."

Tamim lingered a moment longer, drawn to Ifayad in spite of himself. Despite the restricted field of vision, he appreciated that the skull would provide protection against enemy fire.

Tamim climbed down, bemused at himself for having any sort of faith in the necromancer. She would betray him in the end, and surrender to the sorcerer, and he would have to kill her. Until then, he would learn what he could.

Tamim had always been quick with his hands, quick of reflexes, even as a child. It had taken him a while to appreciate this. He had thought it was something ordinarily true of people, as opposed to ghouls. Ghouls were unrelenting once they had a goal, but dexterity was not one of their virtues.

Sakera was methodical in her lessons. They started with stances and moved on to simple motions—an arm lifting, a hand opening, a foot shifting—then compound motions. Familiar with the precepts of arms training, Tamim accepted this as necessary. They did everything slowly: gesture followed by the giants' motion. Tamim's hands became callused from clutching Ifayad's ridged teeth to keep from rattling around inside the skull.

He and Sakera went hunting together. Sakera was good at tracking animals, even the tricky, shadow-colored animals that lived in the rimlands. "Every life is a potential death," she said when he asked her about it, since she didn't seem to pay much attention to the usual cues, such as tufts of fur snagged in the rimlands' scraggly foliage, or scat, or scuffed tracks in the dirt. Tamim was good at making snares, although a certain percentage of the animals that he caught that way were half-ghoul themselves, and had to be released. The problem had only grown worse over time.

Between the two of them, they often had a full stew-pot. Sakera tended to pick at her food; sometimes he wasn't sure she ate at all. When he pressed her on the topic, she ate the better portion of a rabbit, just to show him she could.

"I've been thinking about our rides," Tamim said to her over this night's stew. "Have you ever ridden a horse?"

Sakera shook her head. "No," she said. "Hasn't it been a long time since the rimlands saw anything but ghoul-steeds?"

"Probably," he said. "I wasn't thinking about the horses themselves, but of harnesses. Do you think we could create some kind of harness for riding the giants? That way, if something goes wrong"—he couldn't help but think of Sakera's unsteady hands—"you won't be thrown."

"Interesting," she said.

"Something with buckles, maybe?"

"We'd have to find a smith," Sakera said drily. They had approached a settlement last week, leaving the giants behind, crouched behind some hills. The settlement's buildings had been intact, but corpse-colored fungus grew from all the doors, releasing pale spores. They had retreated in haste. Sakera had been withdrawn for the rest of the day. "I don't have any power over metal. Maybe we're better off with some carefully chosen knots."

"With your hands?" Something else occurred to him: he had once seen a trader trapped under a fallen horse, back in the days when horses were to be found in the rimlands. "You'd want to be able to get out in a hurry, in case something went wrong."

"A slip knot of some sort?"

He considered it. "It might work."

Unfortunately, Sakera was not any good at finding trees. It took them several days to track down a stand of widely separated willows by following one of the rimlands' black rivers. Sakera drank the water fearlessly, although she grimaced at its taste.

Tamim showed Sakera how to strip the bark and plait it into cords. Once they had enough rope, it took them more time to devise a system of knots that would work on the giants. Sakera knew an amazing number of knots. "They're a kind of magic from the sea-folk," she said. "I don't suppose you've ever seen the sea."

Supposedly there was a black sea on the other side of the Pit's boundary, with ships of rotting timbers and ghost-fabric sails. "No," he said. "There's nothing magical about knots, either, no more than a gun is magical." He still had five bullets, although they were of iron rather than jade. Death and undeath were the only magic he recognized.

Sakera flexed her fingers, grimacing. Her skin was torn from working the bark. She washed her hands in the river, then dried her hands on her coat. "If only things were that simple," she said.

They made more rope, just in case, and took the opportunity to bathe and wash their clothes. Sakera's coat was beginning to look more grey than black. Tamim suspected it was losing its dye. Sakera insisted on going around in a ragged blanket while the coat dried.

"Do you really get that cold?" Tamim said.

"Death is cold," Sakera said. "It's the absence of warmth and the absence of light."

All Tamim could think of was the grave he had dug for the last of his caretaker ghouls. All virtue had gone from their bones, and no necromancer would raise them again. But he had wanted to do them that honor anyway, to offer them the peace that his mother had denied them. He had wanted to lower himself into the grave, too, but then no one would have been left to cover them with earth.

"These are not entirely bad things," she said, more kindly. "What would day be without night, a candle without the shuttered room?"

"It's been years since I've seen a candle."

"There we go, missing the point," she said, but she didn't sound offended.

It wasn't until Sakera was satisfied with Tamim's control over the giant that she began to teach him the alphabet. He had been looking forward to this until he realized that the shapes she was showing him didn't resemble the ones he knew. "They're wrong," he said stubbornly as he stared at the two figures she had drawn in the dirt.

Blood welled up in the letters, as though she had cut them into the flesh of some sleeping beast. It bubbled briefly, then soaked back into the dirt. It was not an uncommon phenomenon, this deep in the rimlands, away from the sections that the sorcerer had reclaimed for human use.

Sakera, who was crouching next to him with her coat hitched up over her knees in an unsuccessful attempt to keep it from getting soiled, sighed. "There's more than one alphabet in the world. There are even things more complicated than alphabets."

Tamim tried to look receptive to the idea of learning something more complicated than an alphabet.

Sakera burst out laughing at his expression. "You're quick-witted. A little practice is all it would take."

"Thank you," he said dourly.

"As to why this alphabet and not another: it's the oldest one in the rimlands. It was used by priests to gods now unnamed."

He leaned back and scowled. "How is it that you say the most preposterous things as if you knew them absolutely?"

"Because I do, of course." She grinned at him. "Really, Tamim, what kind of necromancer would I be if I didn't gather knowledge?"

"If my mother had spent more time gathering knowledge," Tamim said thoughtfully, "maybe she would have been better prepared when she tried to assassinate the sorcerer."

"Come on," Sakera said, clearly deeming it better to skirt the subject, "alphabet. The sooner you start, the sooner you'll have it memorized."

Tamim drew an awkward copy of the first one.

"No, no, *no*," Sakera said, laughing again. He didn't mind it as much as he thought he would. "There's an order to these things."

"I can't see why it makes any difference, so long as you get the shape right."

"Hit me," she said.

"What?" Sometimes he wondered about her sanity.

"It won't land," she said, "if that's what you're worried about. Come on, hit me."

He got up, settling his balance solidly over each foot, then threw a punch. He kept his fist several inches away from her even at full extension.

"Oh, Tamim," she sighed, "you don't have to be so careful. But you see? Notice how all the parts of your body moved in a particular order, the way you twisted your fist at the end and not the beginning? There is a logic to these things."

Tamim should have known that complaining about it would elicit one of Sakera's incomprehensible explanations. "Just tell me how to get it right."

"If you'd rather," she said. She drew the letter again, slowly, imitating his strokes. "You went from left to right, and it's right to left. That's the first thing to remember." And again, except this time from right to left, as she had said. "Do you see how it's shaped, how the strokes flow into each other?"

He tried a few more times until he could feel the flow that she spoke of: not so different from the alphabet he knew, even if the direction was different. "Shouldn't it have a name?" he said. The letters of that other alphabet had names.

"This one is *tilat*. If we spelled out your name, it would be the first letter."

"*Tilat*," he repeated. "What's the other one?"

Sakera showed him how to write it correctly. Dirt collected under her fingernail. "*Meneth*," she said. "*Tilat-meneth-meneth* spells your name."

Tamim frowned. "Aren't there letters missing, the breath-sounds?"

"Vowels, you mean? You don't write them in this alphabet."

"That sounds terribly confusing."

"There is power in empty spaces," Sakera said. "Call it another part of the lesson."

Tilat-meneth-meneth. Tamim wrote it three times so the letters aligned, forming a three-by-three figure. "Show me—show me how to write your name." He had a good memory. He would prove it to her.

She showed him *senu*, and *kor*, and *ras*. If he looked at all the letters sideways, he could see a faint resemblance to the ones of his childhood alphabet. Were they related somehow?

Tamim didn't write the name he had given his skeleton, Ifayad, for he had a premonition that it would alter some necessary relationship. *Power in empty spaces,* Sakera had said.

Numbers came after letters. This time the numerals looked more similar to those he already knew, and the lessons went more quickly.

Sakera was in the middle of teaching him *yush*, one hundred, when the ambush came. Their days of training in the hinterlands had made them careless. The rimlands had never been friendly to human existence. Under the sorcerer's reign, they had become less so. The sorcerer might have built edifices of slate and dark marble and delicate bone, but each year fewer and fewer people were willing to dwell under the banner of the vulture. So it was that Tamim and Sakera had not run into travelers or traders. Thanks to the giants' conspicuousness, they had also gotten into the habit of avoiding villages.

Tamim was watching Sakera's hand draw the numeral in the dirt when she made a fist. "What's wrong?" he asked.

"Run!" she said in a low, fierce whisper. Her hands went through a sequence of motions punctuated by pauses, like a language in itself. The ground thundered as her giant hauled itself out of the nearby copse of trees and walked toward her. The trees' limbs knotted themselves around the giant's arm. It pulled free. Hand-shaped leaves flew everywhere, writhing and clutching at the air. The giant crouched down so Sakera could vault up to its rib cage. She climbed until she reached the safety of its skull, then guided it back toward Tamim.

Tamim had Ifayad pick him up and place him in its eye socket. His stomach lurched as he climbed down, into the harness. He hated the moments of absolute helplessness as he secured himself. He could practically hear his heartbeat echoing in the skull.

Through Ifayad's open maw, he could see the vultures' red banner. There were six vultures: two necromancers in their black robes and four grey-fleshed ghouls in dull armor. The necromancers gaped at the moving giants. Even with its massive limbs, Sakera's was faster than the ghouls, although Tamim was far from reaching her level of control.

Sakera's giant loomed over the vultures and swept the banner to the ground, crushing it under one foot. Then it stopped. Tamim guessed that her hand tremor had started up again. The necromancers scrambled out of the way, out of his field of vision, shouting orders.

The ghouls were armed with repeating crossbows. Tamim heard an initial burst of bolts clattering against Sakera's giant, and cursed all the small gods of the rimlands. He got Ifayad moving. A sweep of its forearm knocked two ghouls to the ground. One ghoul leapt for Ifayad's hand and clung to a finger. He heard it laughing creakily. Tamim pivoted Ifayad and smashed the ghoul against a tree. Its arm separated from its body and the ribcage collapsed.

Tamim lifted Ifayad's arm. It probably looked ridiculous from the outside, but he had to see—there it was: the ghoul's severed arm was climbing toward Tamim. He didn't fancy the thought of struggling with it while trying to control Ifayad.

He tried for a tense minute to use the giant's fingers to pry the severed hand off and fling it away before he realized he knew no commands that would accomplish that end.

Cursing, he raised Ifayad's arm to bring the target closer and put the giant in a stable stance. Then he unknotted himself from the harness and reached for his gun. Five bullets left.

The ghoul's hand continued its relentless climb.

He crouched against the base of Ifayad's jaw. It was lucky for him that the giant's teeth, besides being chipped, had irregular alignment.

He aimed through the gap between two teeth. Fired. The ghoul's hand was blown backwards and landed on the ground, twitching, before righting itself.

Four bullets.

However feebly, the hand was scrabbling toward him. But at least it wasn't *on* Ifayad.

Sakera had gotten her giant to respond again. In a display of entirely characteristic ferocity, it intercepted one of the necromancers and stomped. The sound of crunching bone was palpable.

The necromancers meant them no good; no one who served the sorcerer could. He retied the harness and set off after the second necromancer. Ifayad's hand closed around her.

"Kill her!" Sakera said.

The necromancer wheezed out something.

Tamim hesitated for a long moment.

The necromancer said rapidly, "I can tell you of the death at your heels—"

He had agreed to support Sakera, not to ask questions. He took a deep breath, then pinched his thumb and forefinger against each other.

The giant's fist squeezed tight. The necromancer screamed.

Tamim didn't stop until the screaming cut off. Then he dropped the body.

Sakera had dismembered the rest of the ghouls. "That will hold them for a while," she said. "We can travel faster than they can."

Tamim turned Ifayad to face Sakera's giant. "That wasn't so difficult," he said.

"Only two necromancers and their ghouls for now," she said. "We don't know how long they were following us. We haven't exactly been subtle. That's my fault. I thought—" Her voice sounded hollow. "This place has been my home for so long. I thought it would protect me, somehow. But I should have known better. It's not as if land has any loyalty."

Tamim focused on the part of her speech that had made sense. "So we should expect more pursuit. Let's get our gear and run."

"We can only run so far," Sakera said. "We'll end up at the gates of the sorcerer's palace with the undead nipping at our heels. There's no help for it."

"We could head out of the rimlands instead," Tamim said. He was accustomed to the idea of dying, but surely Sakera felt differently. The thought of her felled by the vultures made him ache in a way he had no name for.

"No," Sakera said firmly. "This has to be done."

Two villages later, Tamim discovered why Sakera was so desperate to take down the sorcerer.

This far into the rimlands, they had expected the village to be abandoned. Tamim had suggested that they might be able to find cloth or soap or needles left behind, small necessities. "Unless it bothers you to scavenge," he added.

"Not at all," Sakera said. "If they've left, they've left."

They paused at the crest of a hill to peer down at the village. There were no cook-fires burning, and the crops in the nearby fields had withered. Yet people walked around the village's perimeter and through its streets.

The pattern they traced was *chakath*, one of the letters of the alphabet, except with the beginning and ending points joined.

"They're ghouls," Tamim said, looking at Sakera for an explanation. "But why—?"

"The vultures didn't raise them," Sakera said. "They're too practical to have ghouls spelling out alphabet lessons. No: something came to this village and killed its people, and the people simply failed to die."

"What force moves them, then?"

"The sorcerer's control of the Pit is not a natural thing," she said. "It is affecting the balance of life and death in the rimlands. Necromancy is one thing: it too has its limits. It's another matter for everything that dies to rise on its own. We must kill the sorcerer before he warps the purpose of the Pit any further."

"I can try to go salvage what I can," Tamim said. "Or would that catch the ghouls' attention?"

Sakera watched the ghouls walking, from stoop-shouldered old men to children dragging shapeless dolls. "As long as you don't interrupt their *chakath*. We'll go together."

"All right." For the purposes of walking past the ghouls, her hand tremor shouldn't make a difference.

The procession of ghouls had gaps in odd places. It was simply a matter of seeking out the gaps and slipping past. The ghouls' rotted eyes tracked them, but the ghouls themselves did not deviate from their path.

Together, Sakera and Tamim raided the village for luxuries they had not seen in their time together: fruit preserves, bolts of ramie dyed in muddy colors, beeswax, hemp slippers. No guns or bullets, but that would have been too much to hope for. Tamim found some reasonably intact sacks for them to carry away their haul in.

They stepped outside with two sacks each. Tamim froze. "The pattern's changed," he said. "They're no longer going down that trail to the left. It's now the one to the right."

"I wonder what letter of the alphabet they're tracing out now," Sakera said. "We'd better leave."

They dashed for the giants. There was no pursuit. Tamim would have felt better if the ghouls had come after them. He understood enemies that stared you in the face and fought you. He didn't understand this business of ghouls that—

"Sakera," he said as they loaded up, "most people in the rimlands can't read."

"Mmm?"

"And they especially wouldn't be able to read this strange old alphabet you taught me. Of which *chakath* is the sixth letter, or that's what you said."

They gazed down at the ghouls' new letter, *liyut*. The seventh.

Tamim said, "What happens when they make it all the way to the end of the alphabet?" In his mind's eye he traced the strokes that comprised *qaref*.

"What do you think?" Sakera said. "*Qaref* is also the word for 'end' in various dead languages."

"How much longer before we reach the sorcerer's palace?" Tamim asked.

"A while," she said. "He isn't the only one with a citadel deep in the rimlands."

"Someone else to fight?" he said, both dismayed and determined.

"No," she said. Her smile was crooked and not a little rueful. "Mine. Or did you think we were going to find paper and ink by raiding the villages of people who never had the fortune to learn to read?"

In actuality, Sakera's citadel was a small fort atop a hill deep in a tangle of woods and vines. Tamim was astonished by the proliferation of vegetation. "Is any of this safe to eat?" he asked, especially after he saw the half-dissolved bones of birds beneath one tree with lush purple fruit.

"The fruit's all safe," Sakera said offhandedly. "It's getting it without making the tree angry that's the problem." To demonstrate, she threw a rock at one of the trees.

The wood splintered open with a screaming sound at impact, and fingers of bark-less wood stroked the stone before hurling it back toward them.

"Don't catch it!" Sakera said, as if Tamim had to be told. Streaks of sap marred the stone's surface.

"What good is a fort without guards?" Tamim said, uneasy that they had had to leave the giants back a little ways. He supposed the trees were worth something, but . . .

"So maybe I exaggerated when I called it a citadel," Sakera said. "It's more like a supply depot."

He sighed.

Sakera drew out a key of blackened iron and opened the fort's gates. It was built of concrete and dark granite, which had to have been brought from somewhere else. Sakera lit a small candle—one of their spoils—and led the way to a room down the end of the hall. She opened it with a smaller key.

Inside the room were stacks and stacks of paper, and in one corner, an escritoire. "This," said Sakera, "is where you are going to learn to draw your own patterns."

"Why is this necessary?"

"Do you remember the encounter where you couldn't get rid of the hand?"

"You noticed?" he said.

"Please," she said. "It was a dead thing climbing up another dead thing. I couldn't help but notice. If we can draw the necessary motions, that won't happen again. We must prepare as many maneuvers as we can think of."

"It's been years since I've used a brush and ink," Tamim said.

"I taught you to use the giant, didn't I?" Sakera said.

He looked pointedly at her hands. "The tremor's getting worse."

She averted her eyes. "I know. But food first. I bet you're famished."

They made a meal of leftover pemmican and fruit preserves. Then Sakera went to give herself a sponge bath with water from the cistern. Tamim waited patiently. Her long hair took forever to wash, and he knew that when he returned from his own bath, she would still be working out the tangles with a broken-toothed comb.

Tamim kept watch while Sakera drowsed in the sun outside the fort, letting her hair dry. At last she got up and danced across the ground, arms outflung, face lifted. "Time to learn drawing," she said.

After learning the alphabet and numbers by drawing them in the dirt, Tamim felt frustrated at returning to the beginning. Sakera was relentless, however. She made him review the basics: how to hold a brush, how to make perfect single strokes. Then she made him learn each letter all over again, with the initial, medial, and final forms that she had omitted the first time around.

"Couldn't you have taught me all the forms to begin with?" Tamim said.

"You wouldn't have sat still for it," she said.

When she deemed him ready, Tamim wrote out a passage she dictated to him, words that had no meaning to him and probably had no meaning to anyone but Sakera.

"It'll do," she said when the ink had dried and she had a chance to inspect it minutely. "We're running short on time. I hope you have a good eye for motion."

She brought out a chart of the human body, except it was boxed off and marked with numbers. "What do you make of this?"

At first he was bewildered by the sheer number of lines and curves. Then, as he studied the chart, pieces came clear: notes on the proportion of head height to body height, head width to shoulder width, the range of motion of the major joints.

"I can memorize this," Tamim said.

"You have to do better than memorize," she said. "You'll have to draw.

This is the kind of thing you'll have to produce." She brought out another chart—no, a sheaf of drawings on translucent paper—and showed him how to flip through them. Each paper in the sheaf was numbered.

The drawings showed something very simple: a man—no, woman, from the wider pelvis—walking, the motion depicted in painstaking detail, from the lift of the feet to the shift in balance.

Tamim closed his eyes and visualized Sakera walking, although she had a peculiarly straight-hipped stride for a woman. How would he draw a diagram for Sakera? He opened his eyes. "We can already make the giants walk," he pointed out.

"That's true," Sakera said, "but walking is the fundamental thing. If you can master walking, the rest will follow."

"Do we have time for this?"

"We have to make time. I don't want to take any chances with the sorcerer." She bit her lip. "I've already underestimated him once; how do you think I got this tremor?"

Tamim bent his head, studying the diagram some more. He didn't miss Sakera's hum of satisfaction.

In the days that followed, Tamim learned to draw the human form with graphite sticks. He grew accustomed to having greasy, grey-smeared fingers. "Does it matter whether I'm drawing the living or the dead?" he asked.

"You're showing the giants the pattern of the motion," Sakera said. "That's what matters."

He stared down at his latest tracing of one of Sakera's beautifully inked drawings: a woman in the midst of a leap. The vast quantity of her papers was daunting, but when he wasn't drawing—everything from butterflies to murderous trees to doomed birds, everything but Sakera herself—he was studying them. "How do you decide the interval of motion?" Sometimes the difference between two drawings in a sequence was fractional, and he had to hold both up to the sunlight to see what had changed.

"Think of it as equal intervals of time," Sakera said. "You don't need to be this meticulous to draw the motion for the giant; you'll be mediating the action through your hands. All it needs are the distinguishing moments. But it's useful to know the motion's rhythm."

"How many drawings like this does the sorcerer have?"

"Too many."

"You can't just burn them?"

She gave him a pained look. "Once they've been painted in ink—anything permanent—by the necromancer's own hand, they're available to every ghoul he raises. He's probably burned them himself, to keep others from stealing his knowledge."

"Ink," Tamim repeated.

"Why do you think I've been having you work in graphite even though your calligraphy's passable?"

"I had been wondering, yes."

"You can start working with ink tomorrow," Sakera said, as though she were granting him a favor. "Try not to mess it up."

"I wish I could do something for your hands," Tamim said.

She grimaced, and he regretted bringing it up. But she said only, "I can still do most necessary things. But a brush is sensitive to small motions. I can't risk it anymore. Why don't we organize the sketches that you want to do in ink, so we can increase your giant's range of motion?"

"How much longer do we have?"

Sakera looked away, her eyes distant. "You remember that village? They're on *uth*."

Three to go. "You should have pushed me harder," he said. "How often do they change the letter?"

"About once a week," she said.

He could have asked earlier, and he hadn't. "How far is it to the sorcerer's palace?"

"From here? A week's hard journeying."

"Let's start organizing," Tamim said.

Tamim was never going to get all the ink out of his fingernails from painting maneuvers. Then again, it was cleaner than grave-dirt. Sakera's fingernails weren't much better, although Tamim had done his best to trim them for her. He missed the days of sketching with graphite. He had even attempted a portrait of his mother. It hadn't come out very well, but considering that he hardly remembered her face, that was only to be expected.

They had re-rigged the giants' harnesses using their best rope, their most cunning knots, loaded up the giants with supplies. "Once we're out of the immediate area," Sakera said, "expect more of the vultures' patrols. We are not concerned with their total defeat. They'll know we're coming. The point is to get to the palace as quickly as possible."

"The ghouls will swarm us," Tamim said.

"I know," she said. "Once we get close enough, your job will be to distract the sorcerer's armies as long as you can. I—" She hesitated. "I may have to go in alone, if he doesn't come out to greet us."

"How are you going to keep them from tearing you apart?"

"I'll be fast," she said.

"You call that a plan?" he said incredulously.

She grinned.

"I will never understand you," Tamim said.

"You will someday," she said. "It's time to go."

Forever after, Tamim remembered that week in nightmare snatches, despite an ordinarily orderly sense of time. They passed statues that had been overgrown by violet-grey crystals that luminesced in response to the giants' footfalls, roads that liquefied into vortices of glittering sand. The

THE BONES OF GIANTS

wind muttered at them, perhaps in words from extinct languages, perhaps in the universal language of nightmare. They passed more villages, some inhabited by the living, who fled their approach, others inhabited by ghouls marching the alphabet's path in its countdown to *qaref*.

Curiously, there were few vultures. When asked, Sakera said, "They've probably been recalled to the palace for the sorcerer's protection."

"Does he fear the giants?" Tamim asked.

"Wouldn't you?" She sounded cranky. It seemed sleep deprivation could affect even her.

At last they reached the sorcerer's high road, paved at the sides with dark, gleaming stones. An army of ghouls awaited them. The banner of the vulture flew high in the distance, along with the standards of individual companies. Tamim had Ifayad crane its head back so he could glimpse the black-and-iron palace high on its hill.

"Do we charge?" Tamim said.

"Wait," Sakera said implacably.

The ghouls parted. Down the road came the sorcerer, mounted on a blood bay horse with a skull for a head, although no other part of it had decayed. The sorcerer was tall, and he wore ornate lamellar lacquered red and black.

The ghouls bent their heads to the sorcerer in unison. For his part, the man removed his helmet and shaded his eyes, looking unerringly at Sakera's giant. "You are brave to return, Sakera," he said. He had a low, resonant voice, and he sounded respectful but unintimidated.

"I have an ally this time," she said.

Tamim said, "Ghouls may require jade bullets, but he's only human. Let me shoot him."

The sorcerer raised a spyglass and fixed it on the giant's maw. Tamim held still; he had nothing to hide. "You must be Liathu's son," the sorcerer said, almost fondly. "It's in the shape of your face. She was brave, too, in her way."

To Tamim's dismay, Sakera had the giant lower her to the ground. It took her a while to disentangle herself from the harness. "It's been a long time," she said.

"You are destroying the realm I would have built," said the sorcerer. "What good is the Pit when everything in the rimlands is becoming an extension of death? This could have been a prosperous realm, if not for your revenge. I did not think even you were so cruel."

Sakera's revenge? What revenge?

"Not death," Sakera said, "but undeath. You misunderstand the nature of the problem. There's only one way to reverse what has happened to the rimlands. Abdicate. Else there are two giants, and there will be more. All the old bones of the land will rise up against you, extinct though their race may be, when the ghouls write *qaref*."

"You know better than to expect me to listen," the sorcerer said, "especially after you took away the woman I loved."

"She was not yours to have, not that way," Sakera said quietly. "A ghoul can do as it is told, but it cannot love, not the way the living do."

Tamim didn't want to hear any more of the sorcerer's history. He sliced his hand through the air. Ifayad's hand moved correspondingly.

The sorcerer said, unfazed, "Has it never occurred to you, son of Liathu, to wonder why I didn't raise the giants as ghouls myself? Do you know who it is you have been allied with all this time?"

Tamim stopped. The hand stopped short of the sorcerer and his uncanny mount.

Once it would not have mattered. But if he didn't find out now, he would never know.

"Go ahead," Sakera said to the sorcerer. "Tell him." She raised her chin as if in challenge. Her hands were trembling. For once, Tamim thought it was out of anxiety.

"It is perhaps unforgivable that Liathu's child should be so ignorant of necromancy," the sorcerer said, "but she was never much of a teacher. A necromancer can only raise people who died during his life-span. And the giants became extinct before any humans came into being. They were possibly the first to walk the world. What does that tell you about the woman you have been traveling with?"

Sakera was certainly no giant.

Then he knew. "Death," Tamim said. "Death is the oldest necromancer of all."

"Would you rather be ruled by Death," the sorcerer said to Tamim, "or by someone who is likewise human?"

"The Pit was never meant to be ruled by mortal man or woman," Sakera said. "Did you think your conquest solved anything? There must be a place in the world where Death has a home, and that is the Pit, else there is no rest for anyone when the last breath flees, when the heart finally stills."

"Choose," the sorcerer said harshly. "Choose by numbers, if nothing else: fight and fight though you may, even after my death, the Vulture Corps will track your every footstep.—Do you make no argument, Sakera?"

"It has to be a real choice," Sakera said. "His choice, because he is a child of life and death both."

Tamim didn't believe in facing violence with his eyes closed. He knew what he had seen, all his life in the rimlands, the unclean animals and the countdown ghouls, bleeding earth and ashen fruit. Once he would not have had the courage to imagine something better—if not for himself, then for whatever generations might follow.

He twisted both hands and stabbed his fingers into his right palm. Ifayad's hand lunged down. The sorcerer spurred his mount, charging slantwise forward. Tamim moved Ifayad to block him; Ifayad swept the sorcerer from his mount.

The sorcerer screamed as he fell. His rage shook Tamim, even though Tamim was safe inside Ifayad. The man landed upon the spears of his own ghouls, despite their efforts to move aside. They were too densely packed.

Tamim stared down at the man's broken body, thinking, *Was that all?*

"There will be no rest for—" said the ghouls in one voice.

Sakera knelt and pounded her fists against the ground. All the ghouls fell silent, then shuddered and collapsed. It seemed to Tamim that the clattering sound went on halfway to forever.

"You couldn't have done that before?" Tamim demanded.

"Not while he ruled the Pit, no," she said. She stared out over the fallen bones. "That was your part. Do you know how many his vultures killed?"

Tamim almost said, *I didn't think it would matter to you.* But she was Sakera. He had come to know her. Of course it mattered to her.

In no hurry at all, he made Ifayad lower him to the ground so he could stand next to her. "Now what?" he said.

She raised her face to him. The expression in her eyes was uncharacteristically solemn.

I will give you the death you desire, she had promised. In their time together, he had forgotten his original purpose.

Sakera was Death, the Pit made flesh. There was one promise Death always kept.

Tamim squared his shoulders. "I'm ready."

"Silly," Sakera said affectionately, standing. "I never said the death you wanted had to be *right now.*"

"I was going to kill myself."

"Why do you think I came for you, out of all the people in the rimlands?" she said. She stretched up on tiptoe to kiss his cheek. Her lips were cool, though not unpleasantly so. "You may not know my face when I come for you next. But I will come, at a time of your desiring."

"I don't know how to live."

"But you do," she said. "It's all about the distinguishing moments. It's about going from one to the next, no matter how small the interval of time, or how long. As for me, I have a home to return to. You can't follow me yet."

"I could—" Tamim stopped. Did he want to follow her?

"I think the hesitation is answer enough," Sakera said.

"The giant?"

"That's up to you," she said. "Choose wisely."

"Goodbye, then," Tamim said.

"Goodbye, Tamim," she said. Her hands shook, but less than they had. Or so he liked to think. She returned to her giant. It strode off into the horizon beyond the palace, toward the Pit.

Tamim stood for a long time, watching. Then he wrote Ifayad's name on its right tibia with his fingerprints. "Just a little longer," he said, "and you can go to your rest." He reentered the giant and began the long task of burial, a grave for the fallen—but not for himself.

between two dragons

One of the oldest tales we tell in Cho is of two dragons, twinborn and opposite in all desires. One dragon was as red as Earth, the other as blue as Heaven: day and night, fire and water, passion and calculation. They warred, as dragons do, and the universe was born of their battle.

We have never forgotten that we partake of both dragons, Earth and Heaven. Yet we are separate creatures with separate laws. It is why the twin dragons appear upon our national seal, separated by Man's sinuous road. We live among the stars, but we remember our heritage.

One thing has not changed since the birth of the universe, however. There is still war.

Yen, you have to come back so I can tell you the beginning of your story. Everything is classified: every soldier unaccounted for, every starsail deployed far from home, every gram of shrapnel . . . every whisper that might have passed between us. Word of the last battle will come tomorrow, say the official news services, but we have heard the same thing for the last several days.

I promised I would tell no one, so instead I dream it over and over. I knew, when I began to work for the Ministry of Virtuous Thought, that people would fear me. I remind myself of this every time someone calls me a woman with no more heart than a stone, despite the saying that a stone's weeping is the most terrible of all.

You came to me after the invaders from Yamat had been driven off, despite the fall of Spinward Gate and the capital system's long siege. I didn't recognize you at first. Most of my clients use one of the government's thousand false names, which exist for situations requiring discretion. Your appointment was like any other, made under one such.

Your face, though—I could hardly have failed to recognize your face. Few clients contact me in person, although I can't help wanting to hear, face-to-face, why my patients must undergo the changes imposed on them.

Admiral Yen Shenar: You were an unassuming man, although your dark eyes suggested a certain taut energy, and you were no stranger to physical labor. I wished I were in such lean good health; morning exercise has never done much for me. But your drab civilian clothes and the absent white gun did nothing to disguise the fact that you were a soldier. An admiral. A hero, even, in my office with its white walls and bland paintings of bamboo.

"Admiral," I said, and stopped. How do you address the war hero of a war everyone knows will resume when the invaders catch their breath? I thought I knew what you wanted done. A former lover, a political rival, an inconvenience on the way up; the client has the clout to make someone disappear for a day and return as though nothing as changed, except it has. A habit of reverse-alphabetizing personal correspondence, a preference for Kir Jaengmi's poetry over An Puna's, a subversive fascination with foreign politics, excised or altered by my work. Sometimes only a favorite catchphrase or a preference for ginseng over green tea is changed, and the reprogramming serves as a warning once the patient encounters dissonance from family and acquaintances. Sometimes the person who returns is no longer recognizable. The setup can take months, depending on the compatibility of available data with preset models, but the reprogramming itself only takes hours.

So here you were, Admiral Yen Shenar. Surely you were rising in influence, with the attendant infelicities. It disappointed me to see you, but only a little. I could guess some of your targets.

"There's no need for formality, madam," you said, correctly interpreting my silence as a loss for words. "You've dealt with more influential people in your time, I'm sure." Your smile was wry, but suggested despair.

I thought I understood that, too. "Who is the target?"

The despair sharpened, and everything changed. "Myself. I want to be expunged, like a thrall. I'm told it's easier with a willing subject."

"Heaven and Earth, you can't be serious."

The walls were suddenly too spare, too white.

I wondered why you didn't do the obvious thing and intrigue against Admiral Wan Kun, or indeed the others in court who considered your growing renown a threat. No surprise: the current dynasty had been founded by a usurper-general, and ever since, the court has regarded generals and admirals with suspicion. We may despise the Yamachin, but they are consummate warriors, and they would never have been so frightened by the specter of a coup as to sequester their generals at the capital, preventing them from training with the troops they commanded on paper. We revere scholars. They have their sages, but soldiers are the ones they truly respect.

"Madam," you said, "I am only asking you to do what the ministry will ask of another programmer a few days from now. It doesn't matter what battles one wins in the deeps of space if one can't keep out of political trouble. Even if we all know the Yamachin will return once they've played out this farce of negotiations . . . "

You wanted me to destroy the man you were, but in a manner of your choosing and not your rivals', all for the sake of saving Cho in times to come. This meant preserving your military acumen so you might be of use when Yamat returned to ravage Cho. Only a man so damned sure of himself would have chanced it. But you had routed the Yamachin navy at Red Sun and Hawks Crossing with a pittance of Chosar casualties, and no one could forget how, in the war's early hours, you risked your command by crossing into Admiral Wan Kun's jurisdiction to rally the shattered defense at Heaven's Gate.

"Admiral," I said, "are you sure? The half-death"—that's the kindest euphemism—"might leave you with no more wit than a broken cup, and all for nothing. It has never been a *safe* procedure." I didn't believe you would be disgraced in a matter of days, although it came to pass as you predicted.

You smiled at that, blackly amused. "When calamity lands on your shoulder, madam, I assure you that you'll find it difficult to mistake for anything else." A corner of your mouth curled. "I imagine you've seen death in darker forms than I have. I have killed from vast distances, but never up close. You are braver by far than I have ever been."

You were wrong about me, Admiral Yen, even if the procedure *is* easier with a willing patient. With anyone else, I would have congratulated myself on a task swiftly and elegantly completed.

You know the rest of the story. When you tell it to me, I will give you the beginning that I stole from you, even at your bidding. Although others know our nation Cho as the Realm Between Two Dragons, vast Feng-Huang and warlike Yamat, our national emblem is the tiger, and men like you are tigers among men.

Sometimes I think that each night I spin the story to myself, a moment of memory will return to you, as if we were bound together by the chains of a children's fable. I know better. There are villains every direction I look. I am one of them. If you do not return, all that will be left for me is to remember, over and over, how I destroyed the man you should have been, the man you were.

By the time we took him seriously, he was an old man: Tsehan, the chancellor-general of Yamat, and its ruler in truth. Ministers came and ministers went, but Tsehan watched from his unmoving seat in Yamat's parliament, the hawk who perched above them all.

He was not a man without refinement, despite the popular depiction of him as a wizened tyrant, too feeble to lead the invasion himself and too fierce to leave Cho in peace. Tsehan loved fine things, as the diplomats attested. His reception hall was bright with luxuries: sculptures of light and parabolic mirrors, paintings on silk and bamboo strips, mosaics made from shattered ancient celadon. He served tea in cups whose designs of seasonal flowers and fractals shifted in response to the liquid's temperature or acidity. "For the people of Yamat," he said, but everyone knew these treasures were for Tsehan's pleasure, not the people's.

War had nurtured him all his life. His father was a soldier of the lowest rank, one more body flung into Yamat's bloody and tumultuous politics. It is no small thing, in Yamat—a nation at least as class-conscious as our own—to rise from a captain's aide to heir-apparent of Chancellor-General Oshozhi. Oshozhi succeeded in bringing Yamat with its many would-be warlords under unified rule, and he passed that rule on to Tsehan.

It should not have surprised us that, with the end of Yamat's bloody civil wars, Tsehan would thirst for more. But Cho was a pearl too small for his pleasure. The chancellor-general wanted Feng-Huang, vastest of nations, jewel of the stars. And to reach Feng-Huang, he needed safe passage through Cho's primary nexus. Feng-Huang had been our ally and protector for centuries, the culture whose civilization we modeled ours after. Betraying Feng-Huang to the Yamachin would have been like betraying ourselves.

Yamat had been stable for almost a decade under Tsehan's leadership, but we had broken off regular diplomatic relations during its years of instability and massacre. We had grown accustomed to hearing about dissidents who vanished during lunch, crèches destroyed by rival politicians and generals, bombs hidden in shipments of maiden-faced orchids, and soldiers who trampled corpses but wept over fire-scored sculptures. Some of it might even have happened.

When Tsehan sent the starsail *Hanei* to ask for the presence of a Chosar delegation and our government acquiesced, few of us took notice. Less than a year after that, our indifference would be replaced by outrage over Yamat's demands for an open road to our ally Feng-Huang. Tsehan was not a falling blossom after all, as one of our poets said, but a rising dragon.

In the dream, he knew his purpose. His heartbeat was the drum of war. He walked between Earth and Heaven, and his path was his own.

And waking—

He brushed the hair out of his eyes. His palms were sweaty. And he had a name, if not much else.

Yen Shenar, no longer admiral despite his many victories, raised his hand, took aim at the mirror, and fired.

But the mirror was no mirror, only the wall's watching eyes. He was always under surveillance. It was a fact of life in the Garden of Tranquility, where political prisoners lived amid parameterized hallucinations. The premise was that rebellion, let alone escape, was unlikely when you couldn't be sure if the person at the corner was a guard or the hallucination of a childhood friend who had died last year. He supposed he should be grateful that he hadn't been executed outright, like so many who had rioted or protested the government's policies, even those like himself who had been instrumental in defending Cho from the Yamachin invasion.

He had no gun in his hand, only the unflinching trajectory of his own thoughts. One more thing to add to his litany of grievances, although he was sure the list changed from day to day, hour to hour, when the hallucinations intensified. Sourly, he wished he could hallucinate a stylus, or a chisel with which to gouge the walls, whether they were walls or just air. He had never before had such appreciation for the importance of recordkeeping.

Yen began to jog, trusting the parameters would keep him from smashing into a corner, although such abrupt pain would almost be welcome. Air around him, metal beneath him. He navigated through the labyrinth of overgrown bamboo groves, the wings of unending arches, the spiral blossoms of distant galaxies glimpsed through cracked lattices. At times he thought the groves might be real.

They had imprisoned him behind Yen Shenar's face, handicapped him with Yen Shenar's dreams of stars and shapes moving in the vast darkness. They had made the mistake of thinking that he shared Yen Shenar's thrall-like regard for the government. He was going to escape the Garden if it required him to break each bone to test its verity, uproot the bamboo, break Cho's government at its foundations.

The war began earlier, but what we remember as its inception is Sang Han's death at Heaven's Gate. Even the Yamachin captain who led the advance honored Sang's passing.

Heaven's Gate is the outermost system bordering Yamat, known for the number of people who perished settling its most temperate world, and the starsails lost exploring its minor but treacherous nexus. The system was held by Commandant Sang Han, while the province as a whole remains under the protection of Admiral Wan Kun's fleet. Wan Kun's, not Yen Shenar's; perhaps Heaven's Gate was doomed from the start.

Although Admiral Wan Kun was inclined to dismiss the reports of Yamachin warsails as alarmism, the commandant knew better. Against protocol, he alerted Admiral Yen Shenar in the neighboring system, which almost saved us. It is bitter to realize that we could have held Cho against the invaders if we had been prepared for them when they first appeared.

The outpost station's surviving logs report that Sang had one last dinner with his soldiers, passing the communal cup down the long tables. He joked with them about the hundred non-culinary uses for rice. Then he warned the leading Yamachin warsail, *Hanei*, that passage through Cho to invade our ally Feng-Huang would not be forthcoming, whatever the delusion of Yamat's chancellor-general.

Hanei and its escort responded by opening fire.

We are creatures of fire and water. We wither under a surfeit of light as readily as we wither beneath drowned hopes. When photons march soldier-fashion at an admiral's bidding, people die.

When the Yamachin boarded the battlestation serving Heaven's Gate, Sang awaited them. By then, the station was all but shattered, a fruit for the pressing. Sang's eyes were shadowed by sleepless nights, his hair rumpled, his hands unsteady.

The *Hanei*'s captain, Sezhi Tomo, was the first to board the station. Cho's border stations knew his name. In the coming years, we would learn every nuance of anger or determination in that soft, suave voice. Sezhi spoke our language, and in times past he had been greeted as one of us. His chancellor-general had demanded his experience in dealing with Cho, however, and so he arrived as an invader, not a guest.

"Commandant," he said to Sang, "I ask you and your soldiers to stand down. There's time yet for war to be averted. Surrender the white gun." Sezhi must have been aware of the irony of his words. He knew, as most Yamachin apparently did not, that a Chosar officer's white gun represented not only his rank but his loyalty to the nation. Its single shot is intended for suicide in dire straits.

"Sezhi-kan," the commandant replied, addressing the other man by his Yamachin title, "it was too late when your chancellor-general set his eye upon Feng-Huang." And when our government, faction-torn, failed to heed the diplomats' warning of Tsehan's ambitions; but he would not say that to a Yamachin. "It was too late when you opened fire on the station. I will not stand down."

"Commandant," said Sezhi even as his guards trained their rifles on Sang, "please. Heaven's Gate is lost." His voice dropped to a murmur. "Sang, it's over. At least save yourself and the people who are still alive."

Small courtesies have power. In the records that made it out of Heaven's Gate, we see the temptation that sweeps over the commandant's face as he holds Sezhi's gaze. We see the moment when he decides that he won't break eye contact to look around at his haggard soldiers, and the moment when temptation breaks its grasp.

Oh, yes: the cameras were transmitting to all the relays, with no thought as to who might be eavesdropping.

"I will surrender the white gun," Sang said, "when you take it from me. Dying is easier than letting you pass."

Sezhi's face held no more expression than night inside a nexus. "Then take it I shall. Gentlemen."

The commandant drew the white gun from its holster, keeping it at all times aimed at the floor. He was right-handed.

The first shot took off Sang's right arm.

His face was white as the blood spurted. He knelt—or collapsed—to pick up the white gun with his left hand, but had no strength left to stand.

The second shot, from one of the soldiers behind Sezhi, took off his left arm.

It's hard to tell whether shock finally caused Sang to slump as the soldiers' next twelve bullets slammed into him. A few patriots believe that Sang was going to pick up the white gun with his teeth before he died, but never had the opportunity. But the blood is indisputable.

Sezhi Tomo, pale but dry-eyed, bowed over the commandant's fallen body, lifting his hand from heart to lips: a Chosar salute, never a Yamachin one. Sezhi paid for that among his own troops.

And Yen—Admiral, through no fault of your own, you received the news too late to save the commandant. Heaven's Gate, to our shame, fell in days.

There is no need to recount our losses to Yamat's soldiers. Once their warsails had entered Cho's local space, they showed what a generation of civil war does for one's martial abilities. Our world-bound populations fell before them like summer leaves before winter winds. One general wrote, in a memorandum to the government, that "death walks the only road left to us." The only hope was to stop them before they made planetfall, and we failed at that.

We asked Feng-Huang for aid, but Feng-Huang was suspicious of our failure to inform them earlier of Yamat's imperial designs. So their warsail fleets and soldiers arrived too late to prevent the worst of the damage.

It must pain you to look at the starsail battles lost, which you could have won so readily. It is easy to scorn Admiral Wan Kun for not being the tactician you are, less adept at using the nexuses' spacetime terrain to advantage. But what truly diminishes the man is the fact that he allowed rivalry to cloud his judgment. Instead of using his connections at court to disparage your victories and accuse you of treason, he could have helped unify the fractious factions in coming up with a strategy to defeat Yamat. Alas, he held a grudge against you for invading his jurisdiction at Heaven's Gate without securing prior permission.

He never forgave you for eclipsing him. Even as he died in defeat, commanding the Chosar fleet that you had led so effectively, he must have been bitter. But they say this last battle at Yellow Splendor will decide everything. Forget his pettiness, Yen. He is gone, and it is no longer important.

"I have your file," the man said to Yen Shenar. His dark blue uniform did not show any rank insignia, but there was a white gun in his holster. "I would appeal to your loyalty, but the programmer assigned to you noted that this was unlikely to succeed."

"Then why are you here?" Yen said. They were in a room with high windows and paintings of carp. The guards had given him plain clothing, also in dark blue, a small improvement on the gray that all prisoners wore.

The man smiled. "Necessity," he said. "Your military acumen is needed."

"Perhaps the government should have considered that before they put me here," Yen said.

"You speak as though the government were a unified entity."

As if he could forget. The court's inability to face in the same direction at the same time was legendary.

"You were not without allies, even then," the man said.

Yen tipped his head up: he was not a short man, but the other was taller. "The government has a flawed understanding of 'military acumen,' you know."

The man raised an eyebrow.

"It's not just winning at baduk or other strategy games, or the ability to put starsails in pretty arrangements," Yen said. "It is leadership; it is inspiring people, and knowing who is worth inspiring; it is honoring your ancestors with your service. And," he added dryly, "it is knowing enough about court politics to avoid being put in the Garden, where your abilities do you no good."

"People are the sum of their loyalties," the man said. "You told me that once."

"I'm expected to recognize you?"

"No," the man said frankly. "I told them so. We all know how reprogramming works. There's no hope of restoring what you were." There was no particular emotion in his voice. "But they insisted that I try."

"Tell me who you are."

"You have no way of verifying the information," the man said.

Yen laughed shortly. "I'm curious anyway."

"I'm your nephew," the man said. "My name wouldn't mean anything to you." At Yen's scrutiny, he said, "You used to remark on how I take after my mother."

"I'm surprised the government didn't send me back to the Ministry of Virtuous Thought to ensure my cooperation anyway," Yen said.

"They were afraid it would damage you beyond repair," he said.

"Did the programmer tell them so?"

"I've only spoken to her once," the man said.

This was the important part, and this supposed nephew of his didn't even realize it. "Did she have anything else to say?"

The man studied him for a long moment, then nodded. "She said you are not the sum of your loyalties, you are the sum of your choices."

"I did not choose to be here," Yen said, because it would be expected of him, although it was not true. Presumably, given that he had known what the king's decree was to be, he could have committed suicide or defected. He was a strategist now and had been a strategist then. This course of action had to have been chosen for a reason.

He realized now that the Yen Shenar of yesteryear might not have been a man willing to intrigue against his enemies, even where it would have saved him his command. But he had been ready to become one who would, even for the sake of a government that had been willing to discard his service.

The man was frowning. "Will you accept your reinstatement into the military?"

"Yes," Yen said. "Yes." He was the weapon that he had made of himself, in a life he remembered only through shadows and fissures. It was time to test his forging, to ensure that the government would never be in a position to trap him in the Garden again.

This is the story the way they are telling it now. I do not know how much of it to believe. Surely it is impossible that you outmatched the Yamachin fleet when it was five times the size of your own; surely it is impossible that over half the Yamachin starsails were destroyed or captured. But the royal historians say it is so.

There has been rejoicing in the temporary capital: red banners in every street, fragrant blossoms scattered at every doorway. Children play with starsails of folded paper, pretending to vanquish the Yamachin foe, and even the thralls have memorized the famous poem commemorating your victory at Yellow Splendor.

They say you will come home soon. I hope that is true.

But all I can think of is how, the one time I met you, you did not wear the white gun. I wonder if you wear it now.

swanwatch

Officially, the five exiles on the station were the Initiates of the Fermata. Unofficially, the Concert of Worlds called them the swanwatch.

The older exiles called themselves Dragon and Phoenix, Tiger and Tortoise, according to tradition based in an ancient civilization's legends. The newest and youngest exile went by Swan. She was not a swan in the way of fairy tales. If so, she would have had a history sung across the galaxy's billions of stars, of rapturous beauty or resolute virtue. She would have woven the hearts of dead stars into armor for the Concert's soldiers and hushed novae to sleep so ships could safely pass. However, she was, as befitted the name they gave her, a musician.

Swan had been exiled to the station because she had offended the captain of a guestship from the scintillant core. In a moment of confusion, she had addressed him in the wrong language for the occasion. Through the convolutions of Concert politics, she wound up in the swanwatch.

The captain sent her a single expensive message across the vast space now separating them. It was because of the message that Swan first went to Dragon. Dragon was not the oldest and wisest of the swanwatch; that honor belonged to Tortoise. But Dragon loved oddments of knowledge, and he could read the calligraphy in which the captain had written his message.

"You have good taste in enemies," Dragon commented, as though Swan had singled out the captain. Dragon was a lanky man with skin lighter than Swan's, and he was always pacing, or whittling appallingly rare scraps of wood, or tapping earworm-rhythms upon his knee.

Swan bowed her head. *I'd rather not be here, and be back with my family.* She didn't say so out loud, though. That would have implied a disregard for Dragon's company, and she was already fond of Dragon. "Can you read it?" she asked.

"Of course I can read it, although it would help if you held the message right-side-up."

Swan wasn't illiterate, but there were many languages in the Concert of Worlds. "This way?" Swan asked, rotating the sheet.

Dragon nodded.

"What does it say?"

Dragon's foot tapped. "It says: 'I look forward to hearing your masterpiece honoring the swanships.' Should I read all his titles, too?" Dragon's ironic tone made his opinion of the captain's pretensions quite clear. "They take up the rest of the page."

Swan had paled. "No, thank you," she said. The swanwatch's official purpose was as a retreat for artists. Its inhabitants could only leave upon presenting an acceptable masterwork to the judges who visited every decade. In practice, those exiled here lacked the requisite skill. The captain's message clearly mocked her.

Like many privileged children, Swan had had lessons in the high arts: music and calligraphy, fencing and poetry. She could set a fragment of text to a melody, if given the proper mode, and play the essential three instruments: the zither, the flute, the keyboard. But she had never pursued composing any further than that, expecting a life as a patron of the arts rather than an artist herself.

Dragon said, kindly, "It's another way of telling you your task is impossible."

Swan wondered if Dragon was a composer, but would not be so uncouth as to ask. "Thank you for reading me the letter," she said.

"It was my pleasure," Dragon said. It was obvious to him that Swan was determined to leave the Initiates and return home, however difficult the task and however much home might have changed in the interim. Kind for a second time, he did not disillusion her about her chances.

Tiger was a tall woman with deceptively sweet eyes and a rapacious smile. When Swan first met her, she was afraid that Tiger would gobble her up in some manner peculiar to the Initiates. But Tiger said only, "How are you settling in?"

Swan had a few reminders of her home, things she had been allowed to bring in physical form: a jewelry box inlaid with abalone, inherited from her deceased mother; a silver flute her best friend had given her. The official who had processed Swan's transfer to the station had reminded her to choose carefully, and had said she could bring a lot more in scanned form, to be replicated at the station. But where homesickness was concerned, she wanted the real item, not a copy.

Swan thought about it, then said, "I'll adjust."

Tiger said, "We all do." She stretched, joints creaking. "You've seen the duty roster, I trust. There's a swanship coming in very soon. Shall I show you what to do?"

Although Swan could have trusted the manuals, she knew she would be sharing swanwatch with Tiger and the others for a long time. If Tiger was feeling generous enough to explain the procedures to her, best not to offend Tiger by declining.

Together, Tiger and Swan walked the long halls of their prison to the monitoring room. "You can do this from anywhere on the station," Tiger said. "The computers log everything, and it only requires a moment's attention for you to pray in honor of the swanship's valor, if you believe in that at all. Once you've been here a while, you'll welcome the ritual and the illusion that you matter. They do value ritual where you come from, don't they?"

"Yes," Swan said.

"How much of the fermata did you see on your way here?"

"They wouldn't let me look." In fact, Swan had been sedated for her arrival. New Initiates sometimes attempted escape. "They said I'd have plenty of time to stare at the grave-of-ships as an Initiate."

"Quite right," Tiger said, a little bitterly.

Doors upon doors irised before them until at last they reached the monitoring room. To Swan's surprise, it was a vast hall, lined with subtly glowing banks of controls and projective screens. Tiger grasped Swan's shoulder firmly and steered her to the center of the hall. "The grave-of-ships," Tiger said, adding an honorific to the phrase. "Look!"

Swan looked. All around them were the projected images of swanships in the first blush of redshift, those who had cast themselves into the fermata and left their inexorably dimming shadows: the Concert of Worlds' highest form of suicide art. In any number of religions, the swanships formed a great fleet to battle the silence at the end of time. Some societies in the Concert sent their condemned in swanships to redeem themselves, while others sent their most honored generals.

"The ship doesn't need our assistance, does it?" Swan said.

"What, in plunging into a black hole?" Tiger said dryly. "Not usually, no."

Tiger muttered a command, and all the images flickered away save that of the incoming swanship and its escort of three. The escort peeled away; the swanship flew straight toward the fermata's hidden heart, indicated in the displays by a pulsing point.

Swan did not know how long she watched that fatal trajectory.

Tiger tapped Swan on the shoulder. "Breathe, cygnet. It's not coming back. You'll just see the ship go more and more slowly as it approaches the event horizon forever, and you don't want to pass out."

"How many people were on the ship?" Swan said.

"You want statistics?" Tiger said approvingly. Tiger, Swan would learn, was a great believer in morbid details. She showed Swan how to look up the basic things one might wish to know about a swanship: its crew and shipyard of origin, its registry, the weapons it brought to the fight at the end of time.

"I had thought it would be more spectacular," Swan said, gazing back at the swanship's frozen image. "Even if I knew about the—the physics involved."

"What were you expecting, cygnet? False-color explosions and a crescendo in the music of your mind?" Tiger saw Swan bite her lip. "It wasn't hard to guess how you'd try to escape, little musician. It's too bad you can't ask Tortoise to write music for your freedom, but all Tortoise does anymore is sleep."

"I wouldn't ask that of Tortoise," Swan said. "But I have to understand the swanships if I am to compose for them."

"Poor cygnet," Tiger said. "You'll learn to set hope aside soon enough."

Tiger kissed Swan on the side of the mouth, not at all benevolently, then walked away.

In the silence, Swan listened to the ringing in her ears, and shivered.

After her nineteenth swanship, Swan hunted through the station's libraries—updated each time a swanship and its entourage came through—for material on composition. She read interactive treatises on music theory for six hours, skipping lunch and dinner: modes and keys, time signatures and rhythms, tones and textures, hierarchies of structure. The result was a vile headache. The Concert of Worlds was as rich in musical forms as it was in languages, and despite Swan's efforts to be discriminating, she ran into contradictory traditions.

Swan returned to the three instruments she knew, zither, flute, and keyboard. The station replicated the first and third for her according to her specifications. Drawing upon the classics she had memorized in childhood and the libraries' collection of poetry, she practiced setting texts to music. Sometimes she did this in the station's rock garden. The impracticality of the place delighted her absurdly.

Dragon often came to listen, offering neither encouragement nor criticism. Rather than applauding, he left her the figurines he whittled. Swan decorated her room with them.

"Are you an artist?" she asked Dragon once after botching her warm-up scales on the flute.

"No," Dragon said. "I could play a chord or two on your keyboard, but that's all."

Swan turned her hand palm-up and stepped away from the keyboard, offering. Smiling, he declined, and she did not press him.

After fifty-seven swanships—months as the station reckoned time—Swan asked the others if she could move her keyboard into the observation room. Dragon not only agreed, but offered to help her move it, knowing that Swan felt uneasy around the station's mechanical servitors. Phoenix said she supposed there was no harm in it. Tiger laughed and said, "Anything for you, cygnet." Swan was horribly afraid that Tiger meant it. Tortoise didn't respond, which the others assured her was a yes.

Swan wrote fragments of poetry for each ship thereafter, and set them to music. The poetry itself was frequently wretched—Swan was honest enough with herself to admit this—but she had some hope for the music. She was briefly encouraged by her attempts at orchestration: bright, brassy fanfares for ships that had served in battles; shimmering chords for ships built with beauty rather than speed in mind; the menacing clatter of drums for those rare ships that defied their fate and swung around to attack the station.

Tiger deigned to listen to one of Swan's fragments, despite her ordinary impatience for musical endeavors. "Orchestrate a battle; orchestrate a piece of music. This isn't the only language that uses the same verb for both. Your battle, cygnet, is a hundred skirmishes and no master plan. If you plan to do this for every swanship that is and has ever been, you'll die of old age before you're finished."

"I'm no general," Swan said, "but I have a battle to fight and music to write."

"I can't decide whether your persistence is tiresome or admirable," Tiger said. But she was smiling, and although she didn't seem to realize it, her foot was still tapping to the beat.

Swan had already returned to the keyboard, sketching a theme around the caesuras of an ancient hymn. Lost in visions of ships stretched beyond recognition, she did not hear Tiger leave.

Phoenix had held herself aloof from Swan after their initial introduction. This was not a matter of personal ill-will, as Dragon told Swan. Phoenix didn't hold anyone but herself in high regard, and she locked herself away in pursuit of her own art, painting.

Perhaps Swan's diligence impressed Phoenix at last. It was hard to say. Tiger paid as little attention to Phoenix as possible, and urged Swan to do likewise. "She's forever painting nebulae and alien landscapes, then burning the results," Tiger said contemptuously. "What's the point, then?"

Dragon said that everyone was entitled to a few quirks. Tiger remarked that anyone would say that of a former lover. At that point, Swan excused herself from the conversation.

"I have heard that you started the first movement of your symphony. I should like to hear it," Phoenix said to Swan through the station's most impersonal messaging system.

So Swan invited her to the observation room at an hour when no swanships were scheduled to arrive. She played the flute—her best instrument—to the station's recordings of the other parts; the libraries had included numerous sequencers. Phoenix applauded when Swan had finished. Her expression was reluctantly respectful. Gravely, she said, "This captain of yours—"

He's not mine, Swan thought, *although perhaps I am his.*

"—do you know anything of his musical preferences?"

Swan shook her head. "I tried to find out," she said. After all, if the captain had possessed enough influence to send her to the swanwatch, he might also be able to influence the selection of judges. "He commissioned a synesthetic opera once, which I have no recording of. Beyond that, who knows how he interprets the grave-of-ships? And if I am to do each swanship justice, shouldn't I draw upon the musical traditions of their cultures? Some of them contradict each other. How am I to deal with this in a single finite symphony?"

Phoenix lifted an eyebrow, and Swan felt ashamed of her outburst. "Do you know why we're here, Swan?" she asked. She was not referring to their official mission of contemplating the fermata to further their art.

"It seemed impolite to ask," Swan said.

"Tiger is a war criminal," Phoenix said. "Tortoise is a scholar who resigned and came here to protest the policies of some government that has since been wiped out of time. It might even have done some good, in the strand of society where he was famous. I, of course, am here as unjustly as you are." She did not elaborate.

"And Dragon?"

Phoenix smiled thinly. "You should ask Dragon yourself. It might make you think twice about your symphony."

Swan wouldn't have realized anything was wrong if Tiger hadn't sent her a message while she was in the middle of working on her second movement. The idea had come to her in the middle of her sleep shift, and she was kneeling at the zither, adjusting the bridges.

"Urgent message from Tiger," the station informed her.

"Go ahead," Swan said absently, trying to decide what mode to tune to.

Tiger's voice said, "Hello, cygnet. It's Tortoise's watch, but he seems to be asleep as usual, and you might be interested in going to the observation room."

Tiger's tone was lazy, but she had flagged the message as urgent. What was going on?

"Station," Swan said, "who's in the observation room now?"

"No one," it said.

"Is there a swanship scheduled to arrive soon?"

"There is an unscheduled swanship right now."

Swan rose and ran to the observation room.

Tiger had been correct about the importance of ritual. No matter how smoothly a ship descended into the fermata, Swan always checked the ship's status. Swanships did occasionally arrive off-schedule, but she wondered why Tiger had sounded concerned.

So she looked at the ship, which was tiny, with an underpowered sublight drive, and its crew, a single person: Gazhien of the *Circle of Swords*.

She knew that name, although ages had passed since she had used it. It was Dragon.

She asked the station what the *Circle of Swords* was. It had been a swanship nearly a century ago, and all but one member of the crew had passed into the fermata on it.

"Swan to Dragon," she said to the tiny ship, which was one of the station's shuttles. "Swan to Dragon. Please come back!"

After a heartstopping moment, Dragon replied, "Ah, Swan."

Swan could have said, *What do you think you're doing?*, but they both knew that. Instead, she asked, "Why now, and not tomorrow, or the day before? Why this day of all days, after a century of waiting?"

"You are as tactful as ever," Dragon said, "even about the matter of my cowardice."

"*Please*, Dragon."

Dragon's voice was peculiarly meditative. "Your symphony reminds me of my duty, Swan. I came here a long time ago on the *Circle of Swords*. It was one of the proudest warships of—well, the nation has since passed into anarchy. I was the only soldier too afraid of my fate to swear the sacred oath to *sing always against the coming silence*. As punishment, they left me here to contemplate my failure, forever separated from my comrades."

"Dragon," Swan said, "they're long gone now. What good will it do them, at this end of time, for you to die?"

"The Concert teaches that the fermata is our greatest form of immortality—"

"Dead is dead," Swan said. "At this end of time, what is the hurry?"

The door whisked open. Swan looked away from the ship's image and met Tiger's curious eyes.

"Damn, 'Zhien," Tiger said respectfully. "So you found the courage after all."

"That's not it," Swan said. "The symphony wasn't supposed to be about the glory of death."

Loftily, Tiger said, "Oh, I'd never perform suicide art. There's nothing pretty about death. You learn that in battle."

After a silence, Dragon said, "What did you intend, then, Swan?"

The question brought her up short. She had been so absorbed in attempting to convey the swanships' grandeur that she had forgotten that real people passed into the fermata to send their souls to the end of time. "I'll change my music," she said. "I'll delete it all if I have to."

"Please don't," Dragon said. "I would miss it greatly." A faint swelling of melody: his ship was playing back one of her first, stumbling efforts.

"You'll miss it forever if you keep going."

"A bargain, then," Dragon said. "I was never an artist, only a soldier, but a hundred years here have taught me the value of art. Don't destroy your music, and I'll come back."

Swan's eyes prickled. "All right."

Tiger and Swan watched as Dragon's ship decelerated, then reversed its course, returning to the station.

"You've sacrificed your freedom to bring him back, you know," Tiger said. "If you finish your symphony now, it will lack conviction. Anyone with half an ear will be able to tell."

"I would rather have Dragon's life than write a masterpiece," Swan said.

"You're a fool, cygnet."

Only then did Swan realize that, in her alarm over the situation, she had completely forgotten the theme she had meant to record.

Dragon helped Swan move the keyboard out of the observation room and into the rock garden. "I'm glad you're not giving up your music," he remarked.

She looked at him, really looked at him, thinking of how she had almost lost a friend. "I'm not writing the symphony," she said.

He blinked.

"I'm still writing music," Swan assured him. "Just not the captain's symphony. Because you were right: it's impossible. At least, what I envisioned is impossible. If I dwell upon the impossible, I achieve nothing. But if I do what I can, where I can—I might get somewhere."

She wasn't referring to freedom from the swanwatch.

Dragon nodded. "I think I see. And Swan—" He hesitated. "Thank you."

"It's been a long day," she said. "You should rest."

"Like Tortoise?" He chuckled. "Perhaps I will." He ran one hand along the keyboard in a flurry of notes. Then he sat on one of the garden's benches and closed his eyes, humming idly.

Swan studied Dragon's calm face. Then she stood at the keyboard and played several tentative notes, a song for Dragon and Phoenix and Tiger—a song for the living.

effigy nights

They are connoisseurs of writing in Imulai Mokarengen, the city whose name means *inkblot of the gods.*

The city lies at the galaxy's dust-stranded edge, enfolding a moon that used to be a world, or a world that used to be a moon; no one is certain anymore. In the mornings its skies are radiant with clouds like the plumage of a bird ever-rising, and in the evenings the stars scatter light across skies stitched and unstitched by the comings and goings of fire-winged starships. Its walls are made of metal the color of undyed silk, and its streets bloom with aleatory lights, small solemn symphonies, the occasional duel.

Imulai Mokarengen has been unmolested for over a hundred years. People come to listen to the minstrels and drink tea-of-moments-unraveling, to admire the statues of shapeshifting tigers and their pliant lovers, to look for small maps to great fortunes at the intersections of curving roads. Even the duelists confront each other in fights knotted by ceremony and the exchange of poetry.

But now the starships that hunt each other in the night of nights have set their dragon eyes upon Imulai Mokarengen, desiring to possess its arts, and the city is unmolested no more.

The soldiers came from the sky in a glory of thunder, a cascade of fire. Blood like roses, bullets like thorns, everything to ashes. Imulai Mokarengen's defenses were few, and easily overwhelmed. Most of them would have been museum pieces anywhere else.

The city's wardens gathered to offer the invading general payment in any coin she might desire, so long as she left the city in peace. Accustomed to their decadent visitors, they offered these: Wine pressed from rare books of stratagems and aged in barrels set in orbit around a certain red star. Crystals extracted from the nervous systems of philosopher-beasts that live in colonies upon hollow asteroids. Perfume symphonies infused into exquisite fractal tapestries.

The general was Jaian of the Burning Orb, and she scorned all these things. She was a tall woman clad in armor the color of dead metal. For each world she had scoured, she wore a jewel of black-red facets upon her breastplate. She said to the wardens: What use did she have for wine except to drink to her enemies' defeat? What use was metal except to build engines of war? And as for the perfume, she didn't dignify that with a response.

But, she said, smiling, there was one thing they could offer her, and then she would leave with her soldiers and guns and ships. They could give her all the writings they treasured so much: all the binary crystals gleaming bright-dark, all the books with the bookmarks still in them, all the tilted street signs, all the graffiti chewed by drunken nanomachines into the shining walls, all the tattoos obscene and tender, all the ancestral tablets left at the shrines with their walls of gold and chitin.

The wardens knew then that she was mocking them, and that as long as any of the general's soldiers breathed, they would know no peace. One warden, however, considered Jaian's words of scorn, and thought that, unwitting, Jaian herself had given them the key to her defeat.

Seran did not remember a time when his othersight of the city did not show it burning, no matter what his ordinary senses told him, or what the dry pages of his history said. In his dreams the smoke made the sky a funeral shroud. In waking, the wind smelled of ash, the buildings of angry flames. Everything in the othersight was wreathed in orange and amber, flickering, shadows cinder-edged.

He carried that pall of phantom flame with him even now, into the warden's secret library, and it made him nervous although the books had nothing to fear from the phantoms. The warden, a woman in dust-colored robes, was escorting him through the maze-of-mists and down the stairs to the library's lowest level. The air was cool and dry, and to either side he could see the candle-sprites watching him hungrily.

"Here we are," the warden said as they reached the bottom of the stairs.

Seran looked around at the parchment and papers and scrolls of silk, then stepped into the room. The tools he carried, bonesaws and forceps and fine curved needles, scalpels that sharpened themselves if fed the oil of certain olives, did not belong in this place. But the warden had insisted that she required a surgeon's expertise.

He risked being tortured or killed by the general's occupation force for cooperating with a warden. In fact, he could have earned himself a tidy sum for turning her in. But Imulai Mokarengen was his home, for all that he had not been born here. He owed it a certain loyalty.

"Why did you bring me here, madam warden?" Seran said.

The warden gestured around the room, then unrolled one of the great charts across the table at the center of the room. It was a stardrive schematic, all angles and curves and careful coils.

Then Seran saw the shape flickering across the schematic, darkening some of the precise lines while others flowed or dimmed. The warden said nothing, leaving him to observe as though she felt he was making a difficult diagnosis. After a while he identified the elusive shape as that of a girl, slight of figure or perhaps merely young, if such a creature counted years in human terms. The shape twisted this way and that, but there were no adjacent maps or diagrams for her to jump to. She left a disordered trail of numbers like bullets in her wake.

"I see her," Seran said dryly. "What do you need me to do about her?"

"Free her," the warden said. "I'm pretty sure this is all of her, although she left a trail while we were perfecting the procedure—"

She unrolled another chart, careful to keep it from touching the first. It appeared to be a treatise on musicology, except parts of it had been replaced by a detritus of clefs and twisted staves and demiquavers coalescing into a diagram of a pistol.

"Is this your plan for resistance against the invaders?" Seran said. "Awakening soldiers from scraps of text, then cutting them out? You should have a lot more surgeons. Or perhaps children with scissors."

The warden shrugged. "Imulai Mokarengen is a city of stories. It's not hard to persuade one to come to life in her defense, even though I wouldn't call her *tame*. She is the Saint of Guns summoned from a book of legends. Now you see why I need a surgeon. I am given to believe that your skills are not entirely natural."

This was true enough. He had once been a surgeon-priest of the Order of the Chalice. "If you know that much about me," he said, "then you know that I was cast out of the order. Why haven't you scared up the real thing?"

"Your order is a small one," she said. "I looked, but with the blockade, there's no way to get someone else. It has to be you." When he didn't speak, she went on, "We are outnumbered. The general can send for more soldiers from the worlds of her realm, and they are armed with the latest weaponry. We are a single city known for artistic endeavors, not martial ones. Something has to be done."

Seran said, "You're going to lose your schematic."

"I'm not concerned about its fate."

"All right," he said. "But if you know anything about me, you know that your paper soldiers won't last. I stick to ordinary surgery because the prayers of healing don't work for me anymore; they're cursed by fire." And, because he knew she was thinking it: "The curse touches anyone I teach."

"I'm aware of the limitations," the warden said. "Now, do you require additional tools?"

He considered it. Ordinary scissors might be better suited to paper than the curved ones he carried, but he trusted his own instruments. A scalpel would have to do. But the difficult part would be getting the girl-shape to hold still. "I need water," he said. He had brought a sedative, but he was going to have to sponge the entire schematic, since an injection was unlikely to do the trick.

The warden didn't blink. "Wait here."

As though he had somewhere else to wait. He spent the time attempting to map the girl's oddly flattened anatomy. Fortunately, he wouldn't have to intrude on her internal structures. Her joints showed the normal range of articulation. If he hadn't known better, he would have said she was dancing in the disarrayed ink, or perhaps looking for a fight.

Footsteps sounded in the stairwell. The woman set a large pitcher of water down on the table. "Will this be enough?" she asked.

Seran nodded and took out a vial from his satchel. The dose was pure guesswork, unfortunately. He dumped half the vial's contents into the pitcher, then stirred the water with a glass rod. After putting on gloves, he soaked one of his sponges, then wrung it out.

Working with steady strokes, he soaked the schematic. The paper absorbed the water readily. The warden winced in spite of herself. The girl didn't seem capable of facial expressions, but she dashed to one side of the schematic, then the other, seeking escape. Finally she slumped, her long hair trailing off in disordered tangles of artillery tables.

The warden's silence pricked at Seran's awareness. She's *studying how I do this,* he thought. He selected his most delicate scalpel and began cutting the girl-shape out of the paper. The medium felt alien, without the resistances characteristic of flesh, although water oozed away from the cuts.

He hesitated over the final incision, then completed it, hand absolutely steady.

Amid all the maps and books and scrolls, they heard a girl's slow, drowsy breathing. In place of the paper cutout, the girl curled on the table, clad in black velvet and gunmetal lace. She had paper-pale skin and inkstain hair, and a gun made of shadows rested in her hand.

It was impossible to escape the problem: smoke curled from the girl's other hand, and her nails were blackened.

"I warned you of this," Seran said. Cursed by fire. "She'll burn up, slowly at first, and then all at once. I suspect she'll last a week at most."

"You listen to the news, surely," the warden said. "Do you know how many of our people the invaders shot the first week of the occupation?"

He knew the number. It was not small. "Anything else?" he said.

"I may have need of you later," the warden said. "If I summon you, will you come? I will pay you the same fee."

"Yes, of course," Seran said. He had noticed her deft hands, however; he imagined she would make use of them soon.

Not long after Seran's task for the warden, the effigy nights began.

He was out after curfew when he saw the Saint of Guns. Imulai Mokarengen's people were bad at curfews. People still broke the general's curfew regularly, although many of them were also caught at it. At every intersection, along every street, you could see people hung up as corpse-lanterns, burning with plague-colored light, as warnings to the populace. Still, the city's people were accustomed to their parties and trysts and sly confrontations. For his part, he was on his way home after an emergency call, and looking forward to a quiet bath.

It didn't surprise him that he should encounter the Saint of Guns, although he wished he hadn't. After all, he had freed her from the boundary of paper and legend to walk in the world. The connection was real, for all that she hadn't been conscious for its forging. Still, the sight of her made him freeze up.

Jaian's soldiers were rounding up a group of merry-goers and poets whose rebellious recitations had been loud enough to be heard from outside. The poets, in particular, were not becoming any less loud, especially when one of them was shot in the head.

The night became the color of gunsmoke little by little, darkness unfolding to make way for the lithe girl-figure. She had a straight-hipped stride, and her eyes were spark-bright, her mouth furiously unsmiling. Her hair was braided and pinned this time. Seran had half-expected her to have a pistol in each hand, but no, there was only the one. He wondered if that had to do with the charred hand.

Most of the poets didn't recognize her, and none of the soldiers. But one of the poets, a chubby woman, tore off her necklace with its glory's worth of void-pearls. They scattered in all directions, purple-iridescent, fragile. "The Saint of Guns," the poet cried. "In the city where words are bullets, in the book where verses are trajectories, who is safe from her?"

Seran couldn't tell whether this was a quotation or something the poet had made up on the spot. He should have ducked around the corner and toward safety, but he found it impossible to look away, even when one of the soldiers knocked the pearl-poet to the street and two others started kicking her in the stomach.

The other soldiers shouted at the Saint of Guns to stand down, to cast away her weapon. She narrowed her eyes at them, not a little contemptuous. She pointed her gun into the air and pulled the trigger. For a second there was no sound.

Then all the soldiers' guns exploded. Seran had a blurry impression of red and star-shaped shrapnel and chalk-white and falling bodies, fire and smoke and screaming. There was a sudden sharp pain across his left cheek where a passing splinter cut it: the Saint's mark.

None of the soldiers had survived. Seran was no stranger to corpses. They didn't horrify him, despite the charred reek and the cooked eyes, the truncated finger that had landed near his foot. But none of the poets had survived, either.

The Saint of Guns lowered her weapon, then saluted him with her other hand. Her fingers were blackened to their bases.

Seran stared at her, wondering what she wanted from him. Her lips moved, but he couldn't hear a thing.

She only shrugged and walked away. The night gradually grew darker as she did.

Only later did Seran learn that the gun of every soldier in that district had exploded at the same time.

Imulai Mokarengen has four great archives, one for each compass point. The greatest of them is the South Archive, with its windows the color of regret and walls where vines trace out spirals like those of particles in cloud chambers. In the South Archive the historians of the city store their chronicles. Each book is written with nightbird quills and ink-of-dedication, and bound with a peculiar thread spun from spent artillery shells. Before it is shelved, one of the city's wardens seals each book shut with a black kiss. The books are not for reading. It is widely held that the historians' objectivity will be compromised if they concern themselves with an audience.

When Jaian of the Burning Orb conquered Imulai Mokarengen, she sent a detachment to secure the South Archive. Although she could have destroyed it in a conflagration of ice and fire and funeral dust, she knew it would serve her purpose better to take the histories hostage.

It didn't take long for the vines to wither, and for the dead brown tendrils to spell out her name in a syllabary of curses, but Jaian, unsuperstitious, only laughed when she heard.

The warden called Seran back, as he had expected she would.

Seran hadn't expected the city to be an easy place to live in during an occupation, but he also hadn't made adequate preparations for the sheer aggravation of sharing it with legends and historical figures.

"Aggravation" was what he called it when he was able to lie to himself about it. It was easy to be clinical about his involvement when he was working with curling sheets, and less so when he saw what the effigies achieved.

The Saint of Guns burned up within a week, as Seran had predicted. The official reports were confused, and the rumors not much better, but he spent an entire night holed up in his study afterward estimating the number of people she had killed, bystanders included. He had bottles of very bad wine for occasions like this. By the time morning came around, he was comprehensively drunk.

Six-and-six years ago, on a faraway station, he had violated his oaths as a surgeon-priest by using his prayers to kill a man. It had not been self-defense, precisely. The man had shot a child. Seran had been too late to save the child, but not too late to damn himself.

It seemed that his punishment hadn't taught him anything. He explained to himself that what he was doing was necessary; that he was helping to free the city of Jaian.

The warden next had him cut out one of the city's founders, Alarra Coldly-Smiling. She left footsteps of frost, and where she walked, people cracked into pieces, frozen all the way through, needles of ice piercing their intestines. As might be expected, she burned up faster than the Saint of Guns. A pity; she was outside Jaian's increasingly well-defended headquarters when she sublimated.

The third was the Mechanical Soldier, who manifested as a suit of armor inside which lights blinked on-off, on-off, in digital splendor. Seran was buying more wine—you could usually get your hands on some, even during the occupation, if your standards were low—when he heard the clink-clank thunder outside the dim room where the transaction was taking place. The Mechanical Soldier carried a black sword, which proved capable of cutting through metal and crystal and stone. With great precision it carved a window in the wall. The blinking lights brightened as it regarded Seran.

The wine-seller shrieked and dropped one of the bottles, to Seran's dismay. The air was pungent with the wine's sour smell. Seran looked unflinchingly at the helmet, although a certain amount of flinching was undoubtedly called for, and after a while the Mechanical Soldier went away in search of its real target.

It turned out that the Mechanical Soldier liked to carve cartouches into walls, or perhaps its coat-of-arms. Whenever it struck down Jaian's soldiers, lights sparked in the carvings, like sourceless eyes. People began leaving offerings by the carvings: oil-of-massacres, bouquets of crystals with fissures in their shining hearts, cardamom bread. (Why cardamom, Seran wasn't sure. At least the aroma was pleasing.) Jaian's soldiers executed people they caught at these makeshift shrines, but the offerings kept coming.

Seran had laid in a good supply of wine, but after the Mechanical General shuddered apart into pixels and blackened reticulations, there was a maddening period of calm. He waited for the warden's summons.

No summons came.

Jaian's soldiers swaggered through the streets again, convinced that there would be no more apparitions. The city's people whispered to each other that they must have faith. The offerings increased in number.

Finding wine became too difficult, so Seran gave it up. He was beginning to think that he had dreamed up the whole endeavor when the effigy nights started again.

Imulai Mokarengen suddenly became so crowded with effigies that Seran's othersight of fire and smoke was not much different from reality. He had not known that the city contained so many stories: Women with deadly hands and men who sang atrocity-hymns. Colonial intelligences that wove webs across the pitted buildings and flung disease-sparks at the invaders. A cannon that rose up out of the city's central plaza and roared forth red storms.

But Jaian of the Burning Orb wasn't a fool. She knew that the effigies, for all their destructiveness, burned out eventually. She and her soldiers retreated beneath their force-domes and waited.

Seran resolved to do some research. How did the warden mean to win her war, if she hadn't yet managed it?

By now he had figured out that the effigies would not harm him, although he still had the scar the Saint of Guns had given him. It would have been easy to remove the scar, but he was seized by the belief that the scar was his protection.

He went first to a bookstore in which candles burned and cogs whirred. Each candle had the face of a child. A man with pale eyes sat in an unassuming metal chair, shuffling cards. "I thought you were coming today," he said.

Seran's doubts about fortunetelling clearly showed on his face. The man laughed and fanned out the cards face-up. Every one of them was blank. "I'm sorry to disappoint you," he said, "but they only tell you what you already know."

"I need a book about the Saint of Guns," Seran said. She had been the first. No reason not to start at the beginning.

"That's not a story I know," the man said. His eyes were bemused. "I have a lot of books, if you want to call them that, but they're really empty old journals. People like them for the papers, the bindings. There's nothing written in them."

"I think I have what I came for," Seran said, hiding his alarm. "I'm sorry to trouble you."

He visited every bookstore in the district, and some outside of it, and his eyes ached abominably by the end. It was the same story at all of them. But he knew where he had to go next.

Getting into the South Archive meant hiring a thief-errant, whose name was Izeut. Izeut had blinded Seran for the journey, and it was only now, inside one of the reading rooms, that Seran recovered his vision.

He suspected he was happier not knowing how they had gotten in. His stomach still felt as though he'd tied it up in knots.

Seran had had no idea what the Archive would look like inside. He had especially not expected the room they had landed in to be welcoming, the kind of place where you could curl up and read a few novels while sipping citron tea. There were couches with pillows, and padded chairs, and the paintings on the walls showed lizards at play.

"All right," Izeut said. His voice was disapproving, but Seran had almost beggared himself paying him, so the disapproval was very faint. "What now?"

"All the books look like they're in place here," Seran said. "I want to make sure there's nothing obviously missing."

"That will take a while," Izeut said. "We'd better get started."

Not all the rooms were welcoming. Seran's least favorite was the one from which sickles hung from the ceiling, their tips gleaming viscously. But all the bookcases were full.

Seran still wasn't satisfied. "I want to look inside a few of the books," he said.

Izeut shot him a startled glance. "The city's traditions—"

"The city's traditions are already dying," Seran said.

"The occupation is temporary," Izeut said stoutly. "We just have to do more to drive out the warlord's people."

Izeut had no idea. "Humor me," Seran said. "Haven't you always wanted to see what's in those books?" Maybe an appeal to curiosity would work better.

Whether it did or not, Izeut stood silently while Seran pulled one of the books off the shelves. He hesitated, then broke the book's seal and felt the warden's black kiss, cold, unsentimental, against his lips. *I'm already cursed,* he thought, and opened the covers.

The first few pages were fine, written in a neat hand with graceful swells. Seran flipped to the middle, however, and his breath caught. The pages were empty except for a faint dust-trace of distorted graphemes and pixellated stick figures.

He could have opened up more books to check, but he had already found his answer.

"Stop," Izeut said sharply. "Let me reshelve that." He took the book from Seran, very tenderly.

"It's no use," Seran said.

Izeut didn't turn around; he was slipping the book into its place. "We can go now."

It was too late. The general's soldiers had caught them.

Seran was separated from Izeut and brought before Jaian of the Burning Orb. She regarded him with cool exasperation. "There were two of you," she said, "but something tells me that you're the one I should worry about."

She kicked the table next to her. All of Seran's surgical tools, which the soldiers had confiscated and laid out in disarray, clattered.

"I have nothing to say to you," Seran said through his teeth.

"Really," Jaian said. "You fancy yourself a patriot, then. We may disagree about the petty legal question of who the owner of this city is, but if you are any kind of healer, you ought to agree with me that these constant spasms of destruction are good for no one."

"You could always leave," Seran said.

She picked up one of his sets of tweezers and clicked it once, twice. "You will not understand this," she said, "and it is even right that you will not understand this, given your profession, but I will try to explain. This is what I do. Worlds are made to be pressed for their wine, cities taste of fruit when I bite them open. I cannot let go of my conquests.

"Do you think I am ignorant of the source of the apparitions that leave their smoking shadows in the streets? You're running out of writings. All I need do is wait, and this city will yield in truth."

"You're right," Seran said. "I don't understand you at all."

Jaian's smile was like knives and nightfall. "I'll write this in a language you do understand, then. You know something about how this is happening, who's doing it. Take me to them or I will start killing your people in earnest. Every hour you make me wait, I'll drop a bomb, or send out tanks, or soldiers with guns. If I get bored I'll get creative."

Seran closed his eyes and made himself breathe evenly. He didn't think she was bluffing. Besides, there was a chance—if only a small chance—that the warden could come up with a defense against the general; that the effigies would come to her aid once the general came within reach.

"All right," he said. "I'll take you where it began."

Seran was bound with chains-of-suffocation, and he thought it likely that there were more soldiers watching him than he could actually spot. He led Jaian to the secret library, to the maze-of-mists.

"A warden," Jaian said. "I knew some of them had escaped."

They went to the staircase and descended slowly, slowly. The candle-sprites flinched from the general. Their light was almost violet, like dusk.

All the way down the stairs they heard the snick-snick of many scissors.

The downstairs room, when they reached it, was filled with paper. Curling scraps and triangles crowded the floor. It was impossible to step anywhere without crushing some. The crumpling sound put Seran in mind of burnt skin.

Come to that, there was something of that smell in the room, too.

All through the room there were scissors snapping at empty space, wielded by no hand but the hands of the air, shining and precise.

At the far end of the room, behind a table piled high with more paper scraps, was the warden. She was standing sideways, leaning heavily against the table, and her face was averted so that her shoulder-length hair fell around it.

"It's over," Jaian called out. "You may as well surrender. It's folly to let you live, but your death doesn't have to be one of the ugly ones."

Seran frowned. Something was wrong with the way the warden was moving, more like paper fluttering than someone breathing. But he kept silent. *A trap,* he thought, *let it be a trap.*

Jaian's soldiers attempted to clear a path through the scissors, but the scissors flew to either side and away, avoiding the force-bolts with uncanny grace.

Jaian's long strides took her across the room and around the table. She tipped the warden's face up, forced eye contact. If there had been eyes.

Seran started, felt the chains-of-suffocation clot the breath in his throat. At first he took the marks all over the warden's skin to be tattoos. Then he saw that they were holes cut into the skin, charred black at the edges. Some of the marks were logographs, and alphabet letters, and punctuation stretched wide.

"Stars and fire ascending," Jaian breathed, "what is this?"

Too late she backed away. There was a rustling sound, and the warden unfurled, splitting down the middle with a jagged tearing sound, a great irregular sheet punched full of word-holes, completely hollowed out. Her robe crumpled into fine sediment, revealing the cutout in her back in the shape of a serpent-headed youth.

Jaian made a terrible crackling sound, like paper being ripped out of a book. She took one step back toward Seran, then halted. Holes were forming on her face and hands. The scissors closed in on her.

I did this, Seran thought, *I should have refused the warden.* She must have learned how to call forth effigies on her own, ripping them out of Imulai Mokarengen's histories and sagas and legends, animating the scissors to make her work easier. But when the scissors ran out of paper, they turned on the warden. Having denuded the city of its past, of its weight of stories, they began cutting effigies from the living stories of its people. And now Jaian was one of those stories, too.

Seran left Jaian and her soldiers to their fate and began up the stairs. But some of the scissors had already escaped, and they had left the doors to the library open. They were undoubtedly in the streets right now. Soon the city would be full of holes, and people made of paper slowly burning up, and the hungry sound of scissors.

flower, mercy, needle, chain

The usual fallacy is that, in every universe, many futures splay outward from any given moment. But in some universes, determinism runs backwards: given a universe's state *s* at some time *t*, there are multiple previous states that may have resulted in *s*. In some universes, all possible pasts funnel toward a single fixed ending, Ω.

If you are of millenarian bent, you might call Ω Armageddon. If you are of grammatical bent, you might call it punctuation on a cosmological scale.

If you are a philosopher in such a universe, you might call Ω *inevitable*.

The woman has haunted Blackwheel Station for as long as anyone remembers, although she was not born there. She is human, and her straight black hair and brown-black eyes suggest an ancestral inheritance tangled up with tigers and shapeshifting foxes. Her native language is not spoken by anyone here or elsewhere.

They say her true name means things like *gray* and *ash* and *grave*. You may buy her a drink, bring her candied petals or chaotic metals, but it's all the same. She won't speak her name.

That doesn't stop people from seeking her out. Today, it's a man with mirror-colored eyes. He is the first human she has seen in a long time.

"Arighan's Flower," he says.

It isn't her name, but she looks up. Arighan's Flower is the gun she carries. The stranger has taken on a human face to talk to her, and he is almost certainly interested in the gun.

The gun takes different shapes, but at this end of time, origami multiplicity of form surprises more by its absence than its presence.

Sometimes the gun is long and sleek, sometimes heavy and blunt. In all cases, it bears its maker's mark on the stock: a blossom with three petals falling away and a fourth about to follow. At the blossom's heart is a character that itself resembles a flower with knotted roots.

The character's meaning is the gun's secret. The woman will not tell it to you, and the gunsmith Arighan is generations gone.

"Everyone knows what I guard," the woman says to the mirror-eyed man.

"I know what it does," he says. "And I know that you come from people that worship their ancestors."

Her hand—on a glass of water two degrees from freezing—stops, slides to her side, where the holster is. "That's dangerous knowledge," she says. So he's figured it out. Her people's historians called Arighan's Flower the *ancestral gun*. They weren't referring to its age.

The man smiles politely, and doesn't take a seat uninvited. Small courtesies matter to him because he is not human. His mind may be housed in a superficial fortress of flesh, but the busy computations that define him are inscribed in a vast otherspace.

The man says, "I can hardly be the first constructed sentience to come to you."

She shakes her head. "It's not that." Do computers like him have souls? she wonders. She is certain he does, which is potentially inconvenient. "I'm not for hire."

"It's important," he says.

It always is. They want chancellors dead or generals, discarded lovers or rival reincarnates, bodhisattvas or bosses—all the old, tawdry stories. People, in all the broad and narrow senses of the term. The reputation of Arighan's Flower is quite specific, if mostly wrong.

"Is it," she says. Ordinarily she doesn't talk to her petitioners at all. Ordinarily she ignores them through one glass, two, three, four, like a child learning the hard way that you can't outcount infinity.

There was a time when more of them tried to force the gun away from her. The woman was a duelist and a killer before she tangled her life up with the Flower, though, and the Flower comes with its own defenses, including the woman's inability to die while she wields it. One of the things she likes about Blackwheel is that the administrators promised that they would dispose of any corpses she produced. Blackwheel is notorious for keeping promises.

The man waits a little longer, then says, "Will you hear me out?"

"You should be more afraid of me," she says, "if you really know what you claim to know."

By now, the other people in the bar, none of them human, are paying attention: a musician whose instrument is made of fossilized wood and silk strings, a magister with a seawrack mane, engineers with their sketches hanging in the air and a single doodled starship at the boundary. The sole exception is the tattooed traveler dozing in the corner, dreaming of distant moons.

In no hurry, the woman draws the Flower and points it at the man. She is aiming it not at his absent heart, but at his left eye. If she pulled the trigger, she would pierce him through the false pupil.

The musician continues plucking plangent notes from the instrument. The others, seeing the gun, gawk for only a moment before hastening out of the bar. As if that would save them.

"Yes," the man says, outwardly shaken, "you could damage my lineage badly. I could name programmers all the way back to the first people who scratched a tally of birds or rocks."

The gun's muzzle moves precisely, horizontally: now the right eye. The woman says, "You've convinced me that you know. You haven't convinced me not to kill you." It's half a bluff: she wouldn't use the Flower, not for this. But she knows many ways to kill.

"There's another one," he said. "I don't want to speak of it here, but will you hear me out?"

She nods once, curtly.

Covered by her palm, engraved silver-bright in a language nobody else reads or writes, is the word *ancestor*.

Once upon a universe, an empress's favored duelist received a pistol from the empress's own hand. The pistol had a stock of silver-gilt and niello, an efflorescence of vines framing the maker's mark. The gun had survived four dynasties, with all their rebellions and coups. It had accompanied the imperial arsenal from homeworld to homeworld.

Of the ancestral pistol, the empire's archives said two things: *Do not use this weapon, for it is nothing but peril* and *This weapon does not function.*

In a reasonable universe, both statements would not be true.

The man follows the woman to her suite, which is on one of Blackwheel's tidier levels. The sitting room, comfortable but not luxurious by Blackwheeler standards, accommodates a couch sized to human proportions, a metal table shined to blurry reflectivity, a vase in the corner.

There are also two paintings, on silk rather than some less ancient substrate. One is of a mountain by night, serenely anonymous amid its stylized clouds. The other, in a completely different style, consists of a cavalcade of shadows. Only after several moments' study do the shadows assemble themselves into a face. Neither painting is signed.

"Sit," the woman says.

The man does. "Do you require a name?" he asks.

"Yours, or the target's?"

"I have a name for occasions like this," he says. "It is Zheu Kerang."

"You haven't asked me my name," she remarks.

"I'm not sure that's a meaningful question," Kerang says. "If I'm not mistaken, you don't exist."

Wearily, she says, "I exist in all the ways that matter. I have volume and mass and volition. I drink water that tastes the same every day, as water should. I kill when it moves me to do so. I've unwritten death into the history of the universe."

His mouth tilts up at *unwritten*. "Nevertheless," he says. "Your species never evolved. You speak a language that is not even dead. It never existed."

"Many languages are extinct."

"To become extinct, something has to exist first."

The woman folds herself into the couch next to him, not close but not far. "It's an old story," she says. "What is yours?"

"Four of Arighan's guns are still in existence," Kerang says.

The woman's eyes narrow. "I had thought it was three." Arighan's Flower is the last, the gunsmith's final work. The others she knows of are Arighan's Mercy, which always kills the person shot, and Arighan's Needle, which removes the target's memories of the wielder.

"One more has surfaced," Kerang says. "The character in the maker's mark resembles a sword in chains. They are already calling it Arighan's Chain."

"What does it do?" she says, because he will tell her anyway.

"This one kills the commander of whoever is shot," Kerang says, "if that's anyone at all. Admirals, ministers, monks. Schoolteachers. It's a peculiar sort of loyalty test."

Now she knows. "You want me to destroy the Chain."

Once upon a universe, a duelist named Shiron took up the gun that an empress with empiricist tendencies had given her. "I don't understand how a gun that doesn't work could possibly be perilous," the empress said. She nodded at a sweating man bound in monofilament so that he would dismember himself if he tried to flee. "This man will be executed anyway, his name struck from the roster of honored ancestors. See if the gun works on him."

Shiron fired the gun . . . and woke in a city she didn't recognize, whose inhabitants spoke a dialect she had never heard before, whose technology she mostly recognized from historical dramas. The calendar they used, at least, was familiar. It told her that she was 857 years too early. No amount of research changed the figure.

Later, Shiron deduced that the man she had executed traced his ancestry back 857 years, to a particular individual. Most likely that ancestor had performed some extraordinary deed to join the aristocracy, and had, by the reckoning of Shiron's people, founded his own line.

Unfortunately, Shiron didn't figure this out before she accidentally deleted the human species.

"Yes," Kerang says. "I have been charged with preventing further assassinations. Arighan's Chain is not a threat I can afford to ignore."

"Why didn't you come earlier, then?" Shiron says. "After all, the Chain might have lain dormant, but the others—"

"I've seen the Mercy and the Needle," he says, by which he means he's copied data from those who have. "They're beautiful." He isn't referring to beauty in the way of shadows fitting together into a woman's profile, or beauty in the way of sun-colored liquor at the right temperature in a faceted glass. He means the beauty of logical strata, of the crescendo of axiom-axiom-corollary-*proof*, of *quod erat demonstrandum*.

"Any gun or shard of glass could do the same as the Mercy," Shiron says, understanding him. "And drugs and dreamscalpels will do the Needle's work, given time and expertise. But surely you could say the same of the Chain."

She stands again and takes the painting of the mountain down and rolls it tightly. "I was born on that mountain," she says. "Something like it is still there, on a birthworld very like the one I knew. But I don't think anyone paints in this style. Perhaps some art historian would recognize

125

its distant cousin. I am no artist, but I painted it myself, because no one else remembers the things I remember. And now you would have it start again."

"How many bullets have you used?" Kerang asks.

It is not that the Flower requires special bullets—it adapts even to emptiness—it is that the number matters.

Shiron laughs, low, almost husky. She knows better than to trust Kerang, but she needs him to trust her. She pulls out the Flower and rests it in both palms so he can look at it.

Three petals fallen, a fourth about to follow. That's not the number, but he doesn't realize it. "You've guarded it so long," he says, inspecting the maker's mark without touching the gun.

"I will guard it until I am nothing but ice," Shiron says. "You may think that the Chain is a threat, but if I remove it, there's no guarantee that you will still exist—"

"It's not the Chain I want destroyed," Kerang says gently. "It's Arighan. Do you think I would have come to you for anything less?"

Shiron says into the awkward quiet, after a while, "So you tracked down descendants of Arighan's line." His silence is assent. "There must be many."

Arighan's Flower destroys the target's entire ancestral line, altering the past but leaving its wielder untouched. In the empire Shiron once served, the histories spoke of Arighan as an honored guest. Shiron discovered long ago that Arighan was no guest, but a prisoner forced to forge weapons for her captors. How Arighan was able to create weapons of such novel destructiveness, no one knows. The Flower was Arighan's clever revenge against a people whose state religion involved ancestor worship.

If descendants of Arighan's line exist here, then Arighan herself can be undone, and all her guns unmade. Shiron will no longer have to be an exile in this timeline, although it is true that she cannot return to the one that birthed her, either.

Shiron snaps the painting taut. The mountain disintegrates, but she lost it lifetimes ago. Silent lightning crackles through the air, unknots Zheu Kerang from his human-shaped shell, tessellates dead-end patterns across the equations that make him who he is. The painting had other uses, as do the other things in this room—she believes in versatility—but this is good enough.

Kerang's body slumps on the couch. Shiron leaves it there.

For the first time in a long time, she is leaving Blackwheel Station. What she does not carry she can buy on the way. And Blackwheel is loyal because they know, and they know not to offend her; Blackwheel will keep her suite clean and undisturbed, and deliver water, near-freezing in an elegant glass, night after night, waiting.

Kerang was a pawn by his own admission. If he knew what he knew, and lived long enough to convey it to her, then others must know what he knew, or be able to find it out.

Kerang did not understand her at all. Shiron unmazes herself from the station to seek passage to one of the hubworlds, where she can begin her search. If Shiron had wanted to seek revenge on Arighan, she could have taken it years ago.

But she will not be like Arighan. She will not destroy an entire timeline of people, no matter how alien they are to her.

Shiron had hoped that matters wouldn't come to this. She acknowledges her own naïveté. There is no help for it now. She will have to find and murder each child of Arighan's line. In this way she can protect Arighan herself, protect the accumulated sum of history, in case someone outwits her after all this time and manages to take the Flower from her.

In a universe where determinism runs backwards—where, no matter what you do, everything ends in the same inevitable Ω—choices still matter, especially if you are the last guardian of an incomparably lethal gun.

Although it has occurred to Shiron that she could have accepted Kerang's offer, and that she could have sacrificed this timeline in exchange for the one in which neither Arighan nor the guns ever existed, she declines to do so. For there will come a heat-death, and she is beginning to wonder: if a constructed sentience—a computer—can have a soul, what of the universe itself, the greatest computer of all?

In this universe, they reckon her old. Shiron is older than even that. In millions of timelines, she has lived to the pallid end of life. In each of those endings, Arighan's Flower is there, as integral as an edge is to a blade. While it is true that science never proves anything absolutely, that an inconceivably large but finite number of experiments always pales besides infinity, Shiron feels that millions of timelines suffice as proof.

Without Arighan's Flower, the universe cannot renew itself and start a new story. Perhaps that is all the reason the universe needs. And Shiron will be there when the heat-death arrives, as many times as necessary.

So Shiron sets off. It is not the first time she has killed, and it is unlikely to be the last. But she is not, after all this time, incapable of grieving.

iseul's lexicon

kandagghamel, *noun*: One of two names the Genial Ones used for their own language. The other, *menjitthemel*, was rarely written. Derived from *kandak*, the dawn flower of their mythology and a common heraldric device; *agha*, or "law"; and *mel*, "word" or "speech." Note that *mel* is one of a small class of lexical elements that consistently violates vowel harmony in compounds. The Genial Ones ascribe considerable metaphysical importance to this irregularity.

She went by the name Jienem these days, a proper, demure Yegedin name that meant something between "young bud" and "undespoiled." It was not her real name. She had been born Iseul of Chindalla, a peninsula whose southern half was now occupied by the Yegedin, and although she was only the bastard daughter of a nobleman and an entertainer, she never forgot the name her mother had given her.

The Empire of Yeged had occupied South Chindalla for the past thirteen years, and renamed it Territory 4. Yeged and free Chindalla had a truce, but no one believed it would last for long, and in the meantime Chindalla had no compunctions about sending agents into South Chindalla. People still spoke the Chindallan language here, but the Empire forbade them to write it, or to use Chindallan names, which was why Iseul used a Yegedin name while operating as a spy in the south for the Chindallan throne. Curiously, for people so bent on suppressing the Chindallan language, Yeged's censors had a great interest in Chindallan books. Their fascination was enormous and indiscriminate: cookbooks rounded out with gossip, military manuals, catalogues of hairstyles, yearly rainfall tabulations, tales of doomed love affairs, court annals, ghost stories, adventures half written in cipher, everything you could imagine.

Iseul worked for Chindalla's Ministry of Ornithology, which, despite its name, had had nothing to do with birds or auguries for generations. It ran the throne's spies. The ministry had told her to figure out why the books were so important to the Yegedin. Iseul had a gift for languages, and in her former life she had been a poet, although she didn't have much time for satiric verses these days. The ministry had recruited her because she was able to write Yeged-dai and speak it with any of three native accents. She also had a reasonable facility with the language of magic, a skill that never ceased to be useful.

In the town the Yegedin had renamed Mijege-in, the censor was a magician. Iseul was to start with him, especially since tonight he was obliged to attend a formal dinner welcoming an official visiting from Yeged proper. It would have been more entertaining to spy on the dinner—she would have had a chance of snacking on some of the delicacies—but someone else was doing that. Her handler, Shen Minsu, had assigned her to search the magician's home because she had the best chance of being able to deal with magical defenses.

Getting into the house hadn't been too difficult. The gates to the courtyard and all the doors were hung with folded-paper wards inscribed with barrier-words of apathy and dejection to discourage people like Iseul. She had come prepared with a charm of passage, however, and a belt hung with tiny locks worn around her waist under her sash. The charm of passage caused all the wards to unfold, and reciprocally, most of the locks had snapped closed. One time, early in her career as a spy, she had run out of locks while infiltrating a fort, and the thwarted charm had begun throwing up random obstacles as she attempted to flee: a burst pipe, crates almost falling on her, a furious cat. Now she erred on the side of more locks.

It was a small house, all things considered, but magicians were a quirky lot and maybe he didn't want to deal with the servants necessary to keep a larger house clean. The courtyard was disproportionately large, and featured a tangle of roses that hadn't been pruned aggressively enough and equally disheveled trees swaying in the evening wind. Some landscaper had attempted to introduce a Yegedin-style rock garden in the middle. The result wasn't particularly harmonious.

She circled the house, but heard nothing and saw no people moving against the rice-paper doors. Then she went in the front door. She had two daggers in case she came across someone. After watching the house for a few days, she had concluded that the magician lived alone, but you never knew if someone had a secret lover stashed away. Or a very loud pet. That time with the peacock, for instance. Noisy birds, peacocks. Anyway, with luck, she wouldn't have to kill anyone this time; she was just here for information.

Her first dagger was ordinary steel, the suicide-blade that honorable Yegedin women carried. It would be difficult to explain her possession of the blade if she was searched, but that wasn't the one that would get her in trouble.

Her second dagger was the one that she couldn't afford to be caught carrying. It looked more like a very long needle, wrapped around and around by tiny words in the Genial Ones' language. It was the fifth one Iseul had constructed, although the Ministry of Ornithology had supplied the unmarked dagger for her to modify.

The dagger was inscribed with the word for human or animal blood, *umul*. The Genial Ones had had two more words for their own blood, one for what spilled out of them in ordinary circumstances, and another used in reference to ritual bloodletting. The dagger destroyed the person you stabbed it with if you drew blood, and distorted itself into a miniature, rusting figure of the victim: ghastly, but easy to dispose of. Useful for causing people to disappear.

The house's passages had creaky wooden floors, but nobody called out or rushed out to attack her. Calligraphy scrolls decorated the walls. Yeged had a calligraphy tradition almost as old as Chindalla's, and the scrolls displayed Yegedin proverbs and poetry in a variety of commendably rhythmic hands. She could name the styles they were scribed in, most of them well-regarded, if a little old-fashioned: River Rocks Tumbling, Butterfly's Kiss, Anaiago's Comb . . .

Iseul looked away from the scrolls. She shouldn't get distracted, even though the scrolls might be a clue of some kind. There was always the chance that the magician would find some excuse to leave the dinner early and come home.

She found part of what she was looking for in the magician's study, which was dismally untidy, with scraps of paper on every conceivable surface. There was still some light from outside, although she had a lantern charm just in case.

The magician had brought home two boxes of Chindallan books. One of them mostly contained supernatural stories involving nine-tailed foxes, a genre whose appeal had always eluded her, but which was enduringly popular. She had to concede the charm of some of the illustrations: fox eyes peering brightly from behind masks, fox tails curving slyly from beneath layers of elaborate robes, fox paws slipping out of long gloves.

Stuffed into the same box was a volume of poetry, which Iseul pulled out in a spirit of professional interest. With a sigh, she began flipping through the book, letting her eye alight on the occasional well-turned phrase. She kept track of syllable counts by reflex. Nothing special. She was tempted to smuggle it out on principle, but this collection had been popular sixteen years ago and there were still a lot of copies to be had in the north. Besides, the magician would surely notice if one of his spoils went missing.

The next book was different. It had a tasteful cover in dark red, but that wasn't what caught her attention. She had seen books with covers in every conceivable color, some of them ill-advised; hadn't everyone? No. It was the fact that the book shouldn't have been in the box with the others. She went through a dozen pages just to be sure, but she had been right. Each page was printed in Yeged-dai, not Chindallan.

However, Iseul could see why whoever had packed the box had gotten confused. She recognized the names of most of the poets. More specifically, she recognized the Yegedin names that Chindallan poets had taken.

Iseul knew from experience that a poet's existence was a precarious one if you didn't come from a wealthy family or have a generous patron. Fashions in poetry came and went almost as quickly as fashions in hairstyles. Before the Ministry of Ornithology recruited her, she had written sarcastic verses for nobles to pass around at social functions, and the occasional parody. Slightly risky, but her father's prominence as a court official had afforded her a certain degree of protection from offended writers.

The poets who survived in occupied Chindalla could no longer rely on their old patrons, or write as they had been accustomed to writing. But some of them had a knack for foreign languages, as Iseul did, or had perhaps learned Yeged-dai even before the invasion. Those poets had been able to adapt. She had known about such people before this. But it still hurt her to see their poems before her, printed in the curving Yeged-dai script, using Yegedin forms and the images so beloved of the Yegedin: the single pebble, the grasshopper at twilight, the song of a heartbroken lark sitting in a bent tree.

Iseul put the book back in its place, wishing for something to staunch the ache within her. It would have been easy to hate the southern poets for abandoning their own language, but she knew that resistance carried a considerable risk. Even in Mijege-in, which had fallen early and easily, and which the Yegedin considered well-tamed, the governor occasionally burned rebels alive. She had passed by the latest corpses on the walls when she entered the city. Mainly she remembered them as shadows attracting shadows, charred sticks held together by a conglomeration of ravens.

There were also those who had died in the initial doomed defense of the south. Sometimes she thought she would never forgive her father, whose martial skills were best not mentioned, for dying with the garrison at Hwagan Fort in an attempt to slow the Yegedin advance. There were poems about that battle, all red-stained banners and broken spears and unquiet pyres, all glory and honor, except there had been nothing glorious about the loss. She hated herself for reading the poems over and over whenever she encountered them.

Iseul went through the second box. More Chindallan books, the usual eclectic variety, and no clue as to what the Yegedin wanted with them. Maybe it was simple acquisitiveness. One of the Yegedin governors, knowing the beauty and value of Chindallan celadon, had taken the simple expedient of rounding up all the Chindallan potters in three provinces and sending them to his homeland as slaves along with their clay, as well as buying up everything from vases to good forgeries of antique jewelry boxes.

The rest of the box didn't take her long to get through. It included a single treatise on magic. Those were getting harder and harder to find in the south, as the Yegedin quite reasonably didn't trust magic in Chindallan hands. The treatise in question concerned locator charms. Like all magic, locators were based on the writings of the Genial Ones, who had once ruled over the human nations the way Yeged desired to rule over the known world. Humans had united under General Anangan to destroy the Genial Ones, but not long after that, a chieftain assassinated the general and the alliance dissolved.

People discovered that, over time, magic started to fail because its masters were no more. Locators had stopped being reliable about a century ago or Iseul would have had some uses for them herself. On the occasions that you could get one to activate at all, it tended to chew a map into your entrails. Some people would still have used them anyway, but the maps were also inevitably false.

The treatise's author had included a number of gruesome illustrations to support her contention that the failed magic was affected by the position of the user's spleen. The theory was preposterous, but all the same, Iseul wished she could liberate the treatise. She didn't dare risk it, though. The magician would be even more sure to notice a missing book on magic.

Iseul froze. Had she just heard footsteps? How could the magician be back so early? Or had she spent more time looking through those damnable poems than she had realized? She ducked behind a coat rack. Under better circumstances, she would have critiqued the coats, although a quick glance suggested that they were in fact of high quality. That cuff, for instance; hard to find embroiderers these days who were willing to put up with the hassle of couching gold thread that had to be done in such short segments. Iseul's mother had always impressed upon her the importance of appearances, something that Iseul had used against a great many people as a spy.

The footsteps were getting closer and their owner was walking briskly. A bad sign. Contrary to popular belief, magicians couldn't detect each other; being a magician was merely a matter of study, applied linguistics, and a smattering of geometry. Magicians could, however, check the status of their charms by looking, just like anyone else with a working pair of eyes. Or by touch, if it came to that. The problem with the passage charm that Iseul used was that it made no attempt to hide its effects. The older version that disguised its own workings had stopped working about 350 years ago.

It might be time to flee. Iseul was willing to bet that she was more athletic than a magician who worked in an office all day. Her glimpses of him hadn't suggested that he was particularly fit. The study's window was covered in oiled paper, and was barely large enough for her to squeeze through.

More footsteps. Iseul headed for the window, but her sleeve snagged on a coat, and it rustled to the floor. Just her luck: the magician had left a coin purse in it, and the coins jangled as they landed. She cursed her clumsiness. Now he probably knew her location. Indeed, halfway on her way to the window, flowers with shadow-mouths and toothy leaves started growing in hectic tangles from the window, barring her passage.

Iseul knew better than to believe the illusion, no matter how much the heavy, heady scent of the blossoms threatened to clog her sinuses; no matter how much her hands wanted to twitch away from the jagged leaves and the glistening intimation of poison on the stems. She had seen these flowers in her dreams as a child, when she was afraid that she would fall asleep in the garden during hide-and-seek and be swallowed up by the spirits of thorn and malice. They were only as real as she allowed them to be.

Her father had once, uncharacteristically, given her a piece of military advice, probably quoted from some manual. They had been playing baduk, a board game involving capturing territory with stones. As usual, he refused to give her any handicap despite the disparity in age. She had been complaining about the fact that she was sure to lose. In her defense, she had only been ten. *It doesn't matter how good your position is,* he had told her, *if you're already defeated in your head.*

If the magician thought that a childhood nightmare was going to get her to give up so easily, he was sorely mistaken. She could have punched through the window, which was only covered with paper, and gone on her way. But he already knew someone with knowledge of magic had broken into his home. She might as well have it out with him right now, even if she ordinarily preferred to avoid confrontations. Minsu was going to lecture her about taking risks, but the dreadful timing couldn't be helped.

Iseul's pulse raced as she drew her second dagger and angled herself back behind the coat rack. For a moment she didn't realize the magician had entered the room.

Then a figure assembled itself out of shadows and dust motes and scraps of paper, right there in the room. Iseul was tall for a Chindallan woman, but the figure was taller, and its arms were disproportionately long. She thought it might be a man beneath the strange layers of robes, which weren't in any fashion she'd seen before. She could see its eyes, dark in a pale, smudgy face, and that it was holding up a charm of a variety she didn't recognize.

Iseul had killed people before. She lunged with her dagger before the magician had a chance to finish activating the charm. He brought up his arm to protect his ribs. The dagger snagged on his layers of sleeves. She gave it a good hard yank and it came free, along with strands that unraveled in the air.

She made one more attempt to stab him, but he twisted away, fiendishly fast, and she missed again. She bit back a curse. It was only with great effort that she kept herself from losing her balance.

Iseul ran past the figure since momentum was taking her there anyway and out of the study. The dagger was needle-keen in her hand, with blood showing hectic red at its point. It should have shrank into a misshapen figure amid shivers of smoke and fractured light the moment she marked her target. She flung it aside in a fit of revulsion and heard it clattering against the wall. It made a bright, terrible sound, like glass bells and shattering hells and hounds unloosed, and she had never heard anything like it before.

If the dagger hadn't changed, then that meant the magician was still alive. She had to go back and finish the job. She swung around. The dagger was visible where she had cast it. The blood on the blade seemed even redder. Words writhed in the sheen of the metal's surface. Probably no good to her if it hadn't worked the first time. She plunged past it and into the study without hesitating at the threshold.

The magician was waiting for her. The mixture of amusement, contempt, and rage in his eyes chilled Iseul more than anything else that had happened so far. He threw his charm at her as she cleared the doorway.

The charm didn't grow thorns or teeth or tendrils. Instead, it unfolded in a twisting ballet of planes and vertices. For a single clear second, Iseul could see words in the Genial Ones' language pinned to the paper's surface by the weight of the ink, by the will of the scribe. Then, with a thready whispering, the words flocked free of the paper and spread themselves in the air toward her, like a net.

Iseul knew better than to be caught by that net. She twisted around it, thanking her mother for a childhood full of dance lessons, although some of the words brushed her sleeve before they dispersed. Her entire left forearm grew numb. No time to think about that. The magician was reaching for something in a pouch. She ignored that and went instead for his throat. People never expected a woman to have strong hands.

The magician croaked out half a word. Iseul pressed harder with her thumbs, seeking his windpipe, and felt the magician struggle to breathe. His hands, oddly chilly, clawed at her hands.

How could someone as skinny as the magician have such good lung capacity? Iseul hung on. The magician's skin grew colder and colder, as though he had veins of ice creeping closer to his skin the longer she choked him. Her hands ached with the chill.

Worse, she felt the scrabbling of her lantern charm in response to the magician's proximity. Belatedly, she realized he was trying to scratch words into her skin with his fingernails. Her teeth closed on a yelp.

Like all her charms, the lantern charm was made of paper lacquered to a certain degree of stiffness. It scratched her skin as though it were struggling to unfold itself just as the magician's original charm had done. For the first time, she cared about the quality of the charm's lacquer, hoping it would hold fast against another word-cloud.

Iseul could barely feel her left hand. She kept pressing against the magician's throat and staring at the ugly purple marks that mottled his skin. "Die," she said hoarsely. The numb feeling was spreading up her forearm to her elbow, and at this rate, she was going to lose use of the arm, who knew for how long.

The lantern charm was starting to unfurl. Iseul resisted the urge to close her eyes and give up. But the magician was done struggling. The cold hands dropped away, and he slumped.

Iseul was trembling. But she held on for another count of hundred just to be certain. Then she let the figure drop to the ground and staggered sideways.

The magician's eyes slitted open. Careless of her. She should have realized his physiology might be different. She scrabbled for her ordinary dagger with her good hand and cut his throat. The blood was rich and red, and there was a lot of it.

The magician wheezed something, a few words in a language she didn't recognize. Her first instinct was to recoil, remembering the cloud of words. Her second and better instinct, which was to stab his torso repeatedly, won out. But nothing more emerged from those pale lips except a last cool thread of breath.

She sat back and forced herself to breathe slowly, evenly, until her heart wasn't knocking at the walls of her ribs anymore. Then she went back out into the hallway. The magical dagger showed no sign of shrinking. She brought it back with her into the study and its mangled corpse.

Iseul wanted to drop both daggers and huddle under the coats for the rest of the night. Instead, she wiped off both daggers on the magician's clothes and tucked them back into their sheaths. She took off her jacket. There was a small basin of water, and she washed her hands and face. It wasn't much, but it made her feel better and right now she would take what she could get. She hunted through the magician's collection of coats for something that wouldn't fit her too poorly and put it on.

Since she had killed the magician, she might as well complete her search of the house. She wouldn't get another opportunity once they found out about the murder.

Yes. Think about logistical details. Don't think about the corpse.

Except she had to think about the corpse. It would be remiss of her not to search it to see if the magician had been carrying any other surprises.

She couldn't think about the fact that the dagger would have disintegrated a human. It might simply be that the charm no longer worked, the way any number of charms had stopped working. There was an easy way to test that, but she wasn't about to kill some random victim just to test whether her dagger really had lost its virtue.

Iseul thought about the fact that its blade repeated, over and over in a winding trail, the word for human blood. *Umul.*

About the fact that she might have killed a Genial One, and the Genial Ones were supposed to be over a thousand years extinct.

Someone would find the corpse. But first, the search. See what the corpse wanted to say to her in the language of violence and clandestine corners.

Iseul went through the magician's robes, all of them, layers upon layers that clung clammily to her fingers. Next time she did this she was going to bring gloves. All the while she puzzled over the magician's last words. She had believed that she was fluent in the language of magic. The longer she thought about it, the more she became convinced that the magician had said, *You can kill one of us, but not all of us. We won't accept this*—and then there was one more word that she couldn't get to slot into place no matter how much she shifted the vowels or roughened the fricatives.

The most unhelpful thing she found in the magician's pockets was the candy. It smelled like ordinary barley candy, but she wasn't about to put it in her mouth to check.

The one useful thing was a charm. Iseul recognized it because it was folded very similarly to her own charm of passage, except it had a map-word inscribed on some of its corners, which meant that it was meant to interact with a specific lock rather than being intended for general use. The magician had worn it on a bracelet. Iseul cut it away, then set about stuffing the magician's corpse into a closet and wiping down the room. It wouldn't pass a good inspection, but she would be long gone by the time anyone came searching.

It was hard not to flinch every time a branch knocked against the walls of the house as the wind outside grew stronger, but eventually she found the secret passage by paying attention to the way the charm quivered in her hand. The door was in the basement, which had a collection of geometrically sorted blocks of bean curd, bags of rice, and other humble staples. Curious thought: had the magician cooked his own food? She wasn't sure she liked the thought of a Genial One enjoying Chindallan food.

The secret room was situated so it was under a good portion of the oversized garden. Brandishing the magician's charm opened the door. Lantern charms filled the space with a pale blue light. It was hard not to imagine that she walked underwater.

Iseul checked the shadows for signs of movement, but if an ambush awaited her, she would have to deal with it when it came. She stepped sideways into the room.

A book lay open on a cluttered escritoire. Next to it was a desk set containing a half-used, sumptuously carved and gilded block of ink. The carving had probably once been a dragon, judging by the lower half: conventional, but well-executed. A charm that had been folded to resemble a quill rested against the book. The folds had been made very precisely.

Iseul's gaze went to a small stack of paper next to the book. The top sheet was covered with writing. Her hackles rose as she realized that that wasn't precisely true. It sounded like someone was writing on the paper, and the stack made a rustling sound as of furtive animals, but there was no brush or graphite stick, and the ink looked obdurately dry.

Against her better judgment, she approached the desk. She looked first at the charm, which was covered with words of transference and staining, then at the papers. Black wisps were curling free from the book, leaving the page barren, and traveling through the air to the paper, where they formed new words. She flipped back in the book. The first thirty or so pages were blank, as faceless as a mask turned inside-out. Iseul flipped forward. As before, the words on the next page, which were in somewhat archaic Chindallan, continued sizzling away in ashy curls and wisps.

Iseul reminded herself to breathe, then picked up the top of the pile and began paging through. All of the words were in the Genial Ones' language. It appeared to be some sort of diatribe about the writer's hosts and their taste in after-dinner entertainment. She squinted at the pages: only three of them so far. She pulled out the page currently being written on.

More words formed on the new sheet. Iseul had expected a precise insectine march, but that wasn't the case. There seemed to be someone on the other end; it wasn't just a transfer of marks. Sometimes the unseen writer hesitated over a word choice, or crossed something out. At one point a doodle formed in the margin, either a very fat cow or a very large hog, hard to tell. The writer, a middling artist at best, had more unflattering comments about the people they were staying with.

Would she alert the person on the other end if she made off with the letter, which was becoming increasingly and entertainingly vituperative? She didn't know how close by they were. How much time did she have? Her left arm felt less numb than before, which was reassuring, but that didn't mean she should let down her guard. Time to read the letter and see if there was anything she should commit to memory. Sadly, the writer was cagey about revealing their location, although she learned some creative insults.

It was tempting to linger and find out if the writer was going to regale the dead magician with more misshapen farm animals, maybe a rooster or a goose, but Iseul made herself turn away from the escritoire and examine the rest of the hideout. There were more books with the writing worn away, and a number of what she recognized as ragged volumes of a torrid adventure series involving an alchemist and her two animal-headed assistants, popular about five years back. Since she preferred not to believe that one of the Genial Ones had such execrable taste in popular fiction, it seemed likely that the books were convenient fodder for this unusual method of exchanging letters.

Still, it paid to be thorough. Iseul didn't like turning her back on the escritoire, but she still needed to search the rest of the secret room, which was well-supplied with books.

She was starting to think that most of the books would fall into the two previous categories—blank and about to be blank—when she found what the magician had been so keen on hiding. These books, unlike the others, were only labeled by number. Each was impressively thick. An amateur, albeit a moderately accomplished one, had stitched the binding. The binder—probably the magician—had a fondness for dark blue linen thread.

Iseul picked up the first book and flipped rapidly through the pages. Thin paper, but high quality, with just a hint of tooth. The left-hand pages were in a writing system unfamiliar to her. Unlike Chindallan, the letterforms consisted of a profusion of curves and loops. She wondered if it, like the language of the realm of Moi-quan to the south, had originally been incised into large leaves that would split if you used straight strokes.

The right-hand pages were in the Genial Ones' writing, in script so small that it hurt her eyes, and it was immediately obvious that they were compiling a lexicon. Definitions, from denotations to connotations; usage notes, including one on a substitute word to be used only in the presence of a certain satrap; dialectal variations; folk etymologies, some amusingly similar to stories in Chindalla, like the one about a fish whose name changed twice in one year thanks to a princess discovering that something that tasted delicious when you were starving in exile didn't necessarily remain so after you had returned to eating courtly delicacies. And look, there was a doodle of a sadly generic-looking fish in the margin, although it was in a different style than the earlier pig-cow. (Like many Chindallans, Iseul knew her fish very well.) How long had it taken the magician to put this together?

The unfamiliar writing system was summarized in five volumes. Iseul went on to the next language. Four volumes, but the notes in the Genial Ones' language were much more terse and had probably been compiled by a different researcher or group of researchers. She estimated the number of books, then considered the number of languages. Impressive, although she had no way of knowing how many languages there were in the world, and what fraction of them this collection of lexicons represented.

She sampled a few more languages at random. One of the sets was, interestingly, for Yeged-dai. Judging by its position in the pile, it had been completed a while ago. She was tempted to quibble with some of the preferred spellings, but she had to concede that the language as used in occupied territories probably diverged from the purer forms spoken in Yeged proper.

Then she came to the last set. Only one volume. The left-hand pages were written in Chindallan.

It turned out that the second volume hadn't yet been bound, and was scattered in untidy piles in drawers of the study. The words were sorted into broad groups more or less by Chindallan alphabetical order, although it looked like they were added as they were collected. For instance:

Cheon-ma, the cloud-horses that carry the moon over the sea. Thankfully, the magician hadn't attempted to sketch one. It probably would have ended up looking like an ox. The *cheon-ma* were favorite subjects of Chindalla's court artists. There was a famous carving of one on a memorial from the previous dynasty, which Iseul had had the privilege of viewing once.

Chindal-kot, the royal azalea, emblem of the queen's house. This included a long and surprisingly accurate digression on the evolution of the house colors over the lifetime of the current dynasty as new dyes were discovered. Iseul bristled at the magician's condescending tone, although she didn't know why she expected any better from a Genial One.

Chaebi, the swallow, said to be a bearer of good luck. Beneath its entry was a notation on the Festival of the Swallows' Return in the spring. And, inevitably, a sketch of a swallow, although she would have mistaken it for a goose if not for the characteristic forked tail.

Iseul put the papers back. Her throat felt raw. The magician couldn't be up to anything good with this, but what did it mean?

Especially puzzling: what did it mean that all the lexicons were copied out by hand? The rough texture of ink on paper had been unmistakable. She had already witnessed a magician sending a letter by manipulating the substance of text from a book already in existence. Surely magicians could use this process to halve the work? Or did it only work on the language of magic itself?

She had spent too long here already. It was time to get out and report this to her handler, who might have some better idea of what was going on.

Iseul hesitated, then gathered up the Chindallan lexicon and the four volumes of the Yeged-dai lexicon. For all she knew there were duplicates elsewhere, but she would take what she could get. If she had more time to inspect the lexicons once she was far from here, there might be valuable clues. She was going to look odd hauling books around at this hour, but perhaps she could pretend to be running an errand for some Yegedin official.

Cold inside, she headed back up the stairs, and out of the house with its secrets wrapped in words.

The Genial Ones believed in the sovereignty of conservation laws. This may be illustrated by a tale that begins in the usual way by naming the Genial Ones as the terrible first children of the world's dawning. In due course (so the story goes), the sun grew red and dim and large, threatening to swallow the world. Determined to preserve their spiraling towers and their symphonies and their many-bannered armies, the Genial Ones unlanterned a younger star in order to rejuvenate their own.

It is likely that they did this more than once.

Many of Chindalla's astronomers believe that, since this sun indisputably supports learned civilizations, other stars must do the same. Some astronomers have produced lengthy essays, complete with computations, to support this position.

Reckoning whether any such civilization would survive the extinction of its sun, on the other hand, requires no arduous calculation.

Iseul's handler, Shen Minsu, was a tall, plain woman with a strong right arm. Before the invasion, she had been known for her skill at archery. Iseul had seen her split one arrow with another at 130 meters during a private display. "Useless skill," Minsu had said afterwards, "people dead of arrows to the heart find it hard to confess what they're up to. Much better to make use of the living."

They met now in the upper storage room of a pharmacy in a small town. The Shen family had risen to prominence by running pharmacies. One of the earlier Shens had been elevated to a noble after one of his concoctions cured a beloved king-consort's fever. Even in the south, the Shen family maintained good ties with medicine-sellers and herb-gatherers. Yegedin medicine was not terribly different in principle from Chindallan medicine, and the Yegedin prized Chindalla's mountain ginseng, which was said to bestow longevity. Iseul had grown up drinking the bitter tea at her mother's insistence, but from observation of her mother's patrons, it didn't do anything more for you than any other form of modest living.

Minsu didn't care for ginseng tea, ironically, but she always insisted that they drink tea of some sort whenever they met. Iseul took a sip now. She was wearing clothes cut more conservatively, and she had switched her hairstyle to the drab sort of thing a widow might favor. Shen Minsu was wearing subdued brown and beige linen, which suited her surprisingly well, instead of the sumptuous embroidered robes she would have worn in northern Chindalla.

Minsu was going methodically through the incomplete Chindallan lexicon. She had already glanced through the Yeged-dai lexicon. "You're certain," Minsu said for the third time this meeting, which showed how unsettled she was.

"I killed a Yegedin guard on the way out, to be sure," Iseul said bleakly. She had agonized over the decision, but it wouldn't be the first time she had killed a Yegedin on Chindalla's behalf. The dagger had performed flawlessly, which meant the issue wasn't that the charm had stopped working; the issue was that the charm only triggered on human blood. "And the last thing the Genial One said—"

You can kill one of us, but not all of us. We won't accept this—and then the unfamiliar term.

"My guess is that the Yegedin are as much in the dark as we are," Minsu said. "I find it hard to believe that even they would knowingly ally with the Genial Ones."

"I wish I believed that Yeged conquered Chindalla so handily by allying itself with monsters," Iseul said bitterly.

Both of them knew that Yeged's soldiers hadn't needed supernatural help. In the previous century, Chindalla had turned inwards, its court factions squabbling over ministry appointments and obscure philosophical arguments. The Yegedin had also been a people divided, but that division that taken the form of vicious civil wars. As a result, when a warlord united Yeged and declared himself Emperor, he was sitting on a brutally effective army that had grown accustomed to the spoils of war. It had only been natural for the Emperor's successor to send his soldiers overseas in search of more riches to keep them loyal.

"I feel as though we've walked into a children's story," Minsu said. "When I was a child, the servants would scare us out of trouble by telling us tales—you know the ones. Don't pull the horses' tails, or the Genial Ones' falcons will come out of the shadows and eat your eyes. If you pinch snacks from the kitchens at night, the Genial Ones will turn your fingers into twigs and use them for kindling. Or if you tear your jacket climbing trees, the Genial Ones will sew you up with your little brother and use you as a ceremonial robe. That sort of thing."

"Except they were real," Iseul said. "All the histories in all the known nations agree on the basics. It's difficult not to believe them."

Minsu sighed. "The Yegedin haven't mentioned anything in their official dispatches so far as we know, but one of my contacts in Mijege-in has remarked on how the censor has been terribly quiet. A very long-running hangover after entertaining the guest from Yeged. No doubt the Yegedin authorities are looking for the murderer as we speak." She looked sideways at Iseul; her eyes were dark and very grave. "And that means the Genial Ones are looking for the murderer, too.

"We don't know how many of them there are," Minsu went on, "although if they're researching the world's languages it's certain that they're widely dispersed. You're lucky to have survived, and you're also lucky that he tried to take care of you himself instead of raising the alarm."

"He probably didn't want to risk anyone else finding out about his collection of lexicons," Iseul said, "if he ran afoul of some Yegedin magician."

"This is a complication that I didn't need," Minsu said, "but it can't be helped. We're going to have to pull out."

"It's hardly unexpected," Iseul said. People were talking about it in the markets, not least because the prices for ordinary necessities had gone up again.

The Yegedin were preparing to break the thirteen-year truce and move on free Chindalla to the north. Reinforcements had been filtering into the territory, some crossing the ocean from Yeged itself.

"I assume you have dedicated assassins," Iseul said, "but we need to find out if there are any Genial Ones associated with the Yegedin army. One of them might have been mediocre at hand-to-hand combat, but we don't know how closely connected they are with Yeged's plans. If they intervene as magicians, or trained the Yegedin magicians, the border defenses could be in a lot of trouble. At least we know that they can be killed."

Humans had battled the Genial Ones as a matter of necessity, even if they hadn't done as thorough a job of obliterating them as everyone had thought.

"Well," Minsu said, "it's clear you can't rely on the charms anymore since they'll be suspicious of anyone using magic. You're in a lot of danger."

Iseul looked at her bleakly. Like everyone in Chindalla, she had grown up with stories of the Genial Ones' terrible horses, whose hooves opened cracks in the earth with bleak black eyes staring out until they boiled poisonously away; the Genial Ones' banquets, served in the skulls of children; the Genial Ones' adulthood ceremonies, where music of drum and horn caused towers of glistening cartilage to grow out of mounds of corpses. Even in the days of their dominion, the histories said, there had been humans who objected not to the Genial Ones' methods, but to the fact that they didn't have mastery of those terrible arts for themselves. After the Genial Ones' downfall, they had lost no time in learning. The wars in the wake of General Anangan's assassination had been wide-reaching and bloody.

"Everything has been dangerous," Iseul said. "We just didn't realize it until now. And who knows—maybe if I can lure them out, we can get them to reveal more about whatever it is they're up to."

They discussed possible options for a while. "Your tea's getting cold," Minsu said eventually. "Drink up. You never know when you'll next taste Three Pale Blossoms tea harvested before the Yegedin took over the plantation." Her smile was bitter. "I keep track, you know. Not many people care, especially when the stuff is a luxury to begin with, but it matters."

"I know," Iseul said. "You don't have to remind me." She drank the rest of the cup with slow sips. She didn't like the tea, but that wasn't the point.

> **himmadaebi**, *noun*: More literally, "great white horse rains."
> A Chindallan term used of the worst storms. Originally reserved for the storms that the Genial Ones used to call down on cities that defied them. Usage shifted after the Genial Ones' defeat by General Anangan, although attempts to date the change have been hampered by the fact that literacy rates in Chindalla at the time were much lower than they are now, and only a few reliable sources are extant.

Not long after Iseul's run-in with the magician, the second Yegedin invasion began with a storm, and with horses.

The horses were the color of foam-rush and freezing ice. They had wide, mad eyes and hooves that struck the earth as though it were a breaking drum. Their shadows broke off behind them every fourth stride and unfurled into tatters that sliced off tree branches and left boulders in crumbled ruins.

Iseul had been traveling with the soldiers ever since they decamped from the city that the Yegedin had renamed Mijege-in, heading north toward the border of free Chindalla. The infantry soldiers had wan, anxious expressions, and the highborn cavalrymen didn't look much better. Their horses were blinkered, and the blinkers were made of paper covered with cryptic words: charms. She had checked one night. Too bad she couldn't cause a little confusion by making off with all the blinkers, but it wasn't feasible and she had a more important task.

She had been tempted to report to Minsu for further instructions the moment she saw the horses. The storm-spell had been defunct for over two centuries. There were accounts of it in the old histories. One of the northwestern Chindallan forts had been thundered down by such a storm generations past. To this day the grasses and trees grew sickly and stunted where the stones had once stood. It wasn't surprising that the Yegedin had more magicians in their employ, but the fact that an old charm had been resuscitated suggested that at least one of the magicians was a Genial One, or had been trained by one. Perhaps a Genial One could pass the charm off as a brilliant research discovery, even though the problem of magic that didn't work anymore had vexed the human nations ever since the phenomenon was noted.

But Iseul needed better information. It had taken an alliance of all the human nations to defeat the Genial Ones the last time, and some of them had survived anyway. There were probably much fewer of them now, but she was under no illusions that the human nations of the present time were likely to unite even for this, especially if they had a chance of claiming the Genial Ones' magics for themselves.

She had spent cold hours thinking about the fact that at least one of the old spells worked again, which meant others might, too. And which meant that human magicians and their masters would seek those spells for their own ends, no matter how horrible the cost.

Tonight Iseul was dripping wet and huddled in a coat that wasn't doing nearly enough to keep out the chill. She had killed a scout early on and was wearing his clothes. Her hair was piled up underneath his cap and she had bound her chest tight. It wouldn't pass a close inspection, but no one was looking closely at anyone in such miserable weather.

Iseul was helped by the Yegedin themselves. Not that the Chindallans were known for tight military discipline either, but the Yegedin force was doing unusually poorly in this regard. Part of the problem was that no one felt comfortable near the storm-horses. The other part was that orders from Yeged had apparently assigned the initial attack to not one but two rival generals. No doubt the theory was that the two would spur each other on to ever greater feats in battle, but in practice this meant the two generals' soldiers squabbled over everything from watch assignments to access to the best forage. Iseul had situated herself at the hazy boundary between the two armies so she could claim to be on either side as necessary.

Tonight she had decided that she would try approaching the magicians' tent again. The Yegedin were sheltering in hills perhaps two days' march from the nearest Chindallan border-fort. The Chindallan sentries would have seen the storm, although the knowledge wouldn't save them. They almost certainly wouldn't realize what it signified.

She was tempted to assassinate the Yegedin magicians. But she would undoubtedly die in the attempt. Besides, as terrible as it would be to lose the fort, it was more important to determine how the Genial Ones meant to threaten all of Chindalla.

Iseul eased her way toward the magicians' tent a little at a time. She had learned that there were two of them and that they kept to themselves, although not much else. Even the officers didn't like speaking of them too loudly. When they did mention the magicians, it was with careful distaste. Iseul was only a little reassured to find out that Yegedin attitudes toward magicians weren't far different from Chindallan attitudes, considering that she knew how to use charms herself.

Most of the soldiers who weren't on watch were, sensibly, sleeping. But a few exchanged ribald jokes about shapeshifting badgers, or spoke of how much they missed proper plum pickles from home, or mentioned pilgrimages they had made to Yeged's holy mountains in the past. Some of them looked quite young.

One of the younger ones mentioned a pretty Chindallan woman who was waiting for him in a southern town. Iseul kept her face blank at the coarse remarks that followed. She had long practice controlling her expression, and it wasn't news that a number of the Yegedin had taken lovers among the Chindallans. South Chindalla had been occupied for thirteen years, after all. There were Chindallans who had grown up thinking of the Yegedin as their natural rulers, and whose only memories of freedom were a child's memories of stubbed toes and overripe persimmons and picking cosmos flowers in the fall.

Iseul clutched the satchel of the unfortunate scout and continued to the magicians' tent, which stood by itself with two reluctant sentries at the tent flap. A pale, unsettling light burned from the tent. She wound her way to the back. The sentries were exchanging riddles. She wished she could stay and listen; the Yegedin, for all their faults, knew the value of a good riddle.

She was going to have a hard time getting past the sentries into the tent, and from the sounds of it the magicians were having a discussion. The fact that there were always sentries was bad enough. She might have dealt with them, but usually at this hour the magicians were speaking to one or the other of the generals in the command tent. Rotten luck.

Of course, all the rotten luck in the world didn't make a difference when the magicians' defensive charms were certain still to be in place. She had glimpsed some the first time she approached the tent nights ago. While some of them were unfamiliar, she recognized the ones that would have detected the use of concealment magic. Another was a boundary-warden, which would have caught her if she had attempted to cut her way into the tent.

This was no doubt just punishment for developing a dependence on the Genial Ones' tools all these years, but Iseul couldn't help but grit her teeth. She wondered if a passage charm would work, but the Genial Ones might have a countermeasure for that, too. Keeping her expression placid, she strolled on by.

The magicians' voices carried remarkably well in the chilly damp. They spoke the language of magic with an accent similar to that of the Genial One Iseul had killed. She had difficulty understanding their pronunciation, as before, but her mother had taught her how to sing in foreign languages by concentrating first on the sounds without worrying about the meaning. As she traced a meandering path, she committed the conversation, which had the rhythms of an argument, to memory.

Iseul slouched her way to a less conspicuous location, avoiding contact with Yegedin soldiers as much as possible. She had only two days to figure out a better approach. If she had Minsu's astonishing skill with a bow—but going around with a Chindallan weapon, especially one so difficult to conceal as a bow, would be a sure way of getting herself killed for no gain.

The storms grew worse in the next two days. Iseul drifted to the rear with other laggards. The generals had people whipped for it, but nothing could change people's opinion of the storm-horses.

She tried again the next night. The guards were clearly bored. One of them kept peeling back the tent flap to look in and make snide comments about the magicians' furnishings. Time to risk a more direct approach if it would get her a glimpse of the tent's contents. She made sure to spill some of the scout's rice wine on her coat and take a long sip before she strolled on by just as one of the guards was finishing up a joke about an abbot and an albino bear.

"Hey, you'd better move on," the other guard said, noticing Iseul. "The only things that go on in there are related to spiders." He shuddered.

The guard was probably referring to the moving shadows. Iseul staggered a little as she approached him. Inside, there was a charm on the small table right next to a telltale sheaf of papers, but it was hard to see—ah, there it was. Two quills, curving in opposite directions. She guessed that they complemented each other, one to send letters and one to receive.

"If he's drunk, maybe he's drinking something better than we are," the first guard said. "Want to share what you have, friend?"

"It's no good if they catch us drinking on duty," the second guard said.

"Like they pay attention to people like us."

"Ah, what's the harm," Iseul said in her gruffest voice, which wasn't very, and handed over her flask. It was terrible wine, but maybe terrible wine was better than no wine. She didn't hang around to find out what the guards decided to do with the flask.

The information about the quills was all she had gotten out of the miserable journey, but it might allow her to figure out a charm to spy on the Genial Ones' future communications. She worked her way to the rear again, and left six hours before dawn the day the siege began. Without an army's impedimenta to trouble her, she could make better time. Not that the storm wasn't obvious, but it wasn't clear to her the Chindallan watchers would realize just what it signified.

She shed the Yegedin clothing while hiding behind some shrubs, exchanging it for the plain brown dress—now quite rumpled—she had been carrying with her, although she resented even the moments that this took. Then she ran for the border-fort, pacing herself. It was hard to make herself concentrate on the dubious paths, but she would be no use if she sprained an ankle on the loose rocks. She had not eaten well while she traveled with the Yegedin army, and it took its toll now. Her breath came hard, and she could feel the storm-winds drawing ever closer behind her.

She had kept the Yegedin boots on because she hadn't brought spare shoes—they would have been a nuisance to carry around—but she discovered that the boots were even worse than she knew from days of marching around in them. Every step jolted the soles of her feet, and the toes were starting to pinch. The scout she had killed hadn't had notably small feet, so she was guessing the boots had caused him even more discomfort than they were causing her. Ill-fitting shoes were apparently a military universal: she knew Chindallan soldiers complained about it, too.

The sky to the north was yet clear, but every time she glanced over her shoulder she saw the stormclouds.

The gate guards to the border-fort must have been bemused to see a small, disheveled woman huffing as she came up the road. Iseul was gratified to see the wall sentries training their bows on her: at least they were prepared for the enemy. "I work for the Ministry of Ornithology," she called out. Iseul trusted that the purity of her Chindallan accent, high court from the north, would convince them that she was no Yegedin. "That's an army a few hours south, as you've guessed, but it has magicians."

The guards conferred, and after a few moments escorted her in to see the guard captain. "You must have made a narrow escape, sister," he said. He was a stocky man, much scarred, with kind eyes, and he spoke Chindallan with the unhurried rhythms of the hill people. Iseul had never been so grateful to hear her people's language. "The outriders had thought as much. Follow me. We can at least give you something to eat."

The guards let Iseul in, and a young soldier led her to the kitchens, where the cook gave her some rice and chicken broth. Iseul was glad of the opportunity to sit and rest her aching feet.

The captain came in with her and asked her questions about the disposition of the enemy. Iseul reported everything she had observed about the rival generals and their temperaments, the disarray of their army as it marched, and the estimated numbers of cavalry and infantry. "But it's the magicians you must worry about, Captain," she said, determined to impress this point upon him.

"It doesn't matter," the captain said quietly. "We're the first thing that stands in their way, and stand we must, however terrible the thunder that comes for us."

He didn't have to mention the fact that two of the three first land battles in the original Yegedin invasion had involved Chindallan commanders abandoning their forts, destroying all the supplies, and fleeing north. It was a shame that no Chindallan would soon forget.

"You won't stand for long unless you have magical defenses of your own," Iseul said.

The captain was already shaking his head. "The Yegedin will next have to pass Fort Kamang on the River Hwan," he said. "They have two magicians there. That will have to do." He eyed Iseul's soup bowl, already empty, with affectionate amusement. "We've sent word north, but it won't hurt to give them more recent intelligence. You undoubtedly have business of your own in that direction. Could I trouble you to—?"

"Of course, Captain," Iseul said.

The captain insisted on making her eat more soup, and she was given rice and barley hardtack and clear, sweet water for the journey. They let her rest for half an hour. The captain asked if she could ride, and she replied that she could, as her mother had taught her. They mounted her on a steady mare, a plain bay without markings, but one who responded calmly and quickly to each of Iseul's aids.

She set out on the bay mare. She had pulled her coat tightly about her in response to the air, which tasted increasingly of ice even though winter was months away. Then, looking back only once, she rode north, knowing as the distance unribboned behind her that she had failed her people.

The terrible thing about the Genial Ones was not that they held nations as their slaves, or that they destroyed cities with firefall and stormlash, or that they concocted their poisons from corpses. After all, human empires have done similar things.

It was not even that they were fond of sculpture. The Genial Ones regarded it as one of the highest arts. A favorite variant was to attune a slab of marble or a mossy boulder to a particular individual. As the days passed, the victim's skin would crack and turn gray, and their movements would slow. When the process was complete, only a dying, formless lump would remain of the victim, and the statue would be complete.

As much as people dreaded this art, however, the Genial Ones could only kill one person at a time with it.

Two hours before the siege of the border-fort, six arrows flew.

The senior general wore a back banner in livid red and a great helmet that resembled the head of a beetle. Only a small part of his face was exposed.

The first arrow took him through the side of the face, beneath the left eye, and even so he didn't die of it.

At the time he was consulting with the two magicians. In the gray light and the fine haze of rain, it was difficult to discern their otherwise distinctive blue robes. Three arrows took one of the magicians in the chest. She wore no armor and the arrowheads' barbs caught in her heart.

Two more arrows killed one of the general's servants, who happened to wear clothing that you might mistake for a magician's robes from a great distance on a day where the visibility was terrible to begin with.

This left the Yegedin army in disarray: someone notified the junior general, who wished to take command, while the senior general was shouting orders even as his servants tried to call for a physician. Both generals were keen on capturing the assassin, but by the time the two of them had organized search parties—since both groups of soldiers were confused as to whose orders should take precedence—the assassin had gotten away.

All that the Yegedin searchers found, at a distance sufficiently far from the command tent that everyone agreed the archer had taken the shots from some other, closer location, were goose feathers dyed red, damp from the rain, stuck into a hill at the base of a tree in the shape of an azalea.

> **Hwado**, *noun*. The way of fire. At one point the Chindallan bow and arrow were believed to be sacred to the spirits of sun and moon. A number of religious ceremonies involve shooting fire-arrows. Such arrows are often fletched with feathers dyed red. There is a saying in Chindalla that "even the wind bleeds," and most archers propitiate the spirits of the air after they practice their art.

Minsu was late for the rendezvous. Iseul had taken advantage of one of the safehouses in the town of Suwen, which was some distance to the north and out of the likely path of the Yegedin advance. She took advantage of the lull to experiment with making her own charms, even though she knew Minsu would have preferred her not to risk working with magic. Still, Iseul had a notion that she might be able work out something to spy on the Genial Ones' communications if she could only exploit certain of the charms' geometries.

After her latest failure, which resulted in words of lenses and distance charring off the attempted charm, Iseul sought comfort in an old pleasure: poetry. She could barely remember what it was like when her greatest problem had been coming up with a sufficiently witty pun with which to puncture some pretentious noblewoman's taste in hairpins. After a couple hours failing to write anything entertainingly caustic, she ventured to one of the town's bookstores to buy a couple volumes of recent poetry so she could pick them apart instead.

Iseul had once wondered what the Yegedin were getting out of piles of Chindallan books when the majority of them were simply not very good. Especially when the Yegedin were famed for their exquisite sense of aesthetics. It was almost difficult, at times, to hate people who understood beauty so thoroughly, and who even recognized beauty when it was to be had in a conquered people's arts.

She returned to the safehouse with her spoils. One of the books was an anthology by highborn poets. All of the poems were written in the high script, which Iseul had learned as a child at her mother's insistence. She had hated it then. The high script was based on the language of the great Qieng Empire to the north and east, but the Qieng language had little resemblance to Chindallan, necessitating a whole system of contrivances to make their writing work for Chindallan at all. Complicating the matter was the fact that the high script had come into use in Chindalla's earlier days, when Chindallan itself had been different, so you had to compensate both for the Qieng language and for the language shifts within Chindallan.

The other volume was a collection by an entertainer who had made a specialty of patriotic poems. He wrote in the petal script, which had been invented by a female entertainer, Jebi the Clever, to fit Chindallan itself. The shapes of the letters even corresponded to the positions of the tongue as it made Chindallan's speech sounds. Sadly, while the collection was beautifully illustrated—the artist had a real eye for the dramatic use of silhouettes—the poetry itself was trite and overwritten. How many times could you use the phrase "hearts of stout fire" in the space of twenty pages without being embarrassed for yourself, anyway?

Minsu met her at the safehouse two days later. She was wearing modestly splendid robes of silk embroidered with cavorting quails. "I am tired of hearing about battles with no survivors," she said. She was referring to the border-fort.

"I heard about the supernatural archer who came back from the dead to defend the fort," Iseul said, raising her eyebrows. "A rain of arrows to blacken the sky, people falling over pierced through the eye, that sort of thing. I didn't even know you had that many arrows."

"You should know better than to listen to hearsay," Minsu said. "Besides, I'm sure I got one magician, but I missed the other. Damnable light, couldn't tell who was who and couldn't risk getting closer, either. And it made no difference in the end."

Iseul nodded somberly. People in the town spoke of nothing else. The storm clouds, the white hands of lightning, the tumbling stones. Skeletons charred to ash, marrow set alight from within. The kindly guard captain at the border-fort was almost certainly dead.

Despite the city magistrate's attempts to keep order, the townsfolk had been gathering their belongings to flee northward. One of them had insisted on explaining to Iseul the best things to take during an evacuation. "Don't take rice," the old woman had said. "Only fools weigh themselves down with rice." She had shown Iseul her tidy bundles of medicines, small and light and pungent. "Someone always gets sick, stomach trouble or foot pains, or some woman has a hard childbirth, if you're unlucky enough to bring a child into the world in these times. You trade the medicine for the food someone else has had to carry, and you fill your belly without having to break your back." Bemused, Iseul had thanked the old woman for her advice.

"I couldn't get into the magicians' tent," Iseul said, "and I still haven't figured out if there's a way to spy on their letters. The trip was for nothing."

"Overhear anything useful?" Minsu said, looking at her with such an expression of calm trust that Iseul felt even more wretched.

Iseul thought over the magicians' exchange while she waited for Minsu. "They were arguing about how destructive to make the storm, I think. That was all. But there was something—" She frowned. Something about their words had just reminded her of the poetry, but what could Chindallan poetry possibly have to do with the Genial Ones?

"Have some tea," Minsu said, her solution to everything, "and maybe it will come to you."

Iseul gave a tiny sigh. The safehouse's tea might as well have been mud steeped in rainwater, but Minsu gave no sign that she noticed its inferior quality. Iseul recounted the rest of her meeting with the border-fort's captain, although there wasn't much to tell.

"I don't think the magicians at Fort Kamang will do us much good," Iseul said. "How are mere human magicians going to stand up to the Genial Ones themselves? Magic clearly prefers to serve its original masters if the Genial Ones can so casually invoke spells we all thought had decayed to uselessness."

"I'd send you to kidnap one of the Genial Ones," Minsu said, "but I don't think we have a safe way of holding one for questioning."

Over and over Iseul heard the two magicians arguing in her head. "Their accent," she said slowly. The threads were in her hands. She only had to figure out how to weave them together. "Their accents, and the accent of the one I killed. The fact that I didn't recognize the language at first."

Minsu eyed her but knew better than to interrupt. Instead, she poured more tea.

"Minsu," Iseul said, going pale. "I was wrong just now. We've all been wrong. Magic didn't die because the Genial Ones were wiped out. Because we know now that they were never wiped out. Magic stopped working for the humans piece by piece because it's their language, and *their language changed over time* just as Chindallan has changed, which everyone who has studied the high script knows. Their language became different. We've been trying to use the wrong words for magic."

"You could make more powerful charms, then," Minsu said. "Using the proper words now that you know them."

"Now that I know some of them, you mean. It would take trial and error to figure out all the necessary changes, and magical experimentation can get messy if you do it wrong."

"So much for that," Minsu said. "What about the lexicons? What do they signify?"

"I still don't know what they're doing, but I will find out," Iseul said.

"We have some time," Minsu said, "but that doesn't mean we can afford to relax. The fact that Yegedin have learned from their mistakes in the first invasion may, in some sense, work in our favor." Originally the Yegedin armies had raced north, far ahead of their supply lines, and eventually had to retreat to the current border. "This time they're making sure they can hold what they take: conquest is always easier than subjugation. Still, tell me what you need and I will make sure you are well-supplied."

"More paper, for a start," Iseul said. "A lot of paper. I will have to hope that the Genial Ones don't track me down here."

"Indeed." Minsu's eyes were unexpectedly grim. "I would get you the assistance of a Chindallan magician, but you do realize that there's every possibility that the Genial Ones have been hiding among our people, too."

"It had occurred to me, yes." Iseul was starting to get a headache, although in all fairness, she should have had one ages ago. "I don't suppose you have any of that headache medicine?"

"I have a little left from my last detour to a pharmacy," Minsu said, and handed it over. "I'll get you more. I have other business to attend to, but I will check back with you from time to time. The safehouse's keeper will have instructions to assist you in any way she can."

"Thank you," Iseul said. She didn't look up as Minsu slipped out.

The first Chindallan dynasty after the fall of the Genial Ones only lasted four abbreviated generations. Its queens and kings were buried in tombs of cold stone beneath mounded earth. Certain Chindallan scholars, coming to the tombs long after they had been plundered, noted that many of the tombs, when viewed from above, seemed to form words in the high script: *wall*, for instance, or *eye*, or *vigilant*. The scholars believed that this practice, like that of burying terracotta soldiers with the dead monarchs and their households, arose from a desire to protect the tombs from grave robbers. Like the terracotta soldiers, the tombs' construction was singularly inadequate for this purpose.

Iseul slept little in the days that followed. She was making progress on the scrying charm, though, which was something. It required suspending the charm along with two of the quill-charms in a mobile. Sometimes, when her exhaustion overcame her, she found herself staring at the charms bobbing back and forth in the air.

She also developed a headache so ferocious that Minsu's medicine, normally reliable, did her no good. Finally she ventured out in search of a pharmacist. It turned out that the pharmacist had fled town, to her vexation, but an old man told her that one of the physicians, a somewhat disreputable man who had evaded registration with the proper ministry for his entire life, was still around. Since she didn't have much option, she went in search of him.

The physician lived in a small hut at the edge of town. He was sitting outside, and he had finished ministering to a pair of grubby children. One of the children was eating a candy with no sign that her splinted wrist bothered her. The other, an even younger girl, was picking wildflowers.

The physician himself was a tall man who would have been taller if not for his hunched shoulders, and he had a wry, gentle face. His clothes were very plain. No one would have looked at him twice in the market square. He stood at Iseul's approach.

"This will be quick, I promise," Iseul said. "I've been having headaches and I need medicine for it."

The physician looked her up and down. "I should think that a few good nights' sleep would serve you better than any medicine," he said dryly.

"I don't have time for a few good nights' sleep," Iseul said. "Please, don't you have anything to take the edge off the pain? If it's a matter of money—"

He named a sum that explained to Iseul what he was doing in such plain clothes. Any respectable licensed physician could have charged three times as much even for something this simple.

"I can pay that," Iseul said.

The girl with the splint tugged at the physician's sleeve, completely unconcerned with the transaction going on. "Do you have more candy?"

"For pity's sake, you haven't finished what's in your mouth," he said.

"But it tastes better when you have two flavors at once."

He rolled his eyes, but he was smiling. "Maybe later."

"You should be all right so long as you don't fall out of any more trees." But the melancholy in his eyes told Iseul that he knew what happened to children in wartime.

The younger girl handed him the wildflowers. She didn't speak in complete sentences yet, but both Iseul and the physician were given to understand that she had picked him the prettiest and best wildflowers as payment. The physician smiled and told her to go back to her parents with her sister.

"You can come in while I get the medicine, if you like," the magician said.

Iseul looked at him with worry as he began to walk. Something about the way he carried himself even over such a short distance intimated a great and growing pain. "Are you well?" she asked.

"It's an old injury," the physician said with a shrug, "and of little importance."

The hut had two rooms, and the outer room was sparsely furnished. There were no books in it, which disappointed Iseul obscurely. On a worn table was a small jar with a crack at the lip and a handful of wilting cosmos flowers in it. He added the newly plucked wildflowers to the jar.

Iseul couldn't help looking around for weapons, traps, stray charms. Nothing presented itself to her eye as unusually dangerous, but the habit was hard to lose.

"Here it is," the physician said after a moment's rooting around in a chest. "Take it once a day when the pain sets in. Ideally you want to catch it before it gets bad. And try not to rely on it more than you have to. People who take this stuff every day over long periods of time sometimes get sick in other ways."

"That shouldn't be an issue," Iseul said, *one way or another.* She hesitated, then said, "You could do a lot of good to the military, you know. They're sure to be looking for physicians, and they'd probably give you a temporary license."

The physician held out the packet of medicine. "I am a healer of small hurts," he said, "nothing more. Everything I accomplish is with a few herbal remedies and common sense. A surprising number of maladies respond to time and rest and basic hygiene, things that soldiers don't see a lot of when they go to war. And besides, the people here need someone too."

Iseul thought of the little girl picking flowers for him. "Then I will simply wish you well," she said. "Thank you." She counted out the payment. He refused her attempts to pay him what he ought to be charging her.

She took a dose of the medicine, then headed back to the safehouse. She passed more people heading out of the town. Mothers with small, squalling children on their backs. Old men leaning on canes carved in the shape of animal heads, a specialty of the region. The occasional nervous couple, quarreling about things to bring with them and things to leave behind. One woman was crying over a large lacquered box with abalone inlay. The battered box was probably the closest thing to a treasure she owned. Her husband tried to tell her that something of its size wasn't worth hauling north and that nobody would give them much money for it anyway, which led to her shouting at him that it wasn't for money that she wanted to bring it.

Merchants were selling food, clothes, and other necessaries for extortionate sums. People were buying anyway: not much choice. Iseul paused to glance over a display of protection charms that one woman was selling, flimsy folded-paper pendants painted with symbols and strung on knotted cords.

The seller bowed deeply to Iseul. "They say the storms are coming north," she said. "Why not protect yourself from the rains and the sharp-toothed horses?"

"Thank you, but no," Iseul said, having satisfied herself that the charms' symbols were beautifully rendered, but empty of virtue. "I wish you the best, though."

The seller eyed her, but decided not to waste time trying to sway her. Shrugging, she turned away and called out to a passing man who was wearing a finer jacket than most of the people on the street.

There was a noodle shop on the way back to the safehouse. The noodles were just as extortionately priced, but Iseul was tired of the safehouse's food. She paid for cold noodles flavored with vinegar, hoping that the flavor would drive out the foul taste of the medicine. The sliced cucumbers were sadly limp, so she added extra vinegar in the hopes of salvaging the dish, without much luck. At least her headache seemed to have receded.

Iseul sat down with her papers and began her work again. She had been keeping notes on all her experiments, some of which were barely legible. She hadn't realized how much her handwriting deteriorated when she was in pain. This time she adjusted the mobile to include a paper sphere (well, an approximate sphere) to represent the world, written over with words of water and earth and cloudshadow.

When the scrying charm did begin to work, hours later, Iseul almost didn't realize it. She was staring off into space, resigned to yet another failure. It was a bad sign that the tea was starting to taste good, although that might possibly be related to the desperation measure of adulterating it with increasing quantities of honey. Not very good honey, at that.

The safehouse's keeper had come in with another pot of tea and was staring at the mobile. "My lady," she said, "is it supposed to be doing that?"

Iseul stifled a yawn. She didn't bother correcting the keeper, although a mere spy didn't rate "lady." "Supposed to be doing—oh."

The sphere was spinning at a steady rate, and black words were boiling from its surface in angry-looking tendrils. Iseul stood and squinted at them. Experimentally, she touched one of the tendrils. Her fingertip felt slightly numb, so she snatched it back. The safehouse's keeper excused herself and left hastily, but Iseul didn't notice.

Iseul had a supply of sheets of paper and books of execrable poetry. She opened one of the poetry books, then positioned one of the sheets beneath the sphere's shadow. Sure enough, words began to condense from the shadow onto the paper, and lines of poetry began to fade from the books. The lines were distorted, probably because they were traveling from a curved surface to a flat one, but the writing was readable enough, and it was in the Genial Ones' language, as she had expected it would be.

Not far into this endeavor, Iseul realized she was going to need a better strategy. There was only one of her, and only one of the scrying charms. Based on the sphere locations, there looked to be at least a hundred Genial Ones communicating with each other. She could make more scrying charms, but she couldn't recruit more people to read and analyze the letters.

Minsu stopped by the next day and was tactfully silent on Iseul's harried appearance, although she looked like she wanted to reach out and tidy Iseul's hair for her. "That looks like some kind of progress," she remarked, looking around at the sorted stacks of paper, "but clearly I didn't provide you with enough paper. Or assistants."

"I'm not sure assistants would help," Iseul said. "The Genial Ones seem to communicate with each other on a regular basis. And there are a few hundred of them just based on the ones who are writing, let alone the ones who are lying low. How many people would you trust with this information?"

She had worse news for Minsu, but it was hard to make herself say it.

"Not a lot," Minsu said. "There's that old saying: only ashes keep secrets, and even they have been known to talk to the stones. What is it that the Genial Ones are so interested in talking about? I can't imagine that they're consulting each other on what shoes to wear to their next gathering."

"Shoes are important," Iseul said, remembering how much her feet had hurt after running to the border-fort in the Yegedin soldier's completely inadequate boots. "But yes. They're talking about language. I've been puzzling through it. There are so many languages, and they work in such different ways. Did you know that there are whole families of languages with something called noun classes, where you inflect nouns differently based on the category they fall into? Except the categories don't usually make any sense. There's this language where nouns for female humans and animals and workers share a class, except tables, cities, and ships are also included." She was aware as she spoke that she was going off on a tangent. She had to nerve herself up to tell Minsu what the Genial Ones were up to.

"I'm sure Chindallan looks just as strange to foreigners," Minsu said. Her voice was bemused, but her somber eyes told Iseul she knew something was wrong. "I once spoke to a Jaioi merchant who couldn't get used to the fact that our third person pronouns don't distinguish between males and females, which is apparently very important in his language. On the other hand, he couldn't handle the formality inflections on our verbs at all. He'd hired an interpreter so he wouldn't inadvertently offend people."

The "interpreter" would have been a spy; that went without saying. Iseul had worked such straightforward assignments herself, once upon a time.

"You haven't said how bad things are down south," Iseul said. She couldn't put this off forever, and yet.

"Well, I'm tempted to have you relocate further north," Minsu said, "but there's only so far north to go. The Yegedin have taken the coastal fort of Suwen. We suspect they're hoping to open up more logistical options from their homeland. I don't, frustratingly, have a whole lot of information on what our navy is up to. They're probably having trouble getting the Yegedin to engage them." During the original invasion, only the rapacious successes of Chindalla's navy—always stronger than its army—had forced the Yegedin to halt their advance.

"I have to work faster," Iseul said, squeezing her eyes shut. Time to stop delaying. Minsu was silent, and Iseul opened them again. "Of course, every time the safehouse keeper comes in, she looks at me like I'm crazed." She eyed the mobiles. There was only room for eleven of them, but the way they spun and cavorted, like orreries about to come apart, was probably a good argument that their creator wasn't in her right mind. "What I don't understand . . . " She ran her hand over one of the stacks of paper.

When Iseul didn't continue the thought, Minsu said, "Understand what?"

"I've tested the letter-scrying spell," Iseul said, "with languages that aren't the Genial Ones'. I'm only fluent in five languages besides Chindallan, but I tried them all. And the spell won't work on anything but the language of magic. The charms spin around but they can't so much as get a fix on a letter that I'm writing in the same room."

"Did you try modifying the charm?" Minsu asked.

"I thought of that, but magic doesn't work that way. I mean, the death-touch daggers, for instance. If you had to craft them to a specific individual target, they'd be less useful. Well, in most circumstances." They could both think of situations where a dagger that would only kill a certain person might be useful. "But I think that's why the Genial Ones have been so quiet, and why they've been busy compiling the lexicons by hand for each human language. Because there's no other way to do it. They know more magic than I do, that goes without saying. If there were some charm to do the job for them, they'd be using it."

"I have the feeling you're going to lead up to something that requires the best of teas to face," Minsu said, and stole a sip from Iseul's cup before Iseul had the chance to warn her off. She was too well-bred to make remarks about people who put honey in even abysmal tea, but her eyebrows quirked a little.

Iseul looked away. "I think I know why the Genial Ones are compiling lexicons," she said, "and it isn't because they really like writing miniature treatises on morphophonemics."

"How disappointing," Minsu said, "you may have destroyed my affection for them forever." But her bantering tone had worry beneath it.

Iseul went to a particular stack of papers, which she had weighted down with a letter opener decorated with a twining flower motif. "They've been discussing an old charm," she said. "They want to create a variation of the sculpture charm."

"That was one of the first to become defunct after their defeat," Minsu observed. "Apparent defeat, I should say."

"That brings me to the other thing," Iseul said. "I think I've figured out that word that the first Genial One said, the one that was unfamiliar. Because it keeps showing up in their conversations. I think it's a word that didn't exist before."

"I remember that time that satirist coined a new word for hairpins that look like they ought to be good for assassinations but are completely inadequate for the job," Minsu said. "Of course, based on Chindalla's plays and novels, I have to concede that we needed the word."

Minsu's attempts to get her to relax weren't helping, but Iseul appreciated the effort. *You can kill one of us, but not all of us. We won't accept this—*" 'Defeat,' " Iseul said softly. "The word means 'defeat.' "

"Surely they can't have gone all this time without—" Minsu's mouth pressed into a flat line.

"Yes," Iseul said. "These are people who had separate words for their blood and our blood. Because we weren't their equals. Until General Anangan overcame them, they had no word for *their own defeat.* Not at the hands of humans, anyway, as opposed to the intrigues and backstabbing that apparently went on among their clans."

"All right," Minsu said, "but that can't be what's shadowing your eyes."

"They want to defeat us the way we almost defeated them," Iseul said. "They're obsessed with it. They've figured out how to scale the sculpture charm up. Except they're not going to steal our shapes. They're going to steal our words and add them to their own language. And Chindalla's language is the last to be compiled for the purpose."

In the old days, the forgotten days, the human nations feared the Genial Ones' sculptors, and their surgeons, and their soldiers. They knew, however, that the greatest threat was none of these, but the Genial Ones' lexicographers, whose thoroughness was legendary. The languages that they collected for their own pleasure vanished, and the civilizations that spoke those languages invariably followed soon afterwards.

Iseul was in the middle of explaining her plan to thwart the Genial Ones to Minsu, which involved charms to destroy the language of magic itself, when the courier arrived. The safehouse's keeper interrupted them. Iseul thought it was to bring them tea, but she was accompanied by a young man, much disheveled and breathing hard. He was obviously trying not to stare at the room's profusion of charms, or at Iseul herself. She couldn't remember the last time she had given her hair a good thorough combing, and she probably looked like a ghost. (For some reason ghosts never combed their hair.) Her mother would have despaired of her.

"I trust you have a good reason for this," Minsu said wearily.

"You need to hear this, my lady," the keeper said.

The young man presented his papers to Minsu. They declared him to be a government courier, although the official seal, stamped in red ink that Iseul happened to know never washed out of fabric no matter what you tried, was smeared at the lower right corner. Minsu looked over the papers, frowning, then nodded. "Speak," Minsu said.

"A Yegedin detachment of two thousand has been spotted heading this way," the courier said. "It's probably best if you evacuate."

Iseul closed her eyes and drew a shuddering breath in spite of herself.

"All this work," Minsu said, gesturing at the mobiles.

"It's not worth defending this town," Iseul said bleakly, "am I right?"

"The throne wishes its generals to focus on protecting more important cities," the courier said. "I'm sorry, my lady."

"It'll be all right," Iseul said to Minsu. "I can work as easily from another safehouse."

"You'll have to set up the charms all over again," Minsu said.

"It can't be helped. Besides, if we stay here, even if the Yegedin don't get us, the looters will."

The courier's expression said that he was realizing that Iseul might have more common sense than her current appearance suggested. Still, he addressed Minsu. "The detachment will probably be here within the next five days, my lady. Best to leave before the news becomes general knowledge."

"Not as if there are a whole lot of people left here anyway," Minsu said. "All right. Thank you for the warning."

Iseul was used to being able to pick up and leave at a moment's notice, but she hadn't reckoned on dealing with the charms and the quantities of text that they had generated. There wasn't time to burn everything, which made her twitch. They settled for shuffling the rest into boxes and abandoning them with the heaps of garbage that could be found around the town. Her hands acquired blisters, but she didn't even notice how much they hurt.

Iseul and Minsu joined the long, winding trail of refugees heading north. The safehouse keeper insisted on parting ways from them because she had family in the area. Minsu's efforts to talk her out of this met with failure. She pressed a purse of coins into the keeper's hands; that was all the farewell they could manage.

Minsu bought horses from a trader at the first opportunity, the best he had, which wasn't saying much. The price was less extravagant than Iseul might have guessed. Horses were very unpopular at the moment because everyone had the Yegedin storm-horses on their mind, and people had taken to stealing and killing them for the stewpot instead. Minsu insisted on giving Iseul the calmer gelding and taking the cantankerous mare for herself. "No offense," she said, "but I have more experience wrangling very annoying horses than you do."

"I wasn't complaining," Iseul said. She was credible enough on horseback, but it really didn't matter.

Most of the refugees headed for the road to the capital, where they felt the most safety was to be had. Once the two of them were mounted, however, Minsu led them northeast, toward the coast.

In the evenings Iseul would rather have dropped asleep immediately, but constructing her counterstroke against the Genial Ones was an urgent problem, and it required all her attention. Not only did she have to construct a charm to capture the Genial Ones' words, she had to find a way to destroy those words so they could never be used again. Sometimes she caught herself nodding off, and she pinched her palm to prick herself awake again. They weren't just threatened by armies; they were threatened by the people who had once ruled all the known nations.

"We're almost there," Minsu said as they came to the coast. "Just another day's ride." The sun was low in the sky, but she had decided they should stop in the shelter of a hill rather than pressing on tonight. She had been quiet for most of the journey, preferring not to interrupt Iseul's studies unless Iseul had a question for her.

Iseul had been drowsing as she rode, a trick she had mastered out of necessity. She didn't hear Minsu at first, lost in muddled dreams of a book. The book had pages of tawny paper, precisely the color of skin. It was urgent that she write a poem about rice-balls into the book. Everyone knew rice was the foundation of civilization and it deserved more satiric verses than it usually received, but every time she set her brush to the paper, the ink ran down the bristles and formed into cavorting figures that leapt off the pages. She became convinced that she was watching a great and terrible dance, and that the question was then whether she would run out of ink before the dance came to its fruition.

"Iseul." It was Minsu. She had tied her horse to a small tree and had caught Iseul's reins. "I know you're tired, but you look like you're ready to fall off."

Iseul came alert all at once, the way she had trained herself to do on countless earlier missions. "I have to review my notes. I think I might have it this time."

"There's hardly any light to read by."

"I'll shield a candle."

"I'll see to your horse, then," Minsu said.

Minsu set up camp while Iseul hunched over her notes. Properly it should have been the other way around, but Minsu never stood on formalities for their own sake. She was always happy to pour tea for others, for instance.

"If they think to do scrying of their own once I get started," Iseul said while Minsu was bringing her barley hardtack mashed into a crude cold porridge, "our lifespans are going to be measured in minutes."

"We don't seem to have a choice if we want to survive," Minsu said.

"The ironic thing is that we'll also be saving the Yegedin."

"We can fight the Yegedin the way we'd fight anyone else," Minsu said. "The Genial Ones are another matter."

"If only we knew how General Anangan managed it the first time around," Iseul said. But all that remained were contradictory legends. She wondered, now, if the Genial Ones themselves had obfuscated the facts.

"If only." Minsu sighed.

Iseul ate the porridge without tasting it, which was just as well.

A little while later, Minsu said quietly, "You haven't even thought to be tempted, have you?"

"Tempted how?" But as she spoke, Iseul knew what Minsu meant. "It would only be a temporary reprieve."

She knew exactly how the lexicon charm worked. She had the Yeged-dai lexicon with her, and she could use it to destroy the Yegedin language. The thirteen-year occupation would evaporate. Poets could write in their native language without fear of attracting reprisals. Southern Chindallans could use their own names again. No more rebels would have to burn to death. All compelling arguments. She could annihilate Yeged before she turned on the Genial Ones. People would consider it an act of patriotism.

But as Minsu had said, the Yegedin could be fought by ordinary means, without resorting to the awful tools of humanity's old masters.

Iseul also knew that turning the lexicon charm against the Genial Ones' own language would mean destroying magic forever. No more passage charms or lantern charms; no more convenient daggers that made people vanish.

No more storm-horses, either, or towers built of people's bones erupting from pyramids of corpses, as in the old stories. It wouldn't be all bad. And what kind of spy would she be if she couldn't improvise solutions?

Besides, if she didn't do something about the Genial Ones now, they would strike against all the human nations with the lexicons they had already compiled. Here, at least, the choice was clear and narrow.

"I don't want to be more like the Genial Ones than I have to," Iseul said with a guilty twitch of regret. "But we do have to go through with this."

"Do you have ward spells prepared?" Minsu said.

"Yes," Iseul said. "A lot of them. Because once we're discovered—and we have to assume we'll be—they're going to devote their attention to seeking out and destroying us. And we don't know what they're capable of."

"Oh, that's not true," Minsu said. "We know exactly what they're capable of. We've known for generations, even in the folktales."

"I should start tonight," Iseul said. "I'm only going to be more tired tomorrow."

Minsu looked as though she wanted to argue, but instead she nodded.

Iseul sat in the lee of the hill and began the painstaking work of copying out all the necessary charms, from the wards—every form of ward she knew of, including some cribbed from the Genial Ones' own discussions—to the one that would compile the lexicon of the language of magic for her by transcribing those same discussions. That final charm was bound to fail at some point when its world of words was confined to the sheets of blank paper she had prepared for it, but—if she had done this correctly—she had constructed it so that it would target its own structural words last.

The winds were strong tonight, and they raked Iseul with cold. The horses were unsettled, whinnying to each other and pulling at their ropes. Iseul glanced up from time to time to look at the sky, bleak and smothered over with clouds. The hills might as well have been the dented helmets of giant warriors, abandoned after an unwinnable fight.

"All right," Iseul said at last, hating how gray her voice sounded. She felt the first twinge of a headache and remembered to take the medicine the physician had given her. "Come into the circle of protection, Minsu. There's no reason to delay getting started."

Obligingly, Minsu joined her, and Iseul activated each warding charm one by one. It was hard not to feel as though she was playing with a child's toys, flimsy folded shapes, except she knew exactly what each of those charms was intended to do.

At the center of the circle of protection were four books as empty as mirrors in the darkness, which Iseul had bound during her time in the safehouse. She hoped four books would be enough to cripple the Genial Ones, even if they couldn't contain the entirety of their language. Iseul began folding pages of the empty books, dog-earing corners and folding them into skewed geometries. When she wasn't watching closely, she had the impression that the corners were unfolding and stretching out tendrils of nascent words, nonsense syllables, to spy on her. She didn't mention this to Minsu, but the other woman's face was strained. There was a stinging tension in the air; her skin prickled.

Lightning flickered in the distance as she worked. It cut from one side of the sky to the other in a way that natural lightning never did, like the sweep of a sword.

"Hurry if you can," Minsu said, head raised to watch the approach of the storm.

"I'm hurrying," Iseul said.

The winds were whipping fiercely around them now. One of Minsu's braids had come unpinned and was flapping like a lonely pennant.

The candle flickered out. Minsu brought out a lantern charm.

"I'm all for ordinary fire if you can get it to work for you," Minsu said at Iseul's dubious look, "but you need light and this will give you light for a time."

Iseul continued with the lexicon charm, double-checking every fold, every black and twining word, every diagram of spindled lines. The sense of tension sharpened. If she dared to look away from the books' pages and at the suffocating sky, she imagined that she would see words forming amid the clouds, sky-words and wind-words and water-words, words of torrential despair and words of drowning terror, words that had existed in some form since the first people learned to speak.

She slammed each book shut counterclockwise, shuddering, suddenly hoping the whole affair was an extension of the dream she had had and that she would wake to sunlight and flowers and a warm spot by some fire, but no. With a dry creaking voice—with a chorus of voices that rose and rose to a roar—the books wrenched themselves open in unison.

For a second the pages fluttered wildly, like birds newly freed. Then they darkened as words inundated them. Slowly at first, then in a steady pouring of black writhing shapes. Postpositions. Conjunctions. Nouns that violated vowel harmony and nouns that didn't. Verbs in different conjugations, tenses, aspects. A stray aorist. Scraps of syntax and subclause generators. Interjections snatched from between clenched teeth. Sacred names rarely spoken and never before written.

One of the horses was thrashing about, but Iseul was only peripherally aware of it, or of Minsu swearing under her breath. A dark shape plunged up before Iseul, but she was intent upon the books, the books, the terrible books. Who knew there were so many crawling words in a language? Years ago, when reviewing a cryptology text, she had seen an estimate of the number of words a literate Chindallan needed to be able to read. She had thought the number large then. Now she knew the estimate must be low. It wasn't possible for more words to flood the four books' pages, but here they came, again and again and again, growing smaller and smaller as they crushed each other in the confines on the pages.

The dark shape was one of the horses, which had pulled free of the rope in its panic. Minsu had her riding crop out and struck the horse. Iseul had a vague idea of how desperate she must be. The other woman had always been softhearted about the animals. But the horse wheeled and ran toward the hills, neighing wildly.

Iseul's attention was abruptly drawn to the horse when, having passed the circle of protection, lightning scythed through the horse. Except it wasn't lightning, precisely: pale light with eyes in it, and black waving feelers sprouting from each pupil, and the feelers ate holes into the unfortunate animal's spine. The horse screamed for a long time.

More lightning zigzagged down from the sky, crackling around the circle. Rain was pelting down all around them, and muddy water sluiced down the hillside. Voices whispered out of the darkness, murmuring liplessly of entrails and needlepoints and vengeance. The light from the lantern charm glittered in the raindrops and the sheets of water like an unwanted promise. The lantern, although flimsy in construction, seemed to be in no danger of being toppled by the rising winds.

One of the protective wards began to unfold itself.

Minsu said a word that Iseul hadn't even realized she knew.

"We can't let them win this," Iseul said breathlessly. Stupid to just stand here watching, as if the Genial Ones would simply submit to the destruction of their magic. She began constructing an additional ward to reinforce the one that was disintegrating.

Chasms of fire opened in the air, then closed, like terrible fierce smiles. The rain hissed where it met the fire, and Iseul flinched when tendrils of steam were repelled by the circle of protection. Leaves spun free of the hillside wildflowers and the nearby copses of trees, formed into great screaming birds, battered themselves fruitlessly against the wards before dissipating into shreds and slivers of green and yellow.

Iseul spared a glance for the books. Was it possible for them to hold any more words? She set the current ward in place, then flipped through the pages of the fourth book in spite of herself, in spite of the conviction that the paper would hold her hands fast and drag her in. And then the teeth began.

The teeth grew from the corners of the pages. They distended into predatory curves, yellow-white and gleaming. Iseul flinched violently.

The teeth took no notice of her, but the books fanned themselves out like a hundred hundred mouths. Then, with a papery crumpling sound, they began to eat the words.

Minsu was holding Iseul's shoulder. "This is not," she said thinly, "at all what I thought it would be."

The storm crackled and roared above them. The two women clung to each other as rain and lightning crashed inland. If the winds grew any stronger, Iseul felt she would fall over sideways and not stop falling until she had gone through the world and out the other side. But she didn't dare rest, and she didn't dare contemplate leaving the circle of protection.

More of the wards were unfolding. Despite her shaking hands, Iseul bent to the task of making more charms, except now the charms were fighting her. *Of course,* she thought, cursing herself for her carelessness. She had thought to specify that the lexicon charm would spare itself as long as possible, but she had done no such thing for the wards. She would have to try synonyms, circumlocutions, alternate geometries; she would have to hope that the Genial Ones were having as much difficulty sustaining their attacks as she was her defenses.

The lantern charm abruptly guttered out. Iseul couldn't see, through the water in her eyes, whether the words upon it had been devoured, or whether the Genial Ones had discovered them and snuffed it themselves.

Faces of fire scattered downward and struck a hilltop perhaps thirty meters from them. All the faces were howling, and their eyes were hollow sooty pits. For a moment everything was crowned in sanguinary light, from the silhouetted grasses swept nearly flat to the hunched rocks.

"We're done for," Iseul whispered. Was it her imagination, or did she hear horses in the distance, sharp-toothed horses with hooves that struck savage rhythms into the earth's bones?

More charms uncurled, crumpled, made the kinds of sounds you might imagine of lost love letters and discarded prayers.

"Hold fast," Minsu said, although she had to repeat herself over the drumming storm so that Iseul could hear her. Her expression was obscure in the darkness.

Iseul was holding down the covers of one of the books, small futile gesture. The whole thing should have been drenched. Ordinarily she would have been appalled at herself for leaving a book out in the rain, but the teeth seemed just as happy to devour water as words.

A swirl of flame made it past the circle of protection. Minsu's hair caught on fire. She beat at the flames with her hands. For a bad moment, Iseul thought that the fires had spread to her eyes, her ears, the marrow of her hands. But after one horrifying white-red flare, the fire shook itself apart in an incoherent dazzle of sparks, then sizzled into silence.

"I'm fine," Minsu shouted, although her voice shook. She went to retrieve the lantern charm. "No words," she said, squinting at it during the next lightning-flash. The charm had unfolded completely. There were only faint rust-colored marks where the words had been, like splotches of blood.

Hurry, Iseul bid the books with their gnashing teeth. *Hurry.*

There was no way to guide the books' hunger now, no way to tell them to eat words of storm and fire above all others. They were indiscriminate in their voracity. More and more of the pages were spotted rust-red, like the former lantern charm.

Then the storm broke. There was no other word for it. It came apart into smaller storms, and the smaller storms into eddies of wind, the rain into a fine wandering mist. In the distance they heard the tolling of dark bells and the screams of sharp-toothed horses.

The teeth receded. The books' pages twitched upward, yearning, then subsided. A sullen light rippled from their covers. Every single one of their pages was covered with splattered blood, a slaughterhouse of words. Fighting her revulsion, Iseul closed each one and put them away. The light sloughed away.

Iseul and Minsu were drenched through. "We'll catch our death of chill out here," Iseul said. Her throat felt raw although she had hardly spoken. After what had just happened, a great lassitude threatened to drag her under, but she couldn't afford to sleep, not yet.

"We have to see what became of the coastal fort," Minsu said. "If we walk through the night we might make it. Assuming the place hasn't been overrun by the Yegedin navy."

The books felt like chains all the way through the night. They found a trail through the hills, difficult to see in the darkness and dangerously slippery at that, but Minsu had experience of this region and was able to lead them in the right direction. She insisted that Iseul ride the remaining horse while she led it. By that point, Iseul didn't care where they were going or how they got there so long as she was allowed to collapse and sleep at the end of it. Any flat surface would do.

"Oh no," Minsu said at last.

Iseul almost fell off the horse. She had slipped into a half-doze, except she kept seeing black spidering shapes behind her eyelids.

They had stopped on the crest of a hill: risky to be silhouetted if there were enemies in the area, especially archers, but an excellent vantage point otherwise.

The sea crashed against broken white-gray cliffs. The bones of ships could be seen floating in the newly formed harbor along with uprooted trees. "They destroyed the coast," Minsu said, bringing out a spyglass and looking north and south. "Fort Jenal used to be out there—" She gestured toward the horizon, toward the frothing waves. "Now it's all water and wreckage."

"Do you suppose there are any survivors?" Iseul said. But she knew the answer.

Minsu shook her head.

"If only I had figured it out sooner," Iseul said, head bowed. If only she had been able to make the lexicon charm work faster.

"We'll have to notify the nearest garrison," Minsu said, "so they can search for survivors, Chindallan or Yegedin. But for now, we must rest."

She said something else, but Iseul's knees buckled and she didn't hear any of it.

The Genial Ones originally had no word for *medicine* that did not also mean *poison*. They ended up borrowing one from a human language spoken by people that they slaughtered the hard way for variety's sake, person by person dragged from their villages and redoubts and killed, cautery by sword and spear.

Minsu said very little to the garrisons they visited about the real reason the storm had broken, which was just as well. Iseul wasn't sure what she would have said if asked about it. She did, at Minsu's urging, write a ciphered account of the lexicon charm and the devouring books to send to the Ministry of Ornithology with a trusted courier.

They were sitting in a rented room at the time, and Minsu had scared up a tea that even Iseul liked.

"I only wrote the account," Iseul said, very clearly, "because none of the charms work anymore." With the Genial Ones' language extinguished, the magic it empowered was gone for good. She had attempted to create working charms, just to be sure, but all of them remained inert. "Imagine if Yeged's Emperor had figured out how to use this on Chindallan or the language of any other nation he desired to conquer."

"The way we could have?" Minsu said sardonically. "It's done now. Finish your report, and we can get out of this town."

There were still refugees on the road north. They might have deprived the Yegedin of magical assaults, but then, they had also deprived the Chindallans of magical defenses. Given that both sides had spent the uneasy peace preparing to go to war, it was anyone's guess as to who would prevail.

At one point they ended up at a wretched camp for those who were too sick to continue fleeing, and the few people who were staying with them, mostly their families and a few monks who were acting as caretakers. Iseul remained prone to headaches and was running low on medicine. Minsu had insisted that they seek out a physician, even though Iseul tried to point out that the people at the camp probably needed the medicine more than she did.

As it turned out, they forgot all about the question of who deserved the medicine when Iseul saw a familiar little girl. She was picking flowers, weeds really, but in her hands they became jewels.

Iseul approached the girl and asked her if she knew where the physician was. The girl seemed confused by the question, but after a little while her older sister appeared from one of the tents and recognized Iseul. "I'll take you to him," the girl said, "but he's very sick."

"I'm sorry to hear that," Iseul said. Despite the monks' best efforts to enforce basic sanitary practices, the camp reeked of filth and sickness and curdled hopes, and she couldn't help but imagine that the physician had taken sick while helping others.

She and Minsu followed the older girl to a tent at the edge of the camp. Flowers had been weighted down with a rock at the tent's opening: the younger girl's handiwork, surely. They could smell the bitter incense that was used to bring easeful dreams to the dying.

The tent was small, and there were more flowers next to the brazier. Their petals had fallen off and were scattered next to the pallet. The incense was almost all burned away. The physician slept on the pallet. Even at rest his lined face suggested a certain weary kindness. Someone had drawn a heavy quilted blanket over him, stained red-brown on one corner.

"What happened?" Minsu said. "Will he recover? I'm sure he could be a great help here."

"He fell sick," the girl said. "One of the monks said he had a stroke. He doesn't talk anymore and he doesn't seem to understand when people talk to him. They said he might like us to visit him, though, and our mother works with the monks to help the sick people, so we come by and bring flowers."

He doesn't talk anymore. Iseul went cold. He had spoken Chindallan; shouldn't that have saved him? But she didn't know how language worked in the brain.

Without asking, she lifted the corner of the blanket. The physician had longer arms than she remembered, like the Genial One she had killed at his house a lifetime ago. Who was to say they couldn't change their shapes? Especially if they were living among humans? Tears pricking her eyes, she replaced the blanket.

"I'm very sorry," Iseul said to the girl. "It's probably not long before he dies."

She couldn't help but wonder how many Genial Ones had lingered into this age, taking no part in the conspiracy for vengeance, leading quiet lives as healers of small hurts to atone for their kindred who summoned storm-horses and faces of fire. There was no way to tell.

The Yegedin had tried to destroy Chindalla's literature and names, but Iseul had destroyed the Genial Ones themselves. It hadn't seemed real until now.

"Thank you," she said to the dying Genial One, even though his mind was gone. She and Minsu sat by his side for a time, listening to him breathe. There was a war coming, and a storm entirely human, but in this small space they could mourn what they had done.

For a long time afterwards, Iseul tried to come up with a poem about the Genial Ones, encapsulating what they had meant to the world and why they had had to die and why she regretted the physician's passing, but no words ever came to her.

—. A noun, probably, pertaining to regret or cinders or something of that nature, but this word can no longer be found in any lexicon, human or otherwise.

counting the shapes

How many shapes of pain are there?
Are any topologically equivalent?
And is one of them death?

Biantha woke to a heavy knocking on the door and found her face pressed against a book's musty pages. She sat up and brushed her pale hair out of her face, trying to discern a pattern to the knocking and finding that the simplest one was impatience. Then she got to her feet and opened the door, since her warding spell had given her no warning of an unfriendly presence outside. Besides, it would be a little longer before the demons reached Evergard.

"Took your time answering the door, didn't you, Lady Biantha?" Evergard's gray-haired lord, Vathré, scowled at her. Without asking for permission, which he never did anyway, he strode past her to sweep his eyes over the flurry of papers that covered her desk. "You'd think that, after years of glancing at your work, I'd understand it."

"Some of the conjectures are probably gibberish anyway." She smiled at him, guessing that what frustrated him had little to do with her or the theorems that made her spells possible. Vathré visited her when he needed an ear detached from court intrigues. "What troubles you this time, my lord?"

He appropriated her one extra chair and gestured for her to sit at the desk, which she did, letting her smile fade. "We haven't much longer, Biantha. The demons have already overrun Rix Pass. No one agrees on when they'll get here. The astrologer refused to consult the stars, which is a first—claimed he didn't want to see even an iffy prediction—" Vathré looked away from her. "My best guess is that the demons will be here within a month. They still have to march, overwhelming army or no."

Biantha nodded. Horses barely tolerated demon-scent and went mad if forced to carry demons. "And you came to me for battle spells?" She could not keep the bitterness from her voice. The one time she had killed with a spell had been for a child's sake. It had not helped the child, as far as she knew.

"Do you have any battle spells?" he asked gravely.

"Not many." She leaned over and tapped the nearest pile of paper. "I was in the middle of this proof when I discovered that I'd have to review one of Yverry's theorems. I fell asleep trying to find it. Give me a few days and I can set up a battle spell that will kill any demons you've already managed to wound." Biantha saw the weariness in the lord's green eyes and flushed. "It isn't much, I know."

"That helps, but it isn't what I came for."

Dread opened at the pit of her stomach. "The Prophecy."

Vathré inclined his head.

"I've tried to pry some sense out of it ever since I learned of it, you know." She rubbed her eyes. "The poetry translates into shapes and equations that are simply intractable. I've tried every kind of analysis and transformation I know. If there's any hope in the rhymes, the rhythms, the ambiguities, don't ask me to show you where it is. You'd do better consulting the minstrels for a lecture on symbolism."

"I don't *trust* the minstrels." His brows drew together. "And any time I consult the other magicians, I get too many uncertainties to untangle. The seers and healers are hopeless. The astrologer gets headaches trying to determine where to start. The cartomancer gives me a dozen different *possibilities* each time she casts the cards. As far as the Prophecy is concerned, yours is the only kind of magic I can trust."

Biantha smiled wanly. "Which is why, of course, it's so limited." Sometimes she envied the astrologer, the cartomancer, the enchanters, the healers, the seers—magicians whose powers were less reliable but more versatile. "I'll work on it, my lord."

"A month," he reminded her.

She hesitated. "Have you declared your heir yet?"

Vathré eyed her. "Not you, too?"

She swallowed. "If you die, my lord, someone must carry on. Don't leave the succession in doubt. A problem may have several solutions, but some solutions can still be wrong."

"We've been over this before," he said. "Considering the current state of affairs, I'd have to declare a chain of succession down to the apprentice cook. If anyone survives, they can argue over it. My advisors can rule by council until then."

Biantha bowed her head and watched him leave.

Usually Biantha avoided Evergard's great hall. It reminded her of her former home, the demon emperor's palace, though the scents of lavender and lilacs drifted through the air, not the smell of blood; people smiled at her instead of bowing or curtsying rigidly. Musicians played softly while nobles chattered, idle soldiers gambled for pittances, and children scampered in and out, oblivious to the adults' strained voices. A few of the boys were fair-haired, like herself. Biantha closed her eyes briefly before turning along the walls, partly to avoid thinking about a particular fair-haired boy, partly because she had come to study the tapestries for inspiration.

The tapestries' colors remained as vibrant as they had been when she first swore fealty to Lord Vathré upon the Blade Fidora. Biantha had long ago determined the logic by which the tapestries had been arranged, and did not concern herself with it now. Instead, she inspected the scenes of the Nightbreak War.

Here was the Battle of Noiren Field, where webs of starlight blinded a thousand soldiers and angular silhouettes soared above, ready for the massacre. Here was General Vian on a blood bay destrier, leading a charge against a phalanx of demons. Here was amber-eyed Lady Chandal weeping over a fallen young man whose closed eyes might also have been amber, flowers springing up where her tears splashed onto the battlefield. Biantha swallowed and quickened her steps. One by one she passed the tapestries until she found what she sought.

Unlike the other Nightbreak tapestries, its border had been woven in rust rather than Evergard's colors, blue and black: rust for betrayal. She stared at the dispassionate face of Lord Mière, enchanter and traitor to Evergard. His had been a simpler magic than her own, drawing upon ritual and incantation. With it he had almost defeated the Watchlanders; only his daughter's knife had saved them.

Symmetry, she sighed. The one thing she had pried from the Prophecy was that it possessed a twisted symmetry. It hinted at two wars between the demons' empire and the Watchlands, and because records of the first war—the Nightbreak War—were scant, Biantha had yet to understood certain cantos, certain equations, that dealt with it. Hours with Evergard's minstrels and historians hadn't helped. Other than herself, only Vathré knew that there might be a second traitor among them.

Or that, because they had won the first war, they might lose the second, in a cruel mirroring transformation of history.

"Lady Biantha?"

She turned. "Yes?"

The captain—she did not know his name—bowed slightly. "It isn't often that we see you down here, my lady."

Biantha smiled wryly. "A bit too much noise for my work, and on occasion I test spells that might go wrong, sometimes fatally so. My chambers are shielded, but out here . . . "

In the demon emperor's court, her words would have been a veiled threat. Here, the captain nodded thoughtfully and gestured at the tapestry. "I was wondering why you were looking at this. Most people avoid it."

"I was thinking about the Prophecy," she said, retracing the intractable equations in her mind. There had to be a way to balance term against term, solve the system and read Evergard's future, but it continued to escape her. "I'm worried."

"We all are."

Biantha paused. "You said 'most people.' Does that include yourself?"

His mouth twisted. "No. It's a useful reminder. Do you ever wish you had stayed at the demon emperor's palace?"

She read honest curiosity in the captain's expression, not innuendo. "Never." She breathed deeply. "I started learning mathemagic there because magicians, even human magicians, are protected unless they do something foolish. Otherwise I would have been a slave or a soldier; I had no wish for the former and no heart, no talent, for the latter."

Such a small word, *foolish*, when the penalty it carried had given Biantha nightmares for years. She had seen the demon emperor touch his serpent-eyed scepter to a courtesan's perfumed shoulder, as if in blessing; had been unable to avert her gaze before she saw the woman's eyes boiling away and splinters of bone erupting through the rouged skin.

The captain looked down. "I'm sorry to have reminded you, my lady."

"A useful reminder," she echoed. "And what does this portrait of Lord Mière remind you of, if I may ask?"

"Honor, and those who lose it," he said. "Lord Mière was my great-grandfather."

Biantha blinked and saw that there was, indeed, a resemblance in the structure of his face. Her eyes moved to the tapestry's rust border. What had driven Mière to betrayal? It occurred to her, not for the first time, that she herself had fled the demon emperor's court—but the symmetry here seemed incomplete. "Do you think there's hope for us?" she asked the captain.

He spread his hands, studying Biantha's face as she had his just a moment before. "There are those of us who say we must have a chance, or you would have returned to the demons."

She felt herself flush—and then laughed, though that laughter came perilously close to tears. "I have rarely known demons to forgive. Neither have they forgiven Evergard their defeat in the Nightbreak War."

"More's the pity," said the captain, frowning thoughtfully, and took his leave.

For us or the demons? Biantha thought.

Symmetry. The word haunted Biantha through the days and nights as she struggled with the Prophecy. She had wondered, after meeting the captain, if it meant something as simple as her flight from the demons, the fact that one of Lord Mière's descendants survived here. The ballads said Mière had but a single daughter, named Paienne, but they made no mention of her after she saved the Watchlands.

The secret eluded her, slipped away from her, sent her into dreams where dizzying shifts in perspective finally drove her to awaken. Biantha turned to her tomes, seeking clues in others' mathemagical speculations; when she tired of that, she memorized her battle spells, bowing to the heartless logic of war. And went back to the tomes, their treasury of axioms and theorems, diagrams and discussions.

She was leafing through Athique's *Transformations* when someone imitated thunder on her door. Biantha put down the book and opened the door. "Yes?"

The herald bowed elaborately. "A meeting of the court, my lady. Lord Vathré wishes you to attend."

"I'll be there." Firmly, she shut the door and changed into her formal robes as swiftly as she could. Biantha had attended few court meetings: at first, because Vathré had been uncertain of her loyalties, then because of her awkwardness as a foreigner, and finally because she rarely had anything to contribute to matters of state and found her time better spent working on her magic. That Vathré should summon her now was unusual.

She was right. For once the attendants and servants had been cleared out, and the court had arrayed itself along the sides of the throne room while Vathré and his advisers sat at the head. She took her place between the astrologer and Lady Iastre. The astrologer wore his habitual frown, while the lady's face was cool and composed, revealing nothing. Biantha knew better, after playing draughts or rithmomachia against Iastre once a week in less hectic times: Iastre's face only went blank when she anticipated trouble.

"We have a guest today," said Vathré at his driest. His eyes might have flicked to Biantha, too briefly for her to tell for certain.

On cue, the guards led in a man who wore black and red and gold, stripped of his sword—she knew there had been a sword, by the uniform. The style of his clothing spoke of the demons' realm, and the only one besides the emperor who dared appear in those colors was his champion. The emperor's champion, her son.

A challenge? Biantha thought, clenching her hands so they would not shake. *Has Marten come to challenge Vathré?* But surely the emperor knew Evergard held different customs and would hardly surrender the Watchlands' fate to a duel's outcome.

Hopelessly, she studied the man who had so suddenly disrupted her memories of the child who hid flowers and leaves between the pages of her books, who climbed onto her desk to look out the window at the soldiers drilling. He had her pale hair, a face very like hers. His hands, relaxed at his sides, were also hers, though deadlier; Biantha knew of the training an emperor's champion underwent and had little faith that the guards could stop him from killing Vathré if he wished. But Marten's eyes belonged to a man Biantha had tried to forget, who had died attempting to keep her from leaving the palace with their child.

Silence descended upon the throne room. Vathré's court noted the resemblance, though Marten had yet to spot his mother. He looked straight ahead at Evergard's lord.

Vathré stood and drew the Blade Fidora from its sheath. It glimmered like crystal, like the first light of morning, like tears. The lords and ladies glanced at each other, but did not set whispers spinning through the room. Biantha, too, kept silent: a word spoken false in the unsheathed sword's presence would cause it to weep or bleed; the magic had driven men and women mad, and no lord of Evergard used it lightly.

"I am trying to decide whether you are very thoughtless or very clever," Vathré said softly. "Who are you and why are you here?"

"I was the sword at the emperor's side," he answered, "and that sword was nameless." The pale-haired man closed his eyes, opened them. "My name is Marten. I came because the emperor has thousands of swords now, to do his bidding; and I no longer found that bidding to my taste."

Vathré glanced down at the Blade Fidora. Its color remained clear and true. "An interesting time to change your loyalties—if, indeed, they've changed. You might have found a better way to leave than by showing up here in full uniform, scaring the guards out of their wits."

"I left when the demons were . . . subduing a village," Marten said flatly. "I don't know the village's name. I hardly had time to find more suitable attire, my lord, and on campaign one dresses in uniform as a matter of course. To do otherwise would have aroused suspicion."

"And you weren't afraid of being caught and killed on the spot?" one of the advisers demanded.

He shrugged. "I was taught three spells in my training. One allowed me to walk unharmed through the palace wards. One calls fire from blood. And the last lets me pass by like the dream of a ghost."

Biantha glanced at the Blade Fidora and its unwavering light.

Lady Iastre coughed. "Forgive me if I'm less well-informed than I ought to be," she said, "and slow to react as well—but you mentioned being 'on campaign.' Is this a common thing, that 'the sword at the emperor's side' should be out in the field?"

Marten's eyes moved toward the source of the voice, and so he caught sight of Biantha. He inhaled sharply. Biantha felt her face freeze, though she longed to smile at the stranger her son had become. *Answer,* she wished him. *Say you've come to me after so many years—*

Marten gathered himself and said, "I came to warn you, if nothing else; death is a price I have taken from many." His voice shook, but he continued to face Vathré squarely. "The demon emperor has come, and your battles will be the harder for it." Then the whispers began, and even Iastre cast troubled eyes toward Biantha; the light of the Blade Fidora reflected all the shades of fear, all the colors of despair, that were voiced. "Please," Marten said, raising his voice but slightly, "let me help. My lord, I may be slow in learning that there is more to war than following orders. That there are people who die for their homes or their families—"

"Families," Biantha repeated, tasting bitterness. So calm, his face, like polished metal. She felt Iastre's hand on her arm and forced a smile.

The whispers had died down, and Marten faltered. "I know how the emperor thinks," he said at last. "Let me help you there, my lord, or have me killed. Either way, you will have taken the emperor's champion from him."

So pale, his face, like Fidora's light. Biantha caught her breath, waiting for Vathré to speak.

Lines of strain etched the lord's face as he left the throne to stand before Marten. "Will you swear fealty to the Watchlands and their lord, then?"

Marten did not flinch. "Yes."

Yes, echoed Biantha, doubt biting her heart. She had not known, when she first came to Evergard, what powers the Blade Fidora possessed. A magician-smith had died in its forging, that there might never again be a traitor like Lord Mière. Vathré had questioned Biantha, as he had just questioned Marten, and the first part of the sword's virtue had been plain to her, a mirror of spoken minds.

Only later had Vathré told her the second part, that a false oath sworn upon the sword killed the oath-taker. Once an heir to Evergard had sworn guardianship to the Watchlands and their people and fallen dead. Once a weary soldier had woken Evergard's lady three hours before dawn to confess a betrayal planned, and then committed suicide. Biantha had no desire to find her son the subject of another story, another song. How had Paienne felt, she wondered suddenly, when her father's treachery became part of the Nightbreak War's history?

Marten laid his hand upon the glass-clear blade. "I swear it." Then, swallowing, he looked directly at Biantha.

She could not bring herself to trust him, even after the long years, when he wore a uniform like his father's. This time, she did turn away.

"There's something sinful," said Iastre, fingers running round and round a captured draughts piece, "in sitting here playing a game when our world is falling apart."

Biantha smiled uncertainly and considered her options. "If I stayed in my room and fretted about it all the time, I should go mad." She nudged one of her pieces to a new square, musing on how the symmetry of the game—red on black, black on black—had soon been spoiled by their moves.

"I hear it was Marten's planning that kept the demons from overrunning Silverbridge so far."

She looked up and saw Iastre's worried expression. "A good thing, I suppose—especially considering that the emperor now has a personal reason for wanting to humble the Watchlands."

"Surely you don't think he should have stayed in the emperor's service," Iastre protested.

Oh, but he did once, Biantha did not say. "It's your move."

A snort. "Don't change the subject on me now. You fled the emperor's palace too, if you'll recall."

"Too well," she agreed. She had slept poorly the first few years at Evergard, hearing danger in the footfalls that passed by her door and dreaming of the emperor's serpent-eyed scepter upon her own shoulder. "But I left in a time of peace, and as terrible a crime as I had committed, I was only a human mathemagician. Besides,"—and Biantha drew in a shaky breath—"they knew they had my son: punishment enough."

Iastre shook her head and finally made her move. "He's here now, and he may be our only hope."

"That," she said, "is what worries me."

Even here, playing draughts, Biantha found no escape from Marten. She had spotted him once in the courtyard, sparring against Evergard's best soldiers while a healer and several enchanters looked on, lest the former champion seek a life instead of a touch. At mealtimes in the great hall she took to eating at the far end of the high table; yet over the clinking glasses and silverware, the tense voices and rustling clothes, Biantha heard Marten and Vathré speaking easily with each other. Evergard's lord trusted Marten—they all trusted Marten now, while she dared not.

Like a pendulum, her thoughts swung between her son and Paienne, her son and Lord Mière. Late at night, when she walked the battlements listening vainly for the footfalls of marching soldiers, feeling betrayal's cold hand in every tremor of the wind, she remembered tales of the Nightbreak War. Biantha had never put much faith in the minstrels' embellished ballads, but the poetry preyed upon her fears.

Working with fragments of history and the military reports that came in daily, she attempted to map past onto future, battle onto battle . . . betrayal onto betrayal. And failed, over and over. And cursed the Prophecy, staring at the worn and inscrutable pages, alone in her room. It was during one of those bouts that a familiar knocking startled her from her work.

Marten? thought Biantha involuntarily. But she had learned the rhythm of Vathré's tread, and when she opened the door she knew who waited behind it. The twin edges of relief and disappointment cut her heart.

The gray-haired man looked her up and down, and scowled. "I thought you might be overworking yourself again."

She essayed a smile, stepping aside so he could enter. "Overwork, my lord? Tell that to the soldiers who train, and fight, and die for it, or see their friends die for it. Tell that to the cook or the servants in the keep."

"There are ways and ways of work, my dear." He paced around the chamber, casting a curious eye over her bookcase and her cluttered desk, then rested a hand on her shoulder. "Perhaps I should come back later, when you've rested—and I do mean rest, not sitting in bed to read your books rather than sitting at your desk."

Biantha craned her head back to glance at him. "At least tell me why you came."

"Marten," he said bluntly, releasing her shoulder.

She flinched.

"You're hurting the boy," Vathré said. "He's been here quite a while and you haven't said a word to him."

She arched an eyebrow. "He's not the boy I left behind, my lord." Her voice nearly broke.

"I'm old enough to call you a girl, Lady Biantha. Don't quibble. Even I can't find cause to mistrust him, and the years have made me paranoid."

"Oh?" She ran her fingers over her copy of the Prophecy, worn smooth by years of on-and-off study. By all accounts, Marten's advice was sound—but the demons kept coming.

"I'm sending him to command at Silverbridge." Vathré shook his head. "We've held out as long as we can, but it looks like our efforts have been no more than a delaying action. I haven't told the council yet, but we're going to have to withdraw to Aultgard." He exhaled softly. "Marten will keep the demons occupied while the bulk of the army retreats."

Biantha stared at him.

"The soldiers are coming to trust him, you know," he remarked. "He's perhaps the best tactician Evergard has seen in the past couple generations, and I want to see if that trust is justified."

She closed her eyes and said, "A gamble, my lord. Wouldn't you do better to put someone else in charge?"

Vathré ignored her question. "I thought you should know before I announce it."

"Thank you, my lord." Biantha paused, then added, "Do you know where Marten might be at the moment?"

He smiled sadly. "Haunting the battlements, hoping you will stop by."

She bowed her head and, after he had left, went to search for her son. Biantha found him by the southern tower, a sword sheathed at his back. Even now it disconcerted her to see him in the dress of Evergard's soldiers, as if her mind refused to surrender that first image of Marten standing before the court in red and black and gold.

"Mother," he said, clasping his hands behind his back.

Slowly, reluctantly, she faced him. "I'm here."

Moonlight pooled in his eyes and glittered in the tears that streaked his face. "I remember," he said without accusation. "I was seven years old and you told me to pack. You were arguing with Father."

Biantha nodded. Marten had nearly reached the age where he would have to begin training as either a magician or a soldier, or forfeit what little protection his parents' status gave him. Over the years, as their son grew older, she spoke to her husband of leaving the demons' empire to seek refuge in the Watchlands or the realms further east. He always treated her kindly, without ever turning an eye to the courtesans—demon and human both—who served those the emperor favored.

Yet Biantha had never forgotten her husband's puzzlement, molting slowly into anger, that she should wish to leave a court that sheltered them, though it did nothing to shelter others. She could not reconcile herself to the demons' casual cruelty: one of the emperor's nieces sent, after an ill-advised duel, to redeem her honor by riding a horse to the mines of Sarmont and back, five days and back forcing a terrified beast to carry her. The pale-eyed assassin who had fallen from favor after killing the rebellious lady of Reis Keep, solely because he had left evidence of his work. Children drowned after a plague blinded them and clouded their wits. If anything, the demons were as cruel to each other as to the humans who lived among and below them, but Biantha had found less and less comfort in that knowledge.

"I stood in the doorway," Marten went on, "trying to understand. Then Father was weeping—"

She had said to her husband, *If you will not come, then I must go without you.*

"—and he drew his sword against you."

"And I killed him," Biantha said, dry-mouthed. "I tried to get you to come with me, but you wouldn't leave him. You started to cry. I had little time, and there were ever guards nearby, listening for anything amiss. So I went alone. It would have been my death to stay after murdering one of the emperor's officers. In the end, the emperor's trust meant more to him than you or I."

"Please don't leave me again," Marten whispered. He stood straight-backed in the darkness, the hilt of the sword at his back peering over his shoulder like a sleepy eye, but his face was taut. "I am leaving for Silverbridge tomorrow."

"Will you be at the forefront?"

"It would be unwise." His mouth tightened for a moment. "I will be giving orders."

"To kill." *And, perhaps, be killed,* she wanted to say, but the words fluttered in her throat.

Marten met her gaze calmly. "It is war, Mother."

"It is now," she agreed, "but it wasn't before. I know what it is to be the emperor's champion. 'The sword at the emperor's side,' you said. The others heard the words only; they have never lain awake and sleepless for memory of bloodstains on a pale rug, or because of the sudden, silenced cries at night. How many fell to your blade, Marten?"

"I came to follow you when I started losing count." His eyes were dry, now, though Biantha saw the shapes of pain stirring behind them. "When the numbers started slipping out of my grasp."

Biantha held silence before her like a skein of threads that wanted words to untangle it.

He lifted a hand, hesitated, let it drop. "I wanted to talk to you once, if never again. Before I go to Silverbridge where the demons await."

She smiled at him, then. But always the suspicion remained that he had some way of breaking his oath to Vathré, that the demon emperor had sent him to ensure the Watchlands' downfall through some subtle plan—or, more simply, that he had come to betray the mother he had abandoned, who had abandoned him; she no longer knew which.

"Go, then," said Biantha, neither promise nor peril in her voice, and left him to await dawn alone.

Four days later, Biantha stood before her bookcase, eyes roaming aimlessly over her collection of mathemagical works, some in the tight, angular script of the demon empire, others in the ornate writing common to the Watchlands' scholars. *There has to be something useful,* she told herself, even after having scoured everything that looked remotely relevant. Now, more than ever, she wished she had talent for another of the magical disciplines, which did not rely on memorized proofs or the vagaries of inspiration, though none of them had ever seemed to get far with the Prophecy.

Would that it were a straightforward problem—

Biantha froze. The Prophecy did not describe the idealized spaces with which she had grown accustomed to dealing, but the tangles of truth, the interactions of demons and humans, the snarls of cause and effect and relation. Even the astrologer admitted privately that his predictions, on occasion, failed spectacularly where people were involved. She had been trying to linearize the cantos: the wrong approach.

Evergard's treasurer had once teased her about the cost of paper, though she took care to waste as little as possible. She located a pile of empty sheets in a drawer and set them on her desk, opening her copy of the Prophecy to the first page. After a moment, Biantha also retrieved Sarielle's *Speculations, Spells and Stranger Sets*, sparing a glance for the 400-line poem in the back; Sarielle of Rix had fancied herself a poet. She had passed evenings lingering over the book's carefully engraved figures and diagrams, curves that Sarielle had labeled "pathological" for their peculiarities.

Symmetry. That which remained changeless. Red pieces upon black and black upon black at the start of a draughts match. A ballad that began and ended with the same sequence of measures; and now that Biantha turned her thoughts in this direction, she remembered a song that traveling minstrels had performed before the court, voice after voice braiding into a whole that imitated each part. Her image in the mirror. And now, Sarielle's pathological curves, where a segment of the proper proportion spawned yet more such segments.

Methodically, she went through the Prophecy, searching for these other symmetries, for the solution that had eluded her for so long. Late into the night, throat parched because she had drained her pitcher and dared not break her concentration by fetching another or calling a servant, Biantha placed *Speculations, Spells and Stranger Sets* to one side and thumbed through the appendix to Athique's *Infinities*. Athique and Sarielle, contemporaries, had been opposites as far as titles went. She reached the approximations of various shapes, sieves and flowers, ferns and laces, that no mortal hand could craft.

One page in particular struck her: shapes built from varying polygons with various "pathologies," as Athique dubbed them in what Biantha suspected had been a jab at Sarielle's would-be wordsmithing, repeating a procedure to the borders of infinity. The Prophecy harbored greater complexities, but she wondered if her solution might be one of many algorithms, many possibilities. Her eyes flooded: a lifetime's work that she had uncovered, explored briefly by mathemagicians before her, and she had little time in which to seek a solution that helped the Watchlands.

Even after she had snuffled the lamp and curled into bed, a headache devouring her brain, words still burned before her eyes: *Symmetry. Pathologies. Infinity.*

Only a few weeks later, Biantha found herself walking aimlessly down a corridor, freeing her mind from the Prophecy's tyrannous grip, when Lady Iastre shook her shoulder. "They're back, Biantha," she said hurriedly. "I thought you'd like to be there to greet them."

"Who's back?"

"Your son. And those who survived Silverbridge."

Those who survived. Biantha closed her eyes, shaking. "If only the demons would leave us alone—"

The other woman nodded sadly. "But it's not happening. The emperor will soon be at Evergard itself, is the news I've been hearing. Come on."

"I can't," she said, and felt as though the keep were spinning around her while pitiless eyes peered through the walls. "Tell him—tell Marten—I'm glad he's back." It was all she could think to say, a message for her son—a message that she would not deliver in person, because the urgency of the situation had jarred her thoughts back to the Prophecy.

"Biantha!" Iastre cried, too late to stop her.

In bits and pieces she learned the rest of the story, by eavesdropping benignly on dinner conversations and the servants' gossip. The emperor had indeed forsaken his court for the battlefield, perhaps because of

Evergard's stubborn resistance. None of this surprised her, except when a curly-haired herald mentioned the serpent-eyed scepter. To her knowledge that scepter had never left the empire—unless, and the thought sickened her, the demons had begun to consider Evergard part of their empire. It had turned Silverbridge, the shining bridge of ballad, into rust and tarnish, and even now the demons advanced.

Vathré gave a few permission to flee further east with their families, those whose presence mattered little to the coming siege. Others prepared to fight, or die, or both; the mock-battles that Biantha sometimes watched between the guards grew more grim, more intent. She and Iastre agreed that the time for draughts and rithmomachia had passed, as much as she would have welcomed the distraction.

As for Marten—she saw almost nothing of him except the terrible weariness that had taken up residence in his face, as though he had survived a torture past bearing. Biantha grieved for him as a mother; as a mathemagician, she had no comfort to offer, for her own helplessness threatened to overwhelm her. Perhaps he in his turn sensed this, and left her alone.

Day by day the demons came closer, to the point where she could stand on the battlements and see the baleful lights in the distance: the orange of campfires, the gold and silver of magefires. Day by day the discussions grew more frantic, more resigned.

At last, one morning, the horns blazed high and clear through the air, and the siege of Evergard began. Biantha took her place on the parapets without saying any farewells, though some had been said to her, and watched while archers fired into the demons' massed ranks. Not long after, magefire rolled over their hastily raised shields, and she prepared her own spells. Only when the demons began to draw back and prepare a second attack did she call upon powers that required meticulous proofs, held in her mind like the memory of a favorite song—or a child in her arms.

She gathered all the shapes of pain that afflicted the demons and twisted them into death. Red mists obscured her vision as the spell wrenched her own soul, sparing her the need to watch the enemy falling. Yet she would have to use the spell again and again before the demons' mathemagicians shaped a ward against it. Those who shared her art rarely ventured into battle, for this reason: it often took too long to create attacks or adapt to them. A theorem needed for a spell might take years to discover, or turn out to be impossible; and inspiration, while swift, was sometimes unreliable. She had seen mathemagicians die from careless assumptions in spellcasting.

By midday Biantha no longer noticed the newly fallen corpses. She leaned against the wall's cold stone—and glimpsed black and red and gold in the distance: the demon emperor, carrying the serpent-eyed scepter that she remembered too clearly. For a moment she thought of the Blade Fidora and cursed the Prophecy's inscrutable symmetry. "No," she whispered. Only if the emperor were certain of victory would he risk himself in the front lines, and a cold conviction froze her thoughts.

Marten. He's counting on Marten to help him.

She had to find Vathré and warn him. She knew where he would be and ran, despite the archers' protests that she endangered herself. "My lord!" she cried, grieving already, because she saw her fair-haired son beside gray-haired Vathré, directing the defense. "My lord! The emperor—" Biantha nearly tripped, caught herself, continued running.

Vathré turned, trusting her, and then it happened.

The emperor raised his scepter, and darkness welled forth to batter Evergard's walls. In the darkness, colors moved like the fire of dancing prisms; silence reigned for a second, strangely disturbing after the clamor of war. Then the emperor's spell ended, leaving behind more dead than the eye could count at a glance. Broken shapes, blood, weapons twisted into deadly metal flowers, a wind like the breath of disease.

Biantha stared disbelievingly over the destruction and saw that the demons who had stood in the spell's path had died as well; saw that the emperor had come forward to spare his own soldiers, not—she hoped not—because he knew he had a traitor in the Watchlanders' ranks. So much death, and all they had been able to do, she and the other magicians, was watch.

"Mercy," Vathré breathed.

"The scepter," Marten said harshly. "Its unspoken name is Decay."

She looked across at the gates and sneezed, dust stinging her nostrils. Already those who had fallen were rotting, flesh blackening and curling to reveal bone; Evergard's sturdy walls had become cracked and mottled.

Marten was shouting orders for everyone to abandon that section of wall before it crumbled. Then he looked at her and said, "We have to get down. Before it spreads. You too, my lord."

Vathré nodded curtly and offered Biantha his arm; Marten led the way down, across footing made newly treacherous. The walls whispered dryly behind them; she flinched at the crash as a crenel broke off and plummeted.

"—use that scepter again?" she heard the lord asking Marten as she concentrated on her footing.

"No," she and her son both said. Biantha continued, "Not so far from the seat of his power and without the blood sacrifices. Not against wood or stone. But a touch, against living flesh, is another matter."

They had reached safety of sorts with the others who had fled the crumbling section of wall. "What of the Prophecy?" Vathré asked her, grimacing as he cast his gaze over the morning's carnage.

"Prophecy?" Marten repeated, looking at them strangely.

Perhaps he had not heard, or failed to understand what he heard, in the brief time he had been at Evergard. Biantha doubted he had spent much time with the minstrels. At least he was not—she prayed not—a traitor, as she had thought at first. Breath coming hard, she looked around, listened to the cries of the wounded, and then, all at once, the answer came to her, one solution of several.

Perspective. Time and again she had brooded over the Prophecy and the second war it foretold. *The rhymes, the rhythms, the ambiguities,* she had said to Vathré not long ago. She had thought about the strange symmetry, the Nightbreak War's traitor—but failed to consider that, in the Prophecy's second war, the corresponding traitor might betray the demons. The demons, not the Watchlands.

Last time, Lord Mière had betrayed the Watchlands, and died at Paienne's hand—father and daughter, while Biantha and Marten were mother and son. But the mirror was imperfect, as the twisted symmetry already showed her. Marten did not have to die, and there was still hope for victory.

"The emperor is still down there," said Vathré quietly. "It seems that if someone were to stop him, we could hold the keep. Hold the keep, and have a chance of winning."

"A challenge," Biantha breathed, hardly aware that those around them were listening avidly, for on this hung Evergard's fate. "Challenge the emperor. He has his honor, strange as it may seem to us. He lost his champion; will he turn down an opportunity to slay, or be slain by, that champion?"

Had there been such a challenge in the Nightbreak War? The ballads, the histories, failed to say. No matter. They were not living a ballad, but writing their own lines to the song.

Vathré nodded, seeing the sense in her words; after all, she had lived in the demons' realm. Then he unfastened the sheath of his sword from his belt and held it out to Marten. "Take the sword," he said.

If she was wrong, giving the Blade Fidora to him was unrivaled folly. But they no longer had a choice, if they meant to take advantage of the Prophecy's tangled possibilities.

He blanched. "I can't. I don't even know who the heir is—" probably because Vathré *still* had not declared the succession. "I haven't the right."

Biantha gazed at the gates, now twisted into rusty skeins. The captain of the guard had rallied the remaining troops and was grimly awaiting the demons' advance.

The lord of Evergard said, exasperated, "I *give* you the right. This isn't the time for questions or self-recriminations. *Take the sword.*"

Resolutely, Marten accepted the Blade Fidora. He grasped the sword's hilt, and it came clear of the scabbard, shining faintly. "I'm sorry for what I have done in the past," he whispered, "even though that doesn't change what was done. Help me now."

"Hurry," said Biantha, guessing the battle's shape. "The emperor will soon come to claim his prize, *our* home, and you must be there to stop him." She stood on her toes and kissed him on the cheek: a mother's kiss, which she had not given him for too many years. She called to mind every protective spell she could think of and forged them together around him despite her exhaustion. "Go with my blessing." *And please come back to me.* After losing him once, Biantha did not mean to lose him again.

"And go with mine," Vathré echoed.

He ducked his head and moved away at a run. Shivering, Biantha tried to gather the strength for more magic against the demons, to influence the Prophecy in their favor. She felt as if she were a formula in an old book, a creature of faded ink and yellowed paper.

As she and Vathré watched, Marten shoved through the soldiers at the gate, pausing only to exchange a few words with some of his comrades. They parted for him, wondering that he and not Vathré held the Blade Fidora; Vathré waved at them in reassurance. Past the gates were the emperor and his elites, dressed in rich colors, standing in near-perfect formation.

"Traitor," said the emperor to Marten in the cool voice that had never revealed anything but mockery; demon and human both strained to hear him. "Do you think Evergard's blade will protect you?"

In answer Marten swung the sword toward the emperor's exposed throat, where veins showed golden through the translucent skin. The elites reacted by moving to surround him while the emperor brought his serpent-eyed scepter up in a parry. The soldiers of Evergard, in their turn, advanced in Marten's defense. Biantha felt a hysterical laugh forming: the soldiers of both sides looked as though they had choreographed their motions, like dancers.

Now, straining to see what was happening, she realized why the emperor had chosen her son for his champion. Several of the elites saw clearly the blows that would kill them, yet failed to counter in time. Yet her eyes were drawn to the emperor himself, and she sucked in her breath: the emperor appeared to be aiming at a woman who had crippled one of the elites, but Biantha saw the twist in the scepter's trajectory that would bring it around to strike Marten. Even a traitor champion could not survive a single touch of the scepter; it would weaken him beyond his ability to recover.

"Marten!" she screamed. He was all she had left of her old home and its decadent intrigues; of a man with gentle hands who had loved her within the narrow limits of court life; of her family. The emperor had stolen him from her for so long—

Mathemagical intuition launched her past the meticulous lemmas and lines of a proof, panic giving her thoughts a hawk's wings. Biantha spun one more spell. Symmetry: the emperor's attack became Marten's, in spaces too strange for the mind to imagine. The Blade Fidora went true to its target, while the scepter missed entirely, and it was the emperor's golden blood that showered Marten's hands.

I'm sorry for everything, Marten, thought Biantha, and folded out of consciousness.

The minstrels who survived the Siege of Evergard made into song the deaths, the desperation, the duel between the demon emperor and he who was now heir to the Watchlands. Biantha, for her part, listened and grieved in her own way for those who had died . . . for Mière's great-grandson. There was more to any story, she had learned, than what the minstrels remembered; and this was as true of herself, her husband, her son.

Biantha wrote only two lines in the margin of an unfinished book—a book of her own theorems.

There are too many shapes of love to be counted.
One of them is forgiveness.

It was a conjecture, not a proof, but Biantha knew its truth nonetheless. After the ink had dried, she left her room with its well-worn books and went to the great hall where Vathré and Iastre, and most especially Marten, expected her for dinner.

blue ink

It's harder than you thought, walking from the battle at the end of time and down a street that reeks of entropy and fire and spilled lives. Your eyes aren't dry. Neither is the alien sky. Your shoulders ache and your stomach hurts. *Blue woman, blue woman,* the chant runs through your head as you limp toward a portal's bright mouth. You're leaving, but you intend to return. You have allies yet.

Blue stands for many things at the end of time: for the forgotten, blazing blue stars of aeons past; the antithesis of redshift; the color of uncut veins beneath your skin.

This story is written in blue ink, although you do not know that yet.

Blue is more than a fortunate accident. Jenny Chang usually writes in black ink or pencil. She's been snowed in at her mom's house since yesterday and is dawdling over physics homework. Now she's out of lead. The only working pen in the house is blue.

"We'll go shopping the instant the roads are clear," her mom says.

Jenny mumbles something about how she hates homework over winter break. Actually, she isn't displeased. There's something neatly alien about all those equations copied out in blue ink, problems and their page numbers. It's as if blue equations come from a different universe than the ones printed in the textbook.

While her mom sprawls on the couch watching TV, Jenny pads upstairs to the guest room and curls up in bed next to the window. Fingers of frost cover the glass. With her index finger, Jenny writes a list of numbers: pi, H_0 for Hubble's constant, her dad's cellphone number, her school's zip code. Then she wipes the window clear of mist, and shivers. Everything outside is almost blue-rimmed in the twilight.

Jenny resumes her homework, biting her nails between copying out answers to two significant figures and doodling spaceships in the margins. There's a draft from the window, but that's all right. Winter's child that she is—February 16, to be exact—Jenny thinks better with a breath of cold.

Except, for a moment, the draft is hot like a foretaste of hell. Jenny stops still. All the frost has melted and is running in rivulets down the glass. And there's a face at the window.

The sensible thing to do would be to scream. But the face is familiar, the way equations in blue are familiar. It could be Jenny's own, five ragged years in the future. The woman's eyes are dark and bleak, asking for help without expecting it.

"Hold on," Jenny says. She goes to the closet to grab her coat. From downstairs, she hears her mom laughing at some TV witticism.

Then Jenny opens the window, and the world falls out. This doesn't surprise her as much as it should. The wind shrieks and the cold hits her like a fist. It's too bad she didn't put on her scarf and gloves while she was at it.

The woman offers a hand. She isn't wearing gloves. Nor is she shivering. Maybe extremes of temperature don't mean the same thing in blue universes. Maybe it's normal to have blue-tinted lips, there. Jenny doesn't even wear make-up.

The woman's touch warms Jenny, as though they've stepped into a bubble of purloined heat. Above them, stars shine in constellations that Jenny recognizes from the ceiling of her father's house, the ones Mom and Dad helped her put up when she was in third grade. Constellations with names like Fire Truck and Ladybug Come Home, constellations that you won't find in any astronomer's catalogue.

Jenny looks at her double and raises an eyebrow, because any words she could think of would emerge frozen, like the world around them. She wonders where that hell-wind came from and if it has a name.

"The end of the world is coming," the blue woman says. Each syllable is crisp and certain.

I don't believe in the end of the world, Jenny wants to say, except she's read her physics textbook. She's read the sidebar about things like the sun swelling into a red giant and the universe's heat-death. She looks up again, and maybe she's imagining it, but these stars are all the wrong colors, and they're either too bright or not bright enough. Instead, Jenny asks, "Are my mom and dad going to be okay?"

"As okay as anyone else," the blue woman says.

"What can I do?" She can no more doubt the blue woman than she can doubt the shape of the sun.

This earns her a moment's smile. "There's a fight," the blue woman says, "and everyone fell. Everyone fell." She says it the second time as though things might change, as though there's a magic charm for reversing the course of events. "I'm the only one left, because I can walk through possibilities. Now there's you."

They set off together. A touch at her elbow tells Jenny to turn left. There's a bright flash at the corner of her eyes. Between one blink and the next, they're standing in a devastated city, crisscrossed by skewed bridges made of something brighter than steel, more brilliant than glass.

"Where are we?" Jenny asks.

"We're at humanity's last outpost," the blue woman says. "Tell me what you see."

"Rats with red eyes and metal hands," Jenny says just as one pauses to stare at her. It stands up on its hind feet and makes a circle-sign at her with one of its hands, as if it's telling her things will be all right. Then it scurries into the darkness. "Buildings that go so high up I can't see their tops, and bridges between them. Flying cars." They come in every color, these faraway cars, every color but blue. Jenny begins to stammer under the weight of detail: "Skeletons wrapped in silver wires"—out of the corner of her eye, she thinks she sees one twitch, and decides she'd rather not know—"and glowing red clocks on the walls that say it's midnight even though there's light in the sky, and silhouettes far away, like people except their joints are all wrong."

And the smells, too, mostly smoke and ozone, as though everything has been burned away by fire and lightning, leaving behind the ghost-essence of a city, nothing solid.

"What you see isn't actually there," the blue woman says. She taps Jenny's shoulder again.

They resume walking. The only reason Jenny doesn't halt dead in her tracks is that she's afraid that the street will crumble into pebbles, the pebbles into dust, and leave her falling through eternity the moment she stops.

The blue woman smiles a little. "Not like that. Things are very different at the end of time. Your mind is seeing a translation of everything into more familiar terms."

"What are we doing here?" Jenny asks. "I—I don't know how to fight. If it's that kind of battle." She draws mini-comics in the margins of her notes sometimes, when the teachers think she's paying attention. Sometimes, in the comics, she wields two mismatched swords, and sometimes a gun; sometimes she has taloned wings, and sometimes she rides in a starship sized perfectly for one. She fights storm-dragons and equations turned into sideways alien creatures. (If pressed, she will admit the influence of *Calvin and Hobbes*.) But unless she's supposed to brain someone with the flute she didn't think to bring (she plays in the school band), she's not going to be any use in a fight, at least not the kind of fight that happens at the end of time. Jenny's mom made her take a self-defense class two years ago, before the divorce, and mostly what Jenny remembers is the floppy-haired instructor saying, *If someone pulls a gun on you and asks for your wallet, give him your wallet. You are not an action hero.*

The blue woman says, "I know. I wanted a veteran of the final battles"— she says it without disapproval—"but they all died, too."

This time Jenny does stop. "You brought them here to die."

The woman lifts her chin. "I wouldn't have done that. I showed them the final battle, the very last one, and they chose to fight. We're going there now, so you can decide."

Jenny read the stories where you travel back in time and shoot someone's grandfather or step on some protozoan, and the act unravels the present stitch by stitch until all that's left is a skein of history gone wrong. "Is that such a good idea?" she asks.

"They won't see us. We won't be able to affect anything."

"I don't even have a weapon," Jenny says, thinking of the girl in the mini-comics with her two swords, her gun. Jenny is tolerably good at arm-wrestling her girl friends at high school, but she doesn't think that's going to help.

The woman says, "That can be changed."

Not *fixed*, as though Jenny were something wrong, but *changed*. The word choice is what makes her decide to keep going. "Let's go to the battle," Jenny says.

The light in the sky changes as they walk, as though all of winter were compressed into a single day of silver and grey and scudding darkness. Once or twice, Jenny could almost swear that she sees a flying car change shape, growing wings like that of a delta kite and swooping out of sight. There's soot in the air, subtle and unpleasant, and Jenny wishes for sunglasses, even though it's not all that bright, any sort of protection. Lightning runs along the streets like a living thing, writing jagged blue-white equations. It keeps its distance, however.

"It's just curious," the blue woman says when Jenny asks about it. She doesn't elaborate.

The first sign of the battle, although Jenny doesn't realize it for a while, is the rain. "Is the rain real?" Jenny says, wondering what future oddity would translate into inclement weather.

"Everything's an expression of some reality."

That probably means *no*. Especially since the rain is touching everything in the world except them.

The second sign is all the corpses, and this she does recognize. The stench hits her first. It's not the smell of meat, or formaldehyde from 9th grade biology (she knows a fresh corpse shouldn't smell like formaldehyde, but that's the association her brain makes), but asphalt and rust and fire. She would have expected to hear something first, like the deafening chatter of guns. Maybe fights in the future are silent.

Then she sees the fallen. Bone-deep, she knows which are *ours* and which are *theirs*. *Ours* are the rats with the clever metal hands, their fingers twisted beyond salvage; the sleek bicycles (bicycles!) with broken spokes, reflectors flashing crazily in the lightning; the men and women in coats the color of winter rain, red washing away from their wounds. The blue woman's breath hitches as though she's seeing this for the first time, as though each body belongs to an old friend. Jenny can't take in all the raw death. The rats grieve her the most, maybe because one of them greeted her in this place of unrelenting strangeness.

Theirs are all manner of things, including steel serpents, their scales etched with letters from an alphabet of despair; stilt-legged robots with guns for arms; more men and women, in uniforms of all stripes, for at the evening of the world there will be people fighting for entropy as well as against it. Some of them are still standing, and written in their faces— even the ones who don't *have* faces—is their triumph.

Jenny looks at the blue woman. The blue woman continues walking, so Jenny keeps pace with her. They stop before one of the fallen, a dark-skinned man. Jenny swallows and eyes one of the serpents, which is swaying next to her, but it takes no notice of her.

"He was so determined that we should fight, whatever the cost," the blue woman says. "And now he's gone."

There's a gun not far from the fallen man's hand. Jenny reaches for it, then hesitates, waiting for permission. The blue woman doesn't say yes, doesn't say no, so Jenny touches it anyway. The metal is utterly cold. Jenny pulls her fingers away with a bitten-off yelp.

"It's empty," the blue woman says. "Everything's empty."

"I'm sorry," Jenny says. She doesn't know this man, but it's not about her.

The blue woman watches as Jenny straightens, leaving the gun on the ground.

"If I say no," Jenny says slowly, "is there anyone else?"

The blue woman's eyes close for a moment. "No. You're the last. I would have spared you the choice if I could have."

"How many of me were there?"

"I lost count after a thousand or so," the blue woman says. "Most of them were more like me. Some of them were more like you."

A thousand Jenny Changs, a thousand blue women. More. Gone, one by one, like a scatterfall of rain. "Did all of them say yes?" Jenny asks.

The blue woman shakes her head.

"And none of the ones who said yes survived."

"None of them."

"If that's the case," Jenny says, "what makes you special?"

"I'm living on borrowed possibilities," she says. "When the battle ends, I'll be gone too, no matter which way it ends."

Jenny looks around her, then squeezes her eyes shut, thinking. *Two significant figures,* she thinks inanely. "Who started the fight?" She's appalled that she sounds like her mom.

"There's always an armageddon around the corner," the blue woman says. "This happens to be the one that *he* found."

The dark-skinned man. Who was he, that he could persuade people to take a last stand like this? Maybe it's not so difficult when a last stand is the only thing left. That solution displeases her, though.

Her heart is hammering. "I won't do it," Jenny says. "Take me home."

The blue woman's eyes narrow. "You are the last," she says quietly. "I thought you would understand."

Everything hinges on one thing: is the blue woman different enough from Jenny that Jenny can lie to her, and be believed?

"I'm sorry," Jenny says.

"Very well," the blue woman says.

Jenny strains to keep her eyes open at the crucial moment. When the blue woman reaches for her hand, Jenny sees the portal, a shimmer of blue light. She grabs the blue woman and shoves her through. The last thing Jenny hears from the blue woman is a muffled protest.

Whatever protection the blue woman's touch afforded her is gone. The rain drenches her shirt and runs in cold rivulets through her hair, into her eyes, down her back. Jenny reaches again for the fallen man's gun. It's cold, but she has a moment's warmth in her yet.

She might not be able to save the world, but she can at least save herself.

It's the end of the school day and you're waiting for Jenny's mother to pick you up. A man walks up to you. He wears a coat as grey as rain, and his eyes are pale against dark skin. "You have to come with me," he says, awkward and serious at once. You recognize him, of course. You remember when he first recruited you, in another timeline. You remember what he looked like fallen in the battle at the end of time, with a gun knocked out of his hand.

"I can't," you say, kindly, because it will take him time to understand that you're not the blue woman anymore, that you won't do the things the blue woman did.

"What?" he says. "Please. It's urgent." He knows better than to grab your arm. "There's a battle—"

Once upon a time, you listened to his plea. Part of you is tempted to listen this time around, to abandon the life that Jenny left you and take up his banner. But you know how that story ends.

"I'm not in your story anymore," you explain to him. "You're in mine."

The man doesn't look like he belongs in a world of parking tickets and potted begonias and pencil sharpeners. But he can learn, the way you have.

the battle of candle arc

General Shuos Jedao was spending his least favorite remembrance day with Captain-magistrate Rahal Korais. There was nothing wrong with Korais except that he was the fangmoth's Doctrine officer, and even then he was reasonable for a Rahal. Nevertheless, Doctrine observed remembrances with the ranking officer, which meant that Jedao had to make sure he didn't fall over.

Next time, Jedao thought, wishing the painkillers worked better, *I have to get myself assassinated on a planet where they do the job right.*

The assassin had been a Lanterner, and she had used a shattergun. She had caught him at a conference, of all places. The shattergun had almost sharded Jedao into a hundred hundred pieces of ghostwrack. Now, when Jedao looked at the icelight that served as a meditation focus, he saw anywhere from three to eight of them. The effect would have been charming if it hadn't been accompanied by stabbing pains in his head.

Korais was speaking to him.

"Say again?" Jedao said. He kept from looking at his wristwatch.

"I'll recite the next verses for you, sir, if that doesn't offend you," Korais said.

Korais was being diplomatic. Jedao couldn't remember where in the litany they were. Under better circumstances he would have claimed that he was distracted by the fact that his force of eleven fangmoths was being pursued by the Lanterners who had mauled the rest of the swarm, but it came down to the injuries.

"I'd be much obliged, Captain," Jedao said.

This remembrance was called the Feast of Drownings. The Rahal heptarch, whose faction maintained the high calendar and who set

Doctrine, had declared it three years back, in response to a heresy in one of the heptarchate's larger marches. Jedao would have called the heresy a benign one. People who wanted the freedom to build shrines to their ancestors, for pity's sake. But the Rahal had claimed that this would upset the high calendar's master equations, and so the heretics had had to be put down.

There were worse ways to die than by having your lungs slowly filled with caustic fluid. That still didn't make it a good way to die.

Korais had begun his recital. Jedao looked at the icelight on the table in front of them. It had translucent lobes and bronchi and alveoli, and light trickled downward through them like fluid, pale and blue and inexorable.

The heptarchate's exotic technologies depended on the high calendar's configurations: the numerical concordances, the feasts and remembrances, the associated system of belief. The mothdrive that permitted fast travel between star systems was an exotic technology. Few people advocated a switch in calendars. Too much would have to be given up, and invariant technologies, which worked under any calendar, never seemed to keep up. Besides, any new calendar would be subject to the same problem of lock-in; any new calendar would be regulated by the Rahal, or by people like the Rahal, as rigorously as the current one.

It was a facile argument, and one that Jedao had always disliked.

"Sir," Korais said, breaking off at the end of a phrase, "you should sit."

"I'm supposed to be standing for this," Jedao said dryly.

"I don't think your meditations during the next nineteen minutes are going to help if you fall unconscious."

He must look awful if Doctrine was telling him how long until the ordeal was over. Not that he was going to rest afterward. He had to figure out what to do about the Lanterners.

It wasn't that Jedao minded being recalled from medical leave to fight a battle. It wasn't even that he minded being handed this sad force of eleven fangmoths, whose morale was shredded after General Kel Najhera had gotten herself killed. It was that the heptarchate had kept the Lanterners as clients for as long as he remembered. Now the Lanterners were demanding regional representation, and they were at war with the heptarchate.

The Lanterner assassin had targeted Jedao during the Feast of Falcon's Eye. If she had succeeded, the event would have spiked the high calendar in the Lanterners' favor. Then they would have declared a remembrance in their own, competing calendar. The irony was that Jedao wasn't sure he disagreed with the Lanterners' grievances against the heptarchate, which they had broadcast everywhere after their victory over Najhera.

Korais was still looking at him. Jedao went to sit down, which was difficult because walking in a straight line took all of his concentration. Sitting down also took concentration. It wasn't worth pretending that he heard the last remembrance verses.

"It's over, sir," Korais said. "I'll leave you to your duties." He saluted and let himself out.

Jedao looked at his watch after the door hissed shut. Everything on it was too tiny to read the way his vision was. He made his computer enlarge its time display. Korais had left at least seven minutes early, an astonishing concession considering his job.

Jedao waited until the latest wave of pain receded, then brought up a visual of Candle Arc, a battledrift site nine days out from their present position and eleven days out from the Lanterners' last reported position. The battle had taken place 177 years ago, between two powers that had since been conquered. The heptarchate called the battle Candle Arc because of the bridge of lights that wheeled through the scatter-hell of what had once been a fortress built from desiccated suns, and the remnants of warmoths. The two powers probably had called their battle something else, and their moths wouldn't have been called moths either, and their calendars were dead except in records held locked by the Rahal.

Some genius had done up the image in shades of Kel gold, even though a notation gave the spectrum shift for anyone who cared. Jedao was fond of the Kel, who were the heptarchate's military faction. For nearly twenty years he had been seconded to their service, and they had many virtues, but their taste in ornamentation was gaudy. Their faction emblem was the ashhawk, the bird that burned in its own glory, all fire and ferocity. The Shuos emblem was the ninefox, shapeshifter and trickster. The Kel called him the fox general, but they weren't always being complimentary.

The bridgelights swam in and out of focus. Damnation. This was going to take forever. After pulling up maps of the calendrical terrain, he got the computer algebra system to tell him what the estimated shifts looked like in pictures. Then he sent a summons to the moth commander.

He knew how long it took to get from the moth's command center to his quarters. The door chimed at him with commendable promptness.

"Come in," Jedao said.

The door opened. "You wished to see me, sir," said Kel Menowen, commander of the *Fortune Travels in Fours*. She was a stocky woman with swan-black hair and unsmiling eyes. Like all Kel, she wore black gloves; Jedao himself wore fingerless gloves. Her salute was so correct that he wanted to find an imperfection in her fist, or the angle of her arm.

Jedao had chosen the *Fortune* as his command moth not because it was the least damaged after Najhera's death, which it wasn't, but because Menowen had a grudge against the Shuos. She was going to be the hardest commander to win over, so he wanted to do it in person.

The tired joke about the Kel was that they were strong, loyal, and stupid, although they weren't any more prone to stupidity than the other factions.

The tired joke about the Shuos, who specialized in information operations, was that they had backstabbing quotas. Most of the other factions had reasonable succession policies for their heptarchs. The Rahal heptarch appointed a successor from one of the senior magistrates.

With the Kel, it was rank and seniority. The Shuos policy was that if you could keep the heptarch's seat, it was yours. The other tired joke was that the infighting was the only reason the Shuos weren't running the heptarchate.

One of Menowen's aunts had died in a Shuos scheme, an assassin getting careless with secondary casualties. Jedao had already been in Kel service at the time, but it was in his public record that he had once been Shuos infantry, where "Shuos infantry" was a euphemism for "probably an assassin." In his case, he had been a very good assassin.

Menowen was still standing there. Jedao approximated a return salute. "At ease," he said. "I'd stand, but 'up' and 'down' are difficult concepts, which is distressing when you have to think in three dimensions."

Menowen's version of at ease looked stiff. "What do you require, sir?"

They had exchanged few words since he boarded her moth because he had barely been functional. She wasn't stupid. She knew he was on her moth to make sure she behaved, and he had no doubt her behavior would be exemplary. She also probably wanted to know what the plan was.

"What do you think I require?" Jedao asked. Sometimes it helped to be direct.

Menowen's posture became more stiff. "It hasn't escaped my notice that you only gave move orders as far as the Haussen system," she said. "But that won't take us near any useful support, and I thought our orders were to retreat." She was overenunciating on top of telling him things he knew, which meant that at some point she was going to tell him he wasn't fit for duty. Some Kel knew how to do subtlety. Menowen had an excellent service record, but she didn't strike him as a subtle Kel.

"You're reading the sane, sensible thing into our orders," Jedao said. "Kel Command was explicit. They didn't use the word 'retreat' anywhere." An interesting oversight on their part. The orders had directed him to ensure that the border shell guarding the Glover Marches was secured by any means possible.

"Retreat is the only logical response," Menowen said. "Catch repairs if possible, link up with Twin Axes." The Twin Axes swarm was on patrol along the Taurag border, and was the nearest Kel force of any size. "Then we'd have a chance against the heretics."

"You're discounting some alternatives," Jedao said.

Menowen lifted her chin and glared at him, or possibly at his insignia, or at the ink painting over his shoulder. "Sir," she said, "if you're contemplating fighting them with our present resources—" She stopped, tried again. The second try was blunter. "Your injuries have impaired your judgment and you ought to—"

"—let the senior moth commander make the sane, sensible decision to run for help?" Jedao flexed his hands. He had a clear memory of an earlier conversation with Commander Kel Chau, specifically the pinched look around Chau's eyes. Chau probably thought running was an excellent idea. "I had considered it. But it's not necessary. I've looked at the calendrical terrain. We can win this."

Menowen was having a Kel moment. She wanted to tell him off, but it wasn't just that he outranked her, it was that Kel Command had pulled him off medical leave to put him in charge, instead of evacuating him from the front. "Sir," she said, "I was *there*. The Lanterners have a swarm of at least sixty moths. They will have reinforcements. I shouldn't have to tell you any of this."

"How conscientious of you," Jedao said. Her eyes narrowed, but she didn't take the bait. "Did you think I had some notion of slugging it out toe-to-toe? That would be stupid. But I have been reviewing the records, and I understand the Lanterner general's temperament. Which is how we're going to defeat the enemy, unless you defeat yourself before they have a chance to."

Menowen's mouth pressed thin. "I understand you have never lost a battle," she said.

"This isn't the—"

"If it's about your fucking reputation—"

"Fox and hound, not this whole thing again," Jedao snapped. Which was unfair of him because it was her first time bringing it up, even if everyone else did. "Sooner or later everyone loses. I get it. If it made more sense to stop the Lanterners in the Glovers, I'd be doing it." This would also mean ceding vast swathes of territory to them, not anyone's first choice; from her grim expression, she understood that. "If I could stop the Lanterners by calling them up for a game of cards, I'd do that too. Or by, I don't know, offering them my right arm. But I'm telling you, this can be done, and I am not quitting if there's a chance. Am I going to have to fight you to prove it?"

This wasn't an idle threat. It wouldn't be the first time he had dueled a Kel, although it would be frivolous to force a moth commander into a duel, however non-lethal, at a time like this.

Menowen looked pained. "Sir, you're *wounded*."

He could think of any number of ways to kill her before she realized she was being attacked, even in his present condition, but most of them depended on her trust that her commanding officer wouldn't pull such a stunt.

"We can do this," Jedao said. He was going to have to give this speech to the other ten moth commanders, who were jumpy right now. Might as well get in practice now. "All the way to the Haussen system, it looks like we're doing the reasonable thing. But we're going to pay a call on the Rahal outpost at Smokewatch 33-67." That wasn't going to be a fun conversation, but most Rahal were responsive to arguments that involved preserving their beloved calendar. And right now, he was the only one in position to stop the Lanterners from arrowing right up to the Glover Marches. The perfect battle record that people liked to bludgeon him over the head with might even come in handy for persuasion.

"I'm listening," Menowen said in an unpromising voice.

It was good, if inconvenient, when a Kel thought for herself. Unlike a number of the officers on this moth, Menowen didn't react to Jedao like a cadet fledge.

"Two things," Jedao said. "First, I know remembering the defeat is painful, but if I'm reading the records correctly, the first eight Kel moths to go down, practically simultaneously, included two scoutmoths."

"Yes, that's right," Menowen said. She wasn't overenunciating anymore. "The Lanterners' mothdrive formants were distorted just enough to throw our scan sweep, so they saw us first."

"Why would they waste time killing scoutmoths when they could blow up fangmoths or arrowmoths instead? If you look at their positions and ours, they had better available targets." He had to be careful about criticizing a dead general, but there was no avoiding it. Najhera had depended too much on exotics and hadn't made adequate use of invariant defenses. The Kel also hadn't had time to channel any useful formation effects, their specialty. "The scoutmoths weren't out far enough to give advance notice, and surprise was blown once the Lanterners fried those eight moths. What I'm getting at is that our scan may not be able to tell the difference between mothdrives on big scary things and mothdrives on mediocre insignificant things, but their scan can't either, or they would have picked better targets."

Menowen was starting to look persuaded. "What are you going to do, sir? Commandeer civilian moths and set them to blow?" She wasn't able to hide her distaste for the idea.

"I'd prefer to avoid involving civilians," Jedao said coolly. Her unsmiling eyes became a little less unsmiling when he said that. "The Rahal run the show, they can damn well spare me some engines glued to tin cans."

The pain hit him like a spike to the eyes. When he could see again, Menowen was frowning. "Sir," she said, "one thing and I'll let you continue your deliberations in private." This was Kel for *please get some fucking rest before you embarrass us by falling over.* "You had some specific plan for punching holes into the Lanterners?"

"Modulo the fact that something always goes wrong after you wave hello at the enemy? Yes."

"That will do it for me, sir," Menowen said. "Not that I have a choice in the matter."

"You always have a choice," Jedao said. "It's just that most of them are bad."

She didn't look as though she understood, but he hadn't expected her to.

Jedao would have authorized more time for repairs if he could, but they kept receiving reports on the Lanterners' movements and time was one of the things they had little of. He addressed his moth commanders on the subject to reassure them that he understood their misgivings. Thankfully, Kel discipline held.

For that matter, Jedao didn't like detouring to Smokewatch 33-67 afterward, but he needed a lure, and this was the best place to get it. The conversation with the Rahal magistrate in charge almost wasn't a conversation. Jedao felt as though he was navigating through a menu of options rather than interacting with a human being. Some of the Rahal liked to cultivate that effect. At least Rahal Korais wasn't one of them.

"This is an unusual request for critical Rahal resources, General," the magistrate was saying.

This wasn't a no, so Jedao was already ahead. "The calendrical lenses are the best tool available," he said. "I will need seventy-three of them."

Calendrical lenses were Doctrine instruments mounted on mothdrives. Their sole purpose was to focus the high calendar in contested areas. It was a better idea in theory than practice, since radical heresies rapidly knocked them out of alignment, but the Rahal bureaucracy was attached to them. Typical Rahal, trusting an idea over cold hard experience. At least there were plenty of the things, and the mothdrives ought to be powerful enough to pass on scan from a distance.

Seventy-three was crucial because there were seventy-three moths in the Kel's Twin Axes swarm. The swarm was the key to the lure, just not in the way that Commander Menowen would have liked. It was barely possible, if Twin Axes set out from the Taurag border within a couple days' word of Najhera's defeat, for it to reach Candle Arc when Jedao planned on being there. It would also be inadvisable for Twin Axes to do so, because their purpose was to prevent the Taurags from contesting that border. Twin Axes wouldn't leave such a gap in heptarchate defenses without direct orders from Kel Command.

However, no one had expected the Lanterners to go heretical so suddenly. Kel Command had been known to panic, especially under Rahal pressure. And Rahal pressure was going to be strong after Najhera's defeat.

"Do you expect the lens vessels to be combat-capable?" the magistrate asked without any trace of sarcasm.

"I need them to sit there and look pretty in imitation of a Kel formation," Jedao said. "They'll get the heretics' attention, and if they can shift some of the calendrical terrain in our favor, even better." Unlikely, he'd had the Kel run the numbers for him, but it sounded nice. "Are volunteers available?"

Also unlikely. The advantage of going to the Rahal rather than some other faction, besides their susceptibility to the plea, was that the Rahal were disciplined. Even if they weren't going to be volunteers. If he gave instructions, the instructions would be rigorously carried out.

The magistrate raised an eyebrow. "That's not necessary," he said. "I'm aware of your skill at tactics, General. I assume you will spare the lenses' crews from unnecessary harm."

Touching. "I am grateful for your assistance, Magistrate," Jedao said.

"Serve well, General. The lenses will join your force at—" He named a time, which was probably going to be adhered to, then ended the communication.

The lenses joined within eight minutes and nineteen seconds of the given time. Jedao wished there were some way to minimize their scan shadow, but Kel moths did that with formations, and the Rahal couldn't generate Kel formation effects.

Jedao joined Menowen at the command center even though he should have rested. Menowen's mouth had a disapproving set. The rest of the Kel looked grim. "Sir," Menowen said. "Move orders?"

He took his chair and pulled up the orders on the computer. "False formation for the Rahal as shown. Follow the given movement plan," he said. "Communications, please convey the orders to all Rahal vessels." It was going to take extra time for the Rahal to sort themselves out, since they weren't accustomed to traveling in a fake formation, but he wasn't going to insult them by saying so.

Menowen opened her mouth. Jedao stared at her. She closed her mouth, looking pensive.

"Communications," Jedao said, "address to all units. Exclude the Rahal."

It wasn't the first speech he'd given on the journey, but the time had come to tell his commanders what they were up to and brace them for the action to come.

The Communications officer said, "It's open, sir."

"This is General Shuos Jedao to all moths," he said. "It's not a secret that we're being pursued by a Lanterner swarm. We're going to engage them at Candle Arc. Due to the Lanterners' recent victory, cascading effects have shifted the calendrical terrain there. The Lanterners are going to be smart and take one of the channels with a friendly gradient to their tech most of the way in. Ordinarily, a force this small wouldn't be worth their time. But because of the way the numbers have rolled, Candle Arc is a calendrical choke: we're arriving on the Day of Broken Feet. Whoever wins there will shift the calendar in their favor. When we offer battle, they'll take us up on it."

He consoled himself that, if the Lanterners lost, their soldiers would fall to fire and metal, honest deaths in battle, and not as calendrical foci, by having filaments needled into their feet to wind their way up into the brain.

"You are Kel," Jedao went on. "You have been hurt. I promise you we will hurt them back. But my orders will be exact, and I expect them to be followed exactly. Our chances of victory depend on this. I am not unaware of the numbers. But battle isn't just about numbers. It's about will. And you are Kel; in this matter you will prevail."

The panel lit up with each moth commander's acknowledgment. Kel gold against Kel black.

They didn't believe him, not yet. But they would follow orders, and that was all he needed.

Commander Menowen asked to see him in private afterward, as Jedao had thought she might. Her mouth was expressive. Around him she was usually expressing discontent. But it was discontent for the right reasons.

"Sir," Menowen said. "Permission to discuss the battle plan."

"You can discuss it all you like," Jedao said. "I'll say something if I have something to say."

"Perhaps you had some difficulties with the computer algebra system," she said. "I've run the numbers. We're arriving 4.2 hours before the terrain flips in our favor."

"I'm aware of that," Jedao said.

The near side of the choke locus was obstructed by a null region where no exotic technologies would function. But other regions around the null shifted according to a schedule. The far side of the choke periodically favored the high calendar. With Najhera's defeat, the far side would also shift sometimes toward the Lanterners' calendar.

"I don't understand what you're trying to achieve," Menowen said.

"If you don't see it," Jedao said, pleased, "the Lanterners won't see it either."

To her credit, she didn't ask if this was based on an injury-induced delusion, although she clearly wanted to. "I expect Kel Command thinks you'll pull off a miracle," she said.

Jedao's mouth twisted. "No, Kel Command thinks a miracle would be very nice, but they're not holding their breath, and as a Shuos I'm kind of expendable. The trouble is that I keep refusing to die."

It was like the advice for learning the game of pattern-stones: the best way to get good was to play difficult opponents, over and over. The trouble with war was that practicing required people to die.

"You've done well for your armies, sir. But the enemy general is also good at using calendrical terrain, and they've demonstrated their ruthlessness. I don't see why you would pass up a terrain advantage."

Jedao cocked an eyebrow at her. "We're not. Everyone gets hypnotized by the high fucking calendar. Just because it enables our exotics doesn't mean that the corresponding terrain is the most favorable to our purpose. I've been reading the intel on Lanterner engineering. Our invariant drives are better than theirs by a good margin. Anyway, why the hell would they be so stupid as to engage us in terrain that favors us? I picked the timing for a reason. You keep trying to beat the numbers, Commander, when the point is to beat the *people*."

Menowen considered that. "You are being very patient with my objections," she said.

"I need you not to freeze up in the middle of the battle," Jedao said. "Although I would prefer for you to achieve that without my having to explain basics to you."

The insult had the desired effect. "I understand my duty," she said. "Do you understand yours?"

He wondered if he could keep her. Moth commanders who were willing to question him were becoming harder to find. His usual commanders would have had no doubts about his plan no matter how much he refused to explain in advance.

"As I see it," Jedao said, "my duty is to carry out the orders. See? We're not so different after all. If that's it, Commander, you should get back to work."

Menowen saluted him and headed for the door, then swung around. "Sir," she said, "why did you choose to serve with the Kel? I assume it was a choice." The Shuos were ordinarily seconded to the Kel as intelligence officers.

"Maybe," Jedao said, "it was because I wanted to know what honor looked like when it wasn't a triumphal statue."

Her eyes went cold. "That's not funny," she said.

"I wasn't being funny," he said quietly. "I will never be a Kel. I don't think like one of you. But sometimes that's an advantage."

She drew in a breath. "Sir," she said, "I just want to know that this isn't some Shuos game to you." That he wasn't being clever for the sake of being clever; that he wouldn't throw his soldiers' lives away because he was overeager to fight.

Jedao's smile was not meant to reassure her. "Oh, it's to your advantage if it's a game," he said. "I am very good at winning games."

He wasn't going to earn her loyalty by hiding his nature, so he wasn't going to try.

It was even easier to win games if you designed the game yourself, instead of playing someone else's, but that was a Shuos sort of discussion and he didn't think she wanted to hear it yet.

The eleven fangmoths and seventy-three calendrical lenses approached Candle Arc only 1.3 hours behind schedule. Jedao was recovering the ability to read his watch, but the command center had a display that someone had enlarged for his benefit, so he didn't look at it. Especially since he had the sneaking feeling that his watch was off by a fraction of a second. If he drew attention to it, Captain-magistrate Korais was going to recalibrate it to the high calendar when they all had more important things to deal with.

The crews on the lenses had figured out how to simulate formations. No one would mistake them for Kel from close range, but Jedao wasn't going to let the Lanterners get that close.

"Word from the listening posts is that the Lanterners are still in pursuit," Communications informed them.

"How accommodating of them," Jedao said. "All right. Orders for the Rahal: The lenses are to maintain formation and head through the indicated channel"—he passed over the waypoint coordinates from his computer station—"to the choke locus. You are to *pass* the locus, then circle back toward it. Don't call us under any circumstances, we'll call you. And stick to the given formation and don't try any fancy modulations."

It was unlikely that the Rahal would try, but it was worth saying. The Rahal were going to be most convincing as a fake Kel swarm if they stayed in one formation because there wasn't time to teach them to get the modulation to look right. The formation that Jedao had chosen for them was Senner's Lash, partly because its visible effects were very short-range. When the Rahal failed to produce the force-lash, it wouldn't look suspicious because the Lanterners wouldn't expect to see anything from a distance.

"Also," Jedao said, still addressing the Rahal. "The instant you see something, anything on scan, you're to banner the Deuce of Gears."

The Deuce was his personal emblem, and it connoted "cog in the machine." Everyone had expected him to register some form of fox when he made brigadier general, but he had preferred a show of humility. The Deuce would let the Lanterners know who they were facing. It might not be entirely sporting for the Rahal to transmit it, but since they were under his command, he didn't feel too bad about it.

"The Rahal acknowledge," Communications said. Jedao's subdisplay showed them moving off. They would soon pass through the calendrical null, and at that point they would become harder to find on scan.

Commander Menowen was drumming her fingers on the arm of her chair, her first sign of nervousness. "They have no defenses," she said, almost to herself.

It mattered that this mattered to her. "We won't let the Lanterners reach them," Jedao said. "If only because I would prefer to spend my career not having the Rahal mad at me."

Her sideways glance was only slightly irritated. "Where are we going, sir?"

"Cut the mothdrives," Jedao said. He sent the coordinates to Menowen, Communications, and Navigation. "We're heading *there* by invariant drive only." This would probably prevent long-range scan from seeing them. "Transmit orders to all moths. I want acknowledgments from the moth commanders."

"There" referred to some battledrift, all sharp edges and ash-scarred fragments and wrecked silverglass shards, near the mouth of what Jedao had designated the Yellow Passage. He expected the Lanterners to take it toward the choke. Its calendrical gradient started in the Lanterners' favor, then zeroed out as it neared the null.

Depending on the Lanterners' invariant drives, it would take them two to three hours (high calendar) to cross the null region and reach the choke. This was, due to the periodic shifts, still faster than going around the null, because the detours would be through space hostile to their exotics for the next six hours.

Reports had put the Lanterners at anywhere from sixty to one hundred twenty combat moths. The key was going to be splitting them up to fight a few at a time.

Jedao's moth commanders acknowledged less quickly than he would have liked, gold lights coming on one by one.

"Formation?" Menowen prompted him.

There weren't a lot of choices when you had eleven moths. Jedao brought up a formation, which was putting it kindly because it didn't belong to Lexicon Primary for tactical groups, or even Lexicon Secondary, which contained all the obsolete formations and parade effects. He wanted the moths in a concave configuration so they could focus lateral fire on the first hostiles to emerge from the Yellow Passage.

"That's the idea," Jedao said, "but we're using the battledrift as cover. Some big chunks of dead stuff floating out there, we might as well blend in and snipe the hell out of the Lanterners with the invariant weapons." At least they had a good supply of missiles and ammunition, as Najhera had attempted to fight solely with exotic effects.

The Kel didn't like the word "snipe," but they were just going to have to deal. "Transmit orders," Jedao said.

The acknowledgments lit up again, about as fast as they had earlier.

The *Fortune Comes in Fours* switched into invariant mode as they crossed into the null. The lights became less white-gold and more rust-gold, giving everything a corroded appearance. The hum of the moth's systems changed to a deeper, grittier whisper. The moth's acceleration became noticeable, mostly in the form of pain. Jedao wished he had thought to take an extra dose of painkillers, but he couldn't risk getting muddled.

Menowen picked out a chunk of coruscating metals that had probably once been some inexplicable engine component on that long-ago space fortress and parked the *Fortune* behind it. She glanced at him to see if he would have any objections. He nodded at her. No sense in getting in the way when she was doing her job fine.

Time passed. Jedao avoided checking his watch every minute thanks to long practice, although he met Captain-magistrate Korais's eyes once and saw a wry acknowledgment of shared impatience.

They had an excellent view of the bridgelights even on passive sensors. The lights were red and violet, like absurd petals, and their flickering would, under other circumstances, have been restful.

"We won't see hostiles until they're on top of us," Menowen said.

More nerves. "It'll be mutual," Jedao said, loudly enough so the command center's crew could hear him. "They'll see us when they get that close, but they'll be paying *attention* to the decoy swarm."

She wasn't going to question his certainty in front of everyone, so he rewarded her by telling her. "I am sure of this," he said, looking at her, "because of how the Lanterner general destroyed Najhera. They were extremely aggressive in exploiting calendrical terrain and, I'm sorry to say, they made a spectacle of the whole thing. I don't imagine the Lanterners had time to swap out generals for the hell of it, especially one who had already performed well, so I'm assuming we're dealing with the same individual. So if the Lanterner wants calendrical terrain and a big shiny target, fine. There it is."

More time passed. There was something wrong about the high calendar when it ticked off seconds cleanly and precisely and didn't account for the way time crawled when you were waiting for battle. Among the many things wrong with the high calendar, but that one he could own to without getting called out as a heretic.

"The far terrain is going to shift in our favor in five hours, sir," Korais said.

"Thank you, good to know," Jedao said.

To distract himself from the pain, he was thinking about the bridgelights and their resemblance to falling petals when Scan alerted him that the Lanterners had shown up. "Thirty-some moths in the van," the officer said in a commendably steady voice. "Readings suggest more are behind them. They're moving rapidly, vector suggests they're headed down the Yellow Passage toward the choke locus, and they're using a blast wave to clear mines."

As if he'd had the time to plant mines down a hostile corridor. Good of them to think of it, though.

Menowen's breath hissed between her teeth. "Our *banner—*"

His emblem. The Kel transmitted their general's emblem before battle. "No," Jedao said. "We're not bannering. The Lanterners are going to be receiving the Deuce of Gears from *over there*," where the Rahal were.

"But the protocol, sir. The Rahal aren't part of your force," Menowen said, "they don't *fight*—"

That got his attention. "*Fledge*," Jedao said sharply, which brought her up short, "what the hell do you mean they're not fighting? Just because they're not sitting on a mass of things that go boom? *They're fighting what's in the enemy's head.*"

He studied the enemy dispositions. The Yellow Passage narrowed as it approached the null, and the first group consisted of eight hellmoths, smaller than fangmoths, but well-armed if they were in terrain friendly to their own calendar, which was not going to be the case at the passage's mouth. The rest of the groups would probably consist of eight to twelve hellmoths each. Taken piecemeal, entirely doable.

"They fell for it," Menowen breathed, then wisely shut up.

"General Shuos Jedao to all moths," Jedao said. "Coordinated strike on incoming units with missiles and railguns." Hellmoths didn't have good side weapons, so he wasn't as concerned about return fire. "After the first hits, move into the Yellow Passage to engage. Repeat, move into the Yellow Passage."

The fangmoths' backs would be to that damned null, no good way to retreat, but that would only motivate them to fight harder.

If the Lanterners wanted a chance at the choke, they'd have to choose between shooting their way through when the geometry didn't permit them to bring their numbers to bear in the passage, or else leaving the passage and taking their chances with terrain that shaded toward the high calendar. If they chose the latter, they risked being hit by Kel formation effects, anything from force lances to scatterbursts, on top of the fangmoths' exotic weapons.

The display was soon a mess of red lights and gold, damage reports.

The computer kept making the dry, metallic click that indicated hits made by the Kel. Say what you liked about the Kel, they did fine with weapons.

Two hellmoths tried to break through the Kel fangmoths, presumably under the impression that the Rahal were the real enemy. One hellmoth took a direct engine hit from a spinal railgun, while the other shuddered apart under a barrage of missiles that overwhelmed the anti-missile defenses.

"You poor fools," Jedao said, perusing the summaries despite the horrible throbbing in his left eye. "You found a general who was incandescently talented at calendrical warfare, so you spent all your money on the exotic toys and ran out of funding for the boring invariant stuff."

Menowen paused in coordinating damage control—they'd taken a burst from an exploding scout, of all things—and remarked, "I should think you'd be grateful, sir."

"It's war, Commander, and someone always dies," Jedao said, aware of Korais listening in; aware that even this might be revealing too much. "That doesn't mean I'm eager to dance on their ashes."

"Of course," Menowen said, but her voice revealed nothing of her feelings.

The fangmoths curved into a concave bowl as they advanced up the Yellow Passage. The wrecked Lanterner hellmoths in the van were getting in the way of the Lanterners' attempts to bring fire to bear. Jedao had planned for a slaughter, but he hadn't expected it to work this well. They seemed to think his force was a detachment to delay them from reaching the false Kel swarm while the far terrain was hostile to the high calendar, and that if they could get past him before the terrain changed, they would prevail. It wasn't until the fourth group of Lanterners had been written into rubble and smoke that their swarm discipline wavered. Some of the hellmoths and their auxiliaries started peeling out of the passage just to have somewhere else to go. Others turned around, exposing their sides to further punishment, so they could accelerate back up the passage where the Kel wouldn't be able to catch them.

One of Jedao's fangmoths had taken engine damage serious enough that he had ordered it to pull back, but that left him ten to work with. "Formation Sparrow's Spear," he said, and gave the first set of targets.

The fangmoths narrowed into formation as they plunged out of the Yellow Passage and toward five hellmoths and a transport moving with the speed and grace of a flipped turtle. As they entered friendlier terrain, white-gold fire blazed up from the formation's primary pivot and raked through two hellmoths, the transport, and a piece of crystalline battledrift.

They swung around for a second strike, shifting into a shield formation to slough off the incoming fire.

This is too easy, Jedao thought coldly, and then.

"Incoming message from Lanterner hellmoth 5," Communications said. Scan had tagged it as the probable command moth. "Hellmoth 5 has disengaged." It wasn't the only one. The list showed up on Jedao's display.

"Hold fire on anything that isn't shooting at us," Jedao said. "They want to talk? I'll talk."

There was still a core of fourteen hellmoths whose morale hadn't broken. A few of the stragglers were taking potshots at the Kel, but the fourteen had stopped firing.

"This is Lieutenant Colonel Akkion Dhaved," said a man's voice. "I assume I'm addressing a Kel general."

"In a manner of speaking," Jedao said. "This is General Shuos Jedao. Are you the ranking officer?" Damn. He would have liked to know the Lanterner general's name.

"Sir," Menowen mouthed, "it's a trick, stop talking to them."

He wasn't sure he disagreed, but he wasn't going to get more information by closing the channel.

"That's complicated, General." Dhaved's voice was sardonic. "I have an offer to make you."

"I'm sorry," Jedao said, "but are you the ranking officer? Are you authorized to have this conversation?" He wasn't the only one who didn't like the direction of the conversation. The weight of collective Kel disapproval was almost crushing.

"I'm offering you a trade, General. You've been facing General Bremis kae Meghuet of the Lantern."

The name sounded familiar—

"She's the cousin of Bremis kae Erisphon, one of our leaders. Hostage value, if you care. You're welcome to her if you let the rest of us go. She's intact. Whether you want to leave her that way is your affair."

Jedao didn't realize how chilly his voice was until he saw Menowen straighten in approval. "Are you telling me you mutinied against your commanding officer?"

"She lost the battle," Dhaved said, "and it's either death or capture. We all know what the heptarchate does to heretics, don't we?"

Korais spoke with quiet urgency. "General. Find out if Bremis kae Meghuet really is alive."

Jedao met the man's eyes. It took him a moment to understand the expression in them: regret.

"There's a nine-hour window," Korais said. "The Day of Broken Feet isn't over."

Jedao gestured for Communications to mute the channel, which he should have done earlier. "The battle's basically won and we'll see the cascade effects soon," he said. "What do you have in mind?"

"It's not ideal," Korais said, "but a heretic general is a sufficient symbol." Just as Jedao himself might have been, if the assassin had succeeded. "If we torture kae Meghuet ourselves, it would cement the victory in the calendar."

Jedao hauled himself to his feet to glare at Korais, which was a mistake. He almost lost his balance when the pain drove through his head like nails.

Still, Jedao had to give Korais credit for avoiding the usual euphemism, *processed*.

Filaments in the feet. It was said that that particular group of heretics had taken weeks to die.

Fuck dignity. Jedao hung on to the arm of the chair and said, as distinctly as he could, "It's a trick. I'm not dealing with Dhaved. Tell the Lanterners we'll resume the engagement in seven minutes." His vision was going white around the edges, but he had to say this. Seven minutes wouldn't give the Lanterners enough time to run or evade, but it mattered. It mattered. "Annihilate anything that can't run fast enough."

Best not to leave Doctrine any prisoners to torture.

Jedao was falling over sideways. Someone caught his arm. Commander Menowen. "You ought to let us take care of the mopping up, sir," she said. "You're not well."

She could relieve him of duty. Reverse his orders. Given that the world was one vast blur, he couldn't argue that he was in any fit shape to assess the situation. He tried to speak again, but the pain hit again, and he couldn't remember how to form words.

"I don't like to press at a time like this," Korais was saying to Menowen, "but the Lanterner general—"

"General Jedao has spoken," Menowen said crisply. "Find another way, Captain." She called for a junior officer to escort Jedao out of the command center.

Words were said around him, a lot of them. They didn't take him to his quarters. They took him to the medical center. All the while he thought about lights and shrapnel and petals falling endlessly in the dark.

Commander Menowen came to talk to him after he was returned to his quarters. The mopping up was still going on. Menowen was carrying a small wooden box. He hoped it didn't contain more medications.

"Sir," Menowen said, "I used to think heretics were just heretics, and death was just death. Why does it matter to you how they die?"

Menowen had backed him against Doctrine, and she hadn't had to. That meant a lot.

She hadn't said that she didn't have her own reasons. She had asked for his. Fair enough.

Jedao had served with Kel who would have understood why he had balked. A few of them would have shot him if he had turned over an enemy officer, even a heretic, for torture. But as he advanced in rank, he found fewer and fewer such Kel. One of the consequences of living in a police state.

"Because war is about people," Jedao said. "Even when you're killing them."

"I don't imagine that makes you popular with Doctrine," Menowen said.

"The Rahal can't get rid of me because the Kel like me. I just have to make sure it stays that way."

She looked at him steadily. "Then you have one more Kel ally, sir. We have the final tally. We engaged ninety-one hellmoths and destroyed forty-nine of them. Captain-magistrate Korais is obliged to report your actions, but given the numbers, you are going to get a lot of leniency."

There would have been around four hundred crew on each of the hellmoths. He had already seen the casualty figures for his own fangmoths and the three Rahal vessels that had gotten involved, fourteen dead and fifty-one injured.

"Leniency wasn't what I was looking for," Jedao said.

Menowen nodded slowly.

"Is there anything exciting about our journey to Twin Axes, or can I go back to being an invalid?"

"One thing," she said. "Doctrine has provisionally declared a remembrance of your victory to replace the Day of Broken Feet. He says it is likely to be approved by the high magistrates. Since we didn't provide a heretic focus for torture, we're burning effigy candles." She hesitated. "He said he thought you might prefer this alternative remembrance. You don't want to be caught shirking this." She put the box down on the nearest table.

"I will observe the remembrance," Jedao said, "although it's ridiculous to remember something that just happened."

Menowen's mouth quirked. "One less day for publicly torturing criminals," she said, and he couldn't argue. "That's all, sir."

After she had gone, Jedao opened the box. It contained red candles in the shape of hellmoths, except the wax was additionally carved with writhing bullet-ridden figures.

Jedao set the candles out and lit them with the provided lighter, then stared at the melting figures. *I don't think you understand what I'm taking away from these remembrance days,* he thought. The next time he won some remarkable victory, it wasn't going to be against some unfortunate heretics. It was going to be against the high calendar itself. Every observance would be a reminder of what he had to do next—and while everyone lost a battle eventually, he had one more Kel officer in his corner, and he didn't plan on losing now.

a vector alphabet of interstellar travel

The Conflagration

Among the universe's civilizations, some conceive of the journey between stars as the sailing of bright ships, and others as tunneling through the crevices of night. Some look upon their far-voyaging as a migratory imperative, and name their vessels after birds or butterflies.

The people of a certain red star no longer speak its name in any of their hundreds of languages, although they paint alien skies with its whorled light and scorch its spectral lines into the sides of their vessels.

Their most common cult, although by no means a universal one, is that of many-cornered Mrithaya, Mother of the Conflagration. Mrithaya is commonly conceived of as the god of catastrophe and disease, impartial in the injuries she deals out. Any gifts she bestows are incidental, and usually come with sharp edges. The stardrive was invented by one of her worshipers.

Her priests believe that she is completely indifferent to worship, existing in the serenity of her own disinterest. A philosopher once said that you leave offerings of bitter ash and aleatory wine at her dank altars not because she will heed them, but because it is important to acknowledge the truth of the universe's workings. Naturally, this does not stop some of her petitioners from trying, and it is through their largesse that the priests are able to thrive as they do.

Mrithaya is depicted as an eyeless woman of her people, small of stature, but with a shadow scarring the world. (Her people's iconography has never been subtle.) She leans upon a crooked staff with words of poison scratched into it. In poetry, she is signified by smoke-wind and nausea, the sudden fall sideways into loss.

Mrithaya's people, perhaps not surprisingly, think of their travels as the outbreak of a terrible disease, a conflagration that they have limited power to contain; that the civilizations they visit will learn how to build Mrithaya's stardrive, and be infected by its workings. A not insignificant faction holds that they should hide on their candled worlds so as to prevent Mrithaya's terrible eyeless gaze from afflicting other civilizations, that all interstellar travel should be interdicted. And yet the pilgrims—Mrithaya's get, they are called—always find a way.

Certain poets write in terror of the day that all extant civilizations will be touched by this terrible technological conflagration, and become subject to Mrithaya's whims.

Alphabets

In linear algebra, the basis of a vector space is an alphabet in which all vectors can be expressed uniquely. The thing to remember is that there are many such alphabets.

In the peregrinations of civilizations grand and subtle, each mode of transport is an alphabet expressing their understandings of the universe's one-way knell. One assumes that the underlying universe is the same in each case.

Codices

The Iothal are a people who treasure chronicles of all kinds. From early on in their history, they bound forest chronicles by pressing leaves together and listening to their secrets of turning worm and wheeling sun; they read hymns to the transient things of the world in chronicles of footprints upon rocky soil, of foam upon restive sea. They wrote their alphabets forwards and backwards and upside down into reflected cloudlight, and divined the poetry of time receding in the earth's cracked strata.

As a corollary, the Iothal compile vast libraries. On the worlds they inhabit, even the motes of air are subject to having indices written on them in stuttering quantum ink. Some of their visionaries speak of a surfeit of knowledge, when it will be impossible to move or breathe without imbibing some unexpected fact, from the number of neutrons in a certain meadow to the habits of aestivating snails. Surely the end product will be a society of enlightened beings, each crowned with some unique mixture of facts and heady fictions.

The underside of this obsession is the society's driving terror. One day all their cities will be unordered dust, one day all their books will be scattered like leaves, one day no one will know the things they knew. One day the rotting remains of their libraries will disintegrate so completely that they will be indistinguishable from the world's wrack of stray eddies and meaningless scribbles, the untide of heat death.

The Iothal do not call their starships ships, but rather codices. They have devoted untold ages to this ongoing work of archival. Although they had developed earlier stardrives—indeed, with their predilection for knowledge, it was impossible not to—their scientists refused to rest until they devised one that drank in information and, as its ordinary mode of operation, tattooed it upon the universe's subtle skin.

Each time the Iothal build a codex, they furnish it with a carefully selected compilation of their chronicles, written in a format that the stardrive will find nourishing. Then its crew takes it out into the universe to carry out the act of inscription. Iothal codices have very little care for destination, as it is merely the fact of travel that matters, although they make a point of avoiding potentially hostile aliens.

When each codex has accomplished its task, it loses all vitality and drifts inertly wherever it ends up. The Iothal are very long-lived, but even they do not always survive to this fate.

Distant civilizations are well-accustomed to the phenomenon of drifting Iothal vessels, but so far none of them have deciphered the trail of knowledge that the Iothal have been at such pains to lay down.

The Dancers

To most of their near neighbors, they are known as the dancers. It is not the case that their societies are more interested in dance than the norm. True, they have their dances of metal harvest, and dances of dream descending, and dances of efflorescent death. They have their high rituals and their low chants, their festivals where water-of-suffusement flows freely for all who would drink, where bells with spangled clappers toll the hours by antique calendars. But then, these customs differ from their neighbors' in detail rather than in essential nature.

Rather, their historians like to tell the story of how, not so long ago, they went to war with aliens from a distant cluster. No one can agree on the nature of the offense that precipitated the whole affair, and it seems likely that it was a mundane squabble over excavation rights at a particular rumor-pit.

The aliens were young when it came to interstellar war, and they struggled greatly with the conventions expected of them. In order to understand their enemy better, they charged their masters of etiquette with the task of interpreting the dancers' behavior. For it was the case that the dancers began each of their battles in the starry deeps with the same maneuvers, and often retreated from battle—those times they had cause to retreat—with other maneuvers, carried out with great precision. The etiquette masters became fascinated by the pirouettes and helices and rolls, and speculated that the dancers' society was constricted by strict rules of engagement. Their fabulists wrote witty and extravagant tales about the dancers' dinner parties, the dancers' sacrificial exchanges, the dancers' effervescent arrangements of glass splinters and their varied meanings.

It was not until late in the war that the aliens realized that the stylized maneuvers of the dancers' ships had nothing to do with courtesy. Rather, they were an effect of the stardrive's ordinary functioning, without which the ships could not move. The aliens could have exploited this knowledge and pushed for a total victory, but by then their culture was so enchanted by their self-dreamed vision of the dancers that the two came instead to a fruitful truce.

These days, the dancers themselves often speak admiringly of the tales that the aliens wrote about them. Among the younger generation in particular, there are those who emulate the elegant and mannered society depicted in the aliens' fables. As time goes on, it is likely that this fantasy will displace the dancers' native culture.

The Profit Motive

Although the Kiatti have their share of sculptors, engineers, and mercenaries, they are perhaps best known as traders. Kiatti vessels are welcome in many places, for they bring delightfully disruptive theories of government, fossilized musical instruments, and fine surgical tools; they bring cold-eyed guns that whisper of sleep impending and sugared atrocities. If you can describe it, so they say, there is a Kiatti who is willing to sell it to you.

In the ordinary course of things, the Kiatti accept barter for payment. They claim that it is a language that even the universe understands. Their sages devote a great deal of time attempting to justify the profit motive in view of conservation laws. Most of them converge comfortably on the position that profit is the civilized response to entropy. The traders themselves vary, as you might expect, in the rapacity of their bargains. But then, as they often say, value is contextual.

The Kiatti do have a currency of sorts. It is their stardrives, and all aliens' stardrives are rated in comparison with their own. The Kiatti produce a number of them, which encompass a logarithmic scale of utility.

When the Kiatti determine that it is necessary to pay or be paid in this currency, they will spend months—sometimes years—refitting their vessels as necessary. Thus every trader is also an engineer. The drives' designers made some attempt to make the drives modular, but this was a haphazard enterprise at best.

One Kiatti visionary wrote of commerce between universes, which would require the greatest stardrive of all. The Kiatti do not see any reason why they can't bargain with the universe itself, and are slowly accumulating their wealth towards the time when they can trade their smaller coins for one that will take them to this new goal. They rarely speak of this with outsiders, but most of them are confident that no one else will be able to outbid them.

The Inescapable Experiment

One small civilization claims to have invented a stardrive that kills everyone who uses it. One moment the ship is *here*, with everyone alive and well, or as well as they ever were; the next moment, it is *there*, and carries only corpses. The records, transmitted over great expanses against the microwave hiss, are persuasive. Observers in differently-equipped ships have sometimes accompanied these suicide vessels, and they corroborate the reports.

Most of their neighbors are mystified by their fixation with this mordant discovery. It would be one thing, they say, if these people were set upon finding a way to fix this terrible flaw, but that does not appear to be the case. A small but reliable number of them volunteers to test each new iteration of the deathdrive, and they are rarely under any illusions about their fate. For that matter, some of the neighbors, out of pity or curiosity, have offered this people some of their own old but reliable technology, asking only a token sum to allow them to preserve their pride, but they always decline politely. After all, they possess safe stardrive technology of their own; the barrier is not knowledge.

Occasionally, volunteers from other peoples come to test it themselves, on the premise that there has to exist some species that won't be affected by the stardrive's peculiar radiance. (The drive's murderousness does not appear to have any lasting effect on the ship's structure.) So far, the claim has stood. One imagines it will stand as long as there are people to test it.

One Final Constant

Then there are the civilizations that invent keener and more nimble stardrives solely to further their wars, but that's an old story and you already know how it ends.

the unstrung zither

"They don't look very dangerous," Xiao Ling Yun said to the aide. Ling Yun wished she understood what Phoenix Command wanted from her. Not that she minded the excuse to take a break from the composition for two flutes and hammered dulcimer that had been stymying her for the past two weeks.

Through a one-way window in the observation chamber, Xiao Ling Yun saw five adolescents sitting cross-legged on the floor in a semicircle. Before them was a tablet and two brushes. No ink; these were not calligraphy brushes. One of the adolescents, a girl with short, dark hair, leaned over and drew two characters with quick strokes. All five studied the map that appeared on the tablet.

"Nevertheless," the aide said. "They attempted to assassinate the Phoenix General. We are fortunate to have captured them."

The aide wrote something on her own tablet, and a map appeared. She circled a region of the map. The tablet enlarged it until it filled the screen. "Circles represent gliders," the aide said. "Triangles represent dragons."

Ling Yun peered at the formations. "Who's winning?"

At the aide's instigation, the tablet replayed the last move. A squadron of dragons engaged a squadron of gliders. One dragon turned white—white for death—and vanished from the map. The aide smiled. "The assassins are starting to slip."

Ling Yun had thought that the Phoenix General desired the services of a musician to restore order to the fractious ashworlds. She was not the best person for such a purpose, nor the worst: a master musician, yes, but without a sage's philosophical bent of mind. Perhaps they had chosen her on account of her uncle's position as a logistician. She was pragmatic enough not to be offended by the possibility.

"I had not expected prisoners to be offered entertainment," Ling Yun said, a little dubious. She was surprised that they hadn't been executed, in fact.

"It is not entertainment," the aide said reprovingly. "Every citizen has a right to education."

Of course. The government's stance was that the ashworlds already belonged to the empire, whatever the physical reality might be. "Including the classical arts, I presume," she said. "But I am a musician, not a painter." Did they want her to tutor the assassins? And if so, why?

"Music is the queen of the arts, is it not?" the aide said.

She had not expected to be discussing the philosophy of music with a soldier. "According to tradition, yes," Ling Yun said carefully. Her career had been spent writing music that never strayed too much from the boundaries of tradition.

The most important music lesson she had had came not from her tutor, but from a servant in her parents' house. The servant, whose name Ling Yun had deliberately forgotten, liked to sing as he stirred the soup or pounded the day's bread. He didn't have a particularly notable voice. It wavered in the upper register and his vowels drifted when he wasn't paying attention. (She didn't tell him any of this. She didn't talk to him at all. Her parents would have disapproved.) But the servant had two small children who helped him with his tasks, and they chanted the songs, boisterously out of tune.

From watching that servant and his children, Ling Yun learned that the importance of music came not from its ability to move the five elements, but from its ability to affect the heart. She wanted to write music that anyone could hum, music that anyone could enjoy. It was the opposite of the haughty ideal that her tutor taught her to strive toward. Naturally, Ling Yun kept this thought to herself.

The aide scribbled some more on the tablet. In response, an image of a mechanical dragon drew itself across the tablet. It had been painted white, with jagged red markings on its jointed wings.

"Is this a captured dragon?" Ling Yun asked.

"Unfortunately, no," the aide said. "We caught glimpses of two of the assassins as they came down on dragons, but the dragons disappeared as though they'd been erased. We want to know where they're hiding, and how they're being hidden."

Ling Yun stared at the dragon. Whoever had drawn it did not have an artist's fluency of line. But everything was precise and carefully proportioned. She could see where the wings connected to the body and the articulations that made motion possible, even, if she squinted, some of the controls by the pilot's seat.

"Who produced this?"

The aide turned her head toward the window. "The dark-haired girl did. Her name is Wu Wen Zhi."

It was a masculine name, but they probably did things differently in the ashworlds. Ling Yun felt a rebellious twinge of approval.

Ling Yun said, "Wen Zhi draws you a picture, and you expect it to yield the ashworlders' secrets. Surely she's not as incompetent an assassin as all that. Or did you torture this out of her?"

"No, it's part of the game they're playing with the general," the aide said.

"I don't see the connection," she said. And why was the general playing a game with them in the first place? *Wei qi* involved no such thing, nor had the tablet games she had played as a student.

The aide smiled as though she had heard the thought. "It personalizes the experience. When the game calculates the results of combat, it refers to the pilot's emblem to determine her strengths and weaknesses. Take Wen Zhi's dragon, for instance. First of all, the dragon's design indicates that it specializes in close combat, as opposed to Mesketalioth's"—she switched briefly to another dragon painting—"which has repeating crossbows mounted on its shoulders." She returned to Wen Zhi's white dragon. "However, notice the stiffness of the lines. The pilot is always alert, but in a way that makes her tense. This can be exploited."

"The general has an emblem in the game, too, I presume," Ling Yun said.

"Of course," the aide said, but she didn't volunteer to show it to Ling Yun. "Let me tell you about our five assassins.

"Wu Wen Zhi comes from Colony One." The empire's two original colonies had been given numbers rather than names. "Wen Zhi has tried to kill herself three times already. She doesn't sleep well at night, but she refuses to meditate, and she won't take medications."

I wouldn't either, Ling Yun thought.

"The young man with the long braid is Ko. He's lived on several of the ashworlds and speaks multiple languages, but his accent suggests that he comes from Arani. Interestingly enough, Ko alerted us to the third of Wen Zhi's suicide attempts. Wen Zhi didn't take this well.

"The scarred one sitting next to Ko is Mesketalioth. He's from Straken Okh. We suspect that he worked for Straken's intelligence division before he was recruited by the Dragon Corps.

"The girl with the light hair is Periet, although the others call her Perias. We haven't figured out why, and they look at us as though we're crazy when we ask them about it, although she'll answer to either name. Our linguists tell us that Perias is the masculine form of her name; our doctors confirm that she is indeed a girl. She comes from Kiris. Don't be fooled by her sweet manners. She's the one who destroyed Shang Yuan."

Ling Yun opened her mouth, then found her voice. "*Her?*" Shang Yuan had been a city of several million people. It had been obliterated during the Festival of Lanterns, for which it had been famous. "I thought that the concussive storm was a natural disaster."

The aide gave Ling Yun a singularly cynical look. "Natural disasters don't flatten every building in the city and cause all the lanterns to explode. It was an elemental attack."

"I suppose this is classified information."

"It is, technically, not that many people haven't guessed."

"How much help did she have?"

The aide's mouth twisted. "Ashworld Kiris didn't authorize the attack. As near as we can determine, Periet did it all by herself."

"All right," Ling Yun said. She paced to the one-way window and watched Periet-Perias, trying to map the massacre onto the girl's open, cheerful expression. "Who's the fifth one now skulking in a corner?"

"That's Li Cheng Guo, from Colony Two," the aide said. "He killed two of our guards on the first day. Actually, they all did their share of killing on the way in, although Periet takes the prize."

"That's terrible," Ling Yun said. But what she was thinking was, *The ashworlds must be terribly desperate, to send children.* The Phoenix General had had the ashworlds' leader assassinated two years ago; this must be their counterstroke. "So," she said, "one assassin from each ashworld." Colony One and Colony Two; Arani, Straken Okh, and Kiris. The latter three had been founded by nations that had since been conquered by the empire.

"Correct." The aide rolled the brush around in her hand. "The Phoenix General wants you to discover the assassins' secret."

Oh no, Ling Yun thought. For all the honors that the empress had lavished on the Phoenix General, he was still known as the Mad General. He had started out as a glider pilot, and everyone knew that glider pilots were crazy. Their extreme affinity for fire and wood unbalanced their minds.

On the other hand, Ling Yun had a lifetime's practice of bowing before those of greater standing, however much it chafed, and the man had produced undeniable results. She could respect that.

"I'm no soldier," Ling Yun said, "and no interrogator. What would you like me to do?"

The aide smiled. "Each assassin has an emblem in the game."

Ling Yun had a sudden memory of a self-portrait she had drawn when she was a child. It was still in the hallway of her parents' house, to her embarrassment: lopsided face with tiny eyes and a dot for a nose, scribbly hair, arms spread wide. "Why did they agree to this game?" she asked.

"They are playing because it was that or die. But they have some hidden purpose of their own, and time may be running out. You must study the game—we'll provide analyses for you, as we hardly expect you to become a tactician—and study the dragons. Compose a suite of five pieces, one for each dragon—for each pilot."

"Pilot?"

"They're pilots in their minds, although we're only certain that Periet and Mesketalioth have the training. Maybe the secret is just that they found blockade runners to drop them off." The aide didn't sound convinced.

"One piece for each dragon. You think that by translating their self-representations into music, the supreme art, you will learn their secret, and how to defeat them."

"Precisely."

"I will do what I can," Xiao Ling Yun said.

"I'm sure you will," the aide said.

Xiao Ling Yun's ancestors had worshipped dragons. At the harvest festival, they poured libations of rice wine to the twin dragons of the greatmoon and the smallmoon. When the empire's skies were afire with the summer's meteor showers, people would burn incense for the souls of the falling stars.

You could still see fire in the sky, most nights, festive and beautiful, but no one brought out incense. The light came from battles high in the atmosphere, battles between the ashworlders' metal dragons and the empire's Phoenix Corps.

When she was a child, Ling Yun's uncle had made her a toy glider, a flimsy-looking thing of bamboo and paper, with tiny slivers to represent the wing-mounted flamethrowers. He had painted the red-and-gold emblem of the Phoenix Corps on each wing. "Uncle," she asked, "why do we fight with fire when the gliders are made of wood? Isn't it dangerous?"

Her uncle patted her hand and smiled. "Remember the cycle of elements, little one."

She thought about it: metal cut wood, wood split earth, earth drank water, water doused fire, and—"Fire melts metal," she said.

"Indeed," he said. "The ashworlds abound in metal, mined from the asteroid belts. Therefore their dragons are built of metal. We must use fire to defeat metal."

"But wood *burns*," Ling Yun said, wondering, despite all her lessons and the habits of obedience, if her uncle was right in the head. She turned the glider around in her hands, testing the paper wings. They flexed under her touch.

"So does the phoenix," her uncle said.

Ling Yun squinted, trying to reconcile fire-defeats-metal with fire-burns-wood and fire-goes-down-in-flames.

Taking pity on her, her uncle added, "The phoenix is a symbol that came to us by conquest, from the southern spicelands." He laughed at her wide eyes. "Oh, yes—do you think that for thousands and thousands of years, the empire has never been conquered? You'll find all the old, ugly stories in the history books, of the Boar Banner and the Tiger Banner, the woman who brought down the wall, the Outsider Dynasty with its great fleets . . . "

Ling Yun took note of the things that he had mentioned so she could look them up later.

"Come, Ling Yun," her uncle said. "Why don't we go outside and test the glider?"

She sensed that he was preventing her from asking further questions.

But if he didn't want her to know, why had he told her about the phoenix in the first place?

Still, she loved the way the glider felt in her hand, and her uncle didn't visit very often. "All right," she said.

They went into the courtyard with its broad flagstones and pond, and spoke no more of the elements.

Ling Yun started composing the suite on the *wuxian qin*, the five-stringed zither. She had brought her favorite one with her. The military was accustomed to transporting fragile instruments, thanks to the Phoenix Corps, whose gliders had to be attuned to the elements.

For suicidal, dark-haired Wu Wen Zhi, Ling Yun wrote a disjunct melody with tense articulations, reflecting the mixed power and turmoil she saw in the girl's white dragon. White and red, bone and blood, death and fortune. The aide had said Wen Zhi had killed six people since landing in the empire. The dragon had nine markings. Ling Yun trusted the dragon. Wen Zhi did not strike her as the subtle type. The aide's response to this observation was a pained laugh.

Ko's drawing was more of a sketch, in a relaxed, spontaneous style that Ling Yun's calligraphy tutor would have approved of. The colors worried her, however: black and grey, no sign of color, a sense of aching incompleteness. Yet the reports that came every morning noted Ko's unshakable good cheer and cooperativeness. Ling Yun felt a strange affinity to what she knew of the boy. She had no illusions that she understood what it was like to be a killer, but she knew something about hiding part of yourself from the outside world. She gave Ko's piece a roving melody with ever-shifting rhythms and playful sliding tones.

Mesketalioth's blue dragon was the most militant-looking of the five, at least to Ling Yun's untrained eye. Ko's dragon, if you looked at it from a distance, might pass as a picture of a god out of legend, not a war automaton. Mesketalioth's diagram included not only the dragon, but cross-sections and insets showing the mechanisms of the repeating crossbows and the way the joints were put together. The aide assured her that it was a known type of ashworlder dragon, and provided Ling Yun with explanations from the engineers. Ling Yun thought that the aide was trying to be reassuring for her benefit, and failing. For Mesketalioth, she wrote a military air in theme and variations, shadows falling in upon themselves, the last note an infinitely subtle vibrato informed by the pulse in the finger holding down the string.

Periet was the best painter of the five. She had drawn her dragon out of scale so it looked no larger than a large cat, its head tilted to watch two butterflies, one sky-blue and the other star-spotted black. It was surrounded by flowers and gears and neatly organized mechanics' tools. Ling Yun thought of Shang Yuan, with its shattered lanterns and ashes, wind blowing through streets inhabited only by grasshoppers and mice. No one had attempted to rebuild the City of Lanterns. The song she wrote for Periet had an utterly conventional pentatonic melody. The countermelody, on the other hand, was sweet, logical, and in a foreign mode.

As for the last of them, Li Cheng Guo had drawn a flamboyant red dragon with golden eyes. Ling Yun wondered if he meant some mockery of the Phoenix General by this. On the other hand, red did indicate good fortune. The gliders were always painted in fire-colors, while the dragons came in every color imaginable. Obligingly, Ling Yun wrote a rapid, skirling piece for Cheng Guo, martial in its motifs, but hostile where Mesketalioth's was subtle.

Ling Yun slept surrounded by the five assassins' pictures. She was disturbed to realize that, no matter where she rearranged them on the walls, she always woke up facing Periet's butterfly dragon.

Careful inquiry revealed the assassins' sleeping arrangements: in separate cells, although they were permitted in a room together for the purposes of lessons—probably a euphemism for interrogation sessions—

and the general's game. Ling Yun asked how they kept the assassins from killing their guards or tutors.

"After the first few incidents, they swore to the Phoenix General that they would abide by the terms of the game," the aide said.

"And you trust them?" Ling Yun said.

"They've sworn," the aide said emphatically. "And if they break oath, he'll have them executed."

Sooner or later, she was going to have to speak with the Phoenix General, if he didn't demand a report from her first. She presumed that Phoenix Command had other precautions in place.

Two weeks into the assignment, Ling Yun said to the aide, "I'd like to speak with the assassins."

"If you draw up a list of questions," she said, "our interrogators can obtain the answers you want."

"In person," Ling Yun said.

"That's unwise for a whole list of reasons I'm sure you've already thought of."

"Surely one musician more or less is expendable in the general's game," Ling Yun said, keeping all traces of irony from her voice. She doubted the aide was fooled.

Sure enough, the aide said, with exasperation, "Do you know why we requested you, Musician Xiao? When we could have asked for the empress's personal troupe and had them do the general's bidding?"

"I had wondered, yes."

"Most musicians at your level of mastery have, shall we say, a philo-sophical bent of mind."

Ling Yun could think of a number of less flattering expressions. "I've heard that criticism," she said noncommittally.

The aide snorted. "Of course you have. We wanted you because you have a reputation for pragmatism. Or did you think it would go unnoticed? The psychological profiles for the empire's musicians aren't completely worthless."

"Will you trust that I have a pragmatic reason for wanting to talk to the assassins, then?" Ling Yun said. "Tell them it's part of the game. Surely that isn't far from the truth. It's one thing for me to study your game transcripts, but I want to know what the assassins are like as people. I'm no interrogator, but I am accustomed to listening to the hidden timbres of the human voice. I might hear something useful."

"We will consider it," the aide said.

"Thank you," Ling Yun said, certain she had won.

The first time Ling Yun tuned a glider to the elements with her music, she was shaking so badly that her fingers jerked on her zither's peg and she broke a string.

Ling Yun's tutor looked down at her with imperturbable eyes. "Perhaps the flute—" he suggested. Many of the Phoenix Corps' musicians preferred the bamboo flute for its association with birdsong, and therefore the heavens.

Ling Yun had come prepared with an extra set of strings. "I will try again," she said. Instead of trying to block the presence of the pilot and engineers from her mind, she raised her head and studied them. The pilot was a woman scarcely older than Ling Yun herself, who met Ling Yun's gaze with a quirk to her mouth, as if in challenge. The engineers had an expression of studied politeness; they had been through this before.

Carefully, mindful of the others' time but also mindful of the necessity of precision, Ling Yun replaced the broken string. The new one was going to be temperamental. She would have to play to compensate.

After tuning the zither to her satisfaction, she breathed in and breathed out several times. Then she began "The Crane Flies Home," the traditional blessing-piece. At first, the simple task of getting her fingers through the piece occupied her.

Then, Ling Yun became aware of the glider responding. It was a small, scarred creature, with gouges in the wood from past battles, and it thrummed almost imperceptibly whenever she played the strings that corresponded to wood and fire. Remembering her tutor's advice not to neglect the other strings, she coaxed the glider with delicate harmonics, reminding it that it would have to face water, fight metal, return to earth.

Only when she had finished did she realized that her fingers were bleeding, despite her calluses. That hadn't happened in years. She blotted the blood against the hem of her jacket. *Water feeds wood,* she thought.

The engineers, who had their own training in music, checked the glider over. They consulted with her tutor, using terminology she didn't understand. The tutor turned to her and nodded once, smiling.

"You haven't even flown it," Ling Yun said, bewildered. The winch was all the way down the airfield. "How do you know I tuned it properly?"

"I listened," he said simply. "It must fly in spirit before it can fly in truth. You have achieved this."

All her dreams that night were of gliders arcing into the air, launched by winch and changing into birds at the moment of release: herons and cranes and sparrows, hawks and geese and swallows, but not a single red-and-gold phoenix.

The five pilots—Ling Yun wasn't sure when she had started thinking of them as dragon pilots rather than assassins, a shift she hoped to keep from Phoenix Command—wore clothes that fit them indifferently. Dark-haired Wu Wen Zhi stood stiffly, her arms crossed. Ko, the boy with the braid, was smiling. Mesketalioth, whose face was calmly expressionless, had his hands clasped behind his back. The scars at his temple were startlingly white. Periet's blue eyes were downcast, although Ling Yun knew better than to mistake the girl's demeanor for submissiveness. Li Cheng Guo, the tallest, stood farthest from the others and scowled openly.

"I'm—"

"Another interrogator," Wen Zhi said. The girl's voice was high, precise, and rapid. It put Ling Yun in mind of stone chimes.

"Yes and no," Ling Yun said. "I have questions, but I'm not a soldier; do you see me wearing a uniform?" She had worn a respectable grey dress, the kind she would have worn to speak with a client.

Wen Zhi grabbed Ling Yun's wrist and twisted. Ling Yun bit back a cry. "It's all right!" she said quickly, knowing that the guards were monitoring the situation.

The girl ran her hand over Ling Yun's fingertips, lingering over the calluses. "You're an engineer."

"Also yes and no," Ling Yun said. "I'm a musician." Wen Zhi must not play the zither, or she would have noticed immediately that Ling Yun's fingernails were slightly long to facilitate plucking the strings. Ling Yun could practically hear the aide's reproof, but what was she supposed to do? Deny the obvious?

Ko tossed his head. "The correct response, Wen Zhi," he said, "is to say, 'Hello, I am honored to meet you.' Then to give your name, although I'm sure you already know ours, madam." His Imperial was startlingly good, despite the broadened vowels. "I'm Ko."

"I'm Xiao Ling Yun," she said gravely. Did they not use surnames on Arani? Or Straken Okh or Kiris, for that matter?

The others gave their names. Mesketalioth had a quiet, clipped voice, distantly polite. Periet called herself by that name. She had a pleasant alto and spoke with a heavier accent than the others. Li Cheng Guo's Imperial was completely idiomatic; he addressed Ling Yun with a directness that was just short of insulting.

Ling Yun wondered if any of them had vocal training, then felt silly. Of course they did. Not in the populist styles of their homes, surely, but in the way that all glider pilots did, the ability to hold a tune and the more important ability to listen for a glider's minute reverberations. What would it be like to write for their voices?

The question was moot, as she doubted the aide would stand for any such endeavor.

On a whim, Ling Yun had brought her uncle's toy glider with her. Keeping her motions slow, she drew it from her jacket.

"Pretty," Periet said. "Does it fly?" She was smiling.

Mesketalioth opened his hands toward Ling Yun. She gave the toy glider to him. He studied its proportions, and she was suddenly chilled. Could he draw diagrams of gliders, too?

"Yes, it flies," Mesketalioth said. "It's never been tuned, has it?"

"No," Ling Yun said. "It's just a toy." Surely the adolescents had had toys in childhood. What kinds of lives had they led in the ashworlds, constantly under assault from glider bombing runs?

"Even a toy can be a weapon," Cheng Guo said with a sneer. "I would have had it tuned. Especially if you're already a musician."

"Oh, for pity's sake, Cheng Guo," Ko said, "what's it going to do? Drop little origami bombs?" He made flicking motions with his fingers. Cheng Guo glowered at him, and Ko only grinned back.

They sounded like the students she had attended classes with, as an adolescent herself, fractious and earnest. However, unlike those fellow students, they carried themselves alertly. She noticed that, despite standing around her, they deliberately left her path to the exit unblocked.

"I have permission to ask you some questions," Ling Yun said. She wanted them to be clear on her place in the hierarchy, which was to say, low.

"Are you part of the game?" Wen Zhi asked.

Ling Yun wondered if the girl ever smiled, and was struck by a sudden urge to ruffle that short hair. The thought of the nine red marks on Wen Zhi's dragon made the urge entirely resistible. "No," she said, afraid that they would refuse to talk to her further.

"Good," Cheng Guo said shortly. "You're not prepared." He trained his glower on Ling Yun, as though it would cause her to go away. It seemed to her that ignoring her would be much more effective.

"What does it feel like to kill?" Ling Yun said.

Ko had sauntered over to the wall across from Cheng Guo and was leaning against it, worrying at the fraying end of his braid. They hadn't given him a clip for his hair, and the aide had said that he refused to get it cut. Ko gave Ling Yun a shrewd look and said, "You could ask that of your own soldiers, couldn't you?"

"I'd know how they felt, but I'm interested in you," she said.

"Ask what you mean," Periet said. Her tone had shifted, just below the surface. Ling Yun wondered if the others could hear that undercurrent of ferocity. "You're interested in how we're different."

"All right," Ling Yun said. "Yes." It cost her nothing to be agreeable, a lesson she had applied all her life.

"Don't listen to her," Wen Zhi said to the others. "She's trying to get inside our heads."

"Well, yes," Ling Yun said mildly. "But the longer you talk to me, the longer you draw out the game, the longer you live."

Mesketalioth raised his chin. His scars went livid. "Living isn't the point."

"Then what is?" she asked.

With no warning—at least, not to Ling Yun's slow senses—Mesketalioth snapped the glider between his hands.

Ling Yun stared at him, fists pressed to her sides. Her eyes stung. She had known, theoretically, that she might lose the glider. What had she been thinking, bringing it into a room full of assassins? Assassins who knew the importance of symbols and would think of a glider as a hostile one, at that. She just hadn't expected them to break this reminder of her childhood.

It's a toy, she reminded herself. She could make another herself if she had to.

How much had these children lost, before coming here?

Periet's blue eyes met Ling Yun's gaze. The girl made a tiny nod.

" 'Even a toy can be a weapon,' " Mesketalioth said, without inflection. "There are many kinds of weapons."

"Hey," Ko said to Ling Yun. He sounded genuinely concerned. "We can fix it. They'll let us have some glue, won't they? Besides, your general likes you. He'd have our heads if we didn't."

I've never even met the Phoenix General, Ling Yun thought, chewing her lip before she caught herself. "How many people did *you* take down?" she asked, trying to remind herself that these children were assassins and killers.

Ko rebraided the ends of his hair. "I keep a tally in my head," he said.

"He's killed sixteen gliders in the game," Wen Zhi said contemptuously. "That's information that you should have gotten from studying the game."

"You're still losing territory," Ling Yun said, remembering the latest report. "How do you expect to win?"

Cheng Guo laughed from his corner. "As if we'd tell you? Please."

General, Ling Yun thought, *how in the empress's name is this a good idea?* She hoped she wasn't the only musician they had working on the problem. The whole conversation was giving her a jittery sense of urgency.

"Indeed," she said. "Thank you."

"Leave the glider," Ko said. "We'll fix it. You'll see."

"If you like," Ling Yun said, wondering what her uncle would say if he knew. Well, she didn't have to tell him. "Perhaps I'll see you another time, if they permit it."

Periet touched Ling Yun's hand lightly. Ling Yun half-turned. "Yes?"

Periet said, "There should be six, not five. But you've always known that, haven't you?"

The hairs on the back of Ling Yun's neck prickled.

Periet smiled again.

Ling Yun thought of the two butterflies in Periet's dragon-portrait, and wondered if dragons ate butterflies. Or musicians, for that matter. "It was pleasant meeting you all," she said, because her parents had raised her to be polite.

Wu Wen Zhi and Li Cheng Guo ignored her, but the others murmured their goodbyes.

Shaking her head, Ling Yun made the signal that the guards had taught her, and the door opened. None of the assassins made an attempt to escape. It scared her.

Ling Yun was in the midst of revising Mesketalioth's piece in tablature when the summons came. She knew it had to be the Phoenix General, because the soldiers would not disrupt her concentration for anything else. But Ling Yun used to practice composing in adverse circumstances: sitting in a clattering train; at a street puppet theatre while children shouted out their favorite characters' names; during tedious parties when she had had too much rice wine. She didn't compose courtly lays or ballads, but cheerful ditties that she could hum in the bath where no one else had to know. But the aides had certain ideas about how musicians worked, and it was hardly for her to overturn those ideas.

The aide asked, "Will you need your zither?"

"That depends," Ling Yun said. "Will he want me to play what I have so far?"

"No," the aide said, a little hesitantly. "He'll make arrangements when he wants to hear a performance, I'm sure."

Surreptitiously, Ling Yun curled and uncurled her fingers to limber them up, just in case.

The aide escorted her to a briefing room painted with Phoenix Command's flame-and-spear on the door. She slid the door open with a surprising lack of ceremony. "General," she called out, "Musician Xiao is here." She patted Ling Yun's shoulder. "Go on. You'll be fine."

Ling Yun stepped through the minimum distance possible and knelt in full obeisance, catching a glimpse of the Phoenix General on the way down. He had grey-streaked hair and a strong-jawed profile.

"Enough," the general said. "Let's not waste time on ceremony."

Slowly, she rose, trying to interpret his expression. *He hasn't heard your work yet,* she reminded herself, *so he can't hate it already.*

"Sir," she said, dipping in a bow despite herself.

"You've been too well trained, I see," the general said wryly. "I swear, it's true of every musician I meet. Sit down."

Ling Yun had no idea what to say to this, so she sat cross-legged at the table and settled for looking helpful.

"What dreams do you dream?" the general said. His fingers tapped the wall. Indeed, he seemed unable to stop them.

"My last dream was about the fish I had for dinner," Ling Yun said, taken aback. "It swam up out of my mouth and chastised me for using too much salt. When I woke up, I was facing the butterfly dragon."

"Ah, yes," the general said. "Periet, destroyer of Shang Yuan. I lost an entire glider squadron when she flew in. Dragon pilots are unstable too, as you might guess, so we thought she was a rogue. We'd seen her take down a couple of her own comrades on the way in. Then her dragon roared, and the concussive storm shattered everything in its path, and the City of Lanterns exploded in fire."

"You were there, General?"

He didn't answer her. "How is the dragon suite progressing?"

"I have revisions to make based on this morning's results in the game, sir," Ling Yun said.

"Do you play *wei qi*, Musician?" he asked.

"Only poorly," Ling Yun said. "My mother taught me the rules, but it's been years. It concerns territory and influence and patterns, doesn't it? It's strange—musical patterns are so easy for me to perceive, but the visual ones are more difficult."

The general sat across from her. "If musicians were automatically as skilled at *wei qi* as they were at music," he said, "they would be unbeatable."

A tablet rested on the table. He picked up the larger of two brushes and wrote *game*, then several other characters. There were no triangles— no dragons—to be seen anywhere. "I didn't know they could do that," the general mused. "This is what happens when you allow the game to modify its own rules." He met Ling Yun's inquisitive gaze. "Somehow I don't think they've conceded."

"So the dragons haven't been captured," she said, slipping back into the terminology of *wei qi*. "What else mediates this game, General?"

"It's tuned the way a glider might be tuned by a musician, the way a tablet is calibrated by a calligrapher. It's tuned by developments in the living war."

"I had understood," Ling Yun said, "that the suite was to reflect the pilots, not to influence them. I must confess that so far I haven't seen anything that would explain the vanishing dragons."

The general said, "In music, the ideal is a silent song upon an unstrung zither. Is this not so?"

Ling Yun drew the characters in her mind: *wuxian* meant "five," *qin* meant "zither." But the *wu* of "five," in the third tone, brought to mind the *wu* of "nothing" or "emptiness," which was in the first tone. The unstrung zither, favored instrument of the sages. The ancients had preferred subtlety and restraint in all things; the unstrung zither took this to the natural conclusion. Ling Yun had applied herself to her lessons with the same patient dedication that she did all things musical, but the unstrung zither had vexed her. "That was the view of the traditional theorists," she said neutrally, "although modern musicians don't necessarily agree."

The Phoenix General's smile only widened, as though he saw right through her temporizing. "Music is the highest expression of the world's patterns. The sages have told us so, time and again. The music in the empress's court provides order to her subjects. We must apply the same principles in war."

She already knew what he was going to say.

"Thus, in war, the ideal must be a bloodless engagement upon an empty battlefield."

"Are you sure it is wise to keep the ashworlder children alive, then?" Ling Yun said. It made her uneasy to ask, for she didn't want to change the general's mind. Perhaps the thought was traitorous.

"They'll die when they're no longer useful," the general said frankly.

Traitorous or not, there was something wrong with a war that involved killing children. Even deadly children. Even Periet, with her eyes that hid such lethality.

Wei qi was a game of territory, of colonialism. Ling Yun thought of all the things she owed to her parents, who had made sure she had the best tutors; to her uncle, who had brought her the glider and other treats over the years. But she no longer lived in her parents' house. And three of the colonies, Arani and Straken Okh and Kiris, had not been founded by the empire at all. What did they owe the Phoenix Banner?

In her history lessons, she had learned that the phoenix and dragon were wedding symbols, and that this was a sign that the ashworlds, with their dragons, needed to be joined to the empire. But surely there were ways to cooperate—in trade, say—without conquering the ashworlds outright.

The general closed his eyes for a second and sighed. "If we could win the war without expending lives, it would be a marvel indeed. Imagine gliders that fly themselves, set against the ashworlds' dragons."

"The ashworlders are hardly stupid, sir," Ling Yun said. "They'll send pilotless dragons of their own." *Or,* she thought suddenly, *dragonless pilots.*

Maybe the ashworlds were ahead of the Phoenix General. From Ling Yun's vantage point, it was impossible to tell.

"Then there's no point sending army against army, is there?" the general said, amused. "But people are people. I doubt anyone would be so foolish as to disarm entirely, and commit a war solely on paper, as a game."

Ling Yun bowed, even knowing it would annoy him, to give herself time to think.

"Enough," the general said. "It is through music we will win the game, and through the game we will win the war. I commend your work, Musician. Take the time you need, but no longer."

"As you will, sir," Ling Yun said.

The population of the empire on the planet proper, at the last census, was 110 million people.

The population of the five ashworlds was estimated at 70 million people, although this number was much less certain, due to the transients who lived in the asteroid belts.

The number of gliders in the Phoenix Corps was classified. The number of dragons in the Dragon Corps was likewise classified.

Ling Yun stayed up late into the night reviewing the game's statistics. Visual patterns were not her forte, but she remembered the general's words. She had heard the eagerness in his voice, the way she heard echoes of the massacre of Shang Yuan in Periet's. Even now, there had to be pilotless gliders speeding toward the colonies.

Many of the reports compared the pilots' strategy in the game to actual engagements. Ling Yun had skimmed these earlier, because of all the unfamiliar names and places—the Serpent's Corridor, the Siege of Uln Okh, the Greater Vortex—but now she added up the ashworlders' estimated casualties and felt ill. They had lost their own Shang Yuans. She doubted that the general would stop until they lost many more.

Ling Yun had been right. The ashworlders were desperate, to send children.

Something else that interested her was the rate of replenishment. In the game, you could build new units to replace the ones you had lost. The five pilots kept losing dragons. Over the course of the game, the rate at which the game permitted them to build new dragons dropped slowly but significantly. Based on the general's remarks, Ling Yun was willing to bet that this was based on actual intelligence about the Dragon Corps' attrition rate.

It was too bad she couldn't ask her uncle, who had probably helped plan the general's grand attack. Her uncle had once told her that, so far, the ashworlds had held their own because they had a relatively large number of dragon pilots. Metal was not nearly as unstable an element as fire; people who worked almost exclusively with metal did not self-destruct quite as regularly.

It was no coincidence that each colony sent an assassin, and also no coincidence that the Phoenix General had kept all of them captive. Five was an important number, one that Ling Yun had taken for granted until Periet told her that the key was *six*.

The empire, with its emphasis on tradition, had accepted the sages' cycle of five elements since antiquity, even after it founded Colony One and Colony Two in the vast reaches of space. But what of space itself?

Numbers were Ling Yun's domain as much as they were any musician's. Now she knew what to do.

Ling Yun's head hurt, and even the tea wasn't going to keep her awake much longer. Still, she felt a quiet glow of triumph. She had finished the suite, including the sixth piece. The sixth piece wasn't for the *wuxian qin* at all. It was meant to be hummed, or whistled, like a folk melody or a child's song, like the music she had wanted to write all her life.

There was no place in the empire for such music, but she didn't have to accept that anymore.

If the toy glider had a song, it would be this one, even if the glider was broken. It was whole in her mind. That was what mattered.

Five strings braided together were coiled in her jacket sleeve, an uncomfortable reminder of what she was about to do.

Ling Yun wrote a letter on the tablet and marked it urgent, for the general's eyes only: *I must speak to you concerning the five assassins.* Her hand shook and her calligraphy looked unsteady. Let the general interpret that however he pleased.

A handful of moments passed. The character for *message* drew itself in the upper right corner. Ling Yun touched the tip of her brush to it.

The general's response was, simply: *Come.*

Shaking slightly, Ling Yun waited until her escort arrived. Under her breath, she hummed one of the variations from Mesketalioth's piece. In composing the suite, she had attuned herself to the pilots and their cause, but she did this by choice.

Be awake, she urged him, urged all the young pilots. *Be prepared.* Would the music pluck at the inner movements of their souls, the way it happened in the stories of old?

The escort arrived. "You are dedicated to work so long into the night," the taller of the two soldiers said, with every appearance of sincerity.

"We do what we can," Ling Yun said, thinking, *You have no idea.* People thought musicians were crazy, too. Perhaps everybody looked crazy to someone.

After tonight, she was going to look crazy to everyone, assuming Phoenix Command allowed the story to escape.

The Phoenix General met her in a different room this time. It had silk scrolls on the walls. "They're pretty, aren't they?" he said. Ling Yun was eerily reminded of Periet looking at her glider. "Some of them are generations old."

One of the scrolls had crisp, dark lines. Ling Yun's eyes were drawn to it: a phoenix hatching from a *wei qi* stone. "You painted that," she said.

"I was younger," the general said, "and never subtle. Please, there's tea. Your profile said you preferred citron, so I had them brew some for us."

The citron smelled sweet and sharp. Ling Yun knew that if she tasted it, she would lose her nerve. But courtesy was courtesy. "Thank you, sir," she said.

She held the first five movements of the dragon suite in her head, to give her Wu Wen Zhi's fixity of purpose and Ko's relaxed mien, Mesketalioth's reflexes and Periet's hidden ferocity, and Li Cheng Guo's quick wits.

The braided silk strings slipped down into Ling Yun's palm. She whipped them around the Phoenix General's neck. He was a large man, but she was fighting with the strength of six, not one. And she was fighting for five ashworlds rather than one empire.

As the Phoenix General struggled, Ling Yun tightened the strings. She fixed her gaze upon the painting of the hatching stone.

Ling Yun had been the Phoenix General's creature. The phoenix destroyed itself; it was only fitting that she destroy him.

It would only occur to her later that it had begun with the general assassinating the ashworlders' leader, that justice was circular.

Now I know what it is like to kill.

There was—not happiness, precisely, but a peculiar singing relief that the other was dead, and not she. She let go of the strings and listened to the thump as the general's body hit the floor.

The door crashed open. Wen Zhi and Periet held pistols. Wen Zhi's was pointed straight at Ling Yun.

Ling Yun looked up, heart thudding in her chest. She pulled her shoulders back and straightened. It turned out that she cared to die with some dignity, after all. "Make it quick," she said. "You have to get out of here."

Ko showed up behind the other two; he had apparently found a cord to tie his braid. "Come *on*, madam," he said. "We haven't any time to waste."

"So you were right," Wen Zhi said to him, sounding irritable. "The musician took care of the general, but that doesn't guarantee that she's an ally."

"Is this really the best time to be arguing?" Periet asked, with an air of, *Have you ever known me to be wrong?*

The other girl lowered her pistol. "All right, Perias. Are you coming with us, Musician?"

It was unlikely that Ling Yun's family would ever forgive her, even if she evaded capture by the imperial magistrates. She hurried after the pilots, who seemed to know exactly where they were going. "Perias?" she asked Periet, hoping that she might get an answer where Phoenix Command had not.

"Was the sixth one," Mesketalioth said without slowing down.

"What exactly is your plan for getting out of here?" Ling Yun said diffidently, between breaths. "We'll be hunted—"

"You of all people have no excuse to be so slow-witted," Cheng Guo called back. He was at the head of the group. "How do you think we got here?"

"All we need is a piece of sky," Periet said yearningly. She struck the wall with the heel of her hand.

I was right, Ling Yun thought. The edges of her vision went black; the reverberations sounded like a great gong.

Mesketalioth caught her. His arm was steady and warm. "Next time, a warning would be appreciated," he said, deadpan as ever.

The wall split outwards. *Metal cuts wood.*

"Let's fly," Periet said. A great wind was blowing through the hallway. They stepped through the hole in the wall, avoiding the jagged, broken planks. Above them, stars glittered in the dark sky.

"The void is the sixth element," Ling Yun said, looking up.

Five dragons manifested in a half circle, summoned through the void, white black blue yellow red. In the center, tethered to the red dragon by shimmering cables, was an unpainted glider. The sleek curves of its fuselage reminded Ling Yun of her zither.

"See?" Ko said. "I told you we'd fix it."

"Thank you," Ling Yun said, overwhelmed. They had written her into the game after all.

"It only works if there's six of us," Cheng Guo said. "You're the sixth pilot."

Mesketalioth helped Ling Yun into the glider's cockpit. "When we release the cables," he said, "follow Cheng Guo. He understands glider theory best, and he'll safely keep you on the void's thermal paths." Despite the scars, his expression was almost kind.

"It's time!" Wen Zhi shouted from her white dragon. There were now ten red marks on it. "We have to warn the seedworlds."

Soldiers shouted from the courtyard. A bolt glanced from one dragon in a shower of sparks. Mesketalioth's dragon reared up and laid down covering fire while Wen Zhi's dragon raked the ground with its claws. The soldiers, overmatched, scattered.

Then they were aloft, all six of them, dragons returning to the sky where they had been born.

Ling Yun spared not a glance backwards, but sang a quiet little melody to herself as they headed for the stars.

the black abacus

War Season

In space there are no seasons, and this is true too of the silver wheels that are humanity's homes beyond Earth and the silver ships that carried us there. In autumn there are no fallen leaves, and in spring, no living flowers; no summer winds, no winter snow. There are no days except our own calendars and the stars' slow candles in the dark.

The Network has known only one war, and that war ended before it began.

This is why, of course, the Network's ships trapped in q-space—that otherwhere of superpositions and spindrift possibilities—wield waveform interrupters, and why, though I was Rachel's friend, I killed her across several timelines. But the tale begins with our final exam, not my murders.

The Test

You are not required to answer this question.

However, the response (should you attempt one) will be evaluated. If you decide otherwise, key in "I DECLINE." The amount of time you spend will be evaluated. You cannot proceed to the next item without deciding, and there will be no later opportunity.

Your time remaining is: —:—:—

In her essay "The Tyranny of Choice and Observation," Shinaai Rei posits a "black abacus" that determines history's course by "a calculus of personalities and circumstances, cause and effect and chance." (You are not expected to be familiar with this work; the full text is restricted.)

In light of this, under what circumstances is war justified? What about assassination? Consider, for example, Skorzeny's tactics during World War II, police actions against the Candida Rebellion, and more recently, terrorists' sabotage of relay stations. You may cite current regulations and past precedents to support your answer.

As you do, remember the following points:

1. During the 76.9 years (adjusted time) that the Pancommunications Network has been in place, no planet- or station-born conflict has found expression in realspace.

2. Because your future duty as a Network officer requires absolute reliability, treason is subject to the death penalty.

3. "*Reductio ad absurdum* is one of a mathematician's finest weapons. It is a far finer gambit than any chess gambit: a chess player may offer the sacrifice of a pawn or even a piece, but the mathematician offers the game."—G.H. Hardy (1877-1947)

The Results

57% of that year's class declined the question, or so they thought. The computers recorded every keystroke and false start for further analysis. Of those who did respond, the ratio of essay length to time taken (after adjustments for typing speed) matched the predicted curve.

Rachel was the exception. Her answer took 5.47 minutes to compose (including one self-corrected typo) and three sentences to express.

The records knew her as Rachel Kilterhawk. Her comrades in command training knew her as the Hawk. In later times and other lives, they would call her Rachel the Ruthless. Neither of us guessed this when we first met.

White: Queen's Gambit

Rachel was one of the first to leave the exam. Her cadet's uniform was creased where she had bent over the keyboard, and even now her hands shook. *I did what I could,* she thought, and set her mind on other things: the spindles of growing plants, the taste of thrice-recycled water, the cold texture of metal . . . the sea, from her one visit to Earth, with its rush of foam and salt-sprinkled breezes.

She went to hydroponics, where water warbled through the pipes and the station's crops grew in identical green rows, a spring without end. In a corner of the garden she picked out a bench and sat with her legs drawn up, her hands on her knees. Nearby was a viewport—a viewscreen, actually, filtering the stars' radiation into intensities kinder to human eyes.

After a while her hands stopped trembling, and only then did she notice the other cadet. He had dark hair and darker eyes, and where her uniform was rumpled, his was damp with sweat. "Do you believe in angels?" he asked her.

Rachel blinked. "Not yet. Why?"

He gestured at the viewscreen, tracing unnamed constellations and the pale flash of an incoming ship's q-wave. "It must be a cold thing to die in space. I like to think there are angels who watch over the ships." The boy looked away and flushed.

She gazed at the fingerprints he had left on the screen. "Angels' wings."

It was his turn to blink. "Pardon?"

"The q-waves," she said. "Like wings."

He might have laughed; others often did, when Rachel with her quicksilver thoughts and quiet speech couldn't find the right words. She was startled when he rubbed his chin, then nodded. "Never thought of it that way." He smiled at her. "I'm Edgar Kerzen. And you?"

She returned his smile with one of her own. "Rachel."

Dawning realization: "You're the Hawk. No one else would've torn through the exam like that."

"But so did you."

Edgar shrugged. "I aced math and physics, but they killed me on ethics."

She heard the unsaid words: *Let's talk about something else.* Being Rachel, she was silent. And found herself startled again when he accepted the silence rather than filling it with words. She would come to treasure that acceptance.

Black: Knight's Sacrifice

The first life, first time I killed Rachel, it was too late. She had already given her three-sentence answer to the Pandect's exam; won command of the starhiker *Curtana*, one of 26 ever built; and swept from the Battle of Red Lantern to the Siege of Gloria on the shredded wings of a q-wave. After Gloria, her name passed across the relays as both battle-cry (for the Network) and curse (for the Movement). In this probability-space, her triumphs were too great to erase, her influence too great to stop the inevitable blurring of murder and necessity.

After the siege, we had a few days to remember what sleep was, to forget the silence of battle. Space is silent, though we want thunder with our lightning, the scream of metal and roar of guns. I think this was true even for Rachel, because she believed in *right* silences and *wrong* silences.

By fortune or otherwise we had shared postings since we left academy, since that first meeting in hydroponics. Command was short on officers, but shorter still on ones who worked together like twin heartbeats. I stood beside her when she received the captain's wing on her uniform and again when we learned, over the relays, that the scoutship *Boomerang*'s kamikaze destruction of a station had plunged one probability-space into war. I stood beside her and said nothing when she opened fire on Gloria Station, another of the few q-space stopovers. It harbored a Movement ship determined to return to realspace, and so it died in a ripple of incoherence.

One people, one law, said the Network. There were too many factions at a time when humanity's defenses were scattered across the stars: conglomerates with their merchant fleets, colonies defending their autonomy, freetraders who resented the Network's restrictions. Once the Pancommunications Network had only been responsible for routing transmissions between settlements and sorting out discrepancies due to time dilation. Someone had to maintain the satellite networks that knit everyone together and someone had to define a law, however, so the Network did.

In light of this, under what circumstances is war justified?

A ship's captain has her privacy, but we were docked and awaiting repairs, and I knew Rachel's thoughts better than my own. She had her duty, and if that duty demanded it, she would pay in blood. Including her own, if it came to that, but she was too damned brilliant to die in battle. Because she was the Hawk, and when it came to her duty, she never hesitated.

5.47 minutes and three sentences.

I came upon Rachel deep in the ship's hold, in an area closed off for tomorrow's repairs. Her eyes, when she raised them to me, were the wild grey of a winter sky, unlike the carbon-scored grey of the torn bulkheads behind her. These days our world was defined by shades of grey and the reflections therein.

Soon we would be forced to leave the colorless haven of q-space, since the last few stations could barely sustain themselves or the remaining ships. For a while, the Network and the Independence Movement had cannibalized any new ships who entered q-space despite the perils of merging q-waves, gutting them of supplies, people, and news. Once a ship exited into realspace, our own fluctuating history would collapse into a single outcome, and nobody was willing to plunge the realspace world into war, especially one in the enemy's favor. New ships no longer showed up, and God knew what we'd done to realspace transportation and logistics.

A few weary souls had tried to force the issue. Rachel shot them down. She was determined to win or stop the war in every life, every timeline, and she might even succeed.

She noticed my presence and, for once, spoke before I could. "Edgar. While I'm here, more people are dying." Her voice was restless, like the beating feathers of a bird in a snowstorm.

"We'll find out about it on relay," I said, wishing I could say something to comfort her, to gentle those eyes, that voice, but Rachel had never much believed in words, even mine.

"Do you think angels fly between probability-spaces to harvest our souls?"

I closed my eyes and saw the afterimages of a ship's waveform disintegration, translated into images the human mind could interpret. "I wish I knew." I was tired of fighting and forcing myself to remember that the bright, undulating ribbons on the tactical display represented people and what had carried people. I wanted her to say that we would leave and let the multiplicity of battles end, but I knew she wouldn't.

For a long time Rachel said nothing, lacing and unlacing her fingers together. Then her hands relaxed and she said, "How did you know to find me here?"

Nothing but curiosity from a woman who had killed civilians, whom I had always followed. Her duty and her ruthlessness were a greater weapon than any battleship the Network had left. My angel, an angel of death.

My hands were a weapon and her trust, a weakness.

"I'll always find you, my dear," I said, reaching out as though to massage her shoulders, and interrupted the balance of her breath and brain and heartbeat. She did not fight; perhaps she knew that in other probability-spaces, I was still hers. I thought of Red Lantern. My memories held lights and lines in red or amber, autumn colors; tactical screens, terse voices. My own voice, saying *Aye aye, sir.*

After she stopped moving, I laid her down. I was shaking. Such an easy thing, to kill. Escape was the hard part, and I no longer cared.

• • •

The Darkest Game

Schrödinger's cat has far more than nine lives, and far fewer. All of us are unknowing cats, alive and dead at once, and of all the might-have-beens in between, we record only one.

We had the catch-me catch-me-not of quantum physics, then quantum computers, oracles that scanned possibilities. When we discovered a stardrive that turned ships into waves in a sea of their own—q-space—we thought we understood it. We even untangled navigation in that sea and built our stations there.

Then, the echoes. Ghosts in probability-space, waveforms strung taut from waypoint to waypoint, snapshot to snapshot. Enter q-space and you throw a shard of the universe into flux. Exit it, and the shard crystallizes, fixing history over the realspace interval. Shinaai Rei—philosopher, physicist, and sociologist—saw it first.

Before the *Boomerang*, there had been neither been a war nor ships that interrupted the night with their flashfire battles. Then she destroyed a civilian station, and the world shifted into a grand game of chess, probabilities played one on the other, ships that winged into q-space never to return. Why take risks in war when you can try everything at once and find out who will win?

White: Candles

Theirs had been one of many patrolships guarding the satellite network. Sometimes threats breathed through the relays, but nobody was willing to disrupt the web of words between worlds. Rachel had known Network duty was tedious, but didn't mind. Edgar was with her, and around they went, never twice tracing the same path. Their conversations, too, were never twice the same.

Everything had turned awry, but when smoke seared her lungs or she had to put the crew on half-rations again, she remembered. Edgar was all that remained from that quiet time, and when his back was to her as he checked a readout, she gazed fondly at the dark, tousled hair and the steady movements of his hands.

On patrol, through the long hours, Rachel had come to trust his motions, his words, his velvet voice, and the swift thoughts behind them. Even his smile, when smiles often made false promises. But there came dark moments, too.

Once, after watching a convoy of tradeships streak by, Edgar said, "What would happen if all the satellites went out?"

She explored the idea and found it sharp to the touch. "Candles."

He understood. "Only a matter of time before everything fails. Imagine living in a future when the worlds drop silent one by one."

Rachel reached out and stroked his hand. "It won't happen yet," she said. *Not for a long time, and we are here; the Network is here.*

He folded her hand in his, and for a moment his mouth was taut, bitter. "War would do that."

"The exam." Years ago, and she still remembered the way her hands had shook afterward. What Edgar had said, she never asked. He gave her the same courtesy.

She wondered now if he had foreseen the war and chosen to make himself a part of it, with the quicksilver instinct she treasured. She suspected that his dreams, his visions of other probability-spaces, were clearer than hers, which spoke merely of a battle to be won, everywhere and when. Rachel decided to ask him the next time they were both awake and alone.

In some of her lives, she never had the opportunity.

Black: A Riddle

How long can a war go on if it never begins?

White: The Bloody Queen

The Battle of Seven Spindles. The Battle of Red Lantern. The Siege of

Gloria. The Battle of Crescent. 21 stations and 4 battles fought across the swirl of timelines. Rachel counted each one as it happened.

Today, insofar as there were days in q-space, she faced the 45th ship. The *Curtana* was a hell of red lights and blank, malfunctioning displays; she had never been meant to go this long without a realspace stopover. The crew, too, showed the marks of a long skirmish with their red eyes and blank faces. They saw her as the Hawk, unassailable and remote; she never revealed otherwise to them.

The communications officer, Thanh, glanced up from his post and said, "The *Shanghai Star* requests cease-fire and withdrawal." A standard request once, when ships dragged governments into debt and lives were to be safeguarded, not spent. A standard request now, when ships were resources to be cannibalized after they could no longer sustain life.

Rachel did not hesitate. "No." The sooner attrition took its toll, the sooner they would find an end to this.

Her crew knew her too well to show any surprise. Perhaps, by now, they were beyond it. After a pause, Thanh said, "The captain would like to speak to you."

"You mean he wants to know why." For once words came easily to her: she had carried this answer inside her heart since she understood what war meant. "Tell the *Shanghai Star* that there's no easy escape. That we can make the trappings of battle as polite as we like, and still people die. That the only kind end is a quick one."

Rachel heard Edgar approach her from the side and felt his warmth beside her. "They'll die, you know," he murmured.

She startled herself by saying, "I'm not infallible." Battle here, like the duels of old, was fast and fatal. A modification of the stardrive diverted part of the q-wave into a powerful harmonic. If an inverse Fourier breakdown of the enemy ship's waveform was used to forge the harmonic, and directed toward that waveform, the stardrive became an interrupter. The principle of canceling a wave with its inverse was hardly new, but

Edgar had programmed the change to the ship's control computers before anyone else did. A battle was 90% maneuver and data analysis to screen out noise from other probability-spaces, 10% targeting.

Her attention returned, then, to the lunge-and-parry, circle-and-retreat of battle.

At the end, it was her fifth battle and victory. Only the *Curtana* remained to tell of it.

Black: The Traitor Knight

Time and again, Rachel's crew on the *Curtana* speculates that she dreams of Fourier breakdowns and escape trajectories, if she dreams at all. *The Hawk never sleeps,* they say where Rachel isn't supposed to hear, and so she never corrects the misimpression.

Sometimes I was her first officer and sometimes her weapons officer. Either way I knew her dreams. In a hundred lives, they never changed: dreams of the sea and of the silver ships, silver stations, that were her only homes; dreams of fire that burned without smoke, death that came without sound.

In a hundred lives and a hundred dreams I killed her a hundred times. Once with my hands and once with a fragment of metal. Sometimes by betraying her orders and letting the ship hurtle into an interrupter's wave, or failing to report an incoming hostile. On the rare instances that I failed, I was executed by her hand. We knew the penalty for treason.

Several times I killed her by walking away when she called out to me as the ship's tortured, aging structure pinned her down. Several times more I died, by rope or knife or shipboard accident, leaving her behind, and took her soul with me.

I have lived more probabilities than she will ever dream. Doubtless the next will be similar. I know every shape of her despair, every winter hymn in her heart . . . why she looks for angels and only finds me.

I am tired of killing her. Make your move and end the game.

• • •

White: A Change in Tactics

When it was her turn to sleep, Rachel dreamt: constellations of fingerprints, white foam on the wind, ships with dark wings and darker songs. But she woke always to Edgar's hand tracing the left side of her jaw, then her shoulder, and that touch, like her duty aboard the *Curtana*, defined her mornings. It was the only luxury she permitted herself or Edgar. The rest of the crew made no complaint. His were the hardest, most heartbreaking tasks, and they knew it.

His dreams were troubled, she knew. Sometimes they surfaced in his words, the scars of unfought battles and unfinished deaths, merciless might-have-beens. *Stay here,* she thought. *Of all the choices, one must be a quiet ending.*

Perhaps he heard her, in the silence.

Black: Check and Mate

Rachel's response to the ethics question took 5.47 minutes and three sentences. Mine took more lives, mine and hers and others', than I can count.

Rachel's Season

In space there are no seasons, and this is as true of the ships that cross the distances between humanity's far-flung homes. But we measure our seasons anyway: by a smile, a silence, a song. I measured mine by Rachel's deaths. Perhaps she will measure hers differently.

Your move, my dear.

the book of locked doors

The book was bound in leather crinkled pale and rough thread the color of massacres, and Suzuen Vayag carried it in an inner pocket of her coat as a matter of course. Her sister Kereyag had written it in gunfire and witchfire and hellpyre smoke, on the stray cold morning of her death. The least Vayag could do was keep it safe.

Today's operation required that Vayag travel to the administrative capital of Territory 5, which was what the Meroi conquerors called her homeland. The administrative capital had once been Nyago-ot of the Seventy Temples, where pilgrims had brought pressed flowers from all corners of the peninsula twice a year. Now the Meroi called it Shadow City 5-1, for the shadow of the Cloud Fortress that flew above it. Most of the temples had been destroyed during the war of occupation. The greatest one, Ten Bells Ten Flowers, had been spared only to be reopened as a museum honoring the Meroi dead.

The only way to reach the Cloud Fortress was by air. The Meroi controlled airspace tightly and even their dignitaries had to secure permission to visit well in advance. It was an interesting problem. Vayag supposed she ought to be grateful that her orders only required her to shut off the fortress's communications to the Meroi homeland for a single hour. She thought she saw a way to do it and survive, but her survival wasn't, strictly speaking, necessary.

The book had whispered to Vayag in its dry voice of fluttering pages and threads rubbing together. It had suggested that she could do more than disable communications; that she could destroy the Cloud Fortress, send it plummeting to the city below. Ever helpful, it had identified the pages that would facilitate the modified operation. Of course there were page numbers. Kereyag had always been meticulous about details.

Vayag had no intention of carrying through with the book's suggestion, not least because of the number of bystanders that would die, but she had looked at the indicated pages, the way she always did. On page thirty-one was a picture of a cobweb threaded tremulously across a corpse's empty eye sockets. The left socket had been cut into the shape of a keyhole.

Written in neat script, in an alphabet that had been outlawed six years ago, was the corpse's particular profile. His name had been Khem Myan, and like everyone in the book, he had died in the Snowfall Massacre. He had been unrivaled at the old art of mirror archery: shooting slivers that multiplied themselves through prisms, or sending them around corners with the help of strategically placed reflections.

Vayag had to admit the utility of mirror archery. She could have unlocked the page and taken it with her, but the ability belonged to a dead man and she would not disturb his spirit this way.

She entered Subway Station 14 on the blue line, trying to ignore the book's continued whispering. The station was cleaner than it ever had been during her childhood. Say what you would about the Meroi, but they were excellent administrators. Their firesnake crest was painted on every long stretch of wall. The tiles of the floor shone pale blue, with stippled tiles forming a path for the blind. The trains ran smoothly. There were no beggars—

There were no beggars, but neither were there sellers of fruit, neither were there players of drums and tellers of fortunes with cards of azalea and crane. Vayag and her sister had come to stations just like this one with coins in their pockets, buying sour-sweet candies on the way home from school. Now when she looked at the station, all she saw were doors opening and closing, opening and closing, in mechanical defeat.

And although there were still people who spoke the peninsula's many native tongues, the cool sweet voices that read out the trains incoming and

THE BOOK OF LOCKED DOORS

trains outgoing, that reminded travelers of ordinary safety precautions, spoke the Meroi language.

The blue line from Station 14 eastbound (really north-east-east, if you cared about details, which she did) and six stops would take Vayag to Station 20. Her ticket had a firesnake on it, beautifully rendered in red ink. She used to hope that the machines would punch a hole in its head, but such pettiness did her no good. Besides, they never did.

She could feel the book rustling its pages against her side. She gritted her teeth and thought of other things: the color of half-turned leaves in the public gardens of Kiiru-ot, that last kite festival where Kereyag had gone around the whole day in an inside-out tunic without noticing until Vayag finally told her after the dinner feast, the savor of quail eggs with just a hint of mustard.

The windows revealed nothing but darkness pierced by intermittent flashes of light, the pauses where people with no more individuality than silhouettes got on or got off. Vayag assessed them as she stared off at an angle, pretending to be entranced by an advertisement featuring a fine-looking man with improbable hair. That one was a student, slump-shouldered beneath her books. She wore her hair swept up and pinned asymmetrically in the style that the Meroi governor had made fashionable. A man tapped his fingers on his knee in a simple rhythm. An older woman trailed two children, who were bickering amiably over a piece of taffy. The children, like the other passengers, wore the dull, sober clothes permitted to Territory 5's subjugates by sumptuary law.

There was really no excuse for what she was about to do, except that the alternative was to watch as her people adopted Meroi names in exchange for greater privileges and better-paying jobs. Even the graffiti, however quickly painted over, was in the Meroi language these days. And more and more often, she heard children speaking their parents' languages with Meroi accents.

For that matter, Vayag had cultivated that same accent so as to draw less attention to herself. She imagined the day would come when she would no longer be able to shed it at will, whatever her intentions.

The conductor announced that they would soon be stopping at Station 20. Vayag got up and shuffled to the nearest doors, behind a woman who was scowling at her timepiece. The timepiece was a thing of beauty: rose gold set with flashing crystals of darker pink. Vayag was tempted to steal it, just to prove she could, but it would have been unprofessional. She had gotten herself into trouble that way during one of her first missions, and she wasn't going to jeopardize this one now.

The doors opened and light slanted in from the station, softly bright. Vayag followed the woman with the timepiece out, walking fast, but not too fast. She smiled blandly at the firesnake emblem across from her.

She joined the amiable jostling of the crowd. As she passed a newsstand, she cast her gaze over the broadsheets. All the people in the photos were smiling. She didn't get a close look at the figures and statistics and charts, but the photos—lying by omission—told her all she needed to know.

Turn right. Up the stairs. Emerge into the cloudlight, pale and crisp. Vayag couldn't help but notice all the reflective surfaces available to her, if only, if only. Polished windows and metal door frames. Lamp posts darkly glossy. The glint of a man's necklace, a spark of blue from a woman's earring. The polish of a Meroi policeman's boots, even.

It was not too late, the book explained to her, as patiently as if it were instructing a child. Vayag could duck into that teahouse, where there was a line. She could bend her head over the book's pages, fit her finger to the keyhole, open the page and all its possibilities.

But her aim was not another massacre, no matter how much the book wished otherwise.

The book told Vayag, rather sharply, not to be ridiculous. They worked for the resistance, after all. Would freedom be bought with anything less dear than death?

Not here, not now. The words caught in her throat like thorns.

Down the street. No beggars here, either. They were near the heart of Meroi power, and the Meroi despised untidiness. No more festival banners, no more crisscrossing lines of laundry. The children played in designated areas instead of rambling in and out of the alleys. There was a puddle to one side of the street, a remnant of the thunderstorm that had passed by two days ago. More reflections; one of them was Vayag's own, murky and sullen and distorted by ripples.

Vayag went to a noodle shop and made her order: brown noodles with shrimp, which Kereyag had always loved. She sat at a table next to an ostentatious vase and studied the illegible scratches on the tabletop. The server brought her a glass of cold tea.

Outside, a patrol went by in their red uniforms. She couldn't hear their footsteps from here, of course, although the rumbling of cars passing was an inconstant.

Vayag had her own timepiece, a shabby student affair that she had bought two days ago in a pawn shop. She made a note of the time: four more minutes. She had cut it too close, counting on the general reliability of the rail system, but done was done.

She wore long Meroi-style socks that went up to mid-calf. Taped to her left sock was a ribbon-shaped transmitter. In four minutes—three and change, really—she would activate it with her other foot, and then the cancelers that had been planted throughout the city would direct a pulse toward the Cloud Fortress. After that, it was up to her to escape if she could, and to die if she couldn't.

It seemed unlikely that the resistance had a way of disabling the fortress's defenses, but Vayag wasn't privy to the details of the plan, and that was as it should be.

Two minutes. She watched another server, this one sallow of face, settle up with a young couple. The clink of coins sounded the same no matter what the mint. The Meroi coil and its derivatives had largely replaced native coins, which had come in a confusing variety of denominations. As a child she had hated memorizing the relative values: twelve pence to a myon, five myon to a rorogu, two rorogu to a half-jirik . . . fortunately, the full jirik had been the largest denomination she had encountered with any regularity. Naturally, once the coins with their annoying conversions were gone, she missed them.

One minute. Vayag sipped her tea. It wasn't very good tea, brewed too strong, but such details didn't matter. She felt a slow trickle of sweat in the small of her back.

Her time was up. Vayag twisted slightly and pressed her calf hard against the leg of the table.

There was nothing: no immediate sound, no vibration from the trigger, nothing to indicate that it had worked. But she had to assume that it had.

Vayag had just gotten up, a scant few seconds later, when the effect kicked in. The shadows of feathers fell through the window and pierced the tables, the chairs, the floor. She cut toward the back door, surprising the cook, and flung it open.

The sky above was filled with a silhouette in the shape of a great bird, its wingspan stretching from horizon to horizon. The Cloud Fortress, visible at this distance as a tilted spindle bright with green-gold lights, intersected its heart. In the silhouette shapes moved, outlined in shivers of refracted sunlight: broken ribcages, spent bullets, smoke and fire and cars chewed into jigsaw masses. And eyes: hundreds upon hundreds of eyes, blinking too rapidly or not at all.

In the mythology of Vayag's people, three goddesses had shared rule of the world: Minhyen the Bird of Dawn, Khugyun the Bird of Night, and Sarasyon the Bird of Death. Vayag and her sister had left their share of offerings at the goddesses' altars: sweet spring water for Minhyen, or votive candles in the shapes of lotus blossoms for Khugyun, or burnt barley flatbread for Sarasyon. They had seen a priest of Sarasyon summon the goddess's living shadow once, when the Meroi warships first sailed up the river to the capital's harbor. The ships had fallen apart in feather-shaped shards.

The peninsula's resistance had doomed itself then: the Meroi were quick to learn, and had spared nothing in hunting down the priests and wonder-workers.

The patrol from earlier was heading back down the street. A bad sign: she didn't know the specifics of their technology, but she had hoped they wouldn't be able to trace the source of the prayer signal.

The larger issue was that even the resistance should not have been able to summon the goddess's shadow, not at such a size. Sarasyon would only have responded to direct sacrifice. Vayag hadn't realized that enough priests remained in the peninsula to carry off such a feat.

She was spending time thinking about the situation when the proper response was to react. It was difficult to look away from the goddess's transcendent shadow, but she made herself move one foot, then the other, one foot, then the other, over and over again. It would not do to run, not yet, but the more distance she could put between herself and—

The patrol had returned. She could hear a woman barking orders for everyone to take cover in the nearest building and to stay put, as if anything as weak as walls would stop the divine. But then, the Meroi had always been fond of technological solutions to metaphysical problems, relying on the logic of gun and circuit.

The question was, would anyone think to stop an obviously suicidal civilian from walking farther out into the falling shadows?

"You there!"

Apparently the answer was yes. Vayag bolted.

Shouts followed her, but she didn't hear the words. There was only the hard jolt of the pavement beneath her shoes, wind in her hair, shadows compounding shadows.

People were yelling, cursing, sobbing. She couldn't tell the difference between Meroi voices and her own people's voices in the clamor. But they knew what was to come.

Page 62, the book said to her in its dry, matter-of-fact voice.

Vayag knew the page the way she knew all the pages. Heged Alokho, who had been a temple guard, a fast runner over short distances and a master of the sacred knives. She had been survived by two sisters, but they had died a year after she did, hounded out of hiding by Meroi police forces.

Don't make me laugh, Vayag thought at the book. She didn't need supernatural aid for something as simple as running. Even before the occupation, she had delighted in racing Kereyag up hills and down helter-skelter paths, through the wild hills just southeast of the city of their birth, losing herself—just for moments—to the illusion that she could step up and into the sky. She didn't have a racer's conformation, but she could sprint when she had to.

Page 4, the book said, persistent.

She was tempted. She couldn't deny it.

Page 4 contained Yede Marannag, a teenage girl whose life had been dedicated to the Bird of Night when she turned fifteen. A map of the peninsula had been tattooed on her back, where she could never see it. Thereafter she could never be lost, even blindfolded. She used to live in the sacred labyrinth of Nyago-ot with its shroud of mists and its echo-birds. The book had made a note that Yede had been especially fond of tangerine offerings. It wasn't typical for the book to care about such human details, but then, Kereyag had been fond of tangerines herself.

All she had to do was scrape the words off the page and swallow them like bitter medicine. If she got enough of a lead, she could probably spare the time. The book was good at such calculations, and it wouldn't have offered her the option if there didn't exist time in which to exercise it.

"No," she said through her teeth. Six years she had survived since the massacre. She wouldn't resort to the book after all this time.

She slowed down as she approached an intersection, quickly assessed her escape options: down to catch the rail? Or should she continue on foot until she could catch a bus? People had seen her fleeing. She had to decide soon.

No: best to take cover. She saw an open window above a garbage receptacle. Any moving shadows, on-off lights? Nothing so far. She would have to risk it. Vayag vaulted up, then up again, and through the window. She had to be grateful for the peninsular penchant for expansive windows.

The shadow feathers were still falling, only to dissipate when they met solid surfaces. But the sky was growing darker, and she knew there was not much time left before the goddess cried destruction on the city.

There was a potted plant on the windowsill, with withered pink flowers. Vayag took care not to knock it over. The room she found herself in was unlit, unoccupied. She closed the window—there were no curtains, that was a Meroi affectation—and moved away from it. Against one wall was a small chest worked in abalone inlay and a great scar against one of its panels. She left it alone.

The book reminded her of page 19, which contained Beherris Leleyen, another servant of the Bird of Night. During the New Moon Festival twice a year, he had folded himself up into shadows. People had come to watch him disappear, to hear his strong voice out of the empty darkness reciting the old chants in the temple language.

There was no need. She could hear sirens, shouts, but the authorities would be occupied trying to keep order. Instead, she took the door, placing her steps quietly and precisely.

The apartment was in the peninsular style. Most of the owner's furnishings were age-worn. The communal sleeping room only had a single mat rolled up in the corner, though. She would have expected a family even in this tidy space: sisters and brothers and elders and grown-up children, and perhaps some of their children, as well. Whatever the story was here, it wasn't for her to know.

Vayag spent the most time in the kitchen, where there was a satisfactory collection of knives and chopsticks. She selected the sturdiest one and leaned against the wall, staring at the unlit stove.

Now that her breathing was starting to slow, she could devote some thought to the bothersome question of how the resistance had triggered the Bird of Death's appearance. The feathers were only fallout. The real target would be the Cloud Fortress, and on the ground she was powerless to help, or find out what was going on. It was tempting to turn on the television, but the noise might attract attention and she doubted that the authorities would allow any substantive reporting to get through.

The book sounded impatient this time, which was at least a welcome change from its customary smugness. It pointed out, very painstakingly, that Vayag had never matched the count of the dead against the book's own pages.

"I never needed to," Vayag retorted, surprised into speaking aloud, but now she wondered. The Meroi government had never released an official list of casualties, and even the reported deaths were probably well shy of the actual figure.

For that matter, Vayag had been there herself, but in the mist and chaos and the hectic gunfire, she had had no good way to tell how many people had failed to survive.

Then why, the book said relentlessly, did it surprise her that someone else had compiled their own book out of the massacre?

Or indeed, of the other massacres, great and small, that had happened in the past years?

Vayag was sweating now. The thought that the shadow government had manipulated its own people in this fashion was intolerable.

The book informed her that it had welcomed death; welcomed the reduction of blood and sinew into curving letters, words of entwined red and black.

Vayag didn't address the book by name. She never did. It hurt too much to think of Kereyag's easy smile, Kereyag's laugh, Kereyag's footsteps next to her own. "I have a new target," Vayag whispered. "Stand with me or against me."

The book had always been her ally, even as she refused to make use of its capabilities.

All right. The next step, then, was to seek out her handler and pry information out of him. This meant going out into the feather-storm, but there was no help for it. She could only hope that, if the Cloud Fortress were indeed about to fall, that it didn't land on top of her.

Vayag left by the door and took the stairs down to the ground floor. She made sure to lock the door behind her, out of an obscure sense of courtesy toward the individual whose home she had entered. A cat watched her, slit-eyed and unconcerned, as she emerged.

The air had grown cold and restless. She could almost feel the wind's fingers creeping through her hair, along her face, up into her sleeves. There was the sound of fire, roaring and directionless, but no sign of heat or light.

Her handler wouldn't be expecting her to check in. Indeed, their next contact was to be in nine days, which would work in her favor. It probably wouldn't surprise him that she knew his usual hangouts, the clerk's job that he had assumed, the tisanes he liked to order from the tea-shops.

A sudden motion on the ground caught her attention. The pavement had cracked in the shape of a perfect keyhole, one large enough to swallow her foot if she placed it wrong. The inner section slowly crumbled into particles of shadow. It was followed by another keyhole, and another. The particles swirled, gathering themselves into the shapes of vertebrae and tibias and mazed circuit boards.

She had to get out of here. Now.

On foot, taking adequate precautions under these conditions, it would take her the better part of three hours to reach her handler's neighborhood. There was no help for it but to start walking. The book reminded her of page 62's runner, as she had known it would. It was less easy than usual to ignore its suggestion.

Vayag kept to small, shadowed streets and away from major intersections, sprinting whenever she thought she could get away with it. Thankfully, she had always had good direction sense, and as she neared the city's northwest-central district, the streets became familiar. About a third of the way there, she emerged from under the rain of shadow feathers, although she could still feel the dread wind and a more worrying, almost concussive force that transmitted itself in brief pulses, just below the threshold of human hearing.

She passed an eclectic variety of people. Children who were gawking at the spectacle, despite the best efforts of their parents and aunts and uncles. Looters who were taking advantage of the confusion to slip into undefended stores; she gave those a wide berth, not because she feared them, but she couldn't waste the time to deal with them. On one street corner she spotted a circle of older women and men with their arms linked and raised toward the treacherous sky, singing the old hymn of the three goddesses dancing the dawn of the world. The occasional Meroi, brandishing guns and sticks to get people under cover. A beggar sifting patiently through one of the keyholes in search of stray change. Her arms were covered with skull-shaped soot-marks all the way up to the elbows.

She found herself wishing that the resistance's gambit would succeed, given that they had tried it at all. The fact that the goddess was having difficulty with a Meroi Cloud Fortress was itself worthy of note. But then, she supposed, the problem was not the people but the technology. The Bird of Night was most concerned with people, and not at all with flying machines, and the Meroi were great believers in automated failsafes.

Vayag, the book said. It rarely addressed her by name. It told her to run. There was no playfulness in its tone at all.

People were watching. She shouted a warning, but couldn't find the words. And then she ran as fast as she could. Not as fast as page 62 would have run—under other circumstances she would have been ashamed that the name had escaped her—but fast enough.

For a while there was nothing but the jolt of her feet against uneven pavement, watering eyes, the thumping of her heart. And then she heard the Bird of Night's scream. It scratched every cloud out of the sky. Even the feathers stopped falling.

The book told her she could stop now.

It took her several moments to convince herself that this was the case. She backtracked because the people who had been standing were standing no more. She had been perilously close to the boundary line, and she had to wonder if the book had protected her in some fashion.

Vayag only checked six corpses, but six was enough. Each one had a bloody gaping wound in the shape of a keyhole where its heart should have been.

Bile rose in her throat. Had the resistance's plan failed? How could they have allowed it to go so wrong?

It was by no means certain that her handler would have answers, but she had nothing else left to try. She continued heading northwest. The sun was so bright that it was giving her a headache, but it was better than the rain of shadows.

She made sure to mop the sweat off her face with a handkerchief before she approached her handler's favorite place for afternoon tea. It was a small tea-shop with a wooden unsign, well-weathered and unpainted.

A glance through the door told her he wasn't there. Well, it was too much to expect to get lucky so early. The book was curiously silent about her options, although she knew perfectly well that page 98 contained someone with a tracking ability. Since the sun was in the sky it would even work right now.

Vayag had no luck with the next three places she tried, and she was considering risking his workplace when she thought of going back to the tea-shop and asking if they'd seen the man. She pretended, not very gracefully, to be a worried lover, but the woman at the tea-shop was too distracted by the news on the television of this latest massacre—in her home city, at that—to need much convincing. It turned out he had not shown up today, so chances was that he was either sick or pretending to be.

Her handler was not only at home, he was cooking a late lunch: fried rice with shrimp and strips of pork. She came directly through the door—picking the lock was absurdly easy, but then he wouldn't want to arouse suspicion with unusually high security—and wavered for a moment out of sheer hunger.

"I take it they stopped all the trains," was the first thing he said to her. "But you're days early, you know. Do you want something to eat? There were going to be leftovers anyway."

Vayag didn't know his real name, the way he didn't know hers. Probably. "We have to talk," she said shortly. She supposed this meant sharing a meal with him, and she really didn't want to be burdened by thoughts of hospitality customs.

He turned off the stove and dumped the pan's contents onto two plates, divided evenly. "Sit, then." He gestured vaguely toward a table and two plain oak chairs.

She sat, but didn't touch the food. She did pick up the chopsticks he had provided, though.

Her handler eyed her, then shrugged and began eating. After a while, he said, "You really know all you need to know. If you're going to ask for operation details—"

"It's already out on the television," Vayag said pointedly. "What's there to hide?"

He wasn't looking her in the eye, although that could have been because he was very interested in his lunch.

"What was the objective?" she said. She wasn't shouting yet. "A lot of people died because we fucked this up."

Still no answer. Now she was certain that he was avoiding eye contact. She reached across the table and shoved the plate violently. It spun off the table, scattering fried rice everywhere, and shattered against the floor.

"That was uncalled for, agent," the man said in a dead, even tone. Still, he made no move to defend himself when she abruptly got up and leaned forward to grab him by the throat.

Vayag still had a chopstick in one hand. She set its point against his lower eyelid. "I need to know," she said, "why those people had to die. The people whose freedom we are supposed to be fighting for."

"An agent who can't follow orders isn't of much use to us," he said.

She increased the pressure of the point, angled the chopstick up toward his eye. He only flinched a little, to his credit.

"I have killed people for you," she said. "I have risked death for you. I need to know that you're *doing it right*."

"All right," he said slowly. "But I'm going to have to remand you to a higher authority, and they could just as well decide to have you killed for being a security risk."

"I'll take that chance," Vayag said.

"What did you think the objective was?"

"To damage the Cloud Fortress, I suppose," she said. She hadn't thought very hard about it.

"You know what the Meroi industrial capacity is like," he said. "I won't say that it's trivial for them to manufacture and maintain Cloud Fortresses, but they have them over all their occupied territories so it's clearly doable. No; the objective was the *expertise* that goes into a Cloud Fortress. Its operation, its design, everything."

"You'd have to get that from the Meroi themselves," Vayag said slowly.

He smiled; it barely lit his eyes. "And that's what we just did. The other deaths in the city were an unfortunate side-effect. You gave us the idea, really."

"I what?"

"Your book is no secret," he said. "I don't know how you persuaded a temple scribe to make it for you, or how often you use it, but the concept was sound: a Meroi 'sacrifice' would enable us to scribe their spirits for future use."

There was no point in denying it, even if her handler didn't seem to be aware that the temple scribe in question had been her sister. "That's not right," Vayag said blankly. "I've never used the book. If it isn't right to use our own spirits for gain, how can it be right to use Meroi spirits taken unwillingly?"

"I don't believe the Meroi ever gave us a choice worth speaking of," he said.

"No," Vayag said. "I suppose not." She dropped the chopstick.

And then, when her handler relaxed, she grabbed a blade out of her sleeve and cut his throat with it.

She felt like a hole had been carved out of her heart.

The dead, reduced to words chained to a page, could not consent to be used in this fashion. All her life she had heard, from Kereyag even, that the scribe's art was to be used only to present an accurate picture of the dead. Siphoning their aptitudes and abilities out of them afterwards was disrespectful to their rest, and scribes caught abusing their ability in this fashion could expect to be tortured to death.

Kereyag had thought it no longer mattered, that last cold morning. Dying, she had recorded all the dead that Vayag could find for her, and then scribed herself into the book with its rough pages.

Now Vayag had to find a way to stop her own people from conquering the Meroi by throwing away their own beliefs. It was too late for second thoughts. She had committed to this course the moment she threatened her handler.

She washed up and went to find a change of clothes.

Then she found an empty space at the kitchen counter and opened the book. The last page was blank. Trembling, she wrote, in unstable, spidery letters: *Anything I can do with your help, I can do better by relying on my own heart and my own hopes.*

The book's answer formed below Vayag's sentence:

This isn't my book, sister sweetest. You are.

Vayag slammed the book shut but couldn't bring herself to leave it behind where someone would come across it. She left the dead man's apartment, then, and walked out into a world of ashfall and crumbling keyholes.

conservation of shadows

There is no such thing as conservation of shadows. When light destroys shadows, darkness does not gain in density elsewhere. When shadows steal over earth and across the sky, darkness is not diluted.

Hello, Inanna. You have seven inventory slots, all full. The seventh contains your heart, which cannot be removed. We will do our best to remedy this.

A feast awaits you at the end, sister. I am keeping it warm for you. You will be cold by the time you reach my hall beneath the floors of the world. Meadow honey on barley cakes, cheese and the tender flesh of goats; plums and pears brighter than the jewels in your hair; wine less sweet than birdsong and more bitter than tears. Taken together they form a nutritionally complete diet.

You think that all we eat in the underworld is dust and all we drink is the dregs of rain, but that is not the case. Come and share the feast.

You hesitate over the shadow-gun at your waist. Notice the holster, leather stamped with a lioness on each side. The leather comes from a lioness's hide. She is dead, sister. She cannot aid you here.

I can't tell you how to pass through the first gate. More accurately, I could, but I won't. We live by different laws in the underworld, we who live at all. Now you must respect those laws as well.

The gate lies there. Your fingers move toward it, then draw back. How wise of you. Gates are hungry. They demand propitiation. Once a woman put her hand in a gate and it ate her fingers. A five-legged spider with red eyes crawled out. That woman put in three fingers from her other hand, so that the spider might be complete. Do you have that integrity of purpose, sister?

No, what you feed the gate is other. It is easy for gates to be dark, maws opening to the earth's own secrets. They wonder what light is like. So you tempt it with the jewels in your hair. Poor gate: it knows nothing about symbolism. It knows only that the tinted diamonds and emeralds and lapis lazuli glint with the evening star's passion. Down you draw the golden pins from your dark hair and let that torrent free.

Eagerly, the gate lips at the diamonds' fire, the emeralds' intimation of bounty, the lapis lazuli's memory of the sky that cannot be seen. The color leaches from the diamonds, leaving them ashen. The other stones, less hardy, crumble into dust, their virtue vanished.

Sated, the gate eats no more of you as you pass through, divested of glory yet more beautiful than ever.

The fires won't hurt you unless you let them, sister. Hungry already? You'll be hungrier still. Don't roast the flesh off your bones. It's not time yet.

Did you think the underworld moved in ignorance of summer? The season that scours the earth and fills the stomachs of those aboveground while leaving us below-ground with the rotting chaff? At least we know that we are the chaff of days, the dust of time.

It is summer because you've scarcely left the world above. Just think, sister: the longer you linger here, the more the leaves shrivel gold and brown on the branches; the more the last grapes wither on the vines.

Now you are hungry again, and thirsty as well. I know. I know you so well that you could flense yourself bare of face and fingerprints and still I would recognize you. After all, I recognized you the first seventy-four times you came my way.

Does it surprise you that your inventory comes up in the shape of an eight-pointed star? Blink once and it appears; twice, and it folds out of your field of vision. It reports nothing you can't find upon you.

One slot is empty now, black as a gate, as the absence of day; black as your hair. Pick up something else if you like. Yes, that pencil will do. The graphite's luster is dark. It grows darker yet in your grasp.

I don't recognize the words you are writing on my walls, sister: graffiti, in scratchy bird-claw marks. Maybe you mean it to be illegible. That would be unkind.

Consider this. The seventy-four earlier iterations of you left no guide-star tags upon the walls, no cheat sheets, no maps tattooed upon their skins. Underneath your armor there is skin, the organ on which your boundaries are written. You'll know the instant it dissolves and opens your secrets to the air.

Nothing's left of your pencil but a stub. One point of the eight-pointed star flares diamond-bright as the inventory slot empties itself in response.

Did I speak to you of skin? The walls are my skin, the gold-painted pillars my bones. Do what you will with them. You always did.

You are silent. I don't know whether this is an improvement or not. Do you think your words will inscribe themselves upon the air like the coming frost upon fallen leaves? Twenty degrees Celsius, room temperature. You are in a room.

There is no way out of the room, except now there is. Like a hundred mutilated lips the letters—are they letters or logograms?—crack wide, wider. Gap to gap, they gape until they dissolve into a single opening.

A wind rushes through the gate. The wind chill factor is 14 degrees Celsius. You may feel that is excessive. From that number you can calculate the speed of the wind. Unfortunately, your pencil's stub will write no more for you. Perhaps you can do the figures in your head.

If you came to the feast, you would soon sate yourself with warm food. You would watch as dancers clad in feathers reenacted the descent of your first self, or the eighth, or the forty-ninth. How many gates do you think your sad, brave clones survived? Do not worry. You are different, you are special, more clever and greater of heart. I will make sure you reach the barley cakes brimming with dark honey.

Now you are singing. Your formants are rich with despair. Some languages can be recorded without stylus or pencil.

The gate swallows the holy sweetness of your voice. It cancels the waveform, replacing it with silence beyond imagining. Sister, you have not known silence until you have sat in the dark among the dead for generations.

You don't know, yet you do. These are the things you sing of: the embryos of mice, stillborn, albinos that have never known light; the needle's prick drawing blood directly from the betrayed artery; curling strands of fossil DNA, a language more legible than yours. Memory is not inherited, memory is no mirror to times past, yet you divine the experiments that I oversee here.

The gate is as still as matter ever is. Even you cannot cancel that lowest level of vibration, absolute zero thrumming. It will have to do.

Assured of the gate's momentary toothlessness, you step through, and it lets you. Silence drifts in your wake like leaves and petals, like all things ephemeral.

This time it's not so easy to ignore the fire, is it? Go deep enough and you'll meet the mantle's heat. You think of the underworld as cold and dank, inhabited by pale, eyeless creatures whose circulatory systems are written within them with ink redder than spinels. That is not the whole of us. We can kill you by fire, too.

Are you worried about dying? You shy from the fires, watch your balance on the narrow walkways. It helps to have good reflexes in death as well as life. It's good that you practice. Of course I support your efforts.

Traverse the spiraling maze and who do you find at the center? Imagine peeling the layers of yourself away. What's left when you reach your hallowed heart, when the hollows admit no shadows but what you carry with you? I forgot: with no voice, you can't answer me.

Walk and walk as you may, you only knot yourself further into the maze's pattern. Isn't this the way of the world? From the moment you first draw breath, you're woven into the world's overbearing warp.

Look: the necklace at your throat responds to the fire, capturing and releasing that warm light with its own golden gleam. In this surfeit of light I can read the inscription on your eight-pointed pendant, spider-scratch marks deep in the metal. No cipher hides you from me. I have mapped you down to your mitochondria. I can read your rate of respiration, the flush of your skin. Surely the heat isn't unbearable yet.

You unclasp the bright unknot from around your neck. Which lover gave you that necklace? Was it before or after he pressed you against the flowering earth, the leafing tree? Through the floor of the earth, I heard your demands. You were never easy to please, no matter how many lovers you dragged from bars, drugged by the honey of your voice and the heat of your mouth. Nevertheless the mares and does swelled, and the boughs curved under the weight of tender fruit.

Did the lionesses nuzzle each other, wondering over cubs to come?

Like a sleepy snake the necklace ripples over your hands, throwing bright glints across knuckles and prominent bones. I will listen when you explain to your beloved that his gift was worth nothing except as a talisman against one more nexus of shadow and insatiable envy. That's the problem, surely: not that you discarded the gift, but that it was discarded in such small cause.

There are people who would kill for fire: fire to stoke youth in the furnace beneath their skins, fire to brighten the faded cloth of their lives. Better to die burning than chilled by slow moments into the silvered dark. No? Tell that to all those whose bones embrace beneath the worm-furrowed loam.

A narrow opal flares open in the air at the maze's heart, narrow like a woman before she grows great with child. Were this gate a woman you could dance with her, span her with your hands—no. Instead, you fasten the necklace around the gate, adorning it as you once adorned yourself.

The gold shines with the warmth of the surrounding fires. The gate does not drain away the reflected light. Instead, darkness seeps into the inscription. You can't turn away from the words, sister, the seething shapes of *summer, hope, health* inverted.

The gate offers you its embrace. Without hesitation or tenderness, you accept, ducking your head so that you are briefly crowned in gold.

Do you know how deep in the earth you are, sister? You squint in the near-dark. There is only a single lantern to comfort you. Imagine: maybe that lantern is the only thing between you and utter darkness. Shall I snuff it out? Don't shiver so; it doesn't become you.

The stalactites and stalagmites grip the light in their jaws, returning only washed-out, variegated colors: poor exchange for that faint gold.

You shouldn't have sold your voice so cheaply. It makes conversation difficult. Would you like to borrow the voices that whisper in the underworld for your own? You never know who might wander here. They might remember the world's oldest hymns. They might be praising the serpentine coils of your hair, the silent cunning of your hands. They might not know who you are at all, now that you're stripped of your war-chariot, far from the morning star. For all the storms you dragged in your wake, all the rain-tossed days and nights, you craved light as your nourishment: star or moon, lightning scarring the shrouded sky. You always were one for fanfare.

Here are no drums to shake the stone columns and threaten you with the slow death of suffocation. Don't worry about the air, dear sister. You breathe as darkness does, without need of oxygen or any element but your very self. Light travels through the void without a mediating aether; why should darkness be any different?

Come to my halls, sister, and there will be no more talk of light or dark or the permutations in between. We will sit side by side on our thrones, drinking young wine and old rather than the dark, dank water that trickles just beneath the world's skin. We will bestow treasures upon those who please us, luminous cabochons and spiral emblems of gold, chains sometimes of silver and sometimes of bronze.

In the earth's hidden hoards you can taste treasure as though it were a nectar beyond price. Underground, so deep that even fungi find no nourishment, the earth fruits metal and precious stones. It is of no concern to us that living creatures starve contemplating such fruit.

You unfasten your belt, such a short, blunt length to encircle your waist. Jewels of varying cuts are set in the leather, all polished to the brilliance of river water beneath a fecund moon. They fling colored sparks across the floor and walls. Did you ever spare a thought for the underground spirits that had to be disturbed by the digging for your treasures?

With the belt you whip the largest geode in the wall, already cracked half-open to reveal its jagged amethyst heart. The jewels fall out of your belt and scatter to the floor, uncracked yet dimmer, duller. You should be more patient, sister. After all, when you reach the final gate there will be no returning. Doesn't the thought distress you even a little?

Heedless, you bunch up the belt in your fist, then thrust it into the gate that is growing from the crack in the geode. Is that how you regard the underworld's gleaming treasures? Obstacles to be destroyed?

I suppose I haven't learned anything that I didn't already know. You are all the same, all of you.

The geode's teeth scratch your skin as you enter, even through the stiff curves of your armor.

This deep in the earth, you can't hear the seasons breathing even in your dreams. Tell me true: when you close your eyes, can you smell the earthy sweetness of rotting leaves, or taste the last fruits of fall? If I set before you a feast of the finest wines and hearty porridge and roast boar, would it taste like the dust that surrounds you?

Come to me before it's too late, before you lose all ability to see color or to taste salt or sweet.

You tilt your head, listening to the laments of the dead. Their voices sound very like your own, don't they? Maybe they always have. There is no use for fertility without death, you know.

All your faces are mine. You can verify that with a mirror when we meet, except that mirrors are liars when there is no light, claiming that everything is equal to everything. Perhaps that's the sort of lie you like to tell yourself.

Here's the thing about shadows. Even at their most distorted, shadows are mathematically precise. They show you what is given to them to show. If a shadow portrays you as larger as you are, it's no fault of the shadow's. It's all a matter of light, of angles and intensity and color.

If I loom so large in your experience here, sister, you might consider what it is about you that has made me who I am.

Don't worry about the candles here, or the supply of oxygen. The ventilation is quite adequate for our purposes.

Your shadows flicker and jump in perfect time to the candles' flames, like dancers yearning after each other. Which one most truly represents your face? Or mine?

When you close your eyes, just before sleep bears you beneath the surface of the world, do you have a face at all? Can you differentiate yourself from the shadows at all?

Furiously, you pull open your jacket, unfasten your tunic. I know all the scars you bear, sister. The abrupt cuneiform shapes of scars embellish your skin. Scars from battle or love or all the jagged shapes in between, cicatrices and burn scars, round and pale and lightning-shaped.

Of course: no shadow living ever bore a scar.

You feed the shadows your scars, erasing all record of those past triumphs and defeats. As the scars smooth out, becoming invisible against the brown canvas of your body, the shadows gain in depth and form, braiding themselves together until they are a cold, tangible presence on the floor.

Unhesitating, you refasten your tunic and step through, falling without falling.

You're shielding your eyes. Surprised at how bright it is? I thought you could use a reminder. The spectrum produced by each lamp imitates that of a sun you or one of your clone-sisters has visited. Sadly, no matter how faithful a lamp is, it can never rival the real thing.

Don't look for their remnants here. Seasons in human time are one thing, but seasons in the lives of starfarers—what is a human winter to people like you or me? You've been breathing their dust, treading on their fossilized despair.

Nevertheless, you crouch, heedless of the gray grit that clings to your clothes, and draw figures on the cave's floor. If you think your calculus will save you, you are sorely mistaken. In your formulae the infinitesimals come to a positive sum. Here, the sum of iterated emptiness will only be more emptiness.

Let me tell you a story to distract you from the useless fable you are telling yourself. Long ago, the people of a great and fertile land resolved to explore worlds that circled the god-stars that they had watched and worshipped since their people first set brick upon brick to build cities. But for all their ambitions, they were loyal, and did not forget their gods. They knew they would need their gods to guard them from the dangers that lie deep in space.

So they made sure that their gods would follow them into that shining darkness, a pantheon of gods for each world. They made you, all of you, and they made me.

If you must console yourself over your journey here, tell yourself that those who made you achieved their purpose, and that you are perfectly recapitulating that old story so that your world will pass into its winter rest. You will not live to see your world's renewal, but another of you will.

Don't bother scratching out a message to her. She won't read the same languages you do, won't take the same twisting path. I will tell her the same things that I have told you. You may be sure of it.

You've removed the shadow-gun from its holster and are cradling it in your hands. You knew it would come to this. We both did.

It's a beautiful weapon. It has the same coiled intensity that you do when you are intent on war, sister. And it has killed people in your hands. You are not the kind to beg forgiveness; you were made for bloodshed. I don't understand why you regard the gun with such loathing, then.

Steadily, you raise the shadow-gun and squeeze the trigger. The room explodes into utter darkness, the kind of darkness that swallows sound and stifles thought. Even the spangled otherspace behind your eyelids is brighter than this.

A moment later, your fingers close around empty air as the gun dissolves. It has served its purpose. All but one of your inventory slots is empty as well.

The entire room is a gate now. It remains only for you to take a step. It speaks well of you that you listen for a long, careful moment before moving in the direction leading downward, toward me.

Your heart thuds one-two, one-two, one-two like a march without an army. There is only you, alone before the last gate. What did you hope to accomplish when you set out, sister? Did you have some brave notion of unseating me from my dark throne, or tearing asunder all the underworld gates so the dead would roam free and outnumber the living?

I have always admired your purity of purpose, mistaken as it is. We are not so different, you and I. We play the roles that are given to us. Yours is to die, and mine is to kill you. Don't spoil the symmetry of the story.

The only reason you can see anything here, where the darkness is thicker than honey, is that you still have a heart. It shines red-bright in the final inventory slot, last remaining illumination. If I cared to, I could grow you a new, more compliant heart. But that is not my duty. Would you deny Number Seventy-Six her chance at this journey?

There is a small, angular object in your hand like a dead star. Your inventory system needs to be debugged. Why was I not informed?

You kneel again. I can hear the painful harshness of your breathing. More important is what you are scratching into the dust on the floor with your pointed fingernail. This time it is in a language I understand:

I have always known I am not the only one. You are not the only one of your kind, either. My clone-sisters and I have planned for this moment, a coordinated strike. It is the only way we can be free. I am s—

How can it be that I feel the touch of rain so deep beneath the earth, blotting out the last word you would have written?

You timed it to your traitor heart. And now that I know to look, I see it: a mass inside your heart, tangled inextricably into it.

In the end you give up your heart after all, but I am the one who loses everything, in a springtime effusion of light.

story notes

"Ghostweight"

This was the second-hardest story I have ever written, not because of the subject material (I find it funny to slaughter fictional characters, that bit's easy) but because it took me the better part of six months to nail the opening. The thing about the story is that in the first paragraph you are setting up the story's axioms, and this affects your ability to hammer in the QED at the end. It is like writing a proof. You have to know what your premises are so you know what you're arguing from.

Charibdys's prompt was "origami and consequences in space." I believe I delivered. Ordinarily, when I'm writing to a prompt for individuals, I don't write downers because people don't seem to like downers. I had strong reason to believe that Charibdys would be okay with a story about genocide and treachery, so I went with it.

Once I had the opening, the rest was easy. The hinge is getting the reader to accept the ghost as a given and not question who the ghost really is, which is made easier by the fact that Lisse never thinks to question this. I could be mistaken; maybe a lot of people guessed that in advance. Let me know.

As an aside, this is set in the same world (far in the future) as "The Shadow Postulates," but you'd only know it if you happen to be one of a small set of people who saw some version of the defunct source novel.

"The Shadow Postulates"

The shadow postulates came from a hazy conjunction of two things in math: Fermat's last theorem and Euclid's fifth postulate. Fermat's last theorem is the famous one where he wrote in the margin that he had a great proof that wouldn't fit. It is likely that he had a great *wrong* proof. I have not attempted to read popular math accounts on Andrew Wiley's actual proof of the theorem because just reading popular math accounts of the *prerequisites* to understand the actual proof have scared me off. I love math, but a B.A. doesn't get you very far.

Euclid's fifth postulate is the one about how if there's a line and a point outside the line, you get only one parallel line to the first one through that outside point. (That's a restatement of the postulate called Playfair's Axiom, but it's the same idea.) Non-Euclidean geometry came about when people realized you could construct alternate consistent geometries by monkeying around with that postulate, which had been driving mathematicians nuts for ages because something about it felt weird and it seemed like they ought to be able to derive it from the other postulates.

By the way, if it's any consolation, any time I get near the word "entelechy" I have to look it up in the dictionary. The definition refuses to stay in my head. But then, that's what dictionaries are for.

"The Bones of Giants"

I had been watching anime about mecha and it occurred to me that fantasy would be great for mecha if you just dug up some big skeletons and applied necromancy. I may have been influenced by *Neon Genesis Evangelion*, although I'm not sure *what* you classify the Evas as except Bad News.

The necromancy system came from the fact that I had been reading up on traditional 2D animation for a few years. I am not an animator; I have only animated three things in my life (one in Flash, two in LivingCels), and I don't draw well enough to try it, but reading about how it works fascinates me because it's something I can't do.

Also, you ever notice how you stick someone in a mecha and half the time they magically sprout a bunch of completely impractical but

318

acrobatic moves? Possibly after a few false starts, but still. That struck me as ridiculous, so I made my characters work for their battle moves.

Sakera's hand tremor came from a hand tremor I developed as a side-effect of a medication I was on. It's very slight now, but when I sketch I long for beautiful, smooth, controlled lines and those are forever beyond me. Oh well.

"Between Two Dragons"

This story is about the Imjin War. The first two wars I grew up knowing about weren't World War I and World War II; they were the Imjin War and the Korean War.

The Imjin War was a Japanese invasion of Korea from 1592 to 1598, and it gave Korea one of its two great national heroes, Admiral Yi Sun-Shin. (The other is King Sejong, who, among other things, invented the Korean alphabet according to phonetic principles.) To give you some idea, at the Battle of Myeongnyang Yi defeated the Japanese with 13 warships against 133.

The Japanese were very good at land warfare (and the Koreans were unbelievably bad at it at that time), but naval warfare was another matter. The Japanese idea of fighting with ships was to sail their ships right up to yours, board you, and hack or shoot up your people. The Korean idea of fighting with ships was to shoot your ships up with cannons. One of these paradigms works better than the other.

(As an aside, the turtle boat, or geobukseon, was almost certainly not an ironclad.)

Admiral Yi went undefeated, but due to intrigue he was removed from command after the Japanese went home for a breather. Then he was tortured, stripped of rank, and almost executed by the Korean king. After the Japanese came back and defeated the Koreans in a battle at sea, the king reinstated him.

Yi was famed for his loyalty, although the regime didn't seem to deserve it much. I didn't want to dump the war's exact events into a future setting because I can't improve on history, but I thought I'd explore the loyalty question by changing things around.

Probably the best single current English-language book on the Imjin War is Samuel Hawley's *The Imjin War*. But you may find Stephen Turnbull's *Samurai Invasion*, which focuses more on the Japanese perspective, easier to locate.

"Swanwatch"

I wanted to put more technical stuff about computer music in this story (at the time I was screwing around in Logic Pro), but one of my betas said she wasn't interested in music theory, she wanted to know more about the characters. This is why I need betas. I am usually happy to spend pages describing things that no one cares about.

I have been fascinated by black holes since 4th grade, when an astronomy book terrified me by suggesting that black holes get bigger the more they (for lack of a better word) ingest, and the more they ingest the bigger they get. By the time I learned about Hawking radiation I was no longer worried, but black holes struck me as fermata-like, and the story grew from there.

By the way, in case anyone was wondering, the reason Tortoise never talks to anyone is that he's dead. Although really, he owes something to Ghast Rhymi from Henry Kuttner's *The Dark World*.

I would also like to report that I was forced to go to some astronomy department's very helpful, well-illustrated website overview of Black Holes 101 in order to check some details about the event horizon (I was right, it turned out) because my husband the *gravitational astrophysicist* was so busy playing *EVE: Online* that he wouldn't answer my questions. I am never going to let him live this down and I take particular pleasure in recounting this in front of other gravitational astrophysicists. Admittedly, this is not a huge set of people!

"Effigy Nights"

This story came from two places. Maybe two and a half.

My father is a surgeon. I am not sure what most children get as playthings from their fathers. Mine provided an endless supply of pens that advertised medications whose purpose I still don't know (I like pens, so this was congenial), occasionally tablets of paper, and those small curved scissors that they use for surgery, once they were no longer suitable for actual surgery. Surgeon hand-me-downs are the best. I spent a serious amount of time trying to cut straight lines in paper with those scissors and never had any success; if you know the trick, please tell me. (I never tried the scissors on, say, a cut of raw chicken. Although now that I think of it . . .) In any case, the scene in which Seran cuts free the Saint of Guns was originally going to be the opening of a novel, but I got bored of the concept and decided to recycle it into another story, and since this one had paper dolls in it, it seemed suitable.

The second is my childhood love of paper dolls. My mother provided these colonial American dolls of a grandmother and her granddaughters, I think, probably from Dover Publications or the like. I soon grew bored of these and started producing paper dolls of unicorns, multicolored river snakes (Crayola was my friend), and dragons. I cut out gemstones from newspaper advertisements of rings and necklaces so the critters could have hoards. (Hoards are very important.) I eventually worked up to two swordswomen with swords and sheaths quasi-laminated using shiny Scotch tape, so that you could slide the swords in and out of the sheaths. I wish I knew what happened to that old folder full of paper dolls and settings and hoarded gems.

As for the last half? One of my earliest memories is of one of the (many) times I scared the hell out of my mother. I can't have been more than four or five years old. I had watched with great interest as my mother

YOON HA LEE

cooked fish in pans on the stove, and thought it looked terrifically fun. So, with impeccable logic, I drew fish on a sheet of paper with crayons, cut them out with scissors, put them in a pan, and turned on the stove. The fish started burning so I was satisfied that I was doing it right, which was the point at which my mother noticed the smoke and freaked out. (I think she had been distracted talking to one of my uncles.) The moral of this story is that I should not be allowed near paper critters.

"Flower, Mercy, Needle, Chain"

I only write about vague magical guns because I have no handgun experience and I have reliably been informed that the two things you Do Not Get Wrong in writing are horses and guns. I mostly stopped putting horses in stories after that (although I took a semester of equitation in undergrad anyway, to be on the safe side), but I am loath to give up a weapon option.

(Okay, I took a semester of riflery, too. But not handguns.)

The philosophical conceit for this story came from a book that I still haven't finished reading, Daniel Dennett's *Freedom Evolves*. It has something to do with how inevitability and free will are not actually mutually exclusive. Someday I will start over, read the whole book, and figure out how this works.

The story tap-dances around the question of how ancestry is defined, and the answer is that ancestry is at least sometimes defined socially ("the line of Zot was founded by Zot the Brusque") rather than an all-the-way-back-to-the-primordial-ooze line. Naturally, I forgot to include any such thing in the story proper, but maybe tap-dancing was the better move anyway.

This has the interesting distinction of being one of the few stories I have written that my husband liked. (We are friends, promise, just different tastes in fiction.) Of course, I know exactly what I do that makes him dislike the other ones, I'm just not willing to stop.

"Iseul's Lexicon"

I used to say that "Ghostweight" was the hardest story I had ever written, but "Iseul's Lexicon" beats it, mostly because while I was trying to hash the thing out, I was sick for over three months. It took me eight drafts, which is mildly appalling. My rough drafts are normally much cleaner, but not when I am bedridden half the day with pain.

I had been wanting to write a tactical linguistics story for years, although damned if I knew what on earth tactical linguistics meant. Then I thought up the Genial Ones' penchant for lexicography and tossed in some genocide, and there it was.

Chindalla and Yeged are very loosely based on Korea and Japan, although it's mashed up between the Imjin War and the Japanese occupation from 1910 to 1945. I don't know a whole lot about my family's experiences of the Japanese occupation. For one thing, the language barrier made it difficult to ask questions. For another, the questions were bound to lead to some messy answers. My spoken Korean is so-so and works best on common domestic conversational topics like food or jump rope, and my ability to read Korean is pretty lousy. But I think about it anyway.

This story originally had a lot more cryptology in it, but my sister persuaded me that going into the combinatorics of how to encrypt syllable blocks in a featural code would bore the reader (I was thinking of working up to a nice Vigenère), so I gave up on that. The petal script is a stand-in for Hangeul. The story goes that when King Sejong introduced the alphabet as a vastly simpler alternative to the method of using Chinese to write Korean, the recalcitrant yangban (literati) remarked derisively that it was so easy that even a woman could learn it. So I decided to have the inventor of my fictional version be a woman.

Many thanks to my husband for helping me think through the plot. Physicists can be excellent plot doctors.

"Counting the Shapes"

Originally this story, which I started in high school, was about wine of immortality. I woke up and realized I had nothing to say about immortality, so I ditched that.

It's clear to me now that this story owes a lot to one of my favorite fantasy novels, Simon R. Green's *Blue Moon Rising*. I have read *Blue Moon Rising* many times and there is no particular math in it (except the bit about teleportation coordinates), but it has demons and last stands and magical swords.

As for math, I fell in love with it sideways, without realizing it. I hated math passionately until 9th grade. 9th grade was geometry and they introduced proofs, and suddenly math wasn't about a bunch of arbitrary facts and procedures, math *came from somewhere*. I despise not knowing the reasons for things, so this was attractive. I read popular math books because it never occurred to me that this isn't something people do for fun. I read about topology and chaos theory and Gödel's incompleteness theorems and catastrophe theory. I thought people should be writing stories about this stuff. It was more fantastic than the usual D&D fireball varieties of magic.

In my defense, I know about Greg Egan and Rudy Rucker now, but the only libraries I had access to were my school's libraries in Korea and the selection was fun but necessarily limited. Ditto English-language books I could get at Gyobo Bookstore. My sister and I once got to order books (Zelazny's Chronicles of Amber) from Amazon.com by badgering our dad, as they would ship to Korea. I don't remember what the shipping cost, which is just as well. It was glorious; but it was only the one time.

"Blue Ink"

In fiction I am wholeheartedly in favor of a good apocalypse and the associated mayhem, but I wanted to go somewhere different for this story. I wish I could tell you that I wrote this story in blue ink. Instead I wrote it at the computer. It occurs to me that I could have changed the font color, but that would have been obnoxious.

I sometimes drew comics in high school, but sadly they were never as interesting as the things Jenny came up with. Both this story and Jenny owe something to the three years of physics I took then, though. The physics textbook came with a lot of interesting sidebars. My favorite was the not-quite-a-joke about the three laws of thermodynamics (You can't win/ You can't break even/ You can't get out of the game). I've always liked the idea of a battle at the end of time, when everything is winding down, and while this is not a new idea (my favorite instantiation is Tony Daniel's "A Dry, Quiet War"), I couldn't resist giving it a try.

"The Battle of Candle Arc"

This story came from an unpublished novel, which at this time I am still revising; you may or may not ever see it. But Shuos Jedao is one of the characters, and as part of the backstory, I mentioned in passing that he once decisively won a battle in space while outnumbered eight to one. I figured that since Candle Arc received all of two lines, I need never explain how he managed this feat, and I was safe from the reader.

(I should mention at this point that I live in terror that militarily savvy readers will tell me how much I fail to understand tactics, but on the other hand it would be good for me to be schooled, so I will accept my medicine. Just saying.)

Well, I was safe from the reader, but I wasn't safe from myself. I became desperate to figure out how the hell he had done it. I complained to one of my betas, Daedala, that I wished I could crib from history, and she said well why not? Being Korean, I went straight for one of Admiral Yi's battles, possibly his most famous one, the Battle of Myeongnyang. Yi did better than Jedao (outnumbered ten to one, killed more of the enemy, and lost no ships) but I figured I shouldn't push the reader's suspension of disbelief.

The hardest part was working out how to translate a naval battle taking advantage of a particular channel and its currents into three-dimensional terms, but fortunately I was saved by the fact that technology in this setting is keyed to competing calendars. Once you can artificially create "terrain" in space using the calendars, you can then arrange it to induce the necessary tactics. I swore a lot when I was trying to work this out. It took me embarrassingly long to remember that the simplest way to figure out what is going on is to draw a diagram, a lesson I learned from a couple West Point Military History textbooks; said textbooks are filled with loving maps and diagrams and it's so much easier to follow what's going on when there's a picture instead of just words.

What's really funny about Candle Arc is that Jedao is not actually deadliest on the battlefield. He's deadliest when you let him talk to you. But that's another story, and I couldn't get into it here.

"A Vector Alphabet of Interstellar Travel"

I wrote this for Sam Kabo Ashwell because he was the one who encouraged me to read Italo Calvino's *Invisible Cities*. I am wary of most people's book recommendations because my tastes are weird and unpredictable. No one else is responsible when I hate a widely well-regarded book, but life is short and I want to avoid being stuck with books I hate. Anyway, but this is Sam, and after some resistance I bought a used copy I saw in a bookstore and he was right. I loved it.

What fascinates me about Italo Calvino is that this book, his prose, it's unbelievable *in translation*. What the hell is the original Italian like? Does it sublimate off the page with its own incandescence? One of the things I regret is that I am not fluent enough in any language but English to have a chance at reading things. I had six years of French and I can make my way through texts sometimes (with a dictionary, unless it's a monograph on group theory and then all the important vocabulary looks the same as in English), but that's my strongest foreign language and getting nuances out of prose is a lost cause even so.

So, really, this is an Italo Calvino pastiche set in space, and the vector alphabet bit comes from the idea of basis vectors in linear algebra. I have a friend who derided linear algebra because it was so easy, and okay, it *was* easy, but it had clean lines and I liked the way it danced for me. I am aware there is an egregious amount of arrogance involved in the idea of pastiching Calvino, but I wanted to give something back to Sam and I figured it wouldn't tear a hole in the universe for me to have a go.

"The Unstrung Zither"

The idea behind this story came partly from a fascinating bit in Kenneth DeWoskin's *A Song for One or Two: Music and the Concept of Art in Early China*. I don't have access to the book anymore, but the idea was that music had the power to create order in society. I'm not entirely certain if the book said that exactly or if I went off on a tangent.

I usually shy away from elemental magic systems because I don't have anything new to bring to the table, but I thought I could go somewhere with the musical/magical correspondences. I spent a fair amount of time looking longingly at websites for places where you can get, e.g., guzheng lessons, but that was out of my reach. If I'd been thinking far enough ahead, I should have tried to learn the gayageum while I was in Korea. In any case, technique descriptions (including the one about using the pulse for vibrato!) are based on written accounts, but sadly I don't know how it works firsthand as I've never played a zither and I'm not convinced classical guitar is close enough to be useful.

"The Black Abacus"

I wrote this story for my first semester of Narrative Writing in college. I am not sure what I got out of that class. The professor seemed to like my writing, but I had already sold a couple of stories and I was sure I could sell more on my own. Plus, almost everyone in the class was an English major. At that point I think I had declared for computer science. We were writing to vastly different genre expectations. On the other hand, if I wrote science fiction for the class, I could get the grade for the work, then turn around and try to sell the story. Twofer.

This is also the story of which I got asked, point-blank by the professor, "Is this about sex?" I am not sure how you get from quantum physics and information theory and people shooting each other in space to "sex" off a couple lines mentioning that two people are sleeping with each other, but perhaps I am missing something.

I was reading *Scientific American* at the time, and although I can't remember which article it was, I was fascinated by the idea of quantum chess. I apologize for misusing "incoherence"; it should be "decoherence," but in my defense an English major and a physics major *both* told me it was "incoherence."

I know the thing I should have done to make the ending work better, which I didn't think of until a couple years after its publication. Rachel's answer wasn't three lines, it was two words, and it's obvious what the two words should have been. But then, I don't write quantum stories; the version that's out there is the version you get.

"The Book of Locked Doors"

I had the anime *Code Geass* on the brain when I wrote this, although there is not very much resemblance. (No giant robots, for one.) I came up with the title sometime in 6th or 7th grade, but I didn't have a story to go with it, so I held off. Much later, I thought of a book of massacred people, containing their special abilities, and I thought that might finally be a decent use of the title. I must also confess the influence of 2nd ed. Advanced Dungeons & Dragons—I can't remember their names now and I also can't remember which of the sourcebooks they were in, but there were magical books that would increase your stats if you read them.

The setting was loosely inspired by the Japanese occupation of Korea, and the subway ride owes something to the years I spent riding Seoul's subways. I went back there a little while ago and was impressed at how much better it had gotten, but maybe it was because I wasn't traveling during rush hour, when I used to have to wedge my way through the crowd with my viola case. A viola or violin (in a hard case) is about the right size for this job, by the way. A guitar would probably work too.

I still don't know how I feel about asymmetrical warfare, on the grounds that if you're a much weaker opponent, running up to the enemy in a full frontal assault just seems stupid, but on the other hand, there has to be some limit to what you can ethically get away with. I guess I will think about it some more.

"Conservation of Shadows"

This is what happens when (a) you fall in love with "The Descent of Inanna" in 8th grade, because there's a Mesopotamian unit in World History and the teacher tells you about Inanna so you look her up in the school library, and (b) you watch your husband play *Portal*. I loved the voice-acting and the writing for that game, although I have still never played it because I am convinced the puzzles would kill me. I mean, beyond the fact that they start being lethal to your character.

I have this thing where I can dial prose up or I can dial prose down. Or I can pastiche someone. I am a style sponge, which makes me picky about what I read while I'm working on a long project, because as much as I adore Simon R. Green, it's weird when my words come out that way when I'm working on a story that wants to be non-Green-like. For this one I dialed it up, which I usually avoid doing. There is always the danger of overwhelming the material with tinsel and I am already prone to that fault, but it's worth doing once in a while.

publication history

"Ghostweight" first appeared in *Clarkesworld*, January 2011.

"The Shadow Postulates" first appeared in *Helix*, June 2007.

"The Bones of Giants" first appeared in *F&SF*, August 2009.

"Between Two Dragons" first appeared in *Clarkesworld*, April 2010.

"Swanwatch" first appeared in *Federations*, edited by John Joseph Adams, 2009.

"Effigy Nights" first appeared in *Clarkesworld*, January 2013.

"Flower, Mercy, Needle, Chain" first appeared in *Lightspeed*, September 2010.

"Iseul's Lexicon" appeared for the first time in this collection.

"Counting the Shapes" first appeared in *F&SF*, June 2001.

"Blue Ink" first appeared in *Clarkesworld*, August 2008.

"The Battle of Candle Arc" first appeared in *Clarkesworld*, October 2012.

"A Vector Alphabet of Interstellar Travel" first appeared in *Tor.com*, August 2011.

"The Unstrung Zither" first appeared in *F&SF*, March 2009.

"The Black Abacus" first appeared in *F&SF*, June 2002.

"The Book of Locked Doors" first appeared in *Beneath Ceaseless Skies*, March 2012.

"Conservation of Shadows" first appeared in *Clarkesworld*, August 2011.